THE CHAINED PRINCE

BECCA CALDER

THE NEW DOMINION
THE SHADOWED SEA
AETHERIS
THE SHADOWED VEIL
ELUNETH
LUMARIA
ITHRALIS
THE TEMPLE

ORINFAEL
ELVANFAL
TIRNAVEL
The Alderwild
FAERWYN
THE SILVERFANGS
STORMPORT
SINDERFAL
N
W
E
S

CONTENTS

For my husband—who endured fantasy romance immersion boot camp to help me realize my dream. Your love and no-holds-barred feedback made all the difference. You're my real-life hero, even if you roll your eyes at fictional ones.

CONTENT WARNINGS

The Chained Prince is a dark fantasy novel that explores themes of oppression, captivity, and survival in a brutal world. It contains depictions of violence, blood magic, and torture, as well as systemic discrimination, forced assimilation, and reproductive control. While fictionalized through a fantasy lens, some of these elements may resonate with real-world histories of cultural trauma and institutional harm. The story also includes an emotionally abusive relationship, psychological trauma, and elements of coercion, with some romantic interactions involving dubious consent. Characters face captivity, magical experimentation, and the lasting effects of war, grief, and loss. Additionally, there are references to pregnancy-related distress, self-harm, and suicidal ideation. Reader discretion is advised.

PROLOGUE

"Your Majesty?"

Dara'el curled around King Corwin, its shadows writhing at his feet like hungry, restless serpents. He barely noticed. His hands remained pressed against the unyielding stone of his mate's tomb, the chill seeping into his skin, into his bones, just as it had on the day they sealed her away. The crown weighed on his head, its once-brilliant luster dulled. He should have left it behind. It wasn't a king who knelt here, only a grieving male.

Two years.

How had it been two years since the light of his life fell protecting their people? Since she gave her last breath to shield the Eldergreen from the humans who would desecrate it?

"Corwinth."

Elric's use of his true name snapped Corwin from his thoughts. With Lysa gone, it had been years since anyone had dared to speak it —but if anyone had the right, it was the male who had stood at his side for a lifetime.

"What is it?" Corwin dragged himself to his feet, turning to face his oldest friend.

Elric's breath was ragged, his face lined with exhaustion, etched with grief. He had lost his own wife and the mother of his child, the human Healer who had been one of Lysa's closest friends.

"They crossed the ridge," Elric said. "They took the bait. They'll be at the gates by nightfall."

The bait. What a thing to call the bones of the female he loved.

"One last time," he whispered. *Let me protect you one last time.*

The shadows moved with him as he ascended the worn stone steps beside Elric, coiling and uncoiling in restless waves, their edges fraying like tattered silk. They wound around his arms, clung to his shoulders, falling behind him like a living cloak that swept the stairs in his wake.

Soon, they hissed in his ear, a hundred voices speaking as one. *Soon, soon, soon, soon—*

We drink. We break. We feast.

Loose us. Unchain us. Let them drown in the dark.

Though he couldn't hear them, Elric still cast the shadows a wary glance, his fingers twitching toward the hilt of his sword. "They're getting worse."

It wasn't an accusation. Not quite.

Corwin exhaled slowly, watching as the shadows shifted with the movement of his breath. "They won't be a problem."

Elric's silence stretched between them, heavy with unspoken doubt.

Corwin sighed. "Not tonight," he amended. "They hate the New Dominion as much as I do."

For a long moment, Elric held his gaze. Then, with a slow, resigned nod, he let out a breath and continued up the stairs.

They crossed through the sanctuary, its air silent and thick with the weight of the prayers of the handful of warriors clustered around the altar, their heads bowed as they spoke to a Goddess who had not answered them in centuries. Others stood motionless, staring into the flickering light of the sconces, taking one last moment of quiet before the end.

Some bowed low, pressing fists to chests as he passed. Others simply looked at him, their faces full of quiet respect and brittle hope—hope he didn't deserve but felt the weight of all the same.

Corwin paused before the temple doors, turning back to face the warriors gathered before him. Their faces were hard, resolute, the flickering torchlight catching in their battle-worn armor, in the lines of exhaustion and defiance etched into their expressions.

His gaze swept over them, taking in the ragged edges of their cloaks, the nicks in their weapons, the way their fingers clenched white-knuckled around their hilts. But it was their eyes that mattered most.

They burned. Shining with the fire of a people who had nothing left to lose.

Corwin exhaled, rolling his shoulders, the weight of duty settling as heavily as the cold press of his crown—a symbol of a kingdom already lost. They were waiting—for him, for words of courage or reassurance. He had neither.

Instead, he spoke the only truth that mattered.

"We all know who we are fighting for."

Silence met his words, a silence thick with understanding, with purpose. Then, one by one, the warriors bowed their heads—not in submission, but in solemn acknowledgment.

Corwin turned away. The time for words was done.

He pressed his palm to the door. "Let's go."

They lined up in front of the temple. Two hundred fae to hold the temple. Two hundred fae to give their loved ones enough time to flee.

Somewhere far away in the darkness, the sea crashed against the jagged cliffs. The wind whipped over them, carrying the scent of salt and blood. The air felt charged, a gathering storm waiting to break. There was no retreat. They would either hold this ground or die on it.

Corwin drew in a slow breath. *Dara'el* coiled tighter around him, rippling with anticipation as the first figures crossed the ridge. The New Dominion's battle mages didn't bother with stealth as they ground to a halt, their grim faces illuminated by the sickly glow of their enchanted weapons, every one powered with aether that had been ripped from its proper place and bound to their will.

At their center, a black-armored Commander wearing the Arcanum's Eye emblazoned on his breastplate stood motionless. Corwin could feel his gaze on him, caught by the shadows that churned around him, marking him as a target. The Commander cocked his head, hefting a staff so long it could only have been carved from an entire fae femur.

Corwin could feel the trapped aether inside it screaming, even across the battlefield. His heart clenched, and he whispered a silent prayer to the absent Goddess for the poor soul whose body had become a weapon for their oppressors.

That's why the New Dominion was here, instead of hunting the last free fae across Eluneth. Fae bone was a powerful amplifier—and the crypt beneath the temple was a prize the humans could not resist.

What monstrosities could they craft from the remains of generations of fae rulers?

There will be no monstrosities. The voices—usually scattered, hissing and half-mad—coalesced. And for the first time in what felt like years, *dara'el* spoke not as many, but as one.

Release us. We will kill the bone-bearer first.

"Not yet," Corwin said aloud, ignoring the way Elric glanced at him—tracking the way the shadows hissed and writhed with barely contained frustration.

They might be lucid now, but *dara'el* hadn't cared about strategy since Lysa died. They didn't obey him, not anymore. He wasn't even sure they remembered who he was or what they stood for. All they wanted was blood and vengeance—and Corwin wasn't sure he was any different.

Well—tonight, they would both gorge on it.

The commander raised the staff, and the first wave surged forward—a wall of iron and death.

Corwin stepped forward to meet it alone, lifting his hands as he called on the power the Goddess had granted him to protect her people.

And *dara'el* answered.

Shadows poured from him, coiling outward like black smoke made solid. They struck, felling the first humans instantly. One, *dara'el* dragged screaming into the shadows, swallowing him whole before his comrades could even react. Another collapsed, choking on pure darkness as his corrupted blade fell uselessly to the ground. A third raised his staff—but *dara'el* was faster. Its shadows coiled around the man's wrist, twisting—

His scream was lost in the roar as fae forces surged past them, meeting the New Dominion soldiers in a clash of steel and magic. Corwin sucked in a deep breath, nearly choking on the stench of burning aether and scorched bone. It clung to the back of his throat, an abomination of everything they stood for.

Corwin lifted his sword. For the first time in years, he did not feel helpless. *Dara'el* met his command eagerly, rising to stand alongside him instead of against him.

Fae magic belonged to the fae. And tonight, the humans would remember why.

Corwin slashed through the ranks of the humans, shadows surging from him in jagged spears and clawed tendrils, cutting through steel and flesh with the fury of a storm. They churned and consumed, swallowing men whole, wrapping around throats and wrists, dragging them screaming into the abyss.

But for every New Dominion soldier that fell, another stepped over his corpse, pushing forward with relentless, merciless precision.

There were too many of them.

The fae fought viciously, holding the line with blades slicked in human blood and magic burning through the air in wild, desperate arcs. But still, they came.

Arrows whistled through the air, fae warriors crying out as iron tips punched through leather armor with deadly precision. Some fell instantly, never rising. Others stumbled, clutching at the black shafts buried deep in their flesh, gasping against the poison lacing the metal.

Corwin's shadows lashed out, seeking the archers, but the battle mages were waiting for him.

Their stolen magic struck back, tearing into his darkness. The first blast of stolen magic slammed into the ground, scorching black tendrils into nothingness. The second ripped through Corwin's defenses, forcing the shadows to recoil and writhe like wounded beasts.

More arrows. More flames. More destruction.

The fae cried out, forced back step by step until their backs were pressed against the temple walls. At least it was warded—no one who sought to do harm could cross into the sanctuary while the doors stood. As long as that held—

The first blast of magic struck the temple.

Lines of light raced through the foundation, wards flaring as they pulled on ancient power to repel the attack. For a moment, Corwin dared to hope they would hold, desperate to believe that, even outnumbered and outfought, they could still protect their dead.

But then the Commander raised his grisly staff overhead a second time, striking it against the ground. Power broke free with a clap like thunder. The doors groaned under the force of it—then cracked down the center, fractures spreading like lightning across the carved reliefs of fae kings and queens.

Corwin staggered backward as stone split, huge chunks crashing to the floor in a thunder of dust and debris. Moonlight speared through the haze, illuminating the sacred heart of the temple—and beyond it, the door leading down to the crypt.

To Lysa.

Dara'el howled. A scream of fury and grief.

"Corwin—" Elric grabbed his arm, hissing in pain as the shadows sliced across his palm. "We have to fall back now. You can't—"

"They'll defile her tomb." Corwin didn't even recognize his own voice, his throat raw as if he had been the one screaming this entire time. "Just like they have defiled everything else."

"You have to think of the living," Elric said, gripping him harder, shaking him. "Think of Eloria—of Loren. Thorne is still out there searching for him. We can't abandon them. We *can't*." His voice cracked. "Lysa wouldn't want that."

Eloria—*Loren*. Was Loren even alive? For a heartbeat, something inside Corwin bent. Lysa would *always* choose their children over herself.

But then the Commander stepped through the settling dust, his sharp gaze snapping to where Corwin and Elric stood with *dara'el* striking out in fury as it raged around them. He didn't speak as he raised that staff, his eyes meeting Corwin's as he pointed it straight at them.

NO.

The word tore through Corwin's mind like a thunderclap, sending him to his knees as *dara'el* cried out in a single, deafening voice. A sound rose in his throat, too raw to be a scream and too feral to be a word as something inside him *snapped*.

And the shadows erupted.

Dara'el ripped free, surging forward in a maelstrom that poured across the field in an unrelenting tide of death and destruction. The Commander's eyes widened as it reached him. His cry was lost in the cacophony—one scream among hundreds, blurred beyond recognition.

Corwin staggered forward, the shadows parting to let him pass. Ahead of him, a New Dominion mage raised his staff, his lips moving in a desperate incantation—but the words never left his throat as the shadows ripped his heart from his chest.

To Corwin's left, a fae warrior stumbled, aether crackling weakly at his fingertips as the darkness reached for him too. His last breath was a shuddering gasp as the shadows coiled around his limbs, dragging him under.

There was no mercy. Fae or human, friend or foe—it didn't matter. The darkness claimed them all.

Corwin moved as if in a dream, passing bodies he couldn't bear to look at. Faces he knew. Warriors who had fought beside him for decades, their armor torn open like paper. Their hands frozen in the moment before death—reaching for help that never came.

"Corwinth—" Elric staggered through the shadows, wincing as they hissed and recoiled, striking him even now. Dark welts burned across his arms and throat, blood seeping through the rents in his tunic. He stumbled to Corwin's side, breath coming in short, pained gasps.

"Stop them," he begged. "Please—stop them. They're killing all of us."

I can't. Corwin shook his head, the words lodging like glass in his throat as he stared at his best friend. *Dara'el* no longer answered to him. It was past command, past reason. All that was left was rage and ruin, and he had set it free.

Elric's face broke as the shadows curled around him, his lips moving to form his son's name one last time as they consumed him too.

And then Corwin stood alone in the aftermath, each ragged inhale dragging through his lungs like a blade. Shadows slid over the bodies, coiling through the broken remains of fae and human alike—discarded by *dara'el* like spent offerings. Their movements were slow and uncertain, as though even they did not know what to do now that everything was gone.

The New Dominion hadn't conquered Eluneth, but the fae hadn't saved it, either. This wasn't a victory—it wasn't even a defeat. It was annihilation.

Corwin let out a shaking breath, staring down at his hands. They were clean—unmarked. There should have been blood—*something* to condemn him for what he had done. But the darkness left nothing behind.

His knees buckled. Corwin didn't even try to catch himself,

collapsing onto the cold earth and curling his fingers into the dirt—seeking something solid in a world that had become nothing but mist and shadow. His crown sat heavy on his head, its once-polished silver dulled by war, sweat, and blood.

He had done this—killed them all.

Corwin's breath caught on an exhale that was half laughter, half sob. The shadows coiled at his back, curling over his shoulders, twisting into the edges of his vision as they whispered to him with a hundred different voices, all speaking at once. Soft. Coaxing. Waiting.

There was one last thing they had to do.

Corwin closed his eyes. The battle was over, but he would not live to see how the war ended. The shadows curled closer, whispering his name.

And this time, he did not resist.

CHAPTER
ONE

The acrid tang of scorched magic clung to the workshop, the stench of burning aether stinging Araya's nose and making her eyes water. She ignored it, steadying her hand as she etched the final rune into the pendant's silver housing.

Her own power simmered inside her, pulsing in her blood and bone as naturally as her heart beat. The shard of fae bone hummed under her fingertips in response, eager to drink in her magic. She needed to be careful here—bone was one of the better amplifiers, but the Arcanum only allotted a sliver of the precious resource for its foot soldiers. Too much, and the shard would shatter. Too little, and it would be useless to the mage it was meant to serve.

Neither failure was an option.

The Arcanum would never renew her waiver if she wasted their materials—and without it, she had no future at all. Not one she could endure.

"*Freyn'thara, ly'ithra,*" she whispered, her heartbeat picking up as the tiny rune tattooed at the base of her thumb heated. Holding her breath, she used her forceps to carefully nudge the sliver of bone into place before threading a tendril of her own power into it.

For one heart-stopping moment, the pendant trembled under her fingertips. The dissonant whine of compressed aether sliced through the air, setting her teeth on edge. Humans couldn't even hear it, but the sound made every hair on the back of Araya's neck stand up as she grappled with the flow of power, adjusting it with practiced precision.

Finally, with a shudder, it yielded. The screech softened into a low, discordant hum, and the runes she'd carved into the housing holding the shard dimmed. Araya only released the breath she was holding once they had faded completely, sliding the finished amplifier across the workbench.

"Was that your last one, Adept Starwind?" Master Carrow asked from his desk. He didn't look up, his pen scratching faintly as he worked.

"Yes sir." Araya slumped on her stool, her back screaming from the hours she'd spent hunched over her workbench. They were alone in the communal workshop, all the others long gone. She was first in and last out—again.

"How many was that, today?" Carrow rose, crossing the workshop to inspect her work.

"Thirty, sir." Araya held her head high as the Master glanced at her sharply, not working very hard to hide her pride. It was a new record—even for her.

Carrow picked up one of the amplifiers, rolling the pendant between his fingers before testing it. It flared in response, its glow sharp and strong. But the magic itself felt sluggish, lacking the fluidity that came naturally to fae. Human hands could wield magic, but only with help. That's why Araya worked here, in a workshop alongside other fae deemed trustworthy enough to craft and imbue the amplifiers humans needed to wield the power they craved.

"No one else manages that many in a week," Carrow mused, his voice tinged with rare admiration. "And your quality is impeccable, as always. The Arcanum discovered a hidden asset when they granted your waiver, Adept Starwind."

"Thank you, sir." Araya didn't let herself smile, but warmth rose in her chest. She didn't know a single other fae who had risen to the rank of Adept—the highest someone like her could attain. She wouldn't have been able to do it herself without Jaxon's help, even if he had abandoned her when it counted most.

A sharp pang settled under her ribs. This role—menial as it was—was a privilege for her. But she might not even have this for much longer. Her cycle had finally started at twenty-eight years old—late, even for a fae. She had reported it as required, filing for her extension at the same time.

That was six months ago.

Carrow placed the last of her amplifiers into the velvet bag, cinching it closed with a practiced flick of his wrist. Araya watched, swallowing her nerves as she steeled herself to speak.

"Sir...about my waiver?" She hesitated, but pressed forward when Carrow paused to glance up at her. "Have you heard anything?"

"The Arcanum has no shortage of petitions to review," Carrow said. He tucked the bag into his case, carefully securing her day's work. He watched her for a heartbeat, then sighed, his expression softening. "It doesn't go unnoticed, Adept. Your hard work—your dedication. I'm certain they see that."

Araya forced a small smile, lowering her gaze. It didn't matter if it was noticed—not if they took everything from her anyway. At any moment, the Arcanum could strip her of everything she'd worked so hard for. They would tell her she had served well and now it was time to do her duty to the New Dominion. And then they would send her away—to a life she wanted no part of.

"You've done everything you can, Adept," Carrow said. He gave her an almost sympathetic look. "It's up to the Arcanum now."

That wasn't comforting. *Nothing* would be comforting until she had confirmation that she wouldn't end up like the others—her magic stripped away and her worth reduced to what power she could bring to whatever human mage the Arcanum deemed a good match for her bloodline. That was all most fae females were worth to them.

But Araya had spent her whole life showing them she was useful, proving she was worth keeping. It had to be enough.

"Thank you, sir." Araya forced a bitter smile as Carrow gathered his things. "Happy Ascendancy."

Carrow sighed, rubbing the bridge of his nose as he studied her. "Araya...Are you walking home alone tonight?"

Araya blinked. The question caught her off guard—Carrow was not the type to ask personal questions, much less show concern.

"I have my papers—"

"Papers won't stop a mob, Starwind." Carrow exhaled sharply. "You should have left with the others."

"I had work to finish, sir."

"You always do." Carrow shook his head. His tone wasn't unkind, but there was something too close to pity in his eyes, and it made her chest tighten.

"Take care, Araya," he said quietly. "Lock up on your way out."

Araya busied herself at the workbench, reorganizing tools that were already in their place and rubbing imaginary specks of dirt off them with a soft cloth. She didn't let her hands start to shake until the door swung closed behind him, the latch clicking shut and leaving her in silence.

Araya gripped the edge of the table, knuckles white, blinking fast against the sudden burn in her eyes. She pressed a hand to her mouth, stifling a sound that might have been a sob, then slowly sank onto the stool by her bench. For a few long breaths, she let herself feel it all—the fear, the anger, the uncertainty of what tomorrow would look like for her.

Then, like she had done every day for the past six months, she packed it all up into a tiny, neat box and locked it in the back of her mind.

Then she straightened. Wiped her eyes. Thirty amplifiers in one day—that had to count for something, didn't it?

Araya clung to that hope as she moved through the workshop, securing the windows one by one, shutting out the distant roar of the streets below. The celebrations had begun as the sun started to set, filling the city with laughter, drums, and the crackle of fireworks.

For humans, Dominion Day was a night of pride. A night where they toasted the kingdom they had built on stolen magic. But for fae females like Araya, Dominion Day was a night best spent behind locked doors.

The others had left hours ago, slipping away in small, tight-knit groups for safety. No one had asked if she was coming, or invited her to walk with them.

They never did.

Araya had been set apart the moment the Arcanum granted her waiver, permitting Jaxon to sponsor her apprenticeship while her peers were reassigned to workshops and other menial pursuits, only to disappear into the breeding program once their cycles began.

Jaxon hadn't saved her like he'd promised. He'd left her here without a word of explanation, leaving her trapped on the same precipice as every fae female under the Arcanum's authority.

Araya exhaled sharply, pushing the thought to the back of her mind as she hurried through the rest of her cleanup and swept her cloak around her shoulders. It might be summer, but only a fool would walk around tonight without doing everything they could to hide their fae blood.

She fastened the clasp at her throat as the door creaked open behind her. "Did you forget something, sir?"

But it wasn't Carrow who responded, his voice filled with a familiar dry amusement that sent her heart galloping as she whipped around to face him, not believing her own ears.

"You never used to call me *sir*."

"Jaxon," Araya whispered, her traitorous heart skipping a beat.

The last time she'd seen him—Gods only knew, they had never been equals, but it had been as close as they would ever get. Now he stood before her, immaculate in a high-collared black coat trimmed with gold thread. A formal black sash crossed his chest, pinned in place by a gleaming medallion bearing the Arcanum's Eye—marking him not only a Master, but a Commander.

But that smile was the same—smug, self-assured, steeped in privilege and charm. Worse, so was her reaction to it. If Jaxon had been fae, he would have heard her heart betray her. It thundered in her chest, caught somewhere between longing and dread.

The door fell shut behind him, plunging the workshop back into shadow. He prowled toward her, the click of his polished boots ringing out against the stone.

"Are you finished for tonight?" he drawled, his voice as thick and sweet as honey.

"I—" Araya stumbled over her words. "I just finished. I'm meeting Serafina tonight."

"Reschedule," Jaxon suggested. He stepped closer, crowding her. Gods, he even smelled the same—the familiar vanilla perfume of his soap surrounding her. "Come to dinner with me instead, Starling."

Araya stiffened. The old nickname slid between her ribs like a cold knife, cutting straight through the heat he stirred.

"I can't," she said shortly, fighting to keep her voice level. "I didn't even know you were back—you never wrote."

She had. Twice.

The first time was three years ago, when the sting of his abandonment was a raw wound in her battered heart. The second was just six months ago, when desperation drowned out her better judgement.

He hadn't answered either one.

Jaxon tilted his head, watching her. "I wasn't exactly in a position to write, Starling."

That wasn't an answer, and they both knew it. But his hand caught hers before she could pull away, his thumb grazing over the tiny *ly'ithra* rune tattooed at the base of her thumb. The tiny touch sent a spark of warmth through her, curling low in her stomach.

Even when she wanted nothing more than to forget she had ever met Jaxon Shaw, her body remembered.

Gods, she hated herself for that.

"For three years?" she snapped, yanking her hand away. She tried to step back, but the workbench pressed into her spine, leaving her nowhere to retreat.

"I'm making up for it now, Starling," Jaxon murmured. His hand slipped beneath her cloak, tracing tiny, maddening circles on her hip with his fingertips. "Have dinner with me. Serafina will understand."

Araya choked on her incredulous laugh. Serafina absolutely would not understand, though Araya refrained from reminding him that her best friend still despised him. Araya wasn't sure what startled her more—his audacity, or the way her heart still fluttered when he looked at her like that.

"I promised Serafina that I would help with maternity rounds tonight," she said. "She's scheduled for Ravonfar."

"On Dominion Day?" Jaxon's frown deepened, his fingers tightening on her hip as she tried to step out of his arms. "It's a holiday, Araya. Everyone else is celebrating. Why not take a break and enjoy it?"

Enjoy it. The words turned her stomach. "Babies don't care about holidays, Jaxon," she said, forcing a thin smile.

Jaxon didn't answer right away. The silence stretched taut between them, broken only by her own thundering heart in her ears.

"I'll find you after, then," he said finally. "I reserved a table—we can do drinks instead."

He twisted a strand of hair that had escaped her braid around his finger, tracing how it shifted from deep red to dark violet. His thumb grazed the long line of her neck—a featherlight touch that sent goosebumps racing across her skin before he finally dropped his hand, releasing her.

"Jaxon—"

"Don't make me wait too long, Starling," he murmured, softening the warning with a grin that could somehow still ruin her.

Then he was gone.

The door shut behind him with a soft thud, leaving her alone with the lingering scent of vanilla and old regrets.

Araya sagged against the workbench, her breath leaving her in a shaky rush. Only Jaxon Shaw affected her like this—and he knew it. Three years without a single gods-forsaken letter, and in one night, he had undone her.

She shook her head, staring out the window as she pressed a hand to her chest, desperate to slow her galloping heart. She didn't even know if he meant to keep the promise he'd made her three years ago.

Was she a fool for hoping he did?

Araya scowled out the window, not sure she wanted the answer to that question. People thronged the streets around the Aetherium, the celebration in full swing now that night had finally fallen.

"Gods save me." She leapt to her feet, swearing as she yanked her hood up to cover her hair and the clipped tips of her ears. She was so late—Serafina was going to kill her. Healer or not.

———

Revelers clogged the streets around the Aetherium, their wild laughter clashing with the frantic drumbeats and the sharp crack of fireworks overhead. Heat and smoke thickened the air, the acrid taste of spent firepowder burning in her throat.

Araya yanked her hood lower as a man slammed into her shoulder, slurring something unintelligible at her before lurching away. She kept moving, weaving through the crowd without meeting anyone's gaze.

She didn't slow until the towering spires of the Aetherium were behind her, crossing the bridge into the outer districts. The crowds were thinner here, the raucous celebration giving way to a subdued hush as she passed through the shadow of the crumbling wall that separated Ravonfar from the city.

Relief unfurled in Araya's chest as she spotted Serafina waiting near the gate. The Healer spotted her too, greeting her with a scowl.

"You're late." Serafina grabbed Araya's arm, not giving her a chance to catch her breath. "I've been waiting for ages!"

"Sorry—" Araya fumbled out her papers for the guard as Serafina dragged her forward. "Work ran long. And then, you'll never believe it—Jaxon showed up."

"Jaxon?" Serafina snatched her papers back from the guard so abruptly that Araya flinched, half-expecting a reprimand. "What did *he* want?"

"Dinner." Araya handed her own, much thicker packet of papers to the guard with an apologetic smile he didn't bother to return. "But I told him I was meeting you—"

"Hood down," the guard ordered, his fingers curling around the club at his belt.

"Ah, sorry—" Araya shoved her hood back, not giving him an excuse to use it. The humid air clung to her skin as his gaze flicked from her face to the portrait stamped on her papers. Finally, he folded her papers back up, but he didn't hand them back.

"Left hand," he ordered.

The hair on the back of Araya's neck prickled as she held out her hand, palm-down to display the rune tattooed just below the knuckle of her thumb, where the skin stretched thin over bone.

The guard leaned in, his sour breath wafting over her skin as he pressed his fingers roughly into the mark. Her stomach turned, nausea rising in the back of her throat as aether flared under her skin, answering his call obediently—then kept going. A thread of her magic slipped free, leeching away under his touch.

Araya barely checked the instinct to rip her hand away. That power wasn't hers to give or his to take—it belonged to the Arcanum. But if she fought him now, the Arcanum wouldn't be here to keep him from punishing her. All she could do was grit her teeth and close her eyes against the violation of it—

"Is that really necessary?" Serafina snapped.

The guard's lip curled, his fingers lingering a second too long before he finally released her. Her magic recoiled, retreating like a wounded animal as he shoved her papers back into her hand with a grunt.

"Move along, then."

Serafina muttered something vicious under her breath and turned, taking Araya's arm gently but firmly. "Come on."

She shoved through the gate, setting off at a brisk pace that forced Araya to almost trot to keep up, her skin still buzzing with unease as they rushed through the deserted streets.

"Are you alright?" Serafina asked once they were clear, her voice tight with fury. "He's not allowed to do that—why didn't you stop him?"

"Because then he would have beaten me," Araya said flatly. "And I'd be one of your patients instead of your assistant tonight—that would have made us *really* late."

Serafina stopped walking, guilt flickering across her face. "Gods, Araya—"

"It's fine. I'm fine—he didn't take that much." Araya waved her off, already moving again. "Let's just get to the clinic."

"You know I can't do this without you," Serafina said quietly, falling into step beside her.

"You have five apprentices," Araya pointed out, laughing. "Surely one of them can handle checking names off a list."

"I have five *human* apprentices." Serafina sighed, not bothering to hide her frustration. "Half these females wouldn't be here if I didn't have you with me. It doesn't matter that I've spent my whole life helping them—here, they'll never see me as anything but human."

Araya didn't have an answer to that. In some ways, Serafina was more fae than she was. After all, she'd grown up with a half-fae father, while Araya had been raised by human minders in the reeducation camps the Arcanum established for fae orphans, where they'd beaten every bit of fae they could out of her.

But here—just like in the Aetherium—blood trumped everything.

Serafina was only a quarter-fae. No one would ever mistake her blonde hair for spun gold, and her green eyes could have come from her human mother as easily as her half-fae father. She had never needed permission to practice magic. No one had ever pinned her to a table and tattooed a *ly'ithra* rune on her hand, condemning her to a fraction of her power while the rest went to the Arcanum to feed their never-ending thirst for magic.

But Araya was three-quarters fae. A halfblood, by the Arcanum's laws. Even worse, she *looked* fae. From her deep red hair streaked with violet, to her silver eyes, to the way aether pulsed beneath her skin and her clipped ears, marking her as someone who had suffered at the hands of the Arcanum.

And that, to the fae here, made her safe.

They fell into an uneasy silence as they raced through the deserted streets. There were no cheery bonfires here, no bright songs drifting through the air. Here, every broken window and flimsy door was bolted tight, offering no sign of the residents that surely huddled inside.

"So?" Serafina demanded as they walked up to the community hall the Arcanum had reluctantly granted her use of for her maternity clinic. "What did you tell him?"

"I told him I couldn't go," Araya said.

"And he just took no for an answer?" Serafina snorted, handing her papers over to another human guard. "That doesn't sound like Jaxon."

"No," Araya admitted, handing her own papers over. "He wants to get drinks after I'm done here. He said he has a table reserved."

The guard here barely glanced at her papers, stifling a yawn as he handed them back. An interior checkpoint in Ravonfar was pretty much the lowest position a guard could get—Araya wondered what he'd done to deserve it.

"Do you *want* to get drinks with him?" Serafina ducked into the ramshackle building, nodding to the females already lined up waiting for them, many of them clutching heavy bellies.

"Maybe." Araya had too much fae blood to lie to Serafina—no matter how badly she wanted to, the denial stuck in her throat. "For old time's sake."

Serafina made a sound somewhere between a scoff and a snort, but whatever sharp retort she'd been ready to unleash died when one of the waiting females doubled over, a rattling cough overtaking her thin frame. She clutched her swollen stomach, her breath coming in sharp gasps.

Serafina stopped instantly, her irritation evaporating as she slid an arm around the female's shoulders and rubbed slow circles on her back until the spell passed.

Araya slipped past them and ducked into the clinic, blinking hard. She blamed the burn in her eyes on the harsh soap the Healers used to scrub everything down. The astringent tang clung to the air, mingling with the sour stench of damp wood and sweat.

But it wasn't the soap.

It was the line of females, hollow-eyed and desperate for whatever reprieve their wombs could buy them. If they delivered healthy children, they would earn the chance to move to a better district—a safer one, further from the shadowed mists that crept in from the Obsidian Shore. Ravonfar was a pit, one of the grimy corners of Aetheris where fae survived by only the narrowest of margins.

If not for Serafina, she would have ended up here when Jaxon left. And she still might, if the Arcanum declined her waiver and restricted her movements.

Araya cast a quick glance over the clinic, scanning the stained privacy screens and sagging cots to ensure everything was in place before taking her place at the wobbly desk by the door. She checked each female in, flipping quickly through their papers and recording the relevant information for the Arcanum's records.

Every one of them carried marks of their fae heritage, just like she did. Hair that was too bright or too dark, eyes that gleamed with an inhuman hue in the dim light, ears that were either delicately pointed or scarred. Araya avoided looking too closely at any of the fae with clipped ears, unwilling to recognize anyone from her past.

"Araya, can you come here, please?" Serafina's voice was calm, but Araya could see the tension that hid beneath her serene expression.

"She's afraid to talk to me," Serafina whispered as Araya ducked behind the screen, pulling it shut behind them. "Can you try?"

Araya nodded, her throat tight as she stared at the female huddled on the rickety cot, her body curled protectively around her swollen belly. Araya could see the marks of a life in the camps on her skin and body, the jagged edges of her ears not quite hidden by the fall of her black hair. She must have fought when they clipped them.

Araya knelt beside the cot, moving slowly in an effort not to startle her. She had enough nightmares of her own to guess at this female's fear.

"*Vira'thal,*" she murmured, one of the few phrases she remembered of her native tongue that had nothing to do with magic.

The female's head whipped up, her violet eyes wide. Araya stayed perfectly still, letting the female take in her silver eyes, the deep red hue of her hair and the way it darkened to violet, and—most telling of all—the jagged edges of her own ears.

Araya had fought too.

"Velgrim?" the female whispered, her voice so quiet that even Araya's fae hearing struggled to catch it.

"Kaldrath," Araya replied just as softly. *Never speak too loudly*—it was the first of many hard lessons all fae learned in the camps. Humans could hear much better than fae children realized. "What's your name?"

"Eilwen," the female murmured, her voice trembling. "I... I'm from Farhallow. But I heard...they said there was someone in Ravonfar who could help fae like me...if you knew who to ask."

"She helps," Araya said, glancing toward Serafina. The Healer couldn't hear their muttered conversation, but watched with quiet concern. Araya knew her friend bent every rule she could, walking the knife's edge between what was permitted and what was right. Clearly, word of her kindness had traveled.

"You can trust her," Araya added. "She's a quarter fae."

Eilwen's gaze darted between them, her fear almost tangible in the dim light. Slowly, she nodded, her hands twisting in her tattered shawl until her knuckles whitened.

"I didn't report my pregnancy to the Arcanum," she said loudly enough for Serafina to hear, her hushed words heavy with desperation. "The father... isn't the human they matched me with."

"Fae?" Serafina asked, her careful tone betraying no judgment.

Eilwen nodded, tears glimmering in her violet eyes. "He's dead—he didn't even know. I thought... I thought I could hide it, just until the baby was born." Her voice cracked, breaking into a sob as she buried her face in her hands.

Serafina stilled, the dread that flashed over her face echoing the tightness in Araya's chest. Araya had checked her in—that meant the pregnancy had to be recorded. And even if they left the father's name blank, the babe's fae bloodline would be obvious the moment it was born.

"Let's just start with an exam," Serafina said gently, stepping forward. "How far along do you think you are?"

"About seven months," Eilwen whispered, trembling as Serafina helped her stretch out on the cot and lift her thin shirt to expose her swollen belly.

"Are you eating enough?" Serafina asked, her hands moving in careful, practiced motions along Eilwen's abdomen. "Any pain? Cramps?"

Serafina's questions blurred, her gentle voice muffled by the rising pressure in Araya's skull. If the Arcanum decided Araya was more useful as a breeder than a mage, they would deny her waiver. Strip her of her magic. Her name would be reduced to a line on a registry, her worth measured in offspring and obedience.

Her breath hitched. Her vision blurred. She couldn't—she wouldn't—

Eilwen's voice cut through the fog, thin and shaking. "Will they take the baby?"

"They'll try," Serafina said, her expression somber. "But I'll do everything I can to stop them, Eilwen. I promise."

Araya swallowed hard.

Serafina could make promises like that. She could stand tall in front of the Arcanum, bend the rules and take risks—because her human blood shielded her.

Her pulse thundered in her ears as she backed away from the cot. The walls pressed in around her, the air too thin in her lungs. Araya had no shield. She only had her waiver, the thin thread of usefulness she clung to like a lifeline.

She didn't realize she was shaking until her hip bumped the tray of instruments, nearly toppling it. Metal clattered as she fumbled to steady it, barely catching everything.

"I—" Her voice cracked. "I need some air."

She turned and slipped through the curtain without waiting to make sure Serafina even heard her. She had to get out of here—before anyone saw her fall apart.

———

Araya moved on instinct, her feet carrying her out of the clinic and into the night. The guard barely stirred, not bothering to challenge her as she rushed past him.

She didn't think—just walked.

By the time the cobblestones gave way to jagged shards of obsidian, her breath had slowed, blind panic retreating enough that she could think again. She stopped, staring out at the dark waves that stretched out in front of her, gleaming silver in the moonlight until they vanished beneath the ever-present looming wall of mist.

Guilt gnawed at her—she'd promised Serafina she would help. But she couldn't. Not tonight.

A cold wind swept off the water, cutting through her cloak and threading damp fingers through her hair, chilling her despite the warmth of the summer evening. The mist drifted on the current, unraveling in long tendrils that curled over the waves, reaching for the land.

The fae in these districts called it the Shadowed Veil—a lingering remnant of the war that had toppled their king and ripped them from their place in the world. On nights when it thickened, those tendrils billowed over the black glass and reached into the streets, bringing misfortune with it.

Children wasted away, burning with fever. Mothers woke gasping for breath—and when a father left for work and never returned, or a sister vanished on her way home…all the fae could do was blame the mist.

It was nothing but superstition. The mist didn't make the fae sick. It was hunger and poverty that opened the door to disease, and the Arcanum's relentless rationing of magic that let it run rampant through these neighborhoods.

And as for the creatures in the Veil—they were nothing but stories, tales told to keep children from straying too close to shore. Over time, they'd grown teeth and claws, becoming the nightmares of children and adults alike.

At least… that was what Araya had always believed. But standing here, alone in the dark? The certainty she'd clung to wavered.

Araya rubbed absently at the thin scar that stretched across her palm—a mark from years ago when these same sharp stones had bitten into her flesh. The hiss of the waves sounded almost like voices now, a low chorus of whispers rising and falling in rhythm with the tide.

She couldn't make out the words. But the cadence was familiar—too familiar. Like the darkness spoke a language she should have remembered, but couldn't quite grasp.

The whispers sharpened, scraping against her mind and pressing into her skull until—

"Araya?"

The voices vanished, sucked back into the mist as if they had never existed.

Serafina picked her way carefully across the obsidian shards. Her braid was damp, loose strands whipping around her face in the wind. She had changed out of her blue Healer's robes, the sleeves of her plain dress pushed up to her elbows, revealing the faint smudges of soap and water still clinging to her skin.

"What are you doing out here?" she asked.

Araya blinked, disoriented. Had she really been out here long enough for Serafina to finish seeing patients and clean the clinic?

"I just needed some air," she said, forcing her voice to steady as she fought the urge to glance back at the now-motionless mist. "I didn't mean to worry you. Is Eilwen alright? The babe?"

"They're both going to be fine," Serafina replied, stopping beside her. Her voice was calm, but her gaze lingered on Araya's pale face. "Are *you* alright?"

Araya opened her mouth, desperately wishing she could lie. What she would give to say *yes* and sweep all of this under the rug— but it stuck in her throat like shards of glass. She coughed, dislodging the lie and letting the truth slip out instead.

"I started my cycle six months ago." Araya dropped her eyes, unable to face the betrayal she knew she'd find in Serafina's expression. "I didn't tell anyone. I just filed the mandatory report with the Arcanum and sent a letter to Jaxon—but that's it."

Serafina stiffened. Her breath hitched once, like she'd been slapped.

"Jaxon," she repeated, her voice sharp. "That's why he's back then. Swooping in like the vulture he is."

"He could help me—"

"I could have helped you!" Serafina snapped. The words rang out, too loud against the crash of the waves. But her voice hollowed at the end, fraying with hurt. "You should've told *me*."

Araya pressed her arms tight around herself, as if that could keep everything inside from breaking loose. "You can't stop the Arcanum from revoking my waiver."

"And Jaxon can?" Serafina demanded. "You don't need him, Araya. You've served the Arcanum loyally for years. That has to mean something."

"Does it?" Araya laughed, bitter and breathless as she finally looked up to meet Serafina's eyes. "Even for a halfblood?"

The slur hung between them, ugly and heavy. Serafina's face tightened, but she didn't flinch away.

"They've already made exceptions for you," she pressed. "They haven't said anything yet. Maybe they just won't."

"I'm not risking my life on a '*maybe*,'" Araya said flatly. "Jaxon could be my only sure way out of this. He said he'd help me—"

"*Three years ago*," Serafina said. "Before he left you here without a word of warning. He's not here to save you out of the goodness of his heart, Araya. He wants something."

"Of course he does," Araya snapped. "The same thing he's always wanted—*me*."

It hadn't mattered that it was forbidden—not to him. Jaxon always took what he wanted, rules be damned. And when she was his apprentice, what he wanted was *her*.

Or at least, she'd thought it was. Until he left.

Serafina stared at her, eyes wide as the wind lifted the loose hair that had escaped her braid from her face. "Araya...you don't still love him, do you?"

"I don't have the luxury of love," Araya snapped. "There isn't another choice here, Serafina—not for me."

She turned away, black glass crunched under her feet as she stormed toward the street. Sometimes it felt like Serafina lived in a different world than she did. But Araya knew better. Jaxon was young, powerful, and ambitious. Even if he didn't love her, there were worse human mages to tie herself to.

"Araya, wait!" Serafina caught up to her, voice breathless. "If there was another way out—would you take it?"

Araya froze mid-step, her back still to Serafina. "There isn't another way."

"You could leave," Serafina whispered, as if even the wind might carry it to the wrong ears. "If we planned it right—"

"No." Araya spun around so fast the hem of her cloak snapped. "Are you *insane?*" Her voice shook. "Do you have any idea what they'd do to us if someone heard you say that?"

"I'm just saying—"

"No," Araya hissed. "If they catch me even *thinking* about that, they won't just revoke my waiver—they'll collar me. It will be Kaldrath all over again—only worse."

Serafina's lips parted, maybe to apologize, maybe to argue—but Araya didn't wait to find out. If she stopped to listen, even for a second, the hurt roiling in her chest might boil over into something she couldn't take back.

There was a new guard at the gate. He barely glanced at Araya's papers before waving her through, but she still caught the sneer curling at the edges of his mouth.

"Happy Ascendancy," he said.

Araya nodded stiffly, tucking her papers away. She should have thanked him, but twisting the words into a half-truths she could speak would take more energy than she had left.

Serafina fell into step beside her, their footsteps the only sound in the deserted streets. The transition was subtle at first—a few intact windows, a freshly painted door. The streets widened, the golden light from well-tended aetherlamps softening the edges of the darkness. Even the buildings stood straighter, small gardens full of sweet late-summer flowers spilling over wrought iron fences. Somewhere, a woman's laugh drifted through an open window, light and carefree.

When she remembered that this was where Serafina had grown up, Araya could almost forgive her optimism. There was still hope here, even if it was tattered at the edges.

But Serafina's father had died on these streets, murdered for nothing more than daring to exist as a half-fae. Safety was never a guarantee—not for fae.

"That's different," Serafina murmured, breaking the silence as they turned onto their street.

Araya followed her gaze and froze. The carriage stood waiting outside their little house, the Arcanum's Eye gleaming gold on the door against the sleek black finish, a silent reminder of the power it represented.

Jaxon leaned casually against it, his dark eyes glittering as they swept over her. A smirk curved his lips, sharp and knowing.

"Adept Serafina Hart," Jaxon said smoothly, though his attention never wavered from Araya. "Happy Ascendancy."

"Jaxon," Serafina replied, inclining her head just enough to be polite before brushing past him to unlock the door.

Araya swallowed. Her throat was dry. "I need two minutes to change," she said quickly, her gaze darting between Jaxon and the carriage. "Where are we going?"

Jaxon grinned, running his tongue over the blunt edge of his front teeth. "You'll see," he said. "Wear something nice."

It wasn't an answer—not really. Araya hesitated.

"Are you sure?" she asked, fingers worrying the frayed edge of her cloak. "It's Dominion Day."

Tomorrow, Serafina's clinic would be full of fae females—bruised, broken—whispering through swollen lips about the guards who had let their drunken attackers go free. The ones who had laughed. Or worse—joined in.

Araya had seen it before—had scrubbed bloodstains from clinic floors, had watched too many fae swallow back sobs as their futures were decided by someone else.

Jaxon's low laugh curled around her like smoke—thick and

suffocating. He stepped closer, invading her space. "I was the one who reminded you, Starling."

Her breath caught. Gods, he said it so easily—like nothing had changed. Like he still believed she belonged to him. And worst of all, part of her wanted to believe it too.

His fingers grazed her temple, sliding down to tuck a strand of hair behind her ear and tracing the scarred edge with a featherlight touch.

"Wear your hair down tonight. Show your ears—whatever you want." He smiled down at her, reading the objection on her face before she could voice it. "Don't worry, you'll be perfectly safe with me."

Safe. The word sent a chill down her spine. She should say no—it was madness to flaunt her fae features tonight of all nights. But the rejection lodged in her throat, tightening like the collar the Arcanum would lock around her neck if she even considered running from them.

She couldn't be a breeder. She needed Jaxon's help.

"Two minutes," she repeated, her voice steady despite the unease clawing at her chest.

Jaxon's smirk didn't falter. If anything, it deepened—lazy and unshaken.

"I'll wait."

CHAPTER
TWO

Araya stood in front of her battered wardrobe, staring at her reflection in the cloudy mirror. Her meager assortment of dresses hung in a limp, somber line, picked for function rather than style. She ran her fingers over the frayed edges of a pale blue dress, pulling it free. Once, it might have been considered elegant. Now, after countless mendings and adjustments, it looked as tired as she felt.

She sighed, tossing the dress onto the growing pile of rejected options on her neat, narrow bed. Everything she owned felt wrong for this—too plain and too worn. There just weren't many occasions when a halfblood needed a *nice* dress. It wasn't every day she had to beg the man who left her to risk his status to help her keep what little freedom she had left.

Araya reached for her braid, unwinding the ribbon at the end and slowly unraveling it. Deep red waves cascaded over her shoulders, fading into violet as they spilled down her back. She stared at her reflection, her silver eyes stark against the riot of color framing her face. Her stomach churned at the idea of stepping outside like this, on Dominion Day, no less. But Jaxon had told her to wear it down... he'd always loved her hair.

She gathered her hair in her hands, twisting it back into a loose knot at the nape of her neck. It wasn't exactly what Jaxon had requested, but it was more than her usual braid. A compromise... Jaxon had never been good at those. Araya picked up a hairpin, biting her lip as she slid it into place.

"You should wear it down," Serafina said softly from the doorway.

Araya turned, startled by the sadness in Serafina's voice. But her questions caught in her throat when she saw the shimmering silver gown draped across Serafina's arms.

"Is that your mother's dress?" Araya asked, the hairpin slipping from her fingers.

Serafina nodded, her green eyes shining with unshed tears.

"Serafina..." Araya trailed off, brushing her fingers over the delicate fabric.

She remembered Serafina's mother—warm and quick-witted, even after she'd gotten sick. Even though they had only spoken a handful of times, Araya had felt her absence like a ghost when Serafina invited her to move into the house with her.

"I can't take this," she said. "It's one of the only things you have left of her—"

"She would want you to wear it," Serafina interrupted. "She'd understand everything you're doing—even if I don't. I shouldn't have argued with you—you were right. It's not my place to judge your relationship with Jaxon."

The weight of her friend's words pressed against Araya's chest, tightening her throat.

"Thank you," she said when she finally managed to find her voice again. "For understanding."

Araya stood still as Serafina helped her slip into the gown, the gossamer fabric settling over her like a second skin. Impossibly light and soft, it was unlike anything she had ever worn.

Serafina smoothed the gown over Araya's shoulders, her hands lingering as though to steady them both. Then, with deliberate care, she reached for the pins in Araya's hair. One by one, she pulled them free, letting the heavy waves tumble loose.

"You should wear it down," Serafina said again. "You deserve to enjoy yourself tonight. And the... safety Jaxon offers."

Araya inhaled sharply as she stared at her reflection in the cracked mirror. She hardly recognized the female staring back at her. The silver gown made her eyes glow like molten quicksilver, and her unbound hair framed her face in wild waves of flame and shadow. She looked more like a fae princess than a halfblood mage.

Their gazes met in the mirror, and Araya's breath hitched at the raw emotion etched into Serafina's face. The sadness was there, threaded through with fear, but it wasn't the fear of judgment or disapproval—it was the fear of losing her.

Serafina's fingers traced the delicate embroidery near the neckline, her lips pressing into a thin line. "I do understand, you know," she said quietly. "That you're just trying to survive. I just want to make sure you can live with what you feel like you have to do."

Araya turned, her throat suddenly tight.

"Serafina..." Her voice faltered. She wrapped her arms tightly around her friend, holding on harder and longer than she usually would.

"It's just dinner," she murmured, but the words felt thin and hollow.

Serafina just hugged her tighter. "I'll be here when you need me," she whispered. Her voice was steady, but her hands trembled against Araya's back. And when she stepped away, her eyes shone with unshed tears. "Be safe."

"You too," Araya whispered as the door clicked closed behind her best friend.

It felt like a crime to put her ragged, threadbare cloak on over a dress like this. Fortunately, it was warm enough that she didn't really need a cloak if she was going to be with Jaxon. Like he'd said— he'd keep her safe.

Still, she shivered when she stepped outside, the night air brushing over her bare skin, leaving her raw and exposed.

But she bravely lifted the skirt of the dress to avoid stepping on the hem as she descended the stairs, making her way over to where Jaxon leaned against the carriage, absently picking at his nails with a knife. He frowned down at his fingers, the blade catching the lamplight, but his eyes lit up when he saw Araya. He tucked the blade away, a slow smile spreading across his face as he straightened and strode toward her.

"Perfect," he murmured, dragging his gaze over her. His smile deepened as his hand slid down her side, lingering at her waist before his palm finally settled at the small of her back, drawing her closer even as she tensed.

"Still mad at me?" he asked lightly, like it was a private joke instead of an open wound. "Can't say I blame you. But we both know this is exactly where you were always meant to be."

Araya forced a tight smile. It didn't matter that he'd shattered her heart three years ago—he was the only chance she had left.

So she let Jaxon guide her forward, so focused on the hem of her dress and not tripping as he helped her into the carriage that she didn't notice the man already seated inside until she was halfway through the door.

She froze. A rabbit before a predator. Every instinct screaming at her to run. But Jaxon's hand pressed firm against her back, unyielding.

"Get in," he ordered.

Her feet obeyed before her mind caught up. She sank onto the bench opposite High Magister Garrick Shaw, the celebrated Architect of the New Dominion, the highest ranking member of the Arcanum —and Jaxon Shaw's father.

Garrick didn't look up from the stack of parchment in his hands, even when Jaxon slid into the seat beside him and the carriage lurched into motion. He ignored them both completely—as if they were little more than an afterthought he'd attend to once his real work was done.

Araya didn't dare break the silence, but Jaxon only smirked when she caught his eye, maddeningly unbothered.

So she folded her hands in her lap, curling her fingers into the silk of her borrowed gown to still their shaking, and waited for the man who had written the laws she was now trapped beneath to finally acknowledge her.

By the time Garrick Shaw finally looked up, Araya's heart was pounding so loudly she could barely hear her own thoughts.

"You must be Araya Starwind," he said, setting his papers aside at last. "Jaxon has told me a great deal about you."

"High Magister." Araya dipped her head, glad neither man could hear her thundering heart as the carriage jolted over the uneven cobblestones. "I'm sorry—I didn't—"

She trailed off helplessly, staring accusingly at Jaxon. He just grinned at her, his expression lazy and satisfied as she squirmed under his father's scrutiny. Araya looked away, forcing herself to meet Garrick's eyes instead—a mistake. His sharp brown eyes lacked any of Jaxon's easy warmth, pinning her in place as he dissected her with cold, calculating intent.

His lips curved into the faintest semblance of a smile at her unease, a gesture so small it sent a shiver down her spine. Without dropping her gaze, he flicked his fingers, his signet ring glowing as the stack of parchment lifted off his lap and arranged itself into a neat pile on the seat beside him.

Araya stared at the ring—an amplifier, no doubt. Custom made, powerful. He hadn't even thought twice about using power for something so mundane. Meanwhile, the fae in the districts measured every drop of aether like it might be their last.

"Your friend seems stunned into silence," Garrick said, glancing at his son.

"I didn't warn her," Jaxon said with a laugh. "I thought it would be fun to surprise her."

"Jaxon," Araya hissed, heat crawling up her neck to her cheeks.

He just leaned back, drumming his fingers idly on the leather bench as he grinned at her. "I love watching you think on your feet, Starling. You never disappoint me."

Garrick's smile deepened just a fraction. "Jaxon, you'll give the poor girl a heart attack." He shook his head, glancing at her apologetically.

"My apologies, Araya. I didn't mean to startle you," he said. "But when my son finally brings someone to my table, I do like to meet them face to face. Especially someone so…important to him."

His pause before *important* hung in the air like a blade, pressing unseen against her ribs.

"It's no trouble, sir," she said at last, her voice thin but steady enough. "I was just surprised. It's an honor to meet you." The words spilled out too quickly, betraying her nerves.

From the corner of her eye, she saw Jaxon's grin widen, but it did nothing to steady her fraying composure. Her focus remained on Garrick, the man who could shape—or shatter—her future with a single word.

"Araya was helping one of our Healers in Ravonfar," Jaxon said when no one else spoke. "Serafina Hart—she runs the community clinic in North Bend. Araya helps her with maternity rounds in Ravonfar several times a month."

Araya glanced at him, startled that he would know that. Serafina hadn't started dragging her along on maternity rounds until after he'd left, using them as a convenient way to force Araya out of her bed and into the world.

Garrick's eyebrows rose. "An unusual pastime. Do you not find your work at the Aetherium fulfilling?"

"I do," she said carefully, proud that her voice didn't shake. This was no simple question—it was a test. "I'm very grateful to the Arcanum for giving me the opportunity to work. I've simply always enjoyed helping others in my spare time."

Safe. Neutral. She clung to the words like a shield, but even as she spoke them, she knew they wouldn't be enough.

Garrick tilted his head slightly, his gaze narrowing as if he could see straight through her. "Because you're three-quarters fae," he said, his tone devoid of any inflection that might hint at approval or disapproval. "I remember when we approved your waiver. But you've started cycling now?"

"Yes, sir," Araya whispered. "I reported it—I've been waiting for the Arcanum's decision."

"Which we delayed while we considered Jaxon's petition." Garrick sighed, shaking his head with a small smile. "I see we've caused you no small amount of anxiety. Bureaucracy, I'm afraid, is a beast we just cannot seem to slay."

His petition? Araya's eyes flicked to Jaxon, searching for an answer. But his easy charm had vanished, leaving behind an expression she couldn't read.

"Let me put you at ease," the High Magister said—though the glint in his eye suggested he expected the opposite. "My son has requested to acquire your bond from the Arcanum. Do you understand what this entails?"

"I do," Araya managed to say. She twisted her fingers together, darting another desperate gaze toward Jaxon, but he didn't meet her eye. Instead, he jumped to his feet as soon as the carriage lurched to a stop.

"I'll take care of things inside," he said, not even bothering to look back before the door clicked shut behind him, leaving her alone with the High Magister.

"You can, of course, decline," Garrick said when she just stared at him, the silence stretching a moment too long. He smiled—almost kindly. "If you do, there will be no consequences. No one will punish you. I'll simply tell Jaxon it was my decision."

His fingers drummed idly on the stack of papers. "The Magisters are very aware of how some of our mages abuse their power, pressuring our fae wards into... arrangements. This is your choice—we would never condone coercion."

Araya swallowed hard, her pulse thundering in her ears. It was a trap—laid with silk instead of steel, but a trap all the same. This was the price of escaping the fate that other females suffered.

"No," she said. "I—I'm accepting. I was just... surprised. Jaxon and I haven't spoken since he left for Elvanfal."

"I'm afraid that may have been my fault," Garrick's expression softened, and for a heartbeat Araya saw a flash of Jaxon in him.

"I'll admit, I was less than thrilled by his interest in you during his apprenticeship." Garrick's lips twitched, leaving no doubt in Araya's mind that he knew exactly what that interest had entailed. "I had him assigned to Elvanfal to give you the chance to make your own decision. It was the fairest thing to do, given the circumstances."

Araya stared at him, words failing her. He said it like breaking her heart had been some sort of calculated kindness. Did he know how lost she had been? How hurt? She didn't doubt it—after all, he knew everything else about her.

"But he was determined, so I followed your career—You've truly proven yourself these past years, Araya." Garrick smiled, ignoring her turmoil. "It's an excellent match for you. Jaxon is a highly regarded Commander, on track to become a Magister himself. His children will have position—power. Names that open doors you've never even seen."

Araya nodded numbly, biting the inside of her cheek until she tasted blood.

"You will, of course, cease visiting the fae slums," Garrick continued, picking his papers back up and shuffling through them. "Your duties to Jaxon come first. Your place is by his side. In his bed. Not tending to the less fortunate."

"Of course, sir," she said, her voice wooden as the words settled over her like chains. "I understand."

"Good," he said, settling back against the bench with a satisfied smile. "I'll make it official then—" he glanced at his son as the door swung open and Jaxon stepped back into the carriage. "Congratulations, Jaxon."

Jaxon grinned, his triumphant gaze landing on Araya as he offered her his hand, his grip firm and possessive as he helped her to her feet. "I knew she'd make the right decision."

"Araya, it was a pleasure to meet you," Garrick said as Jaxon helped her to the ground. "Enjoy your Dominion Day."

"Thank you, sir," Araya murmured, dipping her head as the carriage rolled away into the night.

Jaxon's arm coiled around her waist, his fingers pressing into her hip. "Relax," he murmured, his lips brushing the scarred edge of her ear. "That was the hard part."

"Was it?" Araya asked, her heart still pounding with adrenaline. "What happens now?"

Jaxon chuckled, pressing a lingering kiss to her temple. "Now we celebrate, Starling."

CHAPTER

THREE

Garrick had assigned Jaxon to Elvanfal——because of her.

The revelation sat in the hollow of Araya's stomach as Jaxon guided her through the crowd, his hand warm against the small of her back. Did he even know that *she* was the reason he'd been stationed there?

She wanted to ask him. Needed to. But she couldn't seem to catch her breath.

While the streets around the Aetherium had been wild with noise and color, this district pulsed with quiet opulence. Garlands laced with gold shimmered in the light of the aetherlamps. Couples and small groups of well-dressed humans gathered around tall tables, drinks in hand, their heads turning as Araya passed them.

The whispers trailed her like shadows, countless eyes catching on her bright hair and clipped ears. *That's one of them*, someone hissed to their companion. *Look at her eyes—*

Araya fought the instinct to turn tail and run. She didn't belong here. Not with these people. Not tonight. Not ever.

"Breathe, Starling," Jaxon murmured, his lips brushing her ear. "We're almost there."

Araya started to nod—but then she saw where *there* was.

"Jaxon—" She stopped short, heels scraping against the cobblestone as she dragged them both to a halt. "That's the Gilded Lily. I can't go in there."

"You can with me," Jaxon said, without a hint of hesitation.

She stared at the golden doors, heart pounding. The Gilded Lily was more than just a bar—it was a monument to human supremacy that catered to the most elite human mages. Deals were struck there. Futures decided. Names erased.

It was no place for a halfblood.

"No," she whispered, shaking her head. "Jaxon, if someone asks for my papers—or checks my rune—"

"They won't," he cut in smoothly. "Not when you're with me."

He tilted her chin up, his touch featherlight but commanding. "You're bonded to me now, Araya. You go where I go."

The certainty in his voice left no room for argument.

She shrank closer to Jaxon as they crossed the threshold, bracing herself for the outcry—but no one even looked twice. Jaxon moved through the room like he owned it—his hand a steady pressure at the small of her back as he guided her with practiced ease, returning nods and murmured greetings as they wound their way through the room.

"Thanks for holding the table." Jaxon clapped a mage Araya vaguely recognized on the shoulder.

"I'm always happy to drink on *Commander Shaw's* tab," the man raised his glass in a mock toast, grinning as Jaxon tucked her in front of him.

"You remember Kai Sterling, don't you?" Jaxon plucked a glass of sparkling wine off a passing tray, setting it in front of her. "He's a runesmith now. Mara Redmond is an illusionist—" the slim, brown-haired woman nodded, offering a pleasant smile "—and Caylin Pryce, forensic spellwright."

Araya nodded politely, nerves twisting her stomach as she instinctively traced the small rune at the base of her thumb. Jaxon's friends—they may have been at the Aetherium with her, but they'd hardly run in the same circles.

But Kai grinned at her, winking like they'd ever done more than exchange a handful of passing glances in the halls. "Jaxon's little prodigy," he said. "It's good to see you again, Araya. It's been years."

"And yet it feels like yesterday," Caylin said icily, swirling the dark wine in her glass. "I guess you never learned anything useful despite all the books Jaxon snuck you."

Araya's grip tightened on her glass, her shaky smile faltering as the dark-haired human woman's smirk sharpened.

"Too bad that's all over for you now," Caylin said, her voice sugar-slick and venom-tipped. "You'll have other duties, won't you? Now that you're bonded."

Araya flushed at the cruel suggestion in the human woman's voice, shame slithering down her spine. She dropped her gaze, knowing there was no retort. Bonded fae had a clear role—and it didn't involve continuing to work.

But Jaxon cut in, steel threading his voice as he glared at the woman across the table. "Oh, Araya isn't done working," he said. "She's going to be assisting me on a special project for the Arcanum."

Caylin's fingers curled around the stem of her glass, her expression shifting from sharp amusement to unease.

"That can't be right." She glanced around, looking for support, but Mara and Kai were suddenly very interested in their drinks.

Her hesitation hardened into anger. "That's not allowed," she snapped. "The regulations on bonded fae are clear. Once a bond is formalized, their employment status is revoked unless they hold a pre-existing magisterial appointment." Her eyes narrowed. "And Araya doesn't."

Jaxon smiled. "Yet."

Caylin's jaw tightened. "That's not how it works, Jaxon. There's a process—waivers, formal appeal. You can't just override Arcanum policy because you want to take your little pet to work. We have rules for a reason—"

Araya stiffened at the word *pet*, but Jaxon's smirk only deepened.

"You're thinking like a bureaucrat, Caylin," he said, steel threading through his voice as he lifted his drink and took a slow sip. "I'm thinking like someone who knows the system."

He set his glass down, leveling a cool gaze at the human woman. "Araya *will* be working with me. Anyone who has a problem with it is welcome to take it up with my father. He's voiced his full support for the arrangement."

The silence that followed was deafening.

Caylin flushed, pink rising to her cheeks as she faltered under the weight of Jaxon's glare. Her fingers tightened around the stem of her glass as she darted a glance around the table, searching for support. But Kai looked away, feigning sudden interest in his drink, and Mara dropped her eyes, studying the grain of the table with rapt fascination.

Clearing her throat, Caylin squared her shoulders, forcing a razor-thin smile. "Well, Araya," she said, her voice dripping with false sweetness. "Let's hope your magic is as impressive as the... other attributes that have captured Jaxon's interest. It would be such a shame if the Arcanum started to believe he only thought with his cock."

Araya flinched at the crude words, losing the battle not to show a reaction.

Jaxon's grip on Araya's waist tightened, his fingers biting into her side. "The only appropriate thing to say to her is 'congratulations,'" he said, pinning Caylin to the spot with the intensity of a predator sizing up its prey. "Now, this is a celebration, Caylin. For Araya. So celebrate—or leave."

The words hung in the air, heavy and final.

Caylin glared at him, but there was nothing left to say. She shoved her chair back with a loud scrape, downing her drink in a single gulp before slamming her glass back down on the table and storming away, her back stiff with anger.

Mara sighed. "Well done, Jaxon," she said dryly. "She'll be unbearable tomorrow."

"Caylin is always unbearable," Kai said, raising his glass. He caught Araya's eye, grinning at her. "Don't judge us all by her, please. Some of us are much more charming."

Araya managed a weak smile, though the heat in her cheeks lingered. "It's fine," she said. The urge to lower her gaze tugged at her, but she resisted, brushing against the back of Jaxon's hand. The gesture was more for herself than him—an attempt to ground the swirling tension inside her.

Conversation and alcohol flowed easily around the table after that, the humans slipping into a practiced camaraderie. Laughter rippled like a stream, light and effortless as they swapped stories and sharp-edged quips, their voices weaving together in a melody Araya didn't know the words to. She nodded and smiled where she thought it was appropriate, but no matter how many friendly glances Kai sent her way or how deliberately Jaxon included her in the banter, Araya couldn't shake the sense of being out of place.

Jaxon's touch was her only anchor. His arm curved around her waist, his firm grip and the warm press of his chest against her back grounding her in place. She wasn't sure if his touch was meant to reassure her or to warn everyone else that she was his, but either way, it worked.

The stares that had followed her through the streets were absent here, the weight of human scrutiny diffused by Jaxon's presence. No one dared openly comment on what Jaxon had so clearly marked as his. The realization left a bitter taste in her mouth, but Araya swallowed it down. The stares were gone, and that counted for something.

"Here, try this," Jaxon murmured, sliding a small plate of food in front of her. "I know you didn't stop to eat."

"Thanks." She offered him a soft smile, touched by the gesture. He was right—she hadn't eaten since lunch, and the wine was already making her head swim. She picked up a small bite, enjoying the explosion of flavors across her tongue.

"Of course, Starling," Jaxon murmured, but his attention was already shifting. His gaze snagged on something across the room, his entire posture sharpening in an instant. The easy confidence he'd carried all evening hardened into something colder and more dangerous.

"Watch her," he ordered abruptly, his voice clipped as he glanced at Kai. The warmth that had laced his tone earlier gone.

Araya blinked. "Jaxon, what—"

But he was already striding away, his presence disappearing into the crowd like a shadow dissolving into darkness.

She gripped the edge of the table, her fingers digging into the lacquered wood. Her papers didn't authorize her to be here—not tonight, not in this district, and certainly not in the Gilded Lily itself.

Jaxon had been her shield. Without him at her side, the room suddenly felt too sharp, too exposed. If someone asked for her identification—if an inquisitor decided to check her status—

"Easy, Araya," Kai said, leaning forward to slide another drink across the table to her. "He'll be back before you know it. Jaxon isn't the only important one here—you're perfectly safe with us. I promise."

Araya forced a breath through her nose, nodding quickly as her shaking fingers closed around the cool glass. She took a small sip, but the sweet drink did nothing to lift the oppressive dread that had settled over her.

"I'm not used to any of this," she admitted.

"I'd imagine you aren't," Mara said. Her smile carried none of the sharpness that had colored Caylin's earlier jabs. "It must feel so different. But I'm sure you'll adjust quickly—luxury is easy to get used to. It really is too bad your friend couldn't come—what was her name again, Kai? Serafina?"

The name hit Araya like a blow, sharp and unexpected. "Jaxon invited Serafina?"

Kai winced, his easy smile faltering. "He had me reach out to her weeks ago—she said she had other plans. I'm sorry, I didn't realize she hadn't told you."

"Maybe she didn't want to spoil it," Mara offered, her expression contrite. "Surprises like this—they can be hard to navigate. Maybe she thought it would be better coming from him?"

Araya nearly laughed. Serafina hated Jaxon—had made her opinion of him blisteringly clear more than once. She wouldn't have kept this quiet out of consideration. Not for him. Not even for Araya.

But Mara's excuse was convenient, and Araya was too exhausted to argue.

"Oh, don't worry about it," she said quickly, forcing a tight, brittle smile onto her face. "The entire night has been one big surprise—what's one more?"

But the room spun around her as she took another big gulp of her drink. The table, the glittering sconces, the gleaming mahogany walls—they all blurred together, pressing in around her. The voices around her faded into a distant murmur, a single thought looping endlessly in her mind.

Serafina had known.

Serafina had *known* Jaxon was coming back for her—for *weeks*. If she hadn't known for sure he was planning to ask for Araya's bond, she must have at least suspected—but she hadn't said a word. The realization struck harder than any insult Caylin could have thrown at her.

Jaxon's laugh rang out, sharp and familiar, cutting through the hum of conversation. Araya's head snapped up, searching until she found him in the crowd.

He wasn't alone.

Araya's skin prickled. The crowd parted around the man who stood beside Jaxon now, like even these people didn't want to get too close to him. He glared at Jaxon with unconcealed disdain, the golden medallion marking him as a Magister gleaming in the dim light.

Jaxon leaned in, saying something that had his smirk curling at the edges of his lips. But the magister didn't react—at least not outwardly. Instead, his gaze flicked toward her.

Araya lowered her eyes before she could stop herself. The instinct was too deeply ingrained—*don't be noticed, don't be seen*—but she could feel the weight of the stranger's stare like a blade pressed against her throat.

She didn't dare look up again—not until Jaxon's hand brushed her shoulder. She leaned into his touch, relieved to find the stranger gone. She never wanted to see that man again.

"Did you set Darian to rights?" Kai asked as Jaxon folded her back into his arms.

Mara set her glass down too hard. "Magister Hale," she corrected sharply. "We still owe him respect—whether you like it or not."

Jaxon scoffed. "I'll give him respect when he earns it," he said with a smirk, smoothing his hands down Araya's sides in long, soothing strokes.

Araya leaned into his touch, but her mind was already spiraling. Darian Hale wasn't just a magister—he was the High Inquisitor.

Twenty-five years ago, the New Dominion had broken the fae, and Darian Hale had ensured they stayed broken. It was his laws that had dictated who could live freely and who would be marked, collared, or caged. His rulings that had decided which fae were *useful* and which ones simply... disappeared.

Jaxon could laugh it off. He had never been on his knees in front of an inquisitor, waiting to see if they would deem him worthy of breathing another day. Darian Hale was the reason she had learned early—before she even understood survival—not to meet human eyes. Not to be noticed.

But now—now he had noticed *her*.

Araya closed her eyes, tipping her head back against his shoulder as the floor swayed under her feet like the deck of a ship. She didn't hear what Kai said next—his words dissolving into the noise around them, breaking like a wave against the jagged edges of her mind.

Jaxon's low laugh rumbled against her back. "I think it's time to get you home, Starling," he murmured, his warm breath ghosting over her skin. "I forgot—you don't really drink."

Araya stifled a wild laugh as Jaxon guided her toward the doors. It wasn't funny—not really. She *never* drank. No fae female did—the dangers of being inebriated and vulnerable were simply too great.

Yet, here she was, in the heart of an affluent human district on the most dangerous night of the year, her senses dulled and her mind murky, clinging to Jaxon's arm.

Her vision blurred, the edges of the world rippling like water as Jaxon settled her onto the plush bench of the waiting carriage. Her stomach lurched as they started moving, the silver gown sticking to her overheated skin.

Cool air brushed her face, laced with the familiar scent of burnt vanilla that always accompanied Jaxon's spells. She blinked hard, trying to focus on his face as he watched her with open concern.

"What's wrong?" Jaxon demanded, scanning her face like he'd find the reason for her panic there. "If you're still worried about Hale, don't be. He can't touch you. I won't let him. You're safe with me, Starling."

Safe. It was a lie wrapped in silk—a word meant for someone else. But if she closed her eyes, Araya could almost believe it, almost convince herself that everything tonight had happened exactly as it was meant to.

But the doubt was insidious, curling through her like smoke, poisoning the air in her lungs. Had she ever truly had a choice? Had Jaxon really saved her—or had she simply stepped into the only cage that had been left open?

Jaxon's hand traced up her back, settling at the nape of her neck. "You're shaking," he murmured, his voice low and coaxing. "Tell me what's wrong, Starling."

"Mira told me you invited Serafina—weeks ago," Araya finally admitted. "How long did you know this was going to happen?"

"Years." Jaxon's fingers stroked her jaw, tilting her chin so she had nowhere else to look. "I made you a promise before I left, Araya. I never intended to break it."

Her stomach twisted. "Then why did you let them send you to Elvanfal? Why didn't you write?"

Jaxon exhaled slowly. But he didn't release her, didn't look away.

"I wanted to request your bond as soon as I was eligible," he said. "But Elvanfal—he told you, right? That was his condition." His thumb brushed along the curve of her cheek, lingering. "He said you deserved time outside my influence to decide what you wanted."

His voice softened, his grip tightening at her waist. "I would have waited longer if I had to. But when I got your letter about your waiver..." He dropped his head forward, pressing his forehead against hers. "I would never let them take your magic from you, Starling. I requested my transfer back that day—before I even talked to my father. And I came to you the second I arrived back in Aetheris."

"You transferred back for me?" Araya's voice cracked.

This hadn't just fallen into place. Jaxon had built it around her, laying the foundation of their future around her long before she even realized what he was doing. While she had agonized over her waiver, drowning under the weight of uncertainty, Jaxon had been maneuvering, ensuring she never had a decision to make at all.

She'd never even been in danger.

She didn't know if she wanted to cry or scream. Probably both. Maybe neither. Instead, she just buried her face in Jaxon's shoulder —because pretending to be fine was suddenly too much work.

Jaxon's grip on her waist tightened, his lips ghosting over her temple in a barely-there touch. "It's over now, Starling," he murmured. "You don't have to worry. I'm never going anywhere without you again. You're mine. And no one—not the Arcanum, not Hale, not anyone—can take you from me."

A shiver trailed down her spine. There was never another ending to this story—only the illusion of one. She could keep fighting it... or she could surrender.

Araya closed her eyes, letting Jaxon's warmth envelop her.

His children would never see the inside of a place like Kaldrath.

They would never wake up wondering if this was the day they were taken away. They would never feel the sharp bite of the shears or the hot wash of blood running down their face as their ears were clipped. They would never feel the sting of a lash for some minor infraction against the endless rules designed to grind them into dust.

And if that meant letting Jaxon shape her future the way he had shaped her past—then maybe it was worth it.

It had to be. Because if it wasn't, then what would even be left of her when he was finished?

Jaxon must have felt her relax, because he shifted, cradling her closer. "You're very drunk, Starling," he murmured. "Let's go home."

CHAPTER
FOUR

The shadows started whispering before she even opened her eyes.

Their voices wove together, an eerie chorus of hushed tones forming words she might have once understood, but had long since lost. The sound curled around her, sinking into her very bones.

She didn't want to be here. Didn't want to see him—not tonight.

But the dream took her anyway.

The damp chill of the dungeon filled her lungs, the stench of decay curling in the air. She knew what she would see before her eyes fluttered open.

It was always the same.

The corridor stretched endlessly before her, lined with iron doors, each one scarred by time and cruelty. Runes, long dead, had been gouged into their surfaces—remnants of a history written in suffering. The Arcanum had used these cells to break any fae who refused to kneel. No matter how much magic they possessed, the Arcanum always found a way to make them beg.

The whispers coiled around her footsteps, swallowing the sound of her bare feet on slick stone. They had always whispered. But tonight, they were trying to tell her something.

She stopped in front of his door. It waited for her. It always did.

It was the only one still alive, pulsing with silver-blue runes that flared to life as her fingers brushed the cold metal. The magic thrummed beneath her touch, rising to a discordant buzz that set her teeth on edge. It rejected her, resisted her presence—but still, it let her through.

Whoever he was, the Arcanum did not want him getting out.

The shadows slithered across her hands as the door swung open, spilling in like smoke. Araya followed them, stepping over the threshold as they coiled up her arms, wrapping around her ribs, pressing at her skin.

They wanted her to understand.

Tonight, he sat on his moldy straw pallet, slumped against the wall with his eyes closed—sleeping, somehow. His wrists were raw beneath the manacles and the iron collar at his throat, as if he had worn them for years.

The shadows rippled at the edges of the room, their whispers turning frantic. They knew something she didn't.

Araya sank to her knees in front of him, the cold stone biting into her skin. She had seen fae males fight the Arcanum's power before, had watched them break and die at human hands—so why did seeing this one unravel her?

She reached out without thinking, her fingers trembling as they brushed over the sharp line of his cheekbone. She didn't know what she meant to do—only that she couldn't stop herself from reaching for him.

She didn't expect him to see her. He never had before. But this time when her fingers brushed his skin his eyes snapped open, freezing her in place for the heartbeat it took for his hand to close around her wrist.

Shock flickered across his face, followed by something even more frightening—recognition. He spoke, his voice so hoarse and cracked from disuse that it took her a long moment to realize he was speaking Valenya. A shiver raced down her spine, the air crackling around her as the shadows' whispers fractured into desperate, pleading cries.

She opened her mouth to tell him that she couldn't understand him—that he would have to speak common, but before a single word could leave her lips, the dream lurched around her. The male dropped her wrist and Araya stumbled back as he rose to his feet with lithe grace and the whispers around them rose to an earsplitting wail.

The shadows wanted her to stay—to listen and understand. But Araya couldn't stop the dream from shattering, breaking into a thousand pieces as it collapsed around her. The last thing she saw before the darkness swallowed her was his bright green gaze—burning and desperate.

And then—nothing.

———

Araya jolted awake, thrashing against the lingering remnants of the dream as it disintegrated around her.

A dream. Just a dream—a nightmare.

Araya took a deep breath, trying to ground herself in the waking world. But—this wasn't her bed. *Her* bed was narrow and hard as rock, with rough, cheap linens and an old, patched quilt. *This* bed wrapped around her like a cloud, and the silk sheets tangled around her limbs smelled faintly of vanilla and sage.

Araya scanned the dimly lit room, her gaze catching on the glint of silver—Serafina's dress, neatly draped over an overstuffed chair. Araya's gaze snapped down to her body, taking in the oversized men's shirt she was wearing.

She was in Jaxon's bed. Wearing his shirt.

Araya dragged a pillow over her face. *Reckless, stupid fool,* she cursed herself. The last thing she remembered clearly was Jaxon guiding her out of the Gilded Lily—had he carried her in from the carriage? Changed her into his shirt and tucked her into his bed?

Had they—?

No. She would have remembered. Wouldn't she?

A flicker of memory surfaced—Jaxon's voice, low and amused, as he'd pulled the blankets over her. His fingers brushing her cheek before retreating. "Sleep, Starling. We'll talk in the morning."

The tension in Araya's chest eased. Jaxon had done exactly what he promised—put her to bed untouched. Relief uncoiled inside her, warm and certain.

And yet...

She pressed her fingers to her temples, trying to ease the dull ache behind her eyes. How much of last night had been her own choice, and how much had been carefully placed in front of her?

Did it even matter? She had what she needed—what she wanted. Jaxon would keep her safe. Forever.

So why did it feel like she had simply followed a path he'd already laid at her feet?

And, most importantly—where was Jaxon now?

Araya threw back the sheets, swinging her legs over the edge of the bed and burying her toes in the plush rug. Jaxon's shirt was long enough to brush her thighs—modest enough, she supposed, to go looking for the man she'd agreed to bond herself to after spending the night in his bed.

She wasn't sure what she expected to find outside the bedroom, but it wasn't the chaos that greeted her.

Trunks lined the walls in haphazard stacks—some shoved into corners, others gaping open, their contents spilling onto the floor. Books and loose parchment cluttered every surface, creating a maze of disarray.

In the middle of it all stood Jaxon, bent over one of the larger trunks, muttering under his breath as he rifled through its contents. His brown hair stuck out in all directions, making him look almost as frazzled as she felt.

Araya couldn't help herself. She let out an involuntary laugh, clapping a hand over her mouth too late.

Jaxon straightened, his head snapping toward her. His expression was uncharacteristically open—so much so that her lingering worries faded. Whatever she'd done, he wasn't angry.

"I'm glad my misery is amusing to you, Starling," he said, gesturing helplessly to the chaos around him. "I think they rolled my trunks back from Elvanfal. Apparently, they wanted to make sure I never find anything again."

"So, you're really back?" Araya asked. She stepped cautiously into the room, picking her way through the mess toward him. "I think I had a dream where you said you'd requested a transfer back to Aetheris."

"I wasn't sure you'd remember," Jaxon replied with a laugh. His gaze swept over her, lingering in a way that made her blush. "You were incredibly drunk."

Araya winced. "I'm sorry—"

"I was the one handing you drinks." Jaxon waved off her apology.

"Kai gave me one," she muttered, twisting the hem of his shirt in her fingers. "Did I—did we—?"

Jaxon's grin widened. "*I* tried to put you to bed fully clothed," he said. "You were the one who insisted on making yourself comfortable. I talked you into the shirt—you fell asleep as soon as I tucked you in."

"And that was all?" she pressed, watching his expression. If he was lying, he gave no sign of it—just that same easy grin, full of amused fondness.

"That was all," he echoed. "The first time I have you again won't be a night you can't remember. You'll have to take advantage of me sober, Starling."

"Gods," Araya groaned, heat flooding her cheeks. She buried her face in her hands. "I'm *so* sorry—"

"Stop apologizing," Jaxon said. His bare feet padded across the floor, circling the trunk between them. His hand touched her chin, tilting her face up to meet his gaze. "I meant what I told you last night, Araya. I was always coming back for you. But I understand how you must have felt when I left."

And just like that, Araya's heart cracked open.

"Don't look at me like I'm saving you," Jaxon laughed, shaking his head. "This isn't some noble sacrifice. I am obviously getting the better end of the deal. Now I have one of the best adepts on the Arcanum's roster at my disposal."

Araya lobbed the parchment ball at him. "I spend all day imbuing amulets."

"You—" He leaned in, pressing his forehead to hers like he used to when they had to sneak around in the dark corners of the Aetherium. "Are wasted on grunt work. It's a crime to let your talent rot. I won't make that mistake."

Her heart stuttered as she met his gaze, their breath tangling in the space between them. "You're really going to let me work?" she asked, disbelief and fragile hope warring in her chest. "Bonded fae females don't get to work—"

"Starling," Jaxon murmured, his smile wicked. "I'm going to insist. Do you have any idea how many times I requested to have you transferred to my division? And those ridiculous old men refused every single time."

"Because you work on fae curses," she whispered. "No one over a third is supposed to touch them. I'm not supposed to—"

"Well, now I make the rules," Jaxon murmured with a low chuckle. "And I have no intention of wasting you locked up in some workshop. Or in my bedroom—though, just to be clear, I want you there, too."

Her heart gave a sharp, uneven thump as his hands settled on her waist, sliding down to her hips. His fingers brushed her bare skin where the shirt ended, sending sparks up her spine.

"They won't let me work on fae curses," she whispered. "There are laws."

Jaxon laughed softly, indulgently. "Starling," he said, his lips brushing hers, "I don't know if you've forgotten—but I'm the High Magister's son."

The words dripped with privilege and arrogance—but Jaxon was one of the few people who might actually have the power to back them up.

He stayed perfectly still as she ran her fingers over the rough stubble that dusted his jaw, tracing his features with a featherlight touch. Finally she wound them into his dark waves, her heart stuttering as she pressed her lips to his.

Jaxon kissed like he owned her. Lips, teeth, and tongue—they all worked to coax gasps and moans from her, his fingers leaving a trail of heat as they swept over her skin. It may have been years since they touched each other, but their bodies remembered. He groaned into her mouth when his hands slipped up, finding her bare under his shirt.

"Gods, Starling," he growled. "Do you have any idea what you do to me?"

"I think I have an idea." She nipped at his lip with one of her sharp canines, careful not to break the skin as she slid her hand between them to trace the hardness pressing against her hip. She squeezed, his startled curse like music to her ears.

Jaxon swept her off her feet, her shriek of laughter echoing through the cluttered room. He crossed to the bedroom in a few quick strides, knocking over more than one pile of books in his haste to kick the bedroom door open. She actually *bounced* on the absurdly soft bed when he dropped her onto it, but Araya didn't get the chance to giggle before he was yanking the shirt over her head.

Araya gasped, arching into his mouth as Jaxon captured the peak of her breast. She tugged at his clothes, urging him without words to get them off.

"My greedy Starling," he said, his lips curling into a smile against her skin. "You were always mine—I just needed you to see it."

The words should have unsettled her. But the way he said them

—the certainty, the warmth—made them feel like a promise instead of a snare. Maybe this was just what safety felt like.

Araya ran her fingers over his chest, tracing the lean contours of his muscles with her nails until his breath hitched, a shudder running through him. By the time he *finally* pressed against her entrance, his voice had dropped to a growl, low and rough with want.

"Tell me, Starling," he coaxed, his lips ghosting over hers. "Tell me you're mine."

"Jaxon—" Araya swallowed, the words catching in her throat as his fingers flexed against her hips. But when his thumb brushed over the sensitive bundle of nerves between her thighs, her resolve melted into heat and hunger.

"I want to *hear* you say it, Starling," he laughed as she nodded frantically, but it came out more like a groan as she arched against him.

"I'm yours," she gasped, her breath hitching at the raw hunger in his eyes. "I'm yours!"

Jaxon hummed in satisfaction, pressing a kiss to her jaw. "Good girl," he said, his voice all silk and steel as his lips trailed fire across her skin.

He took his time, relearning every way she unraveled beneath him. Araya clutched at his shoulders, nails digging into his skin as tension coiled inside her, growing into a wildfire that threatened to consume her entirely.

"I have you, Starling," he whispered, his lips trailing like fire over her skin. "I'll protect you, I promise. Now let go for me."

Her body obeyed before her mind could catch up. The tension inside her snapped, release flooding her in waves of heat and pleasure. He swallowed her cry with another brutal kiss, a guttural groan escaping him as he found his own release.

———

Sunlight filtered through the heavy curtains, casting long, golden streaks across the room. Araya stared at them absently as her fingers drifted over the hard planes of Jaxon's chest, mapping the new scars he carried now.

Jagged slashes marred his skin, some thin and faded, others deep and brutal. A burn stretched across his ribs, paler than the rest, like a brand long since cooled. But it was the smallest one that held her gaze—a silvery line just above his ribs, barely the width of a knife's edge.

Jaxon caught her wrist before she could ask, brushing his lips across her palm. "It's in the past, Starling."

He couldn't seem to stop touching her either. His fingers combed through her hair, the gentle scrape of his nails against her scalp sending shivers of pleasure down her spine.

"So what happens now?" she asked. "Is that really all there is to bonding?"

Jaxon shifted, amusement glinting in his dark eyes as he glanced down at her. "You wanted something more?"

"No...but your father just—" She propped herself up on one elbow, mimicking a flourish with her hand. "And it's done? Is that how it works for everyone, or is it just because you're the High Magister's son?"

"It does have its perks." He laughed, giving her a wicked smile. "You know, he'll probably ask you to call him Garrick—"

"Gods." Araya buried her face in Jaxon's chest. "You're not serious."

"He's not as terrifying as he looks," Jaxon said. He ran his hand down her back, his fingers brushing over each bump of her spine. "He'll be here later—Kai will come by too, to adjust your runes. Your papers need updating, your privileges have to be upgraded..."

He tilted her chin up, pressing a soft kiss to her lips. "All good things, Araya. Things you deserve."

She stared at him, the weight of his words settling heavily in her chest. "And that's it?" she asked softly.

"That's it." Jaxon pulled her back down into his arms. "No more Arcanum oversight, no more waiting or worrying—just the two of us."

"It doesn't feel real," Araya murmured, letting her head drop back to his chest. "Like I skipped the part where I actually earned it."

Jaxon chuckled. "You've earned this a hundred times over," he said. "This is just the official part."

Araya closed her eyes, letting his warmth surround her. "If you say so."

Jaxon's fingers drifted across her back in lazy circles. "Trust me, Starling," he murmured, breath warm against her ear. "This is only the beginning. The Arcanum wants me to lead a new project—something I think you'll find interesting."

Araya lifted her head, her interest piqued. "What kind of project?"

"The fun kind," he said, flashing her a mischievous grin. "But I have to step out for a bit to get things set up for it. Will you be alright here by yourself?"

The question brought her up short. This was going to be her home—or maybe it was already. But the thought of being here by herself, in a neighborhood where she couldn't even walk freely, made her stomach twist.

"Will you be gone long?"

"Not too long," Jaxon assured her, his dark eyes studying her carefully. "You should get some more rest." He pressed a tender kiss to her temple before sliding out of bed and reaching for his clothes.

"I need to return Serafina's dress," Araya said.

"I'll have the courier handle it," Jaxon replied, lacing up his breeches. "They're already going there for your things today."

Of course, he'd already thought of everything. That was Jaxon—always ten steps ahead. But instead of feeling cared for, something about it sat uneasily in her chest, leaving her feeling... boxed in.

"I should be the one to return it," she argued. "I need to talk to her anyway—about why she didn't say anything about you asking for my bond."

Jaxon sighed, turning back to her. "I don't suppose you'd just accept that I asked her not to tell you? I didn't want you worrying about something I was already handling."

Araya's throat tightened. It sounded so reasonable when he said it like that.

"We tell each other everything," she insisted, though her voice lacked the conviction she wanted. "I told her you were here—and she acted surprised. Even though she knew. She *lied* to me, Jaxon."

"I understand why you're upset, but can you really blame her for listening to me, Starling?" Jaxon cupped her face, stroking his thumb over her cheek before trailing down her neck and curling around her waist to pull her close. "She might not like me very much, but she loves you. I'm sure you've kept a secret from her before, haven't you?"

Araya swallowed hard, guilt blooming fast and bitter in her chest. She *had* kept her own secret—but it wasn't like her cycle arriving affected Serafina. At the time, it hadn't felt like a betrayal. But now... maybe it had been. Serafina didn't know how desperate Araya had been—how afraid. How close to the edge.

If she had, maybe she would have told her.

Jaxon sighed. "I'm not saying no, Starling," he said. "But have you thought about what you're going to wear? All you have here is that dress and my shirt."

Her cheeks flushed as her eyes landed on the shirt—still crumpled on the floor, right where they'd left it. She opened her mouth, but the protest didn't come.

Maybe he was right. Either way, fighting over it was pointless.

"I'll have the courier take care of it," she conceded, her voice subdued. "I need to think about what to say to her anyway."

Jaxon's eyes softened, a hint of a smile tugging at his lips as she rose up on her toes, pressing a gentle kiss to his lips.

"Thank you," she murmured. "For everything."

Jaxon pulled back, his smile wide. "Get some rest," he told her, brushing a stray strand of hair from her face. "I won't be long."

Araya nodded, the cold space left in Jaxon's absence already feeling too large. "I'll be here when you get back."

"I know you will, Starling." Jaxon leaned forward, pressing one last lingering kiss to her forehead. "Because this is where you belong."

CHAPTER
FIVE

SHE'D SEEN HIM.

Loren snarled, driving his fist into the stone wall. Pain flared, bright and sharp, as he wrenched against his bindings. The runes etched into the pitted surface flared to life as he strained against them, the cruel iron biting deeply into his raw, mangled flesh.

But the chains held. They always did.

He collapsed onto the moldy straw pallet, trembling with exhaustion and rage, eyes fixed on the manacles that had bound him for half his life. They had weathered over the years, but the runes carved into their surface still gleamed with magic, making them easy to read.

Loris to bind his soul. *Na'vorel* to sap his strength. *Na'ithra* to seal away his magic. All carved into the iron that burned his flesh and chipped away at his soul.

The spells were written in Valenya, but their execution was completely, cruelly human. Between the manacles, the collar, and the years wasted in this cell, Loren's once-formidable power had withered to almost nothing. He couldn't summon enough aether to light a candle, and escape was a dream that had died long ago.

The shadows stirred. Loren tensed, his breath slowing as they inched closer, curling around his feet. Silent, for once. He had felt their presence for years—haunting, watching, whispering. But today... today was different.

They weren't just watching. They were listening.

Loren gritted his teeth, glaring at the inky tendrils. "What do you want from me?" he demanded.

They didn't answer. They never did. But for once, Loren didn't need them to.

They had brought *her* to him.

It wasn't the first time he had seen her. She had haunted him for months, slipping into his dreams like a ghost. He'd almost convinced himself she wasn't real—just a desperate construct conjured by his mind in a last ditch effort to stave off the madness of isolation.

She never spoke. Never looked at him—not until tonight.

Loren closed his eyes, desperate to deny it even as a sick, sinking weight settled in his chest. There was only one reason magic wove fae souls together in dreams. Even now, just thinking of her stirred something deep within him—power he hadn't felt in years, flaring to life like an ember in the dark.

This female was his mate.

Loren curled his aching hands into fists. The absent Goddess was cruel, to dangle her before him now. In another life, he would have sought her out and courted her. He would have knelt at her feet and offered her every piece of himself—his heart, his magic, his name. Everything he had would have been hers.

But in this life?

He could never acknowledge her. Could never admit her existence. Not even if the power she granted him was enough to tip the balance. Because if the Arcanum ever learned he had a mate...

They'd use her. Weaponize her. Tear her apart, piece by piece, just to see what it did to him. And if they ever completed the bond...Goddess help him, he couldn't be responsible for what they'd do to her.

He forced the thought away, shoving it into the depths of his mind and locking it away with all his other unbearable truths, alongside the memories of his parents, his sister, his friends—all the people he had loved and failed to protect.

The best thing he could do—for both of them—was forget she ever existed.

———

LOREN HAD TRIED TO DIE ONCE.

In the beginning, there had been others here. He never saw them, but their voices echoed through the dungeon—cries of pain, defiance, and desperate pleas for mercy that would never come. They had been a grim comfort, proof that he wasn't alone in his suffering.

But one by one, they fell silent.

At first, Loren was relieved. Their suffering had ended—one way or another. But as the years dragged on, the silence seeped into his mind, a creeping, corrosive thing that stripped away even the faintest semblance of hope.

His only companions were the shadows.

They came to him the night the last voice disappeared. A slow trickle of darkness, curling through the cracks in the walls, cold and watchful. He hadn't understood what it meant—had thought, at first, that his father had come for him.

It wasn't until days later, when they didn't leave but no rescue came, that Loren understood.

His father was dead. And his shadows—the ones that always followed the fae crown—they belonged to Loren now.

But they didn't obey him.

When he ordered them to free him, they just coiled around him, useless. They slunk into the corners of his cell when his tormenters came in, watching silently as they cut into his flesh and ripped away pieces of his sanity with their never-ending questions. And when they left him bleeding and broken on the filthy floor, the shadows only drifted over him, whispering things he didn't understand.

Eventually, Loren stopped asking them to help and begged them to kill him instead. But still, they never did anything but whisper—and wait.

Years passed.

No more voices came. Loren had never realized it was possible to feel so hollow, to ache for connection so deeply it felt like a physical wound.

And so, he had decided to end it.

He had curled up on his filthy straw pallet and rejected the rancid scraps they slid into his cell. He had relished the slow unraveling of his body, waiting for his heart to still, for his breath to stop, for death to claim him.

But Garrick Shaw had come before death.

"How long has he been like this?"

Loren barely registered the sound of the cell door opening. But at the familiar voice, his eyes flickered open, sluggish and unfocused as he forced himself to look at the man who had betrayed them all.

The shadows, predictably, were nowhere to be found.

Garrick stood just inside the doorway, studying him with a mix of disdain and calculation. He had aged—fine lines fanning out around his sharp eyes, streaks of gray threading through his dark hair—but the arrogance in his stance, the chill in his gaze, remained unchanged.

Loren hated him.

"You're wasting your time," the guard muttered. "He's given up."

Garrick's lip curled. "Then force him to eat. If he refuses, break his jaw and feed him through a tube."

When the cell door slammed shut, the silence was louder than ever.

How long ago had that been? Years, surely.

And now, Garrick Shaw was back. And this time, he wasn't alone.

The younger man's gaze swept over him, slow and assessing. "This is the prince?" He asked at last, his tone laced with curiosity. "I expected more."

"Don't underestimate him," Garrick said. "He's been in iron for twenty-five years and he's still alive. He's beaten, but he has never been weak."

Loren bared his teeth at them. Garrick would know that, wouldn't he? After all, they'd studied side by side for years, walking the halls of the Aetherium together. Once, Loren had thought of him as a friend.

But humans had never been meant to wield the gifts of the Goddess.

And Garrick Shaw had proved why.

The younger man crouched before him, studying him with the detached curiosity of a scholar examining a broken artifact—valuable, but only if it could be fixed.

"Beautiful work," he murmured, reaching out to trace the collar. "He's been struggling." His eyes flicked to Loren's swollen wrists and the trails of dried blood on his arms. "Why cuffs? Isn't a *ly'ithra* rune more effective?"

"He won't give up his name," for the first time Garrick sounded annoyed. "He hasn't spoken a word to anyone Hale has sent down here to question him in about five years."

"Impressive." The new man sat back on his heels, grinning. "This is going to be fun." He chuckled, turning back to Garrick. "Want to make a wager? Araya breaks the Shadowed Veil in under a year."

Loren bit back a groan. *That's what they wanted?*

The inquisitors had spent years torturing him, starving him, whispering lies in his ears—all in a futile attempt to make him *reveal the secrets of the shadows.*

If only they knew.

He wasn't his father. The shadows didn't answer to him. They watched—they whispered and waited. But they never obeyed him.

Loren exhaled slowly, pressing his head back against the cold stone. The inquisitors would be better off searching the void itself— they would find their answers sooner.

"You're that sure about this female?" Garrick asked. "I'm not the only one you run the risk of disappointing, Jaxon."

Loren's blood ran cold. *Jaxon.* He stared at the younger man, trying to see the dark-haired boy who had once clung to Garrick's robes.

"Completely," Jaxon laughed. "She thinks this whole thing is her idea."

Garrick exhaled, rubbing his fingers over the line grooved between his eyebrows.

"You had everything set up for you," he said. "The Eldergreen project, your own research team—it took years of planning to get you that. And you threw it away to come back and play house with a fae—"

"You act like it was a setback."

"It *was*," Garrick snapped. "The Eldergreen is still crawling with fae magic—"

"Don't be dramatic, father." Jaxon's jaw tightened, but his smirk remained. "You think I should have wasted another decade digging through ruins when I could be making history?"

He gestured lazily toward Loren. "I have bigger things to accomplish now."

Garrick's gaze sharpened. "You have things to prove." His voice was cold, unyielding. "She's good at what she does, but involving her in the actual work—"

"She's done it before." Jaxon waved off his father's concern. "She wasn't supposed to, of course, but she was already doing half my work. I gave her the problem, she worked out the safest sequence, and I cast the spells. She could have saved lives in Elvanfal if the Arcanum wasn't so shortsighted—"

Loren's fingers twitched, his pulse quickening as he forced himself to remain still, his head bowed in feigned disinterest. If the humans hadn't taken the Eldergreen—

Loren clenched his jaw, burying that ember of reckless hope before it could blaze to life. What did it matter to him? There was nothing he could do about it—not when he was chained in the dark like an animal. He'd die in this cell, one day.

"—trust me, she won't be a problem." Jaxon chuckled. "You should have seen her when I told her I wanted her to keep working— she's eager to show her worth in *every* possible way. If she can't break the Veil, at least she'll keep me well entertained until I figure it out myself."

Loren's stomach twisted at the lewd implication. Goddess help that poor female, whoever she was.

"Is there anything else you need to see?" Garrick asked his son. "The workshop down here is fully stocked. If there's anything you need—"

The two men moved back to the door, knocking twice to be let out. Loren listened as their voices and laughter faded, finally leaving him in silence again.

How many years would they spend torturing him this time? Two? Five? Jaxon seemed eager to prove himself—that didn't bode well. Loren sighed. Maybe he could antagonize Garrick's son into finally killing him.

He was so tired. Tired of the shadows, of the cold, of the constant pressure of the iron against his skin. Tired of the despair and hope- lessness. Loren was barely in his fifties. Fae lived a long time—he had at least another 200 years of this.

Loren closed his eyes, whispering another prayer to the absent Goddess for his mate. *Keep her safe. Keep her hidden.*

Because Loren needed her to stay far, far away from Garrick and Jaxon Shaw.

CHAPTER

SIX

Araya lazed in Jaxon's ridiculously comfortable bed, cocooned in soft blankets and the warmth he'd left behind. The sheets smelled like him—his vanilla soap layered over something darker and unmistakably *Jaxon*.

She might have stayed there forever, tangled in the memory of his hands and the lingering heat of his skin—if her body hadn't had other plans. The comfortable haze gave way to a dull ache low in her belly, and a hollow twist in her stomach that refused to be ignored.

Reluctantly, she slipped out of the bed, scooping Jaxon's shirt off the floor as she ducked into the attached bathing chamber to relieve herself. She had to laugh when she caught sight of her reflection, her hair hanging in a wild, tangled halo of red and violet around her face, his shirt swallowing her frame.

Still chuckling, she dug through the drawers until she found Jaxon's comb. She worked it through the worst of the tangles until she could wrestle it back into her customary braid, securing the end with a leather strip and tucking it into the collar of Jaxon's shirt.

Jaxon loved her hair loose and wild—said it made her look like fire. But this made her feel like herself.

Araya wandered back into the chaos of the main living area, picking her way through the disarray as she made her way to the kitchen. A glance into the coldbox confirmed it was empty—no surprise there. In all the years she had known him, Araya had never seen Jaxon Shaw cook so much as an egg.

She did find a glass, marveling at the clear, cool water that flowed from the tap. Even at Serafina's house, the water always ran brown and murky for a few moments before it cleared.

After months of fear and gnawing uncertainty, staring out at the quiet chaos of Jaxon's living room felt almost surreal. He hadn't abandoned her, despite how it looked at the time. And when she'd needed him, he had come before even talking to his father. To know that he had never stopped planning to ask for her bond—it was more than she'd ever expected.

Finishing her water, Araya continued to explore the apartment, making her way to Jaxon's office. While the room was still cluttered with trunks and boxes, Jaxon had clearly started putting an order to the chaos here. Loose parchment was gathered into neat stacks, and rolled maps and diagrams leaned against the walls, waiting to be hung.

Araya ran her fingers over the spines of the books crowding the shelves, taking in the sheer volume of them. Jaxon had always had an impressive collection, but this... this was something else entirely. The sheer wealth of knowledge hoarded here was staggering.

Of course, she had seen the towering shelves of the Aetherium's library, but like all fae she was only allowed into the front room, where the contents were carefully curated within acceptable limits. Only scholars and high-ranking officials were permitted beyond the locked doors. That was simply how it was.

But still, Araya had always wondered.

A flicker of movement caught her eye, drawing her attention past the shelves, beyond the heavy glass doors leading to the balcony. The city stretched beyond, gilded in the soft glow of the late afternoon sun, and for a moment, the books were forgotten.

She drifted toward the doors, pushing them open as warm air brushed against her skin. Stepping outside, she let her gaze sweep over the black spires of the Aetherium. They loomed over the skyline, rising from a tangled maze of winding streets, a monument to power and control.

Trust Jaxon to secure lodging in one of the most desirable neighborhoods in Aetheris. He had everything—wealth, influence, and access to knowledge she could never even have dreamed of. And now, he had her too.

Araya slipped back inside, closing the doors behind her with a soft click. She paused by the desk, running her hand over the rich wood. One of Jaxon's countless leather-bound journals lay open in the center, an uncapped inkwell beside it, as if he'd stood up and walked away mid-thought.

Araya capped the inkwell, unable to keep her eyes from wandering to the journal itself. What kinds of things had he learned and done in Elvanfal?

The temptation was too strong to resist. She flipped it open, revealing pages dense with Jaxon's meticulous handwriting and detailed diagrams. It was a reflection of a mind that never stopped. Jaxon was always thinking, always calculating and analyzing the world around him.

He had been researching the Shadowed Veil.

Araya flipped curiously through page after page of cramped notes, packed full of documentation about interactions with the mists that towered over the Shadowed Sea, highlighting anything that pointed towards the mists being something more sinister than a natural occurrence. Every word drew her in deeper, until the rest of the world faded away.

Jaxon suspected the shadows were a curse. But that didn't make sense—curses unraveled over time, their power eroded by the natural ebb and flow of aether. Even forbidden magic obeyed rules. And yet...

The Shadowed Veil wasn't weakening. If anything, Jaxon's research suggested that it was getting stronger—expanding, even.

Araya stared at the page, searching for another explanation. Maybe he had miscalculated. Maybe his sources were flawed. But Jaxon didn't make mistakes like that.

In one margin, Jaxon had scribbled a reference to another book, *"The Chronicles of Valendral."* The title wasn't familiar to her, but she recognized the shorthand Jaxon had used, indicating that he had this book in his possession.

Araya straightened, running her eyes over the packed shelves. But there were so many books still stacked and scattered everywhere. In the end, it was only by sheer chance that she found it, still tucked away in a trunk and still swaddled in a protective cloth. Only a piece of parchment tucked into the folds with the title scrawled across it in Jaxon's handwriting tipped her off.

Araya unwrapped it eagerly, then nearly dropped it, her eyes widening at the sight of the curling script embossed in silver across the thick, dark leather cover.

This book was written in Valenya.

Her hands shook as she hastily rewrapped the book, nearly dropping it. A sick heat rose in her chest, every instinct screaming at her to shove it back in the trunk—to pretend she'd never even seen it.

Where had Jaxon even found it? These books were supposed to be *gone*—burned with their owners. She shouldn't even be touching it. Not if she wanted to keep her hands—

"Did you find something interesting, Starling?"

Araya gasped, clutching the book to her chest as she whirled around. Jaxon stood in the doorway, his voice light, his smirk familiar—but he wasn't alone. Towering beside him in full regalia was his father, High Magister Garrick Shaw.

For a heartbeat, everything in her went still. The weight of the book in her arms turned molten, scalding her palms. She was going to die. They'd kill her for this, bond or no.

"I—" she stammered. "I'm sorry. The inkwell was uncapped. I didn't—"

"No need to apologize, Starling," Jaxon said. He closed the space between them with easy strides, plucking the book from her hands and tucking it under his arm as if it were nothing more than an old journal.

"Now... were you looking for something? Or just exploring? The courier left your trunk in the hall—" his eyes roved over her, his grin widening into something more playful. "Not that I'm complaining."

Araya glanced down, and the full horror of the situation hit her with mortifying clarity. Not only had she been caught holding a banned book by the most powerful man in the New Dominion, she was wearing his son's shirt—*only* his shirt.

"Excuse me." She darted past Jaxon and his father, racing to the bedroom and slamming the door behind her. Could fae die of mortification? She would have to ask Serafina. Or maybe she would just stay in the bedroom forever.

"Araya," Jaxon's voice came from the other side of the door, followed by a soft knock. "May I come in?"

Couldn't he? This was his apartment, his bedroom. But he'd asked, so Araya stood slowly, pulling the door open. Jaxon didn't push past her or grab her. He just leaned against the doorframe, staring at her with a mixture of amusement and concern.

"I brought your trunk in," he said. "I'm sorry we surprised you."

"Thank you." Araya stepped back, making room for him drag the heavy trunk into the room. It wasn't hers—Jaxon must have lent one of his to pack up her things. He rolled it into the middle of the room, the metal latches clicking softly as they settled.

"The courier confirmed he returned the dress to Serafina as well," Jaxon added, closing the door behind him before untucking the forbidden book from under his arm and dropping it on the night-stand. "Everything is taken care of."

Araya didn't answer. All she could do was stare at the book, sitting innocuously on the nightstand like it didn't carry a death sentence.

"You aren't in trouble, Starling," Jaxon said, following her gaze.

"Why do you even *have* that book?" Araya demanded, unable to keep the edge of panic from her voice.

"Research." Jaxon grinned at her, all easy charm. "Can you read it?"

"Of course not," Araya scoffed. "Can *you*?"

"It takes me a while," Jaxon admitted, shrugging.

Araya gaped at him, but he waved off her shock, as if reading a banned language was just another challenge to overcome. "I promise, Starling, I'll explain everything. But for now, just get dressed and come out—Father was looking forward to dinner with you."

That sounded...stressful. Araya forced herself to nod, but she must not have done a good job hiding her anxiety because Jaxon stepped closer, cupping her face with gentle hands and brushing a chaste kiss over her lips.

"You're allowed to touch anything here, Starling," he said. "Even banned books. Now get dressed and come out and eat something. I know you must be starving, and we have a few logistics to go over—but after that, you'll have the rest of the week to snoop through my things to your heart's content."

———

By the time Araya emerged from the bedroom wearing one of her sensible dresses, Jaxon and his father had cleared the table of Jaxon's clutter and set out a spread of dishes piled high with food. Despite her nerves, the rich scent of roasted meat and seasoned vegetables made Araya's stomach rumble.

"... and then she actually tried to argue with me," the High Magister said, shaking his head as he carved thick slices from the meat. "I had to remind her that mirrors simply reflect the chaos we create."

Jaxon laughed. "I can just picture the look on your face."

The High Magister chuckled, shaking his head as he passed Jaxon a dish of glazed carrots. "You know me, I've never been one for theatrics. But sometimes, it's the only way they'll listen—"

Araya hovered at the edge of the room, feeling like an intruder on this warm familial scene. But Jaxon seemed to sense her there, glancing over his shoulder with a smile.

"Araya, come join us." He set a full plate down at the empty place next to his. "I hope you're hungry."

His hand skimmed her leg as she sat, and Araya ached to lean into the barely there touch—but the High Magister's gaze kept her spine rigid. She had embarrassed herself once in front of him today—she wouldn't do it again.

"Sir," she murmured, inclining her head respectfully. "I apologize for earlier. I wasn't expecting you."

"This is your home now," the High Magister said, arching an eyebrow. "I should be the one apologizing to you, Araya."

"Please don't," Araya laughed weakly. *Home*—the word snagged in her chest, unexpected and too large for her to wrap her head around. She stared down at the table instead, wonderingly taking in the lavish spread.

"Where did all this come from?" she asked. "It looks delicious."

"The Hearth." Jaxon scooped up a bite of meat and potatoes. "We picked it up on our way back from the Aetherium. I don't have any food here."

"I noticed," Araya said, smiling slightly despite her nerves.

"That would be my fault," the High Magister sighed, shaking his head with a rueful smile. "It never occurred to me that the domestic arts would be Jaxon's weakness—"

Jaxon snorted. "I'm perfectly happy with this." He stabbed another piece of meat. "What I don't like is camp food. You should see what they're serving the mages at Elvanfal—"

The conversation flowed on around her until Araya finally relaxed enough to eat. The food was excellent—perfectly seasoned, juicy meat and crisp roasted vegetables. There was even a basket of fresh fruit—juicy and plump without a single bruise.

After a while, Jaxon set down his fork, groaning as he leaned back in his chair. "Gods, I've missed the Hearth." He chuckled, slinging an arm across Araya's shoulders. He stroked the skin along the collar of her dress, grinning when she blushed.

"Father and I had a long talk about what your role would be moving forward," he said. "It's clear to anyone who knows you that you've earned the freedom to expand your work—under my guidance, of course. You'll have your own workshop, right alongside mine. No limitations."

Araya's hand paused over her plate, her fork hovering in midair as she stared at Jaxon. "That sounds... generous."

Jaxon grinned—that familiar, wicked edge flashing just long enough to send a shiver down her spine. He reached into his pocket and produced a small, intricately carved amulet. He placed it gently in her palm, his fingers brushing against hers.

"Have you ever seen one of these before?" he asked.

Araya stared down at the Arcanum's Eye amulet in her hand, wide-eyed. The black disk gleamed, the eye set into its surface shining gold. It buzzed in her hand, charged with magic that would give her access to—well, just about everything.

"Not in person," she breathed.

The only fae she'd ever heard of carrying one of these were half-fae who allied with the Arcanum during the overthrow of the fae monarchy. For her to receive one as a three-quarters fae...it simply wasn't done.

Araya swallowed back tears. "Thank you, Jaxon—and thank you, sir."

Jaxon lifted the pendant from her palm. The delicate golden chain slithered through his fingers, gleaming in the firelight.

"Let me," he said.

Araya's breath caught as he gently brushed her braid to the side, the weight of the pendant settling against her collarbone as he fastened it around her neck. It settled against her skin, charged not only with magic, but with meaning.

There was no undoing it now. She belonged here—with him. To him.

"Perfect," Jaxon whispered.

The High Magister smiled slightly, but there was something pointed in his tone when he said, "Jaxon has worked tirelessly to convince me and the Arcanum that you are a valuable asset. He's sacrificed a very promising career to acquire your bond, Araya."

Jaxon's smile didn't falter. But his fingers tightened, just for a fraction of a second—a slight, instinctive response before smoothing back into a deliberate, measured squeeze.

"Sacrifice?" He echoed, raising his eyebrows. "I'd call it an investment."

The High Magister smiled slightly. "Jaxon did make a compelling case. And his work on the Shadowed Veil is very important to the Arcanum. Have you heard of it?"

Araya choked on her next breath. But Jaxon just rolled his eyes. "Father, really. Don't tease her." His hand found hers under the table, squeezing reassuringly.

"Consider me properly chastised." The High Magister leaned back, hands lifted in mock surrender. "Truly—I meant no offense. Jaxon speaks very highly of your insight—and you certainly seemed engrossed in his notes earlier. I'd be interested to hear what you saw in his findings."

"Oh—" Araya cleared her throat, squirming in her seat under the High Magister's scrutiny. "Well—Jaxon's theory is...intriguing."

Both men stared at her, waiting.

She flushed. "It's just..." She bit her lip, choosing her words carefully. "There's no precedent for a curse to behave like that. Curses decay. They weaken over time unless someone actively maintains them. But this one—" she hesitated, glancing between them. "It's holding. Maybe even growing. So...who's keeping it in place?"

For a beat, no one spoke.

Then Jaxon gave a quiet, almost smug laugh. "See! I told you she'd get there," he said. "It took me a year to come to that conclusion. She did it in minutes."

Araya's breath caught. That had been a test. And she'd walked right into it.

"She did." The High Magister gave a slow nod. "She's as impressive as you said she was, Jaxon."

"Of course she is," Jaxon said, spinning his knife between two fingers. "And she's exactly right—" he grinned at her, his eyes burning with pride and heat. "The Shadowed Veil is more than some cursed fog. It's intelligent. Civilian boats skirt the edges without incident—but send a patrol, and they vanish. No debris. No survivors. Whoever is controlling it, they're shielding something—or someone."

Araya shook her head slowly, her brow furrowed. "But who could even do that?" she asked quietly. "I don't know of any mage who could hold a spell like that in place for decades. It would take immense, constant power."

"You're right." Garrick leaned forward, his expression suddenly serious. "We're considering the possibility of it being the fae king."

"The fae king?" Araya echoed, her gaze flicking between the two men. "But...he's dead—isn't he?"

"Well—" Garrick steepled his fingers, watching her intently. "The shadows were first observed behaving in this manner during the Battle of Eluneth. It seems likely that the Shadowed Veil was Corwin's last, desperate act to protect the fae—but no one actually saw him fall."

Araya stared at him, his words crashing over her like a wave. Everyone knew the fae king had died at Eluneth—everyone. That was the foundation of everything that came after.

If he was still alive...

"It still doesn't make sense," she said. "If it is the fae king, why would the fae be the ones worst affected by it?"

Both men looked at her blankly.

"We—they...the fae in the districts—" Araya glanced between them, stumbling over her words. "It's probably just superstition, but they blame the mists that blow off the Shadowed Veil whenever people get sick...or disappear."

The High Magister tapped a thoughtful finger against his chin. "And they've never reported this to the Arcanum?"

Araya shrugged uneasily. "I've never seen any proof of it. The fae there...they don't have a lot of reasons to trust the Arcanum."

Jaxon's eyebrows lifted slightly—not offended, but clearly surprised.

Garrick merely smiled. "A reasonable response," he admitted. "Jaxon—have you spoken with anyone from the districts?"

Jaxon leaned back in his chair, his brow furrowed. "I haven't... but maybe I should." He glanced at her. "Do you have a recommendation on where to start?"

Araya hesitated, searching for a way to phrase her response without offending him. She wanted to give him a helpful answer, but the thought of Jaxon in the fae districts—it almost made her laugh out loud. The fae of Ravonfar wouldn't speak to him. Most wouldn't even let him see them.

A knock on the door saved her, pulling Jaxon's attention away.

"Ah—that will be Kai," he said, squeezing Araya's leg one more time before standing. "Excuse me."

"They won't talk to Jaxon, will they?" Garrick asked when they were alone, his tone giving her no hint of what kind of answer he wanted or expected.

Araya chose her next words carefully. "Some of them don't even talk to Serafina.

A door opened and closed in the next room, laughter echoing as Jaxon's voice rose in greeting.

"A lot of those females grew up in the camps," she added. "It doesn't make you trusting."

"You grew up Kaldrath," the High Magister observed, his gaze lingering on her scarred ears.

Araya's skin prickled, her mouth going dry—but she was saved having to answer by Kai.

The boisterous human mage practically bounded into the room, the half bow he offered Garrick entirely at odds with his wide grin.

"Sir—always a pleasure to see you," he said. Then, to Araya's shock, he inclined his head to her as well.

"I'm glad you survived us last night," he said warmly. "We'll be able to get your runes settled tonight—sometimes it pays to know people in high places."

Garrick chuckled. "I imagine Araya is already quite familiar with the advantages of having powerful friends."

Araya's ears burned, and even Kai's easy smile faltered as he glanced between them.

"Right—well." He cleared his throat, glancing up as Jaxon walked in with two more glasses of amber liquor. "I just need to talk to Jaxon first and then we can get things sorted out."

"We can use my office," Jaxon offered, handing over one of the glasses. His hand brushed over her shoulders as he passed, and for a heartbeat Araya thought about reaching out to stop him—but he was already gone. "It's a mess in here, but—"

The door clicked shut behind them, cutting Jaxon's voice off abruptly. Now that she was looking for it, Araya caught the faint gleam of *thyn* worked into the ornate scrollwork on the door.

A silencing rune—no wonder she hadn't heard Jaxon and his father come in. They wouldn't hear anything Garrick had to say to her, either.

"I imagine you've guessed that I was not initially in favor of your relationship with my son," Garrick said, swirling his glass. "But Jaxon can be frustratingly persistent—he's convinced you offer a perspective the Arcanum is lacking."

Araya swallowed hard. "I hope I can prove useful, sir."

"I'm sure you do." His gaze didn't waver, pinning her in place with that unwavering authority. "But I want to make sure you understand what it meant—Jaxon coming back here."

"Requesting a transfer back to Aetheris, solely to bond with you —" the High Magister shook his head, sighing. "That wasn't an insignificant decision. He cares for you. Deeply."

Araya watched him warily, waiting for him to continue.

"I won't insult you by asking if you love him." Garrick set his glass down with a soft clink. "But do you trust him? After all, you grew up at Kaldrath." His gaze flicked to her ears again, his expression stern. "Do you still believe he will make the right choices for you —about your magic, your future, your family?"

Araya flushed to the scarred tips of her ears, but this time there was no interruption to save her.

"No offense, sir," she said quietly. "But after Kaldrath? I trust Jaxon far more with those decisions than I trust the Arcanum."

Her heart pounded as silence stretched between them, the High Magister studying her with an expression that betrayed nothing. But finally, the corners of his lips tugged into something almost like a smile.

"I understand." He leaned back in his chair, smiling at her over the rim of his glass. "Let me put you at ease, Araya—you're here with my full support. Everything Jaxon asked for, I approved. I just have one thing to ask from you."

Araya tensed as he took a slow sip from his glass, then set it back down with deliberate care. His gaze lingered on her, steady and unreadable.

"A second chance," he said. "You matter to Jaxon—and he matters to me. I'd rather not be at odds with someone so important to my son."

Araya let out a breath she hadn't realized she was holding. A second chance—she could do that.

"Of course sir," she said, willing her pulse to slow. "I'd like that. Truly."

"Good." His smile widened slightly. "And please, call me Garrick."

"Well, that sounds promising."

Araya twisted as Jaxon crossed the room to squeeze her shoulders, smiling down at her. "Starling, can you go in and get started with Kai while I talk to my father? I'll be right behind you."

"Of course," Araya stood, glancing back at the High Magister—*Garrick*. "Thank you for the conversation, sir—and the opportunity."

"Goodbye, Araya. It was a pleasure speaking with you," Garrick said warmly. "Jaxon will accomplish great things here. I look forward to seeing what you bring to the table."

CHAPTER
SEVEN

ARAYA STEPPED INTO JAXON'S OFFICE, HER GAZE SNAGGING ON THE SPREAD OF runesmithing tools laid out across the desk. Every one of them was iron-tipped—for use on fae. Her fingers twitched, a shiver skimming down her spine before she could stop it.

Focus on now, she told herself, taking a deep breath. This was necessary—once it was done she wouldn't have to think about this again.

Kai looked up from his instruments, a broad grin splitting his face. "Araya," he greeted her warmly, his tone a sharp contrast to the cruel instruments in front of him. "Ready?"

"Is anyone ever ready?" The words slipped out before she could stop them. In Kaldrath, a non-answer like that would have earned her a slap—or worse. But Kai only chuckled.

"I guess not," he conceded. "You're a mage, so I won't bore you with all the basics. You already know you have two primary runes—*ly'ithra* to regulate your magic and *ta'nara* to—" His voice faltered, and he grimaced slightly. "To suppress fertility. Jaxon requested personal control of the *ly'ithra* rune, with *ta'nara* staying as it is for now."

Araya nodded, and Kai's grin widened, his relief evident.

"I'm glad you're both on the same page with that," he said. "It's not always this straightforward."

"Do you do a lot of bondings?" Araya asked, sinking into one of the leather armchairs in front of the desk as she tried not to let her nerves get the better of her.

Kai's grin faltered. "Some." He cleared his throat and busied himself with the iron-tipped instruments on Jaxon's desk. "Most of them are... transactional."

Araya knew the kind he meant. She'd seen them too—formal, hollow things that bound fae females to powerful human mages they barely knew. Technically, there were safeguards in place—even Garrick had ensured she knew she had the right to reject Jaxon's petition.

But accepting meant safety. A warm place to sleep and enough food to eat. The chance to raise your own children, instead of having them ripped from your arms.

How could any female reject that?

"Jaxon's not like that though," Kai said, giving her a lopsided smile. "He cares about you—you're lucky to have him."

Lucky. Araya had said as much herself to Serafina. So why did it feel like Kai had slapped her across the face?

"Anyway—you know that *ly'ithra* is a conduit," Kai continued, oblivious. "It monitors and regulates your magic, ensuring it doesn't overwhelm you or anyone else. Right now, the Arcanum has control over it, siphoning off any excess power before it becomes dangerous."

Araya stared at the instruments laid out on the desk, Kai's words barely registering as her breathing quickened and her heart pounded in her ears. Was she really doing this?

"Araya?" Kai's voice broke through her panic, soft but steady. "Are you with me?"

"Yes," she croaked, forcing herself to meet his gaze.

Kai reached into his kit and placed a small blank on the desk between them. "We'll infuse this with your blood to replace Jaxon's usual amplifier. With the bond, he'll be able to draw power directly from you and store it, instead of relying on the Arcanum."

Araya picked it up, examining the porous, yellowed surface. "Bone," she said, turning it between her fingers. "One of the better amplifiers. How much blood?"

"Just a drop," Kai reassured her. "The power comes from you—all your blood does is link your magic to the amplifier so Jaxon can draw from it." He picked up the iron-tipped needle, pausing when she flinched. "Your runes were done at Kaldrath, right?"

Araya stiffened, but inclined her head slightly.

"I'm sorry," Kai said, true sympathy in his eyes. "The rune work I've seen on fae who came from the camps is...brutal. I wish I could tell you the process is painless, but all I can do is reassure you that I'm an artist—not a butcher."

His gaze flicked to the door as Jaxon entered the room. "It's not uncommon to have some flashbacks during the process. Do you need some time to prepare?"

"She'll be fine," Jaxon said, his hands dropping heavily to her shoulders as he came to stand behind her. "Won't you, Starling?"

Araya nodded, but her breath hitched and her body tensed instinctively as Kai took her hand, the iron needle hovering above her skin. *You're safe*, she told herself. This wasn't Kaldrath. She'd chosen this. Jaxon's hands tightened on her shoulders, the weight grounding her. Or was he restraining her? She didn't know anymore.

The iron needle stung, then tingled as it pricked her finger, a bright red drop of blood welling up immediately. Kai held it over the piece of fae bone, letting that drop fall onto its surface where it was immediately absorbed.

Not so bad—nowhere near the agony that haunted her nightmares.

"Perfect." Kai handed Araya a cloth to press against her finger and passed the amulet to Jaxon. "Put that on, Jaxon. Araya—" he took her hand back, turning it so he could study the rune inked at the base of her thumb. "Don't worry, we'll go as fast as we can. Just stay with me."

Araya nodded, trying to focus on the present and the soothing circles Jaxon was tracing on the back of her neck with his thumbs, but panic surged in her chest, threatening to sweep her away as Kai's magic tugged on a thread of her soul.

"Stay with me, Raya," her mother's voice whispered, ragged with fear. Araya stumbled, struggling to keep up as the sharp shards of black rock shifted under her feet. Dried blood already crusted her arms from an earlier fall, and her legs shook with exhaustion, but her mother's panic kept her moving.

"Just a little further. We're almost safe."

But they weren't. The humans' voices grew louder behind them, and then suddenly, there were soldiers everywhere. Her mother's grip tightened. Too tight.

"She's part human," her mother pleaded as soldiers advanced, shoving Araya behind her. "She grew up here."

"Breathe, Starling," Jaxon's voice whispered, pulling her back into the present. His hands rested heavily on her shoulders, an anchor holding her in place.

Araya flinched, her hand spasming in Kai's grasp as the memories rushed over her. He glanced up at her, something a little too much like understanding in his gaze. *Gods,* was he seeing these too—

"Gods," the human woman shook her head in disgust. "Fae—always with the tricky answers. As if we don't already know her father was half-fae—that makes her three-quarters. Barely human at all."

She grabbed Araya by the chin, turning her face roughly from side to side—inspecting her. "How old is she?"

"Only seven," Araya's mother pleaded. "Please—she's so young—"

"Young enough to forget, if we're careful," the woman said, releasing Araya's chin and shoving her back into the soldier who had ripped her away from her mother's legs. "Take them both. If the mother fights, punish the child."

"Breathe, Starling." Jaxon's voice curled around her like a chain, his grip pinning her to the chair. "Breathe." But the voice wasn't Jaxon's anymore. It was her mother's—

"Keep holding her," Kai said, his voice strained. "This part hurts—"

Araya's hand spasmed. She fought to stay present, to focus on Jaxon's arms around her and the sound of his voice in her ear. She was safe—

Her name was Araya. Her name was Araya. She repeated it over and over, a frantic whisper as the two women pinned her to the chair, another trying to hold her head still.

"Do you want jagged tips for ears?" The woman holding the sharp, silver scissors demanded. "Hold still."

But Araya couldn't. She screamed as the scissors cut through her flesh, the tears running down her cheeks mixing with the blood streaming down the sides of her face.

"Almost there," Kai's voice cut into the memory. Araya wasn't sure if he was talking to her or himself.

They'd promised they would let her mother go if she told them her name.

Rough hands pinned her to a cold, hard table, strapping her arm down with thick leather straps. "Her name is Araya," one of the human women said to the runesmith. The man nodded, wiping blood from his iron-tipped needle.

"It's for your own good," the other woman said when Araya started to scream. Araya could only sob, every stab of the iron needle sending a new wave of pain through her hand, up her arm, and into her very soul.

Araya clenched her jaw, fighting to focus on the now. She was not at Kaldrath. She was not seven years old. She was twenty-eight, sitting in Jaxon's office. She had chosen this—chosen Jaxon.

"You're doing so well," Jaxon murmured, whispering the words into her hair as the tug on her soul worsened, tearing at something buried deep within her. "It's almost over, Starling."

Araya couldn't answer. She couldn't hear anything over the

memory of her mother's screams and the sudden, deafening silence after the human soldier had cut her throat.

"Jaxon," Kai gasped. "Now."

Jaxon leaned over, pricking his finger against the needle Kai offered. A single drop of blood welled up—dark and inevitable.

It fell.

The rune on Araya's hand flared. She cried out, screaming as the bond latched onto her like a trap snapping shut. Hands were on her, holding her down—Jaxon. Strong and reassuring, not the cold, merciless grip from her memories.

"It's done," Kai said finally, his voice tinged with exhaustion.

"You did so well," Jaxon murmured, gathering her into his arms. "It's over now."

Araya couldn't speak, couldn't do anything but shake in Jaxon's arms as something foreign made itself a home inside her skin. It pulsed through her veins like a second heartbeat—*his* heartbeat.

She shuddered, her breath catching as that foreign pulse settled in beneath her skin. She could feel him there—his power entwining itself with hers until she could no more have ripped it out than she could have cut out her own heart.

She'd chosen this, Araya reminded herself. But her magic rebelled, bucking helplessly against the chain she'd allowed them to wrap around her.

"Bucket," Kai said.

Someone shoved a bin in her hands just as her stomach heaved, her body wracked with spasms. Araya vomited, again and again, Jaxon's touch and murmurs of comfort a distant hum against the storm of her memories.

Finally, she had nothing left.

Someone pressed a glass of water into her hands. Araya took a tentative sip, the cool liquid soothing her throat but not the heat curling in her chest. She closed her eyes, trying to focus on the present, but her skin didn't feel like her own, the strange sensation of Jaxon's magic entwined with hers pulsing beneath her breastbone.

"Araya," Jaxon's voice was softer, almost tender, but the underlying steel remained. "Look at me—you're stronger than this. I know you are."

"The worst of it should be over." Kai cleared his throat. "You'll feel... off for a while, but that's normal."

"Great, thank you, Kai—" Jaxon's tone was clipped. "Can you let yourself out?"

"She should actually be observed," Kai said, frowning. "At least for the next few hours. What she went through—it was a lot."

"She'll be fine," Jaxon said, his grip tightening on her shoulders. "I can take care of my own bond, Kai.

Kai hesitated. She felt his eyes on her—sharp, searching—but she couldn't lift her head to meet his gaze.

"She just went through hell," Kai said. "If anything happens—"

"If anything happens, I'll handle it," Jaxon reiterated, his tone final.

Araya barely heard the soft click of the door closing. Her world had narrowed to the quiet pressure of Jaxon's thumb tracing slow, calming circles along her jaw. Soothing her.

"It's done, Starling," he murmured, pressing his lips to the crown of her head. "You're mine now. Let's get you cleaned up."

"I can walk," Araya argued, trying to tug her arm out of Jaxon's grip even as her legs shook.

Jaxon just snorted, half-carrying her down the hallway. He shoved open the bedroom door, lighting the aetherlamps with a flick of his wrist and bathing the luxurious room in a warm, golden glow.

"You're burning up," he said, his deft hands already loosening the laces of her dress and peeling the damp fabric of her chemise away from her clammy skin. Araya shivered, goosebumps racing over her skin at the sudden chill.

"I need—" her voice faltered, her gaze catching on that wide, soft bed. But Jaxon shook his head, steering her toward the bathing chamber instead.

"I know what you need, Starling." He turned the tap, sending water rushing into the massive tub. Steam billowed up, fogging the mirrors and filling the room with the sharp, sweet scent of vanilla and spice.

"Jaxon—" Her protest came out as little more than a groan as he stripped off his own clothes and lifted her in his arms, lowering them both into the rising water.

Araya gasped as the scalding water closed around her, instinctively twisting in his grip. But Jaxon didn't let go.

"Easy," he said, holding her tightly against his chest. "Relax for me, Starling."

She did, eventually. Bit by bit, her muscles loosened. Jaxon kept one arm around her as he reached for the washcloth, running it slowly over her limbs. Then he moved to her hair, unraveling the braid and combing his fingers through the damp strands until she slumped against him, too worn out to keep herself upright.

Her eyes drifted closed. Somewhere in the fog, she heard the splash of water, the shift of movement as Jaxon slid away. Clothing rustled. Then his arms were around her again, lifting her from the water.

She whimpered as the cold air hit her skin, but he didn't pause. He dried her off, wrapped her in a thick towel, and gathered her close.

Relief surged in her chest as he carried her from the bath. The bed was only a few steps away. She didn't care about anything else—just sinking into that softness and letting it all go.

But Jaxon didn't lay her down.

Instead, he settled her on the edge of the bed and kept an arm around her waist, steadying her as he knelt to pull the blankets aside.

"I'm sorry, Starling," he murmured, voice low, almost tender. "But there's one more thing we need to do tonight."

"Jaxon—" Her voice broke on his name, trembling with fatigue and fear. "I can't—"

"This will help," Jaxon insisted. His grip tightened on her arm, his fingers digging into her bicep hard enough to make her eyes water. "I just need to see how much you've been holding back. Trust me."

Trust him. Araya opened her mouth to protest again, but the air rushed from her lungs in an agonized groan as Jaxon's magic pulled tight inside her.

Her own magic slammed into her like a tidal wave as Jaxon pulled at her core, coaxing and commanding. She gasped, doubling over as raw power surged through her veins.

"Jaxon—" she cried, clawing desperately at his wrist. The conduit around his neck swung as he leaned over her, its glow pulsing in time with the beat of the aether in her veins as it bent to his will.

"You're holding back." Jaxon's breath brushed her skin, his lips grazing the shell of her ear. "Let go, Starling."

There was no comfort in his voice, only command. Araya tried to resist, tried to hold on to herself, but his power—*her* power—was relentless, bucking her feeble attempts to collar it. She cried out as the last thread of restraint snapped, her aether exploding outward in a blinding rush.

This was why the Arcanum bound their magic—not to weaken them, but to save them from themselves.

It tore through her—wild and unrelenting. Her power had always been something she could guide, like a current beneath her skin. But this was a flood, and she was drowning in it, swept under by her own power.

Gods, it hurt—

Araya clung to Jaxon's wrist, her gaze locked on his face as she silently begged him to stop, to cut the flow—but he only laughed, his eyes wide and bright with triumph as her power surged through them both.

"Gods," Jaxon breathed, his grip on her tightening. "Do you feel that?" He laughed, staring down at her with awe. "You have no idea how magnificent you are, Starling."

By the time the last surge of power ebbed, Araya sagged against the pillows, black spots dancing at the edges of her vision. Jaxon climbed into the bed beside her, tucking the blankets snugly around them both before pulling her into his arms.

"You can sleep now, Starling," he whispered. "You're safe with me."

Safe. Something about the word rang false, but Araya couldn't find the energy to pull away. Her entire body ached, every shallow breath dragging like broken glass through her lungs.

"You're right where you belong," he murmured, tucking her closer. "And nothing will ever take you from me again."

CHAPTER
EIGHT

Araya hummed softly, shifting the heavy basket against her hip as she made her way through the evening crowd surrounding the Aetherium. The crisp autumn air nipped at her exposed cheeks, but she left her hood down, savoring the bite of the wind. Even after two months, the giddy rush of walking freely—hair unbound, ears uncovered—hadn't faded.

Bonding with Jaxon had given her everything she had ever wanted. Safety. A home—even a place in the Aetherium, though she'd traded the title of *adept* for *miss*.

Though, if she were being picky, she could have done without the dreams.

They were nothing like the nightmares that used to drag her from sleep screaming after Kaldrath—but several nights a week, after falling asleep in the safety of Jaxon's arms, Araya found herself back in that dungeon. The fae male didn't speak to her again, but she knew he saw her. She could feel it in the way his eyes burned, tracking every step she took with a white-hot intensity she couldn't explain.

Araya shook her head, brushing off the lingering unease. Dreams were nothing but echoes of the past. That fae male probably wasn't even real—and if she had known him once, he was surely long gone by now.

She had a future, and it didn't include ghosts.

Araya crossed the street and approached the grand archway that led into the heart of the Aetherium. She paused for just a moment, tilting her head back to take it in. It soared above her, silver-blue veins of magic threaded through the stone so seamlessly they still pulsed with power—all without a single rune.

No mage alive today could replicate it—it was possible no human ever could. The fae mages had been capable of incredible feats. If only they had chosen to share their power, instead of locking it away— hoarding knowledge, refusing to teach anyone beyond their own kind.

What might they have accomplished together, if instead of shutting the world out, the fae had let humans in?

Araya stepped beneath the arch and into the evening bustle of the Aetherium. The grand hall thrummed with life—students in scholar's robes weaving between seasoned mages, Healers in their deep blue cloaks laughing softly with researchers and spellwrights. A pair of black-cloaked Arcanum aides hurried through the throng without stopping, their steps quick and purposeful even as the rest of the hall slowed for dinner. The Arcanum must be meeting on the upper floors—their work never stopped.

A few researchers she'd met through Jaxon nodded in recognition or murmured polite greetings. No one questioned her presence. Araya smiled back, her heart swelling. Mira had been right—this had been easy to get used to.

She was almost to the West Tower when her gaze caught on a group of young fae, all female, huddled near the edge of the hall. They looked to be about the age Araya had been when she first arrived—old enough to have come into their magic, still young enough to look uncertain in it. They must be new—freshly selected by the Arcanum for the honor of learning just enough to serve the New Dominion.

Araya slowed, instinct drawing her toward them. She remembered what it was like to be new here, scared and alone among all these humans.

"You're looking for the East Tower," she said gently, pointing them in the right direction. "Your cohort boards and studies there. The dining hall's on the lower level, with dormitories and classrooms above."

One of them gave a stiff nod, not quite meeting her eyes. Another clutched her satchel like it was a shield. They murmured thanks and moved quickly, skirts brushing the floor as they slipped along the wall, vanishing into the current of robed mages.

Araya watched them go, a pang catching in her chest. She had always told herself she'd earned her place—but sometimes, it was hard to ignore how narrow the path had been.

She and Jaxon were proof that it could work—fae and humans, side by side. Maybe one day, they could show the world.

She climbed the spiraling staircase of the West Tower, the hum of conversation fading behind her. The exertion made her legs burn, but she relished it—each landing she passed was another step away from the frightened child who had once begged the Arcanum to let her learn magic.

No other fae had a workshop in the upper levels of the West Tower.

She adjusted the basket again, almost dropping it as she rounded the corner and barely avoided colliding with Serafina as the Healer hurried down in the opposite direction.

"Araya!" Serafina gasped, stumbling back a step. Her heavy leather satchel slipped from her shoulder and hit the floor with a dull thud.

"Serafina—" Araya's smile faltered as Serafina's gaze flicked past her, sweeping the wide curve of the staircase, as if calculating the fastest way to slip away without causing a scene. "I didn't expect to see you here."

Serafina scooped up her satchel, her knuckles whitening as she clutched the worn leather against her chest. "I was just getting some supplies," she said, flashing a too-bright smile that didn't reach her eyes. "Are you on your way to see Jaxon?"

"I am," Araya answered, suddenly all too aware of the distance between them. When was the last time she had seen Serafina? Not since she bonded with Jaxon. Guilt twisted in her chest.

"I'm sorry I never properly thanked you—for the dress. It was perfect."

"I'm glad." Serafina smiled, but her eyes shone with something sadder. "It looked beautiful on you."

For a moment, neither of them spoke. When had silence between them become so awkward? They had been each other's constants for years—until Araya chose Jaxon.

Serafina swung the bag over her shoulder, shifting to the side like she meant to breeze right past—but Araya took a step forward, desperate to hold onto this interaction with the woman who used to be her best friend.

"You seem busy," she said, nodding to the heavy satchel. "Is it for the clinic? I can't do maternity rounds anymore, but I could ask Jaxon if I could help in the clinic—"

"Oh—no, it's nothing important." Serafina shook her head, though her laugh rang hollow. "I just needed to grab a few things from the infirmary. Don't worry about it. I understand why you can't help now. You have your life—and I'm not part of it. Take care, Araya."

Araya winced. "Serafina—"

But she was already gone, taking the steep stairs two at a time and vanishing around the bend before the word had even left Araya's lips. Araya stared after her. Serafina had been her first friend here— they'd told each other everything. Or at least, she'd thought they had. But now...now Araya wasn't sure if she knew Serafina at all.

Because the infirmary wasn't in the West Tower.

Her best friend had just lied to her.

———

BY THE TIME ARAYA REACHED THE DOOR TO JAXON'S WORKSHOP, SHE HAD almost convinced herself there was a reasonable explanation for Serafina's behavior. She was a master-level Healer—that meant she did, technically, have privileges to access the upper levels of the West Tower. There had to be a logical reason for her behavior.

Araya paused when she heard voices inside Jaxon's workshop, straining her ears. Kai...and Caylin. Wonderful. She glanced at the door to her own workshop, just a door down. It would be easy to slip inside and wait for them to leave, but she had just as much of a right to Jaxon's time as they did. More, even.

Bracing herself, Araya pushed open the door.

Jaxon's workshop was as grand as he was—high, arching windows bathed the space in golden light, illuminating the rows of shelves stacked with tomes, enchanted tools, and half-finished artifacts. From this height, the entire city sprawled out in front of them, offering a clear view of the towering curtain of shadows that loomed over the sea—the Shadowed Veil itself, dark and impenetrable, still guarding its secrets.

Jaxon sat at the scarred workbench, his head bent over a pair of fae daggers. Even from the doorway, Araya could feel the weight of the curse tangled within them—the sharp, strange taste of fae magic clashing with the dissonant hum of the amplifiers Jaxon was using to fuel his work, setting her teeth on edge.

Most cursebreakers would have at least reinforced their wards before dealing with a curse like this. But Jaxon hadn't bothered—his hands didn't even tremble as he wielded his etching tool, tracing delicate runes with confident precision.

"I'm just saying you deserve a break," Kai wheedled, lounging on a stool beside him. "You're working too hard. Everyone needs to have a little fun—we were going to make a night of it. You aren't too good for a little drinking and debauchery, are you?"

"Harassing a cursebreaker while they work is a quick way to end up covered in a blistering rash," Araya warned, setting her basket down on the low table. "Do you think the Gilded Lily will let you in if you're oozing?"

"Araya!" Kai's face lit up, his grin widening when he saw her basket. "Thank the Gods, I'm famished." He darted around the workbench, snatching an apple from the basket and biting into it. "We're trying to convince Jaxon to leave before sunrise—surely you can sway him."

"You put too much faith in my influence," Araya said with a laugh. Jaxon hadn't so much as glanced up from his work, even as Kai loudly lamented his stubbornness. "We all know cursebreaking is Jaxon's true passion."

"Don't bother, Kai," Caylin snarked from one of Jaxon's overstuffed armchairs. "Jaxon's playing house now. Too bad it's not with someone who knows the first thing about keeping one."

"Actually, it's from the Hearth." Araya met Caylin's glare head-on, her smile deliberately calm. She had hoped the human woman's attitude would soften with time, but Caylin still hated her.

"Did you say the Hearth?" Jaxon looked up, blinking owlishly at her through the rune-etched spectacles. "I'm starved."

He flicked his fingers, sealing the last of the curse beneath the web of reinforced enchantment he'd woven, tucking them back into their iron-lined box.

"See?" Kai threw out his arms. "You're underestimating your power over him. He's been staring at those for hours—it's like talking to a statue."

"I can't tonight, Kai," Jaxon said, shaking his head. "I have work to get done." Araya's breath caught as he circled the workbench and brushed a kiss across her lips. Aether sparked between them, the magic in her blood practically singing as his fingers skimmed the edge of her jaw.

Jaxon grinned wickedly at her when he pulled back, his dark eyes smoldering. "I missed you."

"I guess that's our cue," Kai sighed theatrically, tossing his apple core into the bin. "You coming, Caylin? Or are you planning to stand there glaring at Araya all night? Keep it up and people are going to start thinking you're jealous."

"Of what?" Caylin spat. But she stood, making a show of smoothing the wrinkles out of her skirt before storming out of the workshop without a goodbye to any of them.

Kai grinned at Araya, utterly unapologetic. "Enjoy your work, you stuffy old scholars." He gave them a mock bow before backing out of the workshop, closing the door behind them.

Jaxon, seemingly unbothered by the exchange, was already unpacking the basket onto the table. "I like that you get along with them," he remarked.

Araya snorted, pulling out the plates and starting to load one for each of them. "I get along with Kai," she corrected. "Caylin hates me —Mira tolerates me."

Jaxon took his plate and sank onto the couch, kicking his boots up onto the low table. "Caylin is jealous."

Araya arched an eyebrow. "Yes, because human women don't like it when their men bond fae females instead of marrying one of them."

Jaxon tilted his head, amusement glinting in his eyes. "She's jealous because you're twice the mage she will ever be. And it has nothing to do with you being fae and naturally having more power— it's your determination. Caylin doesn't have it. She never will."

Araya flushed. She opened her mouth to argue, but Jaxon cut her off with a playful scowl.

"The only answer I want to hear is, 'Thank you, Master Jaxon Shaw.'"

Araya set her plate aside, then took his from his hands, placing it on the table before swinging a leg over him and settling onto his lap.

His hands tightened on her hips, his breath hitching as she dipped her head toward his.

"Thank you, Master Jaxon Shaw," she murmured against his lips.

Her magic surged toward him, tangling with his in a way she still didn't fully understand. It had been days since he'd siphoned from her, and she was too full again—bloated with power she couldn't burn fast enough. The pressure beneath her skin was nearly unbearable, a slow burn that left her aching and restless.

"Jaxon…" she whispered, pressing her body closer, desperate for even the smallest release. "Please. I need you to take it."

"Gods," Jaxon groaned, his grip on her hips tightening as her magic curled around them both, greedy and insistent. "You're the perfect woman. But I really do have work to do."

"I know," Araya sighed, dragging her nails over his scalp. His head dropped back, and she couldn't resist pressing one more kiss to the exposed column of his throat. "But I need you to come home tonight. I need you."

"I'll be there," he promised, squeezing her hips once more before letting her slide off his lap to claim the seat beside him. "What did you do all day?"

"I spent the whole day locked in your office—reading." Araya nudged his plate back toward him and picked up her own. After safety and security, having an actual library in her home was one of the greatest perks of being bonded to Jaxon.

Jaxon chuckled, ignoring his plate to wrap an arm around her. "Somehow, I'm not surprised. Did you learn anything?"

"I did—" Araya rummaged in her bag until she found her sheaf of notes. "I was going over the translation you found of the Chronicles of Valendral and some other accounts of the fae royal line. I was trying to figure out how a spell could linger more than twenty years past the caster's death. I couldn't come up with anything. If the Shadowed Veil was part of King Corwin's magic it would have dissipated with his death."

Jaxon's brow furrowed as he considered her words, his fingers idly tracing slow, absentminded patterns over the back of her neck.

"But—" Araya flipped her notes open to the passage she had marked earlier. "Shadow powers aren't exactly rare in the royal line —the records you pulled show that every generation has at least one. And there are more than a few references to rulers 'wreathed' or 'crowned' in shadows."

Jaxon leaned in slightly, scanning the note she pointed to. "You don't think it's a metaphor?"

"I don't." Araya frowned down at it. "The more I look at this, the less it feels like a spell. What if it's something else entirely—some kind of hereditary force or entity tied to the royal bloodline?"

Jaxon's eyes narrowed as he skimmed over Araya's notes. "There's no precedent for it."

"True." Araya shrugged, gathering up her pages. "But the fae were secretive. If this was something they meant to keep hidden, maybe no one outside the royal family ever knew the truth." She hesitated, tapping one corner of the parchment. "What I don't understand is—if the power was passed down through the royal line, what happened when the fae king died with no heir to inherit it?"

"That's...an interesting question." Jaxon leaned back slightly, his fingers drifting to the amulet at his throat as he stared past her. The golden setting she'd made for the bone disc gleamed, catching the light of the aetherlamps as he turned it idly between his fingers.

"Too bad there's no way to test it," she said, sliding her research back into her bag. "I guess we'll never know."

Jaxon didn't move as she cleaned up their meal, his thoughtful expression unchanging. For the first time, silence stretched between them—not the easy, comfortable kind, but something heavier, weighted with unspoken thoughts. Like he was deciding how much to say.

"What if someone wore an amulet infused with blood from the

royal line?" Jaxon asked finally. "Do you think the Veil—whatever it is—would respond to them?"

Araya turned slowly. "The Arcanum has the fae king's blood?"

Jaxon's face split into a bright, reckless grin—so full of mischief and excitement it made her stomach flip.

"Tell me, Starling," he said. "How do you feel about breaking a few rules tonight?"

"What about your work?" Araya raised an eyebrow, studying him for some sign of what he intended.

Jaxon's grin widened, giving her no hints. "It will get done—we don't even have to leave the Aetherium for this." He stood, stretching lazily. "Grab your cloak, though—it gets cold down there."

———

If Jaxon's workshop was at the top of the West Tower, then wherever he was leading her had to be buried in the depths of the Aetherium itself. She hadn't even realized the foundation ran this deep. Every step burned, and both of them were breathing hard as they passed the landings for the third and fourth subterranean levels.

Araya sighed in relief when the stairs ended at the fifth, only to groan when Jaxon led her down the hall to yet another set of stairs.

"It's worth it," he laughed. He pressed his hand to the door, blue and silver runes flaring under his touch as it unlocked. "I promise."

This stairway was steeper and longer, lit by dim aetherlamps that cast just enough light to reveal each step, plunging their descent into oppressive gloom. The chill seeped into Araya's bones, every step heavier as if the walls were closing in on her, sealing her fate.

"Almost," Jaxon said, tugging her forward by the hand. "Just through here. You're going to like this part."

They passed through yet another warded door, into a corridor that had partially collapsed. A narrow path had been cleared through the rubble, but it was so tight Araya's shoulders scraped the stone, and Jaxon had to turn sideways in places—though his hand never left hers.

Just as she began to feel like the walls might close in and crush them both, the passage gave way—opening into a vast, echoing chamber. Araya blinked in the dim light, staring at the strange room. It was a temple—or what remained of one. The shattered remnants of idols crunched under her feet as she moved forward, and great chunks had been torn from the walls. A devastating crack split the altar into two, but Araya could still feel the hum of residual power in the room.

Detailed paintings decorated the wall behind it, portraying a history she didn't recognize. Araya stepped back, craning her neck to take in the entirety of it, and her breath caught in her throat.

There, in the very center of the ceiling, was the Valendri Goddess. Araya recognized her from the small portrait her mother had once displayed—a delicate, otherworldly figure surrounded by a halo of ethereal light. Surrounding her, a vivid tableau captured the essence of lost Valendri history and culture in every brushstroke.

"How is this here?" Araya breathed, her voice barely above a whisper as she took in the scene.

"They blocked off the main staircase," Jaxon said, stepping up beside her. "They emptied the graves—"

Araya's stomach turned as she glanced back at the cracked alcoves along the walls. It was one thing to work with processed fae bone—but to see where it came from? That was different.

"—but the temple itself wasn't worth the effort of tearing down."

Araya shivered and tugged her cloak tighter, following Jaxon past the cracked altar. Aetherlamps gave way to rune-inscribed sconces, their thin, sickly light barely illuminating the corridor that stretched ahead of them. Iron doors loomed along both sides, the runes scarring their pitted surfaces long dead—just like the fae they once imprisoned.

"The Arcanum kept their high-value prisoners down here after the Ascendancy," Jaxon said, setting a brisk pace down the hall. "They're down to one at this point, though."

"Master Shaw—" a guard jumped to his feet as they approached the familiar iron-barred door, its surface covered in a labyrinth of runes. "I wasn't expecting—"

"Aeron," Jaxon greeted the guard with an easy smile. "This wasn't planned. We have a theory we need to test."

The guard's eyes flitted to Araya, his gaze lingering on her ears and hair. "Does she have clearance?"

"She's my bond," Jaxon said firmly, his tone leaving no room for protest. "I vouch for her—my father will too, if you make me climb all the way back up there and get him. He hates doing those steps though."

"No need," Aeron said quickly, pulling out a large brass key. "Do you have your key—good."

Araya hardly dared breathe as they turned their keys in unison, magic flaring bright across the blackened door as tumblers clicked. The door cracked open with a low, grinding groan—thick air spilling out like breath from a long-sealed tomb.

"Go ahead, then," Jaxon said, nodding for her to enter first.

She stepped forward, every muscle tense, already knowing what she would see. He looked exactly like he did in her dreams—from the dark fall of his hair to the harsh lines of his too-thin face, and the way his hands rested on his knees, deceptively still. She took another step before she even realized she was moving, dragged forward by that strange tug behind her breastbone.

This had to be another dream. She was asleep—trapped in one of those dreams again, and this time her mind had pulled Jaxon in too, twisting it into something stranger.

Then those emerald eyes snapped open, locking onto hers with such fierce recognition that she gasped aloud, stumbling back into Jaxon's solid chest.

"Easy," Jaxon murmured, laughing as he wrapped an arm around her waist to steady her. He flicked his hand, kindling an aetherlamp as the door groaned shut behind them, locking them inside. "Don't worry, Starling. He hasn't attacked a guard in over a decade."

"Who is he?" Araya's voice wavered as the male's gaze snapped to where Jaxon touched her, his lips curling to reveal a flash of sharp, white teeth.

"Araya Starwind," Jaxon purred, smug satisfaction lacing his voice. "Meet Prince Loren of Valendral—heir to the fae throne."

He dragged his hand down her back, fingertips ghosting over her spine in a silent claim. He met the furious male's gaze, unbothered.

"Do you think his blood will do?"

CHAPTER

NINE

Someone was coming.

Two people—one of them was definitely Jaxon Shaw. Loren had quickly learned the sharp cadence of the young mage's footsteps. His arrival always heralded some new torment, another demand for answers about this so-called Shadowed Veil the humans were so obsessed with.

But the other person—their steps were light, almost soundless. A new guard, maybe? Loren tipped his head back against the wall as keys grated in the lock, closing his eyes and deliberately relaxing his body. He would never give any of them the satisfaction of finding him waiting like a hound straining at its leash.

The door groaned open, iron dragging across stone. The newcomer entered first, the wild pounding of their heart betraying them. Loren stifled a humorless smile. Whoever Jaxon had brought down here, they were terrified.

He inhaled deeply, filtering through the stench of burnt aether. A woman? No—a female. *Fae.* The faint perfume of her magic teased at his senses, fresh and clean like damp earth after a spring rain.

Loren opened his eyes, meeting the frightened silver gaze of his mate.

Loren's world froze. Even the shadows shivered, starting to reach for her before Jaxon stepped in behind her, sending them skittering back into the dark corners of his cell. He ignored them, too stunned to do anything but stare as the shock of seeing her in the flesh rattled him to the core.

Then time began again. She gasped, her eyes widening as she stumbled back a step—straight into Jaxon. Loren snarled, instincts he'd thought long dead filling him with raw, choking rage as the human mage who had caused him so much pain snaked an arm around her waist to steady her.

"Easy, Starling," Jaxon laughed. "He hasn't attacked a guard in over a decade."

Only because attacking the guards never got him anywhere.

Loren bared his teeth, a surge of fierce protectiveness warring with deep despair. Did Jaxon *know*? Could he see the shocked recognition on her face, the way her breath caught? Loren kept his own expression empty, but his mind raced. If Jaxon *suspected*—if he saw even a *hint* of the bond—

"Who is he?" She asked, her voice wobbling.

The worst thing that could have happened to you, Loren answered her silently. They would hurt her because of him—badly. She would have been better off if she never met him.

"Araya Starwind," Jaxon said. "Meet Prince Loren of Valendral. Heir to the fae throne. Do you think his blood will do?"

His blood. Humans always wanted fae blood, fae bone...anything they could use to claim more power than the Goddess ever intended them to have. Loren bared his teeth as Jaxon stroked his hand possessively down the terrified female's back, staking his claim.

"We'll distill it first, of course," Jaxon said. "You know how diffi-cult fae blood can be to work with—and he only has so much."

The female—*Araya, his mate's name was Araya*—swallowed hard, her grip tightening on the case in her hands as she shifted her weight, her shoulders drawing inward as if bracing for what came next.

"Araya is going to collect your blood," Jaxon told Loren. "If you make things difficult for her, I'll do it myself. Trust me, Loren. You don't want that."

She approached him slowly, a small medical kit clenched in her hands. If it was anyone else, he would have fought. But she was already so frightened... Loren didn't care if they beat him—but if they beat her for failing? He wouldn't survive it.

So, Loren sat very, very still as she knelt in front of him. Her scent surrounded him, foreign yet familiar at the same time. It soothed him, even mingled with Jaxon's stench. How close would Jaxon have had to be for his scent to cling to her skin?

"Are you alright?" The words slipped free before he could stop them, his voice raspy from disuse.

Her brow furrowed, confusion clouding her features as she stared at him without a flicker of understanding. He hadn't been sure before, but he couldn't deny it now. His own mate did not speak Valenya. The language of their people, the words that should have been hers by birthright, meant nothing to her.

For the first time in longer than he could remember, something inside Loren broke. Maybe it was his heart. Or maybe it was the last fragile thread of hope he hadn't realized he was still holding onto.

"I'm sorry," Araya murmured in the human tongue, softly enough that Jaxon wouldn't hear. "I'll try not to hurt you."

Loren wanted to laugh, to tell her it wasn't him he was worried about. Instead, he simply held out his arm, squeezing his fist until his veins rose to the surface. Her touch was featherlight, and he barely registered the bite of the blade as it sliced his skin. The pain was insignificant compared to the torment of being so close to her and so utterly unable to help her.

She filled six vials with practiced efficiency despite the way her hands trembled under Jaxon's scrutiny, capping each one and setting it gently in a padded box. When she was done, she pressed a clean cloth to his arm. Her silver eyes softened, a quiet ache lingering in their depths.

Loren couldn't stop himself. He lifted his free hand and rested it on hers.

For a heartbeat, the cell fell away. The stone walls, the iron chains, the ever-present ache of his suppressed magic—it all disappeared as the bond surged between them. Raw and unrelenting, it clawed its way to the surface, the remnants of his magic howling for hers.

"I think he likes you," Jaxon said, voice laced with amusement. "Though I suppose you're the only female he's seen in twenty-five years... No wonder he's so taken with you."

Araya jerked her hand back, dropping the cloth as she scrambled to collect her things. She jumped to her feet, avoiding his eyes.

Loren let her go.

He forced himself to remain seated, even as every instinct screamed at him to protect her. There was nothing to be gained from attacking Jaxon. Even if he caught the human mage by surprise, he wouldn't be able to get her out. The iron around his wrists bit into his skin, a bitter reminder of his helplessness.

Then Jaxon's hand shot out, gripping her arm.

Loren's gaze snapped to the human's hand as it slid down her arm, tugging her towards him like he owned her.

His rage ignited.

The chains groaned as Loren surged to his feet, the manacles biting deep into his ruined skin as he lunged forward. He bared his teeth, the snarl that tore from his throat primal and unrestrained.

"Do not touch her."

Jaxon flinched, his smug expression faltering as he fell back half a step. His brow furrowed, lips parting slightly—processing. Translating. But then he recovered, sneering as he yanked Araya back against his chest. She stumbled, clutching her case to her chest like a lifeline.

"T'sovira, ehn Vael'Thir," he said. The phrasing was stilted, the

cadence mangled beyond recognition. It was Valenya in name only—but Loren still understood him. *Too late, little prince.*

Araya stiffened in his grip, her silver eyes widening with shock and confusion, but Jaxon only sneered as he brushed her braid aside. "I more than touch her," he said in broken Valenya, trailing his fingers deliberately down the long line of her neck. "I *own* her. Her body, her magic, her life—everything she is belongs to me."

"Jaxon—" Araya twisted in his grip, her plea cutting off in a startled yelp as Jaxon roughly slid his hand into her dress.

Loren's vision blurred red.

His instincts roared louder than reason, drowning out any thought of caution. His magic—weak and stifled by years in iron—scraped against his skin as the shadows hissed and writhed in the corners of the cell. He could *feel* them, clawing at the edges of his sanity.

Loren threw himself against his chains, fresh blood trickling down his arms as the iron bit into his ruined skin. The bolts anchoring the chains to the wall groaned under the strain, the metal shrieking in protest.

And then, with a screech of twisting iron, they snapped.

Loren stumbled forward, his chains dragging behind him. Untethered.

For the first time, true fear flickered over Jaxon's face. He took a step back, dragging Araya with him. Loren's heart lurched as she cried out, aether sparking where Jaxon's hand wrapped around her throat. Power surged—with her so close Loren could *feel* it flowing from her and into Jaxon.

The bond recoiled in his chest, bitter disgust flooding his mouth as Jaxon tossed her roughly to the side, freeing his hands. "Do you think breaking your chains changes anything?" He spat, ignoring her broken sobs. "You still don't have your magic."

"I don't need magic to kill you," Loren growled. He took another step forward, his broken chains scraping on the floor behind him. He would rip Jaxon apart with his bare hands before he let him lay another finger on her.

But then she threw herself between them. Power surged—*hers*—rising behind her in an impenetrable wall of magic. Loren staggered to a stop, but the shadows didn't slow, surging across the stone in a tide of darkness. Araya yelped as they wrapped around her, brushing across her skin and curling into the spaces between her fingers, as close to her as they could manage.

Without thinking, Loren took a step towards her. He reached out his hand—but she flinched, and the fear in her silver eyes cut him more deeply than any knife the Arcanum had wielded against him.

Because she wasn't afraid of Jaxon Shaw. She wasn't even afraid of the shadows—she was afraid of *him*.

What did she see when she looked at him? A monster? Snarling and unchained? Loren bit down on the fury still burning in his chest and took a step back, holding his hands up in surrender. Slowly, he lowered himself to the moldy pallet in the corner, careful not to scare her more than he already had.

The shadows drained away reluctantly, shrinking back into the walls and folding into the corners of the cell. Araya's shoulders sagged, her breath coming in quick, shallow bursts. But the wild, shaken fear never left her face.

"I want to leave," Araya whispered, half-glancing over her shoulder. "Now."

Jaxon didn't answer right away, his gaze lingering on where the shadows had wrapped around Araya's hands just a heartbeat too long. Then his lips curled in a slow, satisfied smile.

Loren's stomach twisted, his mouth going dry. Jaxon Shaw had just discovered a new mystery to unravel.

"Of course, Starling," Jaxon said, plucking the padded case from her hands and tucking it under his arm. "But first—be a good girl and put those chains back where they belong."

Araya stiffened, her eyes flicking to Loren's bloody wrists. For a moment, her hand trembled, and Loren thought she might refuse—but then she knelt before him.

"I'm sorry," she whispered, picking up the first chain and pressing it back into place.

Loren didn't move. Didn't speak. Her magic brushed over his skin, soft and gentle, wrapping around the bolts and driving them back into the stone. The iron groaned as it reattached, locking him in place once more.

It took every drop of willpower Loren had to stay on the pallet as she scurried back to Jaxon's side, letting him lead her from the cell. She glanced back once, her brow furrowing as she stared at his bloody wrists, but then Jaxon's hand was on her back, urging her forward.

Loren held his breath as the door groaned shut between them, the aetherlamp flickering and dying a moment later, sealing him in darkness once more. Still, he strained his ears, listening to the echo of their footsteps until they faded away entirely, leaving him with only his useless shadows for company.

He had survived everything the Arcanum had done to him. But this—this was different. His mate had been afraid of him.

A guttural roar tore from his chest, echoing off the walls like the cry of a wild animal caught in a snare. He slammed his fists into the stone floor, welcoming the sharp bloom of pain. Blood smeared across the stone as he struck again and again. He deserved it. Every bruise. Every drop of spilled blood.

He had broken his chains—but she had put them back.

The shadows curled closer, wrapping around his broken hands like a lover's caress. Their whispers echoed his grief, a hundred voices speaking at once as dark tendrils snaked around his wrists and tightened around his heart.

Loren roared again, his voice cracking as the sound collapsed into a hoarse, broken wail. Finally, exhausted, he sank to the floor and cradled his bloodied hands in his lap.

For the first time in years, he let the tears fall.

CHAPTER
TEN

ARAYA CLUTCHED THE VELVET-LINED CASE OF THE FAE PRINCE'S BLOOD TO her chest as they climbed the endless stairs. Neither of them spoke until Jaxon closed the workshop door with a decisive click. A whiff of burnt aether stung her nose as he traced the rune for silence, *thyn* glowing silver-blue against the dark wood.

"Lock those in the safe," he said. "In iron. No sense taking any chances."

Araya nodded, her fingers fumbling as she sealed her entire kit—vials, cloth, everything—into one of the iron-bound boxes meant for cursed objects. The cold metal seared her skin, the sting lingering even after she closed the door on it, as if she could lock the truth away too.

Loren. The male who haunted her dreams wasn't just real—he was the lost heir to the fae throne, imprisoned by the Arcanum for twenty-five years. And the way he'd looked at her... he'd recognized her.

If Jaxon had seen it...

Araya's breath hitched, her heartbeat roaring in her ears as she stared at the locked safe without seeing it. Jaxon would never just brush that off—he'd dig. And if he found out about the dreams... would he call her to task for keeping secrets she hadn't even known she had?

And then there was the magic. She hadn't thought, hadn't reached for a rune, hadn't done anything deliberate. It had just *happened*. The shield, the surge of aether...the shadows. Gods, the *shadows*. She had no idea why that had happened. What possible explanation could there be for how they'd reacted to her? Curling around her like they knew her?

Araya let out a shuddering breath, pressing her hand to her chest as she struggled to compose herself. She would just have to explain —he would listen. Jaxon always listened to her.

She turned, opening her mouth to tell him she had no idea what had happened, but he was already there, his arms caging her against the safe. Araya froze. Her explanations caught in her throat as she braced for the worst—but instead, Jaxon's lips found the curve of her neck.

"That was incredible, Starling," he murmured, pressing slow, hungry kisses against her skin.

She gasped, shivering as he kissed the spot just below her ear. "You're—not angry?"

"How could I be angry? The way you defended me—" he nipped her lightly, laughing when she yelped before soothing the sting with his lips. "It was positively *fae* of you."

He pulled back, watching her with bright, hungry eyes. "Have you always been able to do that?"

"Of course not." Araya wrenched herself from his grip, stepping back and wrapping her arms around herself so he wouldn't see how badly she was shaking. "I've never—I swear—"

"Araya," Jaxon interrupted, watching her with an amusement that felt horribly out of place. "Take a breath, Starling. You're not in trouble."

She stopped, staring at him. How could she not be in trouble? And why didn't he even look surprised?

"It's just power, Starling," he said, soothing, indulgent—like she was being ridiculous. "You know magic theory. You're holding more aether than ever before. It's only natural that you'd start to exhibit more fae traits."

He grinned wider, his voice dipping lower. "You should embrace it—you've never looked more beautiful."

Araya shuddered, pressing her back against the nearest table. The way he was looking at her wasn't affection—it was fascination. He'd let her magic accumulate, *watched* it swell and fester inside her —just to see what it would do. Just to see what *she* would do.

"Are you *studying* me?" Araya snapped. "Is that all this is to you? Another research project? If anyone else had seen that—" she shuddered. She would be in chains right now.

"No one did," Jaxon said. Before she could step away, he reached for her, pulling her flush against him. His hand cupped the back of her neck, fingers tangling gently in her hair. "Except the prince—and he won't tell anyone."

Araya stiffened, but he only smiled, brushing his thumb over her jaw in a gesture that might have looked tender to anyone else.

"You're the first person he's spoken to in years," he murmured, like it was something to be proud of. "You really did play your part brilliantly."

Araya's stomach twisted, bile rising in her throat. "I didn't realize I was supposed to be playing a part."

"You're angry." Jaxon raised his eyebrows, releasing her. "Why?"

"I—" Araya shook her head, trying to dispel the memory of the chained male and the raw, oozing wounds under the iron around his wrists and throat. "It was just so—so ugly."

"It's torture, Araya." Jaxon rolled his eyes. "It *is* ugly."

She stared at him. "But you're not an inquisitor. You're a commander." This wasn't supposed to be his job.

Jaxon smiled faintly, but it didn't reach his eyes. "This one's personal."

He crossed the room, casually pouring himself a drink. "He knew my father—before. It's a brilliant strategy, actually, having me lead his interrogation. The last time he saw me I was barely walking."

"But…" she whispered. "If this project is so important…shouldn't he see a Healer?"

Jaxon turned, glass in hand. "Don't be ridiculous." He sipped, unfazed. "He's fae. He's fine."

"Fine?" The word escaped her lips before she could stop it, sharp with disbelief. This wasn't the Jaxon she remembered—the brilliant human mage who had changed her life by taking an interest in her, who pushed her to apply for a waiver she should never have had a hope of getting.

"He's been in that cell for twenty-five years." Her hands clenched into fists at her sides. "He's not *fine*."

Jaxon turned back to her slowly, like she was the one who had lost her mind. "He's still breathing, isn't he?" he said flatly. "That's all we need from him right now."

Araya looked away, her vision blurring with tears as shame and anger churned in her chest. She needed to get out of this room—away from Jaxon and the horror of what she had just done, before she said something she couldn't take back.

"You still have work to finish," she said, her voice barely above a whisper. "I should go home—"

"No," Jaxon said. "You needed me to siphon from you, didn't you? So you don't *lose control* again."

Araya froze. Her magic thrummed under her skin, restless—but the memory of the cell clung to her like smoke. His hand around her throat. The way he'd wrenched her power from her before it started to flow on its own, tossing her aside just as casually, leaving her gasping in pain on that filthy, cold floor.

"You took enough earlier," she said quietly. "I can wait—"

"You can't." Jaxon's hand shot out, gripping her arm with bruising force. "Like you said, what if someone had seen you?"

"I know," Araya whispered. "But—"

"But what, Araya?" His voice dropped, and she flinched at his use of her name instead of the fond nickname he'd given her all those years ago. "You're mine to protect. Or have you forgotten that?"

"I haven't forgotten," she said. "But you hurt me—in the cell. When you draw on it that fast—"

"I couldn't exactly go slow in the cell with the prince ripping his chains from the wall to get to you, could I?" He huffed, his breath warm against her skin. "But we can go slow now, Starling. Let me take care of you."

"Is this where I pretend I have a choice?" She asked, swallowing hard.

Jaxon leaned back, studying her. "You always have a choice, Starling," he said, his voice soft, almost tender. "But you never say no to me. Now, come here."

He pulled her to the couch, dragging her roughly into his lap when she tried to sit down beside him instead. Her magic pulsed under her skin, rising eagerly to meet him as his hands traced over her sides. She tensed under his touch, bracing for pain—but instead heat bloomed in her chest. It spread through her body like molten gold, soothing her aches and dulling the edges of her exhaustion until she was floating, weightless.

Jaxon sighed against her skin, pleased. "There it is," he whispered, his lips brushing her ear, his breath hot against her skin as his power intertwined with hers. "That's balance, Starling. This is what I give you—what you can't get anywhere else. Remember that."

She buried her face in his neck, a soft moan escaping as he traced lazy, possessive circles on her hip. Shame prickled at the edges of her awareness—but she couldn't hold onto it, not while her magic poured out in slow, steady waves.

But then the pull sharpened. Pleasure twisted, too tight and sharp as warmth bled into pressure. Araya gasped, clutching Jaxon's shirt as his easy draw on her magic turned insistent—demanding. Relentless.

"Jaxon—" she groaned, her voice wavering. "That—it's enough."

But he didn't stop.

"It's dangerous to let power like this fester," Jaxon said, a steel edge under his tender words as his fingers dug harder into her flesh, pinning her in place. "I'm just keeping you safe, Starling."

"*Jaxon*—" she shoved at his chest but he just grunted, then laughed when she clawed at his arms.

"You'd let this destroy you if I stopped now," he said, his fingers digging into her hips as she twisted in his grip. "Stop fighting me, Araya. You're the one making it hurt this time—you need this."

Her body gave in before her mind did.

Her fists unclenched. Her breathing slowed, syncing with his as he kept drawing her power into himself. He was right—she needed this. She needed *him*. No matter how loudly something deep inside her screamed that she didn't.

Jaxon sighed in contentment, loosening his grip to run his free hand down her back in long, soothing strokes. "That's it, Starling. Let go."

And then—finally, he stopped.

"You took too much," Araya gasped, shuddering in his grip. Her voice was slurred and distant—like it belonged to someone else. Cold crawled through her veins, her magic guttering to a flicker.

Jaxon clicked his tongue, shifting her off his lap. She sagged into the couch, too exhausted to support her own weight as he crossed the room to the bar cart. Glass clinked softly as he poured, draining it in a single swallow before turning back to face her.

"I left you with exactly what any unbonded breeding female gets," he said, his voice clipped. "If you didn't have me—this would be your normal."

Araya could only stare at him, her vision blurring. Why would he do that to her? She blinked hard, trying to swallow the tears before he saw them—but of course he did.

He sighed, crossing back to her. His thumb stroked over her cheek, brushing the tears away from the corners of her eyes before tilting her chin up, forcing her to look at him.

"You fought me," he said gently—answering the question she hadn't asked. "You promised to trust me. But you didn't."

"I didn't—" she couldn't focus enough to finish the thought. She hadn't meant to fight him. Had she?

"It's my fault, really," Jaxon said, ignoring her protest. "I've been too lenient with you. But you need to remember, Starling, I give you more because I *want* to. If you ever question me like that again..." he shook his head. "I'll have no choice but to treat you like the rest. Do you understand?"

"Yes, Jaxon," she whispered—because what else could she say?

He smiled down at her, brushing a strand of hair from her face with the backs of his fingers. For a moment, Araya leaned into it— her body betraying her with the instinct to be soothed. To feel safe, even when she knew better. Shame prickled hot in her chest. Why did she always give in to him so easily?

"You'll feel better after you get some sleep," Jaxon said, plucking a blanket off the arm of the couch. He tucked it around her, easing her down onto the cushions. "It's been a hard night, Starling. But you'll feel better in the morning. Now what do you say?"

"Thank you," she murmured, the words spilling automatically from her cracked lips.

"Good girl." He pressed a kiss to her forehead before he straight- ened, smiling down at her.

"Sleep now," he said, already turning back to his work. "I'll wake you when it's time to take you home."

THIS WASN'T REAL. IT COULDN'T BE. BUT NOW ARAYA KNEW IT SOMEHOW was—from the shadows whispering and pooling in the cracks between the stones to the fae prince lounging against the wall, his hands cradled in his lap and his head tipped back, eyes closed. Pretending to sleep.

The dream version of his cell wasn't cold, but she still shivered, wrapping her arms around herself. She couldn't even feel the stone beneath her bare feet this time. Was this her dream? His? Or was it something else entirely?

"Are you going to keep pretending I don't exist?" she demanded.

Loren's eyes stayed closed, but the corner of his mouth twitched. "Would it help if I snored?"

"Did you just make a *joke*?" A laugh bubbled out of her, thin and incredulous. "This isn't funny! Why does this keep happening?"

He opened his eyes slowly, the sharp green gleaming in the strange dim light of the dream. "You tell me, *ael'sura*," he said, flashing her a wicked, sharp smile. "Who do you think I am?"

Araya stared at him, her brow furrowed in confusion. *Sura* was a rune used in Healing—but she was no Healer. The way he said it sounded like a name, or a title.

"Prince Loren of Valendral," she said cautiously. "Heir to the fae throne. Presumed dead—but obviously not."

"Yet." Loren chuckled drily, the sound brittle. He rose in one smooth motion, the chains dragging against the stone with a harsh, metallic rasp. "Is that all you know me as?"

"I don't—" Araya's words cut off as she stared at the fresh blood streaking his arms. It welled around the edges of the manacles, dripping over bruised and bloody knuckles. "Gods—" she stepped forward without thinking. "What *happened*?"

Loren froze as she took his hand, cradling the bruised and broken flesh carefully in her own. He'd hit something—the floor if she had to guess—hard and repeatedly. She didn't have much gift with Healing, but she'd spent enough time with Serafina to guess that he had several broken bones in addition to the terrible wounds from the iron.

"You shouldn't touch me, *ael'sura*." He winced, his voice rough as he gently brushed her hands away. His fingers lingered a moment too long against her skin before falling away, curling into fists at his sides. "Are you alright? If he's hurting you I will kill him—"

"He's not hurting me!" Araya stared at him, her eyes wide with alarm. "You *cannot* kill him, Loren."

"You protected him in my cell, too." He growled, low in his throat. "He doesn't deserve it, *ael'sura*. I saw him take your power. That kind of violation—" he shook his head, like he was too furious to continue. "Do you know what he said about you? He said he owned you—body, magic, and life."

"Well...he does—technically." Araya rubbed the *ly'ithra* rune at the base of her thumb. "He's my bond. We share power all the time. He was just a little too rough with it this time—"

"He's your *what*?" He recoiled like she'd struck him, chains rattling as he jerked a step back. Something jerked in her chest, snapping tight like a thread pulled taut. His gaze dropped to her hand, fixing on the rune inked there. "You gave him your name?"

"All fae give the Arcanum their name," she snapped, not caring for the judgement in his tone. "Jaxon purchased my bond from them —which I consented to. Trust me, it's a better life—"

Loren scoffed, his expression twisting in disbelief. "Fae would never give up their true names."

Araya straightened, indignation flaring hot and bright. Was he accusing her of *lying*? She was nearly as fae as he was—and just as bound by the truth.

"The law mandates that anyone over half-fae surrender their true name and accept the *ly'ithra* rune," she said, her voice heated. "If you refuse, they torture you."

"There are fates worse than torture." Loren bared his teeth at her, the sharp points of his canines flashing. "You gave them the power to do anything they wanted to you."

"I was *seven*." Her voice wavered, but she set her jaw, willing fire into her eyes as she glared at him. "They told me they wouldn't kill my mother if I gave them my name." A bitter laugh scraped her throat. "They lied."

Loren froze, the chains rattling faintly as his grip slackened at his sides. His green eyes flickered with something she couldn't quite place—anger, pity, or perhaps both. "*Ael'sura*—" he started.

Araya cut him off. "They killed her right in front of me before they clipped my ears and inked the *ly'ithra* rune on my hand. Then they sent me to live at Kaldrath. The Arcanum called it a school for fae orphans...but it was more like a prison. They *re-educated* us—anyone caught using a call name or speaking Valenya was beaten until they forgot the words. I saw it happen over and over again."

Loren's face darkened as she spoke, his gaze flicking to the jagged tip of her ear. He opened his mouth but Araya plunged forward, looking away so she wouldn't have to face the pity she was certain she would see in his eyes.

"A lot of us died there. My first week, one of the older boys tried to run. They caught him before he even made it to the gates and hung him up there—as a warning to the rest of us."

"Fae live in slums now," she continued, the heat leaking out of her voice. "Crammed together in crumbling, damp ruins that aren't fit for beasts, let alone people. So many get sick—or disappear. Females...the Arcanum incentivizes breeding with humans, to strengthen their bloodlines—" Loren hissed at that, but Araya ignored him. "Males are drained, worked until they break, then discarded and left to die like trash."

"Your people are being ground down to nothing, *Your Highness*." She forced herself to look up then, to meet the horror in his eyes. "So don't you *dare* judge them for giving up their names. Hate me if you want—but I will *never* be sorry for choosing a life where I'm safe and fed. Where *I* get to raise my children instead of having them ripped from my arms and given to a human family—or worse, sent somewhere like Kaldrath."

"I don't hate you, *ael'sura*," Loren said, his bright eyes shimmering with unshed tears. "I'm just sorry that I wasn't there to protect you."

Araya blinked, startled. An apology was the last thing she had expected.

"I suggested you see a Healer," she said after a moment, her voice quieter now.

"Don't ask for favors on my behalf," Loren said sharply. "I won't have you paying the price."

Araya scowled at him, but before she could argue the dream rippled around them, pitching her forward. Loren caught her, his arms closing around her instinctively. He surrounded her, the sudden contact sending a shock through her like she'd plunged into icy water. Something in her chest *hummed*, reaching—

Loren flinched, releasing her and stepping hastily away.

"What was that?" Araya demanded breathlessly.

"You're waking up," Loren said.

Araya narrowed her eyes at him. That was a *tricky* answer if she'd ever heard one. "That's not—"

He shook his head. "It doesn't matter. You can't tell anyone about these dreams—especially not Jaxon. Promise me you won't—"

Before she could even think about answering, the dream jolted again, shattering into a thousand pieces around her. Araya gasped, dragging air into her lungs like she'd been drowning. Her eyes snapped open, her heart pounding as they locked with Jaxon's warm brown stare.

"Easy, Starling," he murmured, stroking her cheek. "I'm going to take you home now."

Araya nodded, leaning into his warm touch. But her skin still tingled where Loren's hands had been, his words still echoing in her mind. *Don't tell anyone—especially not Jaxon.*

CHAPTER
ELEVEN

The next time Araya opened her eyes, afternoon sunlight spilled across Jaxon's bedroom, painting the rich fabrics with gold and casting intricate shadows over the polished wooden floor. She sat up slowly, her head pounding in time with her heartbeat.

Her power hummed under her skin—stronger than it had been, but a thick fog still clung to the edges of her mind, and even small movements made her head spin. She needed more rest—her body knew it, trying to drag her back into the warm cocoon of Jaxon's bed.

But sleep wouldn't fix this.

She had seen the prince in her dreams again. She had spoken to him—*touched* him. She couldn't keep pretending that he was just a manifestation of her subconscious.

She had to tell Jaxon. Didn't she? At least if she told him now, most of his fury would be directed at the prince instead of her. If she hid it and he found out...Gods. He could leave her like this indefinitely—drained to the point of exhaustion, a shadow of herself. No one would stop him. Most of his peers would probably applaud the decision.

Araya pressed her forehead to her knees, breathing deeply until the iron band around her chest eased.

It should have been easy to choose herself over the practical stranger who haunted her nightmares. But...she couldn't. Loren had already survived decades of iron, pain, and solitude—he had suffered enough. He didn't deserve to be punished for the connection neither one of them had chosen any more than she did.

She would keep it to herself. She had to. Jaxon had never asked about the dreams—never questioned the way she sometimes woke up trembling, breathless, staring into the dark. There was no reason for him to start now.

As long as she was careful... he'd never know.

Araya swung her legs over the edge of the bed, forcing her body to carry her to the bathroom. She washed her face and braided her hair back before stripping out of her sweat soaked nightgown and tugging on a chemise and a warm woolen dress. She needed to get out of the apartment, move her body, and feel the fresh air on her face.

She descended the carved marble stairs carefully, each step echoing softly in the hushed silence. The railing was cold under her palm—winter had crept inside, though the tall double doors were pulled shut against the chill, their dark wood and polished brass gleaming in the light of the chandelier that hung from the tall ceiling.

Jaxon had said this had been a seat of governance at one point— but after the Ascendancy, the Arcanum converted it to housing to meet demand. Most of the fae touches had been removed or covered up, but the sweeping architecture remained, as did the heavy, polished mahogany desk where the doorman sat.

"Miss Starwind," Marcus greeted her, jumping to his feet as she stepped into the atrium. "Are you well? You're quite pale."

"Just a little woozy, Marcus. I'm sure I'll recover quickly." Araya forced a small smile, fisting her hands in her cloak against the urge to pull her hood and hide away from his scrutiny. That wasn't how she lived anymore. "I'm just heading out to pick up some food."

He frowned, glancing at the frost creeping up the tall windows. "Should I call you a carriage?"

"No, thank you." Araya gave him a real smile this time. She liked the older man, with his steady demeanor and unhurried words. Humans were often hard to read, their layers of politeness and ability to lie masking deeper motives, but Marcus always radiated genuine care, going out of his way to make her feel welcome when she bonded with Jaxon.

"The fresh air will do me good," she added, hoping to reassure him.

Still, she almost second-guessed herself when Marcus pulled one of the heavy doors open and the wind tore through the atrium. Her old, threadbare cloak would have been no match for the chill, but the one Jaxon had bought her—lined with plush, white fur and dyed a deep, stately gray—wrapped around her like a shield despite the cold.

The walk back to her old neighborhood took longer than she expected. She had gotten spoiled, riding everywhere in the black carriages Jaxon and his father always used. By the time she finally spotted the familiar wooden sign of the Crust & Kettle swaying in the wind, her cheeks were numb, and the fur around her hood was edged with frost. But the throbbing in her head had receded to a dull ache behind her eyes.

Inside, the smell of fresh bread and simmering stew wrapped around her like a comforting embrace. A blazing fire roared in the hearth, spilling light and warmth into the dining area. Araya had spent many cold nights at one of those worn wooden tables with Serafina, laughing and talking.

Araya approached the counter, letting the warmth seep into her bones as she scanned the chalkboard menu. She ordered far more than she needed—unable to force herself to choose between the creamy comfort of the potato soup and the hearty goodness of the lamb stew, then adding on the wild mushroom soup just for good measure.

"I'll get this all packed up for you," the young female behind the counter said. "If you want to have a seat, I'll bring it over."

Araya turned, scanning the tables for a quiet place to sit and rest—then paused mid-step, heat rising to her face as she spotted Serafina tucked into a shadowed corner. She leaned forward, catching the hand of a broad-shouldered man Araya didn't recognize.

Araya flushed deeper and took a step back—intending to turn back toward the counter and pretend she hadn't seen them. With the way their last conversation had ended, she doubted Serafina wanted to see her at all—but her sudden movement must have caught the Healer's attention.

Serafina's head jerked up, her green eyes widening before she masked her surprise, smoothing her expression into something unreadable.

"Araya," she said, her tone perfectly neutral. "I didn't realize you were coming out this way."

"It wasn't planned." Araya stepped toward them, her gaze flicking between Serafina and the stranger. "Who's this?"

Serafina hesitated, a faint flush coloring her cheeks. "He's—"

"Finn Greenvale." He stood, extending his hand. "I'm a friend of Serafina's."

"Araya Starwind," she returned, shooting another look at Serafina. "I'm...another friend of Serafina's." One who certainly should have known about him—seeing as they'd lived together for the better part of three years.

"A pleasure," Finn said easily, though his sharp brown eyes were calculating, and there was a weight to his words, like he was filing away everything about her. He glanced at Serafina. "Thanks for meeting me—I'll let you two catch up."

He stooped, grabbing a familiar bag from under the table before sauntering toward the door. He moved too gracefully for a human, despite his rounded ears. A casual observer might have been fooled, but Araya had spent enough time around half-fae to recognize the way they carried themselves.

"That was subtle." Araya slid into the chair across from Serafina, not bothering to wait for an invitation. "Who is he really?"

Serafina sighed, rubbing her temples. "It's not—"

"—anything I need to worry about?" Araya finished for her. "You realize that just makes it sound *more* suspicious, right?"

Serafina pressed her lips into a thin line.

Araya drummed her fingers against the tabletop. "Is he a Healer?"

Serafina tensed. "He's a friend."

"Right." Araya let the word hang between them. "And am I supposed to pretend I didn't see him picking up a bag full of supplies you stole from the Aetherium?"

Serafina's flush deepened. "It's not what you think—"

"You don't have any idea what I think," Araya retorted. She shoved back her chair as the waitress approached, intending to take her food and storm out—but as she did, the room tilted sharply. Her vision blurred, the edges of her sight going dark as she grabbed onto the table to stay upright.

"Araya!" Serafina was on her feet in an instant, coming around the table to steady her.

"I'm fine." Araya forced a small smile, waving off the concerned waitress. "Maybe I stood up too fast—"

"Don't try to deflect with me," Serafina snapped. "You're pale as death." She caught Araya's wrist, pressing two fingers to her pulse as her gaze sharpened with the same clinical focus she used on patients. "Are you in pain? What—"

"No pain—" Araya closed her eyes, willing the room to stop spinning. "It's just magic depletion. I'm *fine*, Serafina. I just needed a minute."

"That's a diagnosis, Araya—not an explanation." Serafina scowled. "Magic doesn't just deplete like this—not on its own. Tell me what happened."

Araya hesitated, biting her lip. But Serafina just stared at her, clearly prepared to stand there until Araya told her the truth.

Araya exhaled, her shoulders slumping. "Jaxon siphoned too much," she admitted.

"He *what*?" Serafina's voice was too calm for the rage blazing in her eyes.

"It's not usually like this," Araya said quickly, already regretting saying anything at all. "I just... upset him last night."

Serafina inhaled through her nose, holding the breath before letting it out slowly. "He drained you," she said. It was a statement, not a question. "As a punishment."

"It wasn't—it's just—" Araya shook her head, struggling to find words that didn't stick in her throat as a lie. "He was upset. I pushed him too far. He didn't do anything wrong."

"He didn't do anything *illegal*," Serafina said flatly. "That doesn't mean it wasn't *wrong*." She stood abruptly, picking up Araya's bag of food. "Is your carriage outside?"

"I walked," Araya stood, careful to move more slowly this time. "Really, I'm fine—"

"I'm not letting you walk all the way back to Kingswalk alone in this state," Serafina cut her off. She took Araya by the elbow, guiding her towards the door. "I'd be a bad Healer and a bad friend if I did."

"Are we still friends, then?" Araya asked, the bitterness in her tone surprising even herself.

Serafina's steps faltered, her boots scraping the frozen cobblestones as they stepped out onto the darkening street. She didn't answer. The silence stretched, cold and heavy, pressing into the space between them. Araya swallowed hard, her throat tight, the ache in her chest sharp enough to steal her breath. Maybe she should have expected it...but it still stung.

"When you get home, you should make a tea blend with chamomile, nettle, and a pinch of dried valerian root," Serafina said finally. "It will knock you out for the night, but it will help replenish your magic faster."

"Thanks," Araya sighed, her breath freezing in the air in front of her as she exhaled. "I'll try it. Does it help with dreams?"

"You shouldn't have any with this one," Serafina replied. "Has that been a problem lately?"

"Sometimes," Araya said, ducking her head. Serafina had sat with her through countless nightmares when they roomed together at the Aetherium—but Araya couldn't tell her about Loren. Even Araya wasn't supposed to know he existed. It was safer this way—for Serafina, for Araya...even for Loren.

By the time Jaxon's building finally came into view, Araya's legs were aching, and she was more than a little relieved that Serafina had insisted on walking with her—at least until she recognized the imposing black carriage pulling up out front.

"Who is that?" Serafina asked, her steps slowing as the carriage stopped in front of the building.

"Garrick," Araya said. "Jaxon's father."

"You call the High Magister *Garrick*?" Serafina said. "What is he doing here?"

"He comes for dinner sometimes," Araya said absently. She didn't want to do anything but go inside, eat, and curl up in bed—maybe after a hot bath. "At least I got extra soup."

By the time they reached the building, Garrick was standing beside his carriage, clearly waiting for them.

"Garrick," Araya mustered up a smile from somewhere. "I didn't realize you were coming tonight.

"Araya," he greeted her smoothly, his tone clipped. "This is an unplanned visit." His gaze swept over her, lingering just long enough to feel invasive, before shifting to Serafina. "Who is your friend?"

"Master Serafina Hart, Healer." Serafina inclined her head in a smooth, practiced gesture—but Araya didn't miss the way her jaw tensed, or how her fingers curled tightly around the strap of her bag. "It's an honor to meet you, sir."

"The pleasure is mine," Garrick replied, his dark eyes bright as they assessed her. "Will you be joining us upstairs, Master Hart?"

"No," Serafina said quickly. "I was just making sure Araya got home safely."

"Ah, a loyal friend," Garrick said, his tone almost amused, though the faint smile on his lips never reached his eyes. "An increasingly rare quality."

"Maybe you're making the wrong friends, sir," Serafina said blandly.

Araya's breath caught. What was Serafina thinking? This was the High Magister—no one spoke to him like that. But Serafina didn't so much as blink, holding his gaze with calm, unreadable eyes like she hadn't just insulted one of the most powerful men in the New Dominion.

Araya cleared her throat. "I'm sure she didn't mean—"

Garrick held up a hand, his smile returning, cool and dismissive. "Healers often have... strong opinions. No harm done."

Without waiting for permission—or perhaps choosing to ignore it—Serafina pulled Araya into a tight hug. "Make the tea," she whispered, pressing the bag of food into Araya's arms. Then she stepped back, offered Garrick a cold nod, and turned down the street, walking away with the same composure she'd worn the entire exchange.

Araya watched her go, shaken by the whole interaction—but she didn't have time to dwell on the unease coiling in her chest, not with Garrick standing right there.

"Is Jaxon expecting you?" she asked.

"He's not," Garrick said, his expression unreadable as he gestured toward the door. "Shall we?"

Araya nodded, forcing her legs to move as she followed him toward the door. The warmth of the atrium spilled out as the heavy doors swung open, enveloping her in the scent of polished wood and fresh flowers. She stepped inside, her boots clicking softly against the gleaming marble floor.

Garrick's measured footsteps echoed beside her, his silence pressing down on her like a weight. He said nothing until they reached the grand staircase, his hand closing around her elbow to support her as she faltered on the climb.

"Loyal friends can be invaluable," he said smoothly. "It's a relief when they know which questions to ask... and which to leave unspoken." His sharp gaze lingered on her, the faintest smile brushing his lips. "Especially when it comes to sensitive matters my son is too reckless to take the proper precautions with."

Araya's breath hitched, the weight of Garrick's gaze pinning her in place. *He knew*—he knew Jaxon had taken her down to that cell.

"I didn't tell her anything about what I saw," Araya whispered, fumbling for an answer that might appease him. She was suddenly very relieved she hadn't told Serafina anything, letting her answer directly. "I didn't know—"

"Of course you didn't," Garrick said, his tone as smooth and pleasant as ever. "This certainly isn't *your* fault, Araya. Now, let's go find my son."

———

"JAXON IS PROBABLY IN HIS OFFICE," ARAYA SAID, TOEING OFF HER BOOTS IN the entryway. Jaxon's boots already sat neatly by the door, the warm light of the lamps glinting on the polished leather. His cloak hung on its hook, everything in its place. "Are you staying for dinner? I got plenty of soup—"

"He's not staying."

Araya flinched at the sharpness in Jaxon's voice. She hadn't even heard him approach—but there he was, leaning against the wall. He glared at her, his dark eyes sweeping over her from head to toe as if assessing her for damage.

"Where have you been?" he demanded. "Marcus said you left and refused a carriage."

"I—" Araya stared at him, caught off guard by his anger. "I just picked up dinner. From the Crust & Kettle. I needed some fresh air and I thought some comfort food—"

"If you need fresh air, you go out on the balcony," Jaxon snapped. He pushed off the wall and closed the distance between them in two strides, snatching the bags from her arms before she could react. "You don't *walk* to your old neighborhood."

He set the bags down with a thud, the heavy tureens inside rattling. She'd paid extra for them—once, that would have meant going hungry. But tonight, she hadn't even blinked at the cost. Because of Jaxon.

The thought settled uncomfortably in her chest as she lingered where he'd left her, unsure whether to move or speak.

"That's an odd way of thanking your bond for bringing back dinner, Jaxon," Garrick commented, taking his usual seat at their small table as he watched his son with narrowed eyes. "Araya, you should sit. You look like you're about to collapse where you stand."

"I—" She wanted to say *I'm fine*, but the words stuck in her throat. She looked to Jaxon, instinctively seeking direction—but he was in the kitchen, yanking open drawers and pulling out utensils with more force than necessary.

"Indulge an old man's worry," Garrick said, his gaze unwavering as he inclined his head towards her chair.

Araya sank into her chair, caught between Garrick's cold anger and Jaxon's simmering irritation.

"Eat," Jaxon ordered, setting a bowl of creamy white soup down in front of her and a platter of bread in the center of the table. His hand lingered on her shoulder, heavy and possessive, before he turned to retrieve his own bowl.

"None for me, Jaxon?" Garrick asked.

Jaxon sighed heavily, a muscle in his jaw ticking before he masked it with practiced calm. "Now isn't a good time, Father. I can come to your office tomorrow—"

Garrick laughed, but there was no humor in it. "That's not an option, Jaxon," he said, his voice devoid of any of the usual warmth he had for his son. "Not when Magister Hale was in my office this morning howling about how *my son* brought an *unauthorized fae* into the lower cells."

Jaxon stiffened, rage flashing through his carefully composed expression. "If that guard's running to Hale with every report, then maybe he needs replacing. And if Hale has enough time to monitor a project he was removed from, perhaps he needs more to do."

Garrick sighed, exasperation flashing in his eyes. "Hale is a Magister. You are not." His gaze slid to Araya. "And now, because of your reckless behavior, he has turned his sights on her."

Araya's chest tightened, the soup turning thick and sticky in her mouth. She set her spoon down, her appetite gone.

"Was that your plan?" Garrick asked, his voice sharpening. "Or are you just careless? I taught you to take better care of your possessions than this."

"She's my bond," Jaxon said tightly. "He has no authority—"

"Owning her bond is a privilege, not a right, Jaxon." Garrick cut in, his words razor sharp. "Do you think the Arcanum won't take her back if Hale makes a big enough deal out of this? You know this isn't what I meant when I authorized her to work with you."

Take her back. The words struck Araya like a lash—clean and cruel. Everything she'd fought for was slipping through her fingers before she'd even had the chance to truly hold it. Her heart pounded, every breath sawing out of her lungs in jagged rasps. She would lose everything—Jaxon's protection, the privilege of wielding her magic, the countless tiny freedoms she'd only just started to trust—

She couldn't go back. She wouldn't survive it.

"You said this was my project," Jaxon snapped, his fists clenched at his sides. "My opportunity to prove myself. Hale has had *twenty* years to work on Loren with no results. But in just thirty minutes with Araya? He spoke—*twice.*"

"He spoke to her?" Garrick's expression flickered, a hint of intrigue breaking through his composed mask.

"Spoke, touched—" Jaxon crossed his arms, staring at his father smugly. "How long has it been since he reacted or interacted with anyone Hale sent down there? He broke his chains trying to protect her from me."

"He broke his chains?" Garrick asked sharply.

"Araya put them back." Jaxon said, a note of pride slipping into his voice. "You should have seen his face when he realized she was there by choice."

Garrick exhaled sharply. "She shouldn't have been down there at all, Jaxon."

"She deserved to be there," Jaxon snapped. "You haven't even heard her theory—Hale's team has been stumbling around in the dark without results for years. But Araya came up with an actionable idea without even having all the information."

Jaxon's gaze flicked to Araya, softer for a heartbeat before hardening again as he turned back to Garrick.

"She's the only one who's produced anything actionable in years. She doesn't just deserve access—she deserves credit. She deserves a seat at the table. Whether or not Hale or the rest of the Arcanum like it, she's earned the right to work on this directly."

Garrick pressed his lips together, considering. "You want me to grant her an official clearance."

"If that's what it takes." Jaxon crossed his arms over his chest. "I'm far more concerned about results than I am about arbitrary rules."

"What about her?" Garrick turned his sharp gaze on Araya, staring at her with an intensity that made her spine stiffen. "Have you asked her if this is something she can handle? To be intimately involved in the breaking of one of your own kind—it's not an easy ask, Jaxon."

"I don't have any loyalty to the fae monarchy," Araya whispered, her chest tight.

All she had ever wanted was to live the best life she could—to have a warm bed, enough to eat, the right to practice her magic, and the freedom to breathe without constantly looking over her shoulder. She'd never wanted to be the key to anything—yet here she was, a pawn being positioned for someone else's victory in a war she wanted no part in.

"Of course you don't," Garrick said gently. "No one is questioning your loyalty, Araya. Any fool can see the devotion you have for my son. But even the most finely crafted tools can splinter under strain if they're not handled properly. You've seen more than your share of darkness, Araya. I'd hate to see something so valuable ruined by carelessness."

He glanced back at his son with so much disappointment that Araya squirmed uncomfortably.

"I know how difficult it must have been for you to see a fae in that condition—something Jaxon should have considered before he took you down there." Garrick sighed. "I know it's hard to believe, but Loren and I were friends once. What he's been reduced to—even I find it sad. No one would think less of you if this wasn't something you could do."

Araya shivered as Jaxon's hand fell heavily onto her knee beneath the table, his thumb tracing slow, steady circles. Maybe it was meant to be comforting. But all Araya felt was the leaden reminder of who she owed her privileges to.

"I'll do whatever Jaxon needs me to do," she said.

"Very well." Garrick nodded slowly. "I'll take care of the clearance, then."

Araya sat silently as Jaxon walked his father out, staring down at her soup. It had cooled, its surface thick and congealed. Her appetite was gone anyway, replaced by gnawing unease. She should just brew the tea Serafina recommended and go to sleep—

"Eat, Starling."

Jaxon's hands settled on her shoulders, warm and firm. Araya flinched under the sudden touch, the tickle of his breath on the back of her neck sending a shiver down her spine. "You need your strength."

It wasn't a request.

Araya picked up her spoon with trembling fingers, staring down at the cold, heavy mass of potatoes and cream. Bite after bite, she forced it down. Each bite coating her tongue in a thick, tasteless paste. By the time she set the empty bowl aside, her stomach felt like she'd swallowed a stone.

"Can the Arcanum really revoke our bond?" The question tumbled out before she could stop it, her voice trembling in a way that made her wince. She hated how small she sounded.

"They can," Jaxon murmured, brushing a kiss against the back of her neck as he reached over her shoulder to pick up her dish. "But they won't. Because you're going to prove yourself. By the time you're done here, they'll be giving you a medal."

His words weren't a reassurance—they were a verdict.

The quiet *thunk* of the coldbox closing made Araya flinch. Jaxon moved like a shadow across the kitchen, washing the dishes and stowing away the leftovers. Finally, he tossed the towel over his shoulder and leaned against the counter, studying her.

"You worried me," he said.

Araya lowered her gaze, her cheeks burning. "I'm sorry," she whispered. "You're right—I shouldn't have gone out like that. I thought I could handle it, but if Serafina hadn't been there—"

"You saw Serafina?" Jaxon's voice sharpened, his expression darkening.

"I ran into her at the Crust & Kettle," Araya said, choosing her words carefully. "She walked me home and recommended a tea to help me replenish my magic. I didn't...I didn't tell her anything."

The tension in Jaxon's shoulders eased—slightly. But the furrow in his brow lingered.

"Of course you didn't," he said. "I just remember how hurt you were when she pulled away because of our bond."

"Oh." The lump in Araya's throat tightened. She swallowed hard, the bitterness of that hurt still clinging to her. "It was... I'm fine." She frowned as Jaxon turned away, rummaging through the cabinets until he pulled out the kettle.

"What are you doing?"

Jaxon glanced over his shoulder, that familiar smile tugging at the corner of his mouth. "I'm making the tea, Starling," he said, like it was the most natural thing in the world. "It's the least I can do after pushing you so hard earlier. I shouldn't have taken so much."

Surprise flickered through her exhaustion. "You don't have to—"

"I do." His tone brooked no argument. He moved with steady efficiency, pulling jars from the cabinet. "I was angry, and I took too much from you—that's inexcusable. The least I can do is make you the tea that will help. What did Serafina say to put in it?"

Araya bit her lip, twisting her hands in her lap. First he drained her magic without flinching—and now he was making tea?

"Chamomile, nettle, and a pinch of dried valerian root," she murmured.

Jaxon nodded, measuring each herb with practiced precision. The earthy scent of chamomile and valerian filled the kitchen as the water boiled, its soothing aroma curling around her, loosening the knot of tension in her chest.

Jaxon pulled the kettle off the heat just as it started to whistle, the high-pitched sound fading into silence. He poured the steaming tea through a strainer into a delicate mug, every movement careful and deliberate.

Finally, he crossed the kitchen. He leaned in, his arms bracketing her as he set the mug down, the warmth of his chest pressing lightly against her back. Araya automatically wrapped her hands around the steaming mug, letting the comforting warmth sink into her palms.

"You hurt me," she whispered, her voice barely more than a breath. The words slipped out before she could stop them. Her fingers tightened around the mug. "I wasn't trying to defy you, Jaxon. I was frightened."

"I know, Starling," Jaxon's hands found her shoulders again. His thumbs moved in slow, practiced strokes, kneading at the tension there. His voice was just as soothing, smoothing over the jagged edges of her fear. "I didn't consider what it would be like for you—and then I reacted badly. I'm sorry."

Araya shivered as Jaxon's thumbs traced slow, practiced lines over her shoulders, her wariness flickering under his comforting, familiar touch. She took a sip of the tea, its warmth spreading through her chest like a lazy tide as the bitter herbs settled her stomach.

"It's just this project," Jaxon sighed. "There's so much riding on it. I need to succeed—for us."

"You will." Araya leaned into him, lulled by the comfort he gave so easily. "I know you will."

"I will," Jaxon echoed, his fingers slipping into her hair, gently unpicking her braid. The strands tumbled loose over her shoulders, his touch slow and deliberate. "Because I have you. You're the solution right under the Arcanum's nose, Starling."

The words needled at the edges of her mind, a whisper of warning struggling against the comforting fog. But the tea's warmth tugged her down, dragging her deeper into the haze. She was too tired to hold onto the thought.

Didn't want to.

"Come on," Jaxon murmured, guiding her to her feet with steady hands. His palm rested against her lower back, grounding her as he led her toward the bed.

Araya didn't resist as he tucked her in. The bed's softness cradled her, and Jaxon curled behind her, his warmth wrapping around her like a shield.

"You're safe," he whispered, his lips brushing her temple. "You're always safe with me, Starling."

Her breathing slowed, her body melting into the mattress as her willingness to resist melted away, smothered by warmth and exhaustion. She succumbed to the pull of sleep, letting that dark tide pull her under.

She did not dream.

CHAPTER

TWELVE

Time meant nothing.

Guards came at odd intervals, shoving cold meals through the slot in the iron door. It could have been days or weeks since Jaxon had brought *her* here. Every time Loren closed his eyes, he found himself desperately hoping to find her waiting for him.

She hadn't come.

Loren told himself he was relieved. Better for her—safer—if he never saw her again.

The bond still tugged at him. Raw, insistent—he hated it. Hated how it put her in danger. What if Jaxon knew? What if he had hurt her? The strangled squeal she'd made when the human mage shoved his hand into the neck of her dress haunted Loren's nightmares.

Jaxon had *purchased* her. The thought of it made him sick—that she'd insisted it was her choice made it worse. Did she kneel willingly before the monster that would destroy their people? Did she look up into his eyes and smile?

The shadows stirred at the edges of the cell, sensing his turmoil. They slithered around him, their angry whispers scraping over his mind like shards of glass. They all spoke over each other, their voices a confused cacophony of orders and accusations. Loren could almost never understand them now, except when they chanted *her* name, tearing at the already frayed threads of his sanity.

Somewhere outside, footsteps echoed. Loren's eyes snapped open, his heart hammering in time with the heavy cadence. He knew that gait—Jaxon was back.

The door groaned open, and the shadows scattered like rats, slinking away to hide in the corners of the cell like they always did when someone came. Loren glared after them. What good was being heir to the shadows if they only ever tormented him?

"Your Highness," Jaxon drawled, his smirk firmly in place. The guard closed the door behind him, the key grating in the lock again. "I hope I'm not interrupting. I know you have a busy schedule."

Loren fixed his gaze on the far wall, locking his eyes onto the cracked stone there. His silence had been his shield for years. He'd faltered when he spoke to her—but he wouldn't give Jaxon the satisfaction of getting under his skin a second time.

Jaxon chuckled, shaking his head like a teacher humoring a stubborn pupil. "Back to pretending to be mute? That's fine."

He crossed the cell with measured steps, unrolling his leather kit and hanging it from the hook driven into the wall. The dim light glinted off the tools inside—blades, hooks, clamps—Loren knew the iron-edged bite of every one of them at this point.

"Let's make this easy," Jaxon said, selecting a wickedly curved blade. "Tell me your true name, and we can skip the rest—" he waved the knife lazily. "Maybe I even get you some real food, hm?"

Loren pressed his lips into a firm line. He wouldn't hand over his name—not ever. That Jaxon already had *hers*...that was bad enough. He could use it to make her do anything he wanted—and she wouldn't even have the power, or the knowledge, to fight back.

She'd been seven years old when they took it from her. When they killed her mother in front of her. When they mutilated her body and branded her with their runes. And now *he* owned it—owned her.

Humanity had a lot to answer for. And if Loren ever got the

chance, he would make Jaxon Shaw choke on what he'd stolen from her.

Jaxon sighed, rolling his shoulders before tilting his head until his neck cracked. "Have it your way, then," he said, grinning. "I'll have fun either way." He lifted a hand, flicking his fingers with lazy precision as the burnt stench of his stolen magic filled the cell.

Loren hissed as his bindings wrenched tighter, iron biting deep into the raw, open wounds on his wrists. The manacles glowed faintly, the runes etched into the metal pulsing as they forced Loren's arms out, stretching them painfully wide against the cold stone.

Jaxon closed the distance between them in a few leisurely strides, twirling the knife in his hand. Loren bared his teeth as the man ran his eyes over Loren's pinned body, assessing. Then, almost casually, Jaxon pressed the blade against Loren's shoulder.

Loren swallowed his scream as cold iron bit through the thin, filthy shirt and into his skin. Sharp, searing pain blazed along the thin line. Hot, sticky blood soaked his shirt, spilling down his arm and splashing onto the stones.

"See? I'm trying to be gentle," Jaxon sighed deeply, twisting the blade slightly. "But you make it so difficult."

Loren ground his teeth, locking his jaw as he forced himself to remain silent. He fixed his gaze on the far wall, willing himself to think of nothing but the crack in that stone until Jaxon's voice faded and blurred—

The iron edge scraped bone, wrenching a ragged cry from his throat.

"Focus, Your Highness," Jaxon chided, clicking his tongue softly. "I'm speaking to you."

He stepped back, letting the knife hang lazily at his side as his dark eyes swept over Loren's blood-soaked shirt, admiring his work.

"Araya came up with a very interesting theory about the Shadowed Veil," he said idly. "She doesn't think it's a curse at all. She thinks it's some sort of ancient magic tied to your bloodline. Isn't that a fascinating theory?"

Do not react. Loren hung from his restraints. He ached, every breath coming slow and measured as he fought the instinct to look up and snarl. She was close—too close to the truth.

"It makes sense, doesn't it?" Jaxon continued. "Your ancestors—they must have kept it tethered somehow. But when your father died you didn't step up."

Loren's jaw tightened at the accusation. Only because the Arcanum had him shackled in iron in this cursed cell, where the shadows cowered in corners instead of obeying him. But he couldn't say that, couldn't defend himself. He needed to stay silent.

"It's such a shame, really," Jaxon shook his head. "She's brilliant. She could have been extraordinary—if only she was human."

Loren's fists clenched, the iron shackles biting deeper into his raw wrists. His breath hitched, a slight tremor betraying the storm raging inside him. Jaxon didn't miss it. His expression sharpened, satisfaction gleaming in his dark eyes.

"But you've noticed that, haven't you?" He continued, trailing the tip of his knife across Loren's chest. "Is that why you can't stand the thought of her being with me?"

Loren stared at the crack in the wall, his vision blurring as Jaxon wielded her name like another blade, twisting deeply into an already gaping wound. But the human stepped closer, leaning in until Loren could feel his breath against his blood and sweat-slicked skin.

"She's beautiful, isn't she? So eager to please. And when she touches me..." Jaxon's soft laugh slid under Loren's skin. "You should have seen her last night."

The words dug into Loren like iron barbs, twisting and cruel. His chest heaved, each breath trembling with barely-contained fury. Jaxon didn't just own her name—he owned *her*. Loren pictured those hands on her skin, that voice whispering lies into her ear—and she would have no defense against him.

Blood pooled on his tongue, hot and metallic, and before he could stop himself, Loren twisted his head and spat.

Jaxon's grin faltered, his dark eyes narrowing as he slowly

dragged his hand over his face, studying the blood smeared there. Then, his lips curled into a new smile—one sharper, colder, and infinitely more dangerous.

"Now we're getting somewhere, Your Highness," Jaxon purred. "What is it about her that puts that fire in you? Do you think you can actually do anything to save her?"

Loren stayed silent, his jaw clenched so tightly his teeth ached. Jaxon could never know why he cared so deeply about her.

Jaxon sighed, shaking his head. "So predictable."

He wiped his blade clean, tucking it back into his kit before rolling it up, bundling his tools away. "Don't worry—we have all the time in the world. Who knows—you started down here with my father. Maybe one day it will be my child here torturing you instead of me. Do you think they'll get Araya's hair? It's gorgeous, isn't it? I love seeing it wrapped around my fist—"

A violent snarl ripped from Loren's throat as he strained against his chains, but they didn't give this time.

Not like before.

It hadn't been strength that freed him that night—it had been fear. Fear for *her*, fueling his desperate, all-consuming need to reach her. To save her.

But she didn't need to be saved. She'd *chosen* Jaxon Shaw.

The knowledge burned hotter than iron. She had returned to the man who hurt him, the man who owned her name—who wielded it like a weapon. She had gone back to the man who carved into him like meat. Back to the hands that held the blade. The bond didn't care. It pulled at him anyway—tight, unrelenting, aching with every breath. It refused to let go of her, even as his pride screamed that he should.

Because gods help him... he still wanted her safe.

Jaxon didn't even flinch. He took his time, wiping his blade clean with a deliberate slowness, savoring Loren's ragged breathing.

"Rest up, Your Highness," he said, shouldering his kit and

rapping twice on the door. "Maybe if you cooperate, I'll let you see her again."

The chains loosened as soon as the door slammed shut behind him, dropping Loren's broken body onto the sticky puddle of blood on the stone floor. He retched from the pain, but nothing came up. His head spun, hazy from pain and blood loss.

The shadows slunk out of their corners, coiling around him like silent sentinels now that Jaxon was gone. Their whispers brushed over him, her name echoing in the darkness. They wanted to see her again.

Goddess, so did he.

But it was too dangerous. Jaxon already had her name—if he ever learned she was Loren's mate...he wouldn't need chains. Just her.

CHAPTER

THIRTEEN

Araya descended into the depths of the Aetherium, every reluctant step carrying her closer to the chained prince she never wanted to see again. His shadows pressed in around her—no longer content to linger politely in the corners where they belonged. Instead, they slid through the cracks in the walls and pooled in the seams of the floor, thicker than darkness should be—slithering at the edges of her vision and curling their dark tendrils around her ankles.

"Leave me alone," she whispered. "I don't know what you want."

But they didn't listen.

Their voices rose in a hissing, whispered chorus—like wind through dead branches, or knives dragged over wet stone. The words didn't make sense, not in any language she knew, but they meant something. She could feel it—scraping along the inside of her skull, tugging at memories she'd buried long ago.

She squeezed her eyes shut, gripping the railing until her knuckles ached. It had been weeks since Jaxon first brought her here —long enough that Araya had started to nurture a flicker of hope that the Arcanum would deny Garrick's request for her clearance. But this morning, she'd found the note on her workbench.

Meet me, it read. Jaxon hadn't signed it, hadn't said where to meet him—but she knew. And she knew what would be waiting for her when she got there.

She pressed her palm to the first iron door, that last ember of hope guttering out as the runes carved into it flared silver-blue under her touch. It swung open, confirming exactly what she had dreaded. The Arcanum had granted her clearance. There was no escaping what they wanted from her now.

Get the prince to talk to her. Convince him to trust her. Then betray him.

It was just another task. No different than the others they'd assigned her over the years. Working for them was the price of the freedom they'd allowed her. This was the same.

And yet, it felt different.

Araya had never minded working on amplifiers. The bones were already processed by the time they reached her, and she only ever infused them with her own power...but she didn't want to see the broken prince again. Not even in her dreams.

She'd been brewing herself Serafina's tea every night, chasing the drugged, dreamless sleep it offered.

Araya moved through the desecrated temple, her footsteps nearly silent on the cracked stone floor. She did not stop, refusing to linger under the scrutiny of the shattered idols. She avoided looking at the altar and the ravaged graves altogether, eager to leave this part behind.

She quickened her steps, a strange tug behind her breastbone urging her forward—like someone had hooked her heart on a string and was reeling her in. Araya shook her head, trying to dismiss it as nerves, but the sensation only deepened further into the catacombs she went.

She was almost relieved to see the same guard standing in front of the door to Loren's cell. His gaze flicked to hers, then dropped immediately, his discomfort palpable. Had he been punished for allowing her through last time?

"Miss Starwind," he said, not meeting her eyes. "Master Jaxon asked that you wait in the workshop until he's finished."

"Finished?" Araya asked, frowning. The guard shifted uncomfortably, his gaze darting back to the door behind him. Araya's stomach lurched at the realization—Jaxon was inside.

"He shouldn't be much longer," the guard said, clearing his throat. "The workshop is just down the hall—it will be the only open door. You can't miss it."

Araya hesitated. That pull in her chest surged, urging her to spring forward, to push through the door he guarded. To find *him*. She clenched her fists behind her back, letting the pain of her nails digging into her palms ground her as she shook the feeling off.

"Thank you," she said, pretending not to hear him exhale audibly as she turned away, heading further down the hall.

Bright light spilled from the open workshop door, casting a golden glow into the dank hallway. Araya squinted, half-blinded by the aetherlamps after the calculated dimness of the dungeon. Blinking, she stepped inside, taking in a space that looked more like a field laboratory than a traditional workshop.

Long, communal workbenches stretched across the space, their surfaces cluttered with scattered tools. Mismatched shelves lined the back wall, sagging under the weight of supplies jammed haphazardly wherever they would fit. The air reeked of burning aether and damp stone, all mixed with the lingering undertone of old blood, a sickening mix that turned her stomach.

"Jaxon certainly hasn't done much with the space, has he?"

Araya jumped, startling at the unfamiliar voice. She whirled, finding the man framed in the doorway, his black robes stark against the bright glow of the aetherlamps. His pale blue eyes gleamed, bright and cruel, as they swept the cluttered space with obvious disdain before settling on her.

"I suppose he doesn't have particularly high standards," he continued, stepping forward. "After all, he's insisting on trusting a halfblood female with our most precious secrets."

Araya's stomach dropped as the door swung closed behind him, latching with a quiet *click* that might as well have been a death knell. He prowled closer, his shadow falling over her as she stumbled back until her spine struck the bloodstained wall. She had nowhere else to go.

"But I can see why he's enamored—after all, enchanting a young man rarely requires magic." He stared down at her, his smile thin and cold. "Sometimes, a pretty face and a willing mouth are enough. I'm sure you do everything he asks… don't you?"

Araya flinched, her face flushing under his scrutiny. Shame prickled beneath her skin, and worse—fear. She knew what happened to fae females who found themselves alone with powerful human mages—there was no one to stop him here.

"Magister Hale," she managed to say, her voice shaking.

"You know who I am. Good." The faint smile on his lips didn't touch his pale blue eyes. "I'm sure you can guess that I argued vehemently against this, then. You may belong to Jaxon, but if you compromise this project, I will personally ensure the consequences are… unforgettable. Do you understand me?"

"I understand," Araya said, forcing the words past the lump in her throat.

"Good," Hale said again. He smiled faintly, like he could read her fear as easily as words on a page. "This place is a disaster," he said, turning his sharp gaze back to the room. Air rushed back into Araya's lungs the moment he stepped away, his contempt lingering like a shadow. "Sloppy benches—improper storage. Typical of Jaxon—"

"Are you inspecting my workspaces now?" Araya's heart leapt as Jaxon's voice sliced through the tension, her legs threatening to buckle with relief.

Hale straightened, his lips pressing into a thin line as he turned to face Jaxon. "This isn't your workspace," he said coldly. "It belongs to the Arcanum. You should at least attempt to maintain some semblance of order—"

Jaxon chuckled. "This is how your team left things, Hale." He gestured broadly to the cluttered benches and scattered tools. "If you'd put half the effort into overseeing them as you do interfering with my bond, maybe you would have gotten results."

Hale's face darkened, his pale eyes narrowing to slits. His hands flexed at his sides, but his gaze was icy as it swept over them both.

"Try not to get too attached to your toys, boy." He sneered. "Because when this all falls apart, it won't be the golden son they come for—it will be her."

With that, he turned sharply on his heel, his black robes flaring as he swept from the room like a thundercloud. His sharp footsteps echoed down the hallway, fading quickly into silence.

Araya released a breath she hadn't realized she'd been holding. She stumbled forward, and Jaxon caught her easily, his arms wrapping around her like steel bands as she pressed her face into his chest, trembling.

"Don't let him frighten you, Starling," Jaxon murmured, his hand stroking long lines down her back. "Hale is just bitter because he got outvoted. I'm sorry he surprised you here—he still has clearance, but I'll talk to my father. Hale won't get this close to you again."

Araya clung to him, letting his steady presence ease the tension knotted in her chest. She closed her eyes, breathing in the comforting vanilla scent of his soap. But beneath that comforting scent there was something else—something metallic and acrid. Her nostrils flared as she pulled back, staring at the dried crimson streaking his hands and forearms.

"Jaxon," she breathed, her voice catching. "What happened?"

"I was doing my part, Starling." Jaxon smiled at her, brushing a stray lock of hair behind her ear. "Getting the prince ready for you."

Araya caught her breath, her eyes darting from his hands to his face, searching for answers she wasn't sure she wanted to find. "Ready for me?"

"It's your turn now." Jaxon plucked a worn leather first-aid kit off one of the cluttered workbenches, presenting it to her with a flourish. "Let's see if you can coax a few secrets out of him while you're patching him up."

Araya barely caught the kit, scrambling to follow as he turned, striding into the hall with long steps. "All you need to do tonight is tend to his injuries," he called back, not bothering to look back to see if she followed. "I doubt he'll say much—it will take time before he trusts you enough to reveal anything useful."

"Jaxon—" Araya hurried to keep up, her heart in her throat. She couldn't do this. "I'm not an inquisitor. I can't—"

"You can." Jaxon waved off her protest. "You don't need training, Starling. *You* were what broke him last time."

Araya flushed hot, the pull in her chest sharpening to a burning pain. "But what if—"

"What if what?" Jaxon turned back to her, his dark eyes gleaming in the faint light. "What if he tries to kill you? Trust me, Starling. He's not in any condition to hurt anyone right now."

Araya's stomach turned as Jaxon cupped her face, stroking his thumb along her cheekbone and brushing a kiss over her lips. "And if he does, Aeron is right outside the door. He would never let anything happen to you—right, Aeron?"

"Of course not, sir," the guard said, his focus locked firmly on the opposite wall.

Jaxon's thumb continued its slow, deliberate sweep, his breath warm against her ear. "See? You're perfectly safe," he murmured. "Nothing bad will happen to you as long as you keep being good for me, Starling."

Araya forced herself to nod. His touch, his words, even the tone of his voice—each one was another link in the chain tightening around her.

"That's my Starling," Jaxon said, his grin widening at her obedience. He pressed a fleeting kiss to her temple before releasing her, the absence of his touch more jarring than its presence. "Find me when you're done. I want to hear all about it."

"I'm sorry—about last time, Miss," Aeron said, his voice strained and his eyes locked firmly on the ground. "I didn't know who you were before. It's no excuse—but I...I made a mistake. Master Shaw made that very clear, Miss. I understand now."

Clear. Araya blanched, the word settling uneasily in her chest, dragging her thoughts into darker places. What had Jaxon done to terrify this man? Or had it been Garrick? What would he do to *her* if she failed him?

Araya's fingers tightened around the strap of the first aid kit, the leather biting into her palm. Jaxon was already long gone, his footsteps long since vanished down the hall. There was no way out of this. No excuse clever enough, no soft-spoken evasion that would free her. Jaxon wouldn't accept anything less than total obedience here—even from her. He might care for her, but his true devotion would always be to the Arcanum and the future he was building here.

"Thank you, Aeron," she said, dredging up all the kindness she could muster. "I'm not upset, I never was. You were only doing your job."

Aeron shifted, glancing up at her briefly before his gaze darted back away, landing somewhere over her shoulder. "Just knock twice when you're done," he muttered. "His chains don't let him reach the door."

Araya nodded, the lump in her throat too thick for words as Aeron turned the keys. They grated in the locks, tumblers clicking as they dropped into place, magic illuminating everything in a strange, blue glow for half a heartbeat before it faded away.

The heavy door groaned, creaking open on ancient hinges to yawn open like some ancient maw—wide and waiting to swallow her whole.

Araya stepped forward before she could think better of it, the pull behind her ribs dragging her across the threshold. A heartbeat later, the heavy door slammed shut behind her with a thunderous clang. Araya flinched, barely choking back a scream as she was plunged into instant, absolute darkness.

She stood frozen, breath shallow, listening to the echoing silence that followed. The cell felt alive around her—too still, too quiet, like it was holding its breath. Her heart pounded, each beat a thunderclap in the suffocating black as even her fae sight struggled to adjust.

"Loren?" she called out, her voice shaking.

There was no response, her soft call swallowed almost immediately by the thick air, heavy with the metallic tang of blood, the acrid stench of waste, and the damp rot of moldy straw. She pressed the back of her hand to her mouth, trying not to breathe too deeply as she took another hesitant step toward where she could just barely make out the outline of his body crumpled on the floor.

"Loren," she called again, a little louder. He didn't stir.

She needed light. Turning back to the door, Araya felt her way along the wall, her fingers brushing over the rough, damp stone until they met the cold metal of the sconce. She reached for her aether, sketching the rune for light in the air. For a moment, nothing happened, but then the lamp flared to life with a soft hiss, bathing the cell in its flickering, uneven light.

Araya exhaled shakily, relieved. Now that she had light, she could deal with anything.

But when she turned back to Loren, the first aid kit slipped from her hands, landing on the stone floor with a dull thud as she got her first good look at him. It was worse than she could have imagined. So much worse.

Loren lay crumpled on the cold floor, his blood soaking into the straw scattered haphazardly across the cell, as if he had struggled. His shirt hung from him in tattered, blood-soaked scraps, doing nothing to hide the deep, angry slices that marred his chest and arms, some still oozing blood. Where he wasn't bleeding, dark, mottled bruises spread across his skin.

But it wasn't just the fresh wounds—his ribs jutted sharply beneath his torn shirt, his skin waxy and stretched too thin over hard angles. Some of the bruises were older, faded to sickly yellow, and puckered scars marked where old cuts had healed.

"Oh, Loren," Araya whispered, dropping to her knees beside him. She reached out, but stopped short of touching him, fearing even the gentlest touch would hurt him. His head lolled, his dark matted hair plastered to his ashen skin. If not for the faint rise and fall of his chest, each jagged breath rattling like a dying echo in the stillness, she would have thought he was gone.

She scrambled for the first aid kit, fumbling it open with shaking hands. Her heart sank as she took in the pitiful contents—bandages, clean linen cloths, a small vial of antiseptic...not even a suture kit. Basic, suitable for minor injuries—not...this.

He needed a Healer. A real one. Not her.

"I'm sorry," she whispered, dabbing at one of the cuts on his chest. Loren shuddered under her touch, a low, pained moan escaping his lips. "I'm so sorry," she repeated, her voice choked. "I'm trying to be gentle, I swear."

She worked in silence, her focus narrowing to the rhythm of cleaning and dressing his wounds as best she could. She had to discard his shirt entirely, peeling the tattered, filthy fabric away from his skin with careful fingers. Most of the cuts beneath were shallow and neat, already closing. But the others—some of them were deep, jagged gashes, slicing all the way to the bone. She dressed those carefully, doing her best to pull the edges of the wounds together without a suture kit.

Her breath hitched when she reached his wrists. The iron manacles had bitten deep into the flesh, carving fresh gashes into old scars. Blood pooled in the raw wounds, mixing with dirt and rust, and she bit her lip hard enough to taste copper.

Finally, there was nothing else she could do. Slowly, she gathered the bloodied cloths and the empty vials of antiseptic, tears dripping down her face. When she was done, she stroked her fingers along a small patch of unmarred skin on his face, trying to compose herself. Loren stirred faintly at her touch, but his eyes didn't open. She doubted he even knew she was here.

"I'm so sorry," she whispered one last time, her voice trembling.

Rising slowly, turned to the door, her throat still choked with tears as she knocked twice. The keys grated in the lock and the door opened, letting her back out into the corridor. Aeron waited there, his posture stiff as he locked the door again behind her.

"This one is yours," he said, handing her the second key. "Master Shaw had it made for you. So you can come on your own next time."

Araya swallowed hard, the key in her palm heavier than iron. Of course, there would be a next time. There always would be. Jaxon had no reason to stop. And now, neither did she.

CHAPTER

FOURTEEN

ARAYA HADN'T SEEN JAXON SINCE THE DUNGEON YESTERDAY. HE HADN'T come home until late—long after she'd poured the tea she'd brewed down the drain. Araya had actually wanted her dreams to bring her to him last night, hoping against hope for some small confirmation that he hadn't died in there, alone and cold, because of her.

But she hadn't gotten it.

He was sleeping soundly when she finally slipped out of their bed, dressing in the bathroom and leaving the apartment on silent feet. She wasn't avoiding him. Not entirely. She just wasn't certain she could keep her opinion of what he'd done to Loren behind clenched teeth.

"I might be a while," Araya told the driver as she climbed down from the carriage, balancing her basket of pastries on her hip. "You don't have to wait."

"Sorry, Miss Starwind." The driver didn't meet her eye. "Master Shaw—your Master Shaw—said we're not to leave you anywhere but the Aetherium."

"He—" Araya started, then stopped. She wanted to say Jaxon wouldn't have done that. But he'd been furious the last time she left without a carriage. And this... it did feel like something he would do. But wouldn't he have told her?

"I lived in this neighborhood for years," she said instead. "You really don't have to wait. I'll be fine."

The driver shook his head, gaze fixed just over her shoulder. "I understand, miss. But I still have to stay."

Part of Araya wanted to argue—but no one who worked for the Shaw family disobeyed orders. Not when they came from Jaxon or Garrick. If she argued and tried to force the issue, she would be the one who suffered for it later.

"I'll be quick," she said quietly.

The clinic looked exactly as she remembered it—squat and square, its stone facade softened by ivy and peeling paint. The benches outside were empty at this hour, but later they'd fill with people laughing and chatting as they waited their turn. Just a few months ago, Araya would have sat among them without a second thought. But today, she hesitated on the doorstep, feeling like a trespasser.

Bracing herself, Araya knocked sharply on the cheery blue door, the sound echoing too loudly in the dawn quiet.

Serafina opened the door a moment later, already dressed in her blue Healer's robes, her hair pinned back in the same no-nonsense twist Araya remembered. She said nothing at first, just looked at her —really looked—her eyes pausing on the basket, then flicking past her to the black carriage waiting on the street.

"I brought breakfast," Araya said quietly, lifting the basket between them. "I was hoping we could talk."

For a moment, Serafina didn't move. Her mouth tightened, her expression unreadable, and Araya braced herself for the door to close in her face.

But then, with a tired sigh, Serafina stepped aside. "Of course," she said. "Come in."

———

Serafina poured the tea as Araya unpacked the basket in silence, placing a honey-glazed pastry on each of the two chipped plates.

The clinic was quiet at this hour—only a handful of cots in the back held resting patients, all of them asleep under thin woolen blankets. A low shelf against the far wall overflowed with neatly labeled glass jars and cloth-wrapped bandages, the scent of dried herbs mixing with the sharp tang of antiseptic.

Finally, Serafina took the seat across from her, just as she had hundreds of times before, folding her hands neatly on the scarred workbench that doubled as both a workspace and a kitchen table.

"Now," she said, pinning Araya with a searching look. "Why are you really here?"

Araya looked down at her pastry, twisting the linen towel from the pastry basket between her fingers. She'd had a whole speech prepared—but her gaze snagged on a rust-colored smear beneath one of her nails, and her stomach turned.

She'd always known Jaxon was ambitious—even ruthless. But it had always been bloodless, contained to academics and politics. What he'd done to Loren....it was a cruelty she hadn't expected from him.

And Loren's blood was on her hands too. Literally. She had cleaned his wounds. Cared for him like she wasn't the whole reason Jaxon had tortured him.

But it was necessary, wasn't it? The Arcanum needed to know how to break the Shadowed Veil. Someone had to figure it out—and if it wasn't Jaxon, it would be someone worse. Hale—or someone like him. Wasn't this better?

"Araya?" Serafina's voice cut gently through her thoughts. The Healer watched her, brows drawn and her face pinched with concern. "Is everything alright?"

"Not really." Araya dropped the towel and wrapped her hands around her mug, trying to soak in some comfort from the warmth. "I need some supplies. Bandages, suture kits, antiseptics... and anything you have to treat iron burns."

"Iron burns?" Serafina's spoon clattered against her mug. Her sharp green eyes swept over Araya, searching for injuries. "Are you hurt? Did Jaxon—"

"No," Araya said, too quickly. She took a deep breath, trying to smooth out the edges of her voice. "It's not for me."

"Well whoever it is for needs to see a Healer." Serafina was already on her feet, rummaging through the storage cabinet where they kept the stronger medicines. "Iron burns need proper treatment —not just whatever scraps I can give you. If they can't come here I can come to them—"

"You can't," Araya bit her lip, silently begging Serafina not to ask too many questions. "It's for Jaxon—he doesn't even know I'm here."

Serafina turned slowly, setting the supplies she'd been gathering down on the table. "I'm going to need more than that if you want my help, Araya. What are you doing—are you helping the Arcanum torture someone? Patching them up so they can be hurt again?"

Araya didn't answer. She couldn't. The silence stretched between them—thick and damning.

"*Gods*, Araya." Serafina closed her eyes. "How could you?"

"I don't have a choice," Araya protested. "I'm just doing what I have to do to survive—"

"Survive at what cost, Araya?" Serafina folded her arms, scowling. "Do you think you're the only one they've asked to patch up a prisoner for them? They've asked other Healers—they even came to me. But none of us ever do it. Healers don't treat wounds just to see them reopened. That's not medicine—that's complicity."

Her voice softened, but the disappointment remained. "I thought you believed in that, too. But instead you're letting Jaxon turn you into a tool he can wield."

Araya's breath hitched. "That's not fair," she said. "He's not perfect—but he's trying to fix things. To make things better for the fae. And he actually has the power to do it. He's trying to stop the shadows—"

"He's trying to control the shadows?" Serafina asked sharply.

Araya winced. "I shouldn't have said that—but yes. We think—Jaxon thinks—there's a way to direct them. To harness them. If we can just figure it out, we could keep the shadows off the slums, maybe even lift them entirely."

To her surprise, Serafina's face paled. "And you think that's a good thing?"

"Of course I do." Araya frowned, confused by Serafina's reaction. "Don't you? You're always doing everything you can to help the fae in the districts."

Serafina shook her head, her lips pressed into a thin, tense line. "I can't tell you. Just...leave the shadows alone, Araya. Please."

"We used to tell each other everything," Araya said, staring at Serafina. "There wasn't a single secret between us. When did that change?"

"When you tied yourself to Jaxon." Serafina crossed her arms, her expression cold. "You're the one who made it impossible to tell you anything. Whatever I say could easily end up in his hands--his ties to the Arcanum put us all at risk."

"You work for the Arcanum too, Serafina!" Araya snapped. "Just because you run a community clinic doesn't mean you don't take their gold. How is that any different?"

"Because I'm not bound to them the way you are, Araya." Serafina's voice softened, but the words were no less sharp. "I don't have to wonder who I am when I look in the mirror. Can you say the same?"

Araya shoved her chair back with a loud scrape, her hands shaking as she grabbed her cloak from the back of it. "This was a mistake." She stood, sweeping her cloak around her shoulders. "Sorry to bother you—"

"Wait." Serafina stood, her expression grim. "You're not leaving without what you need."

Araya turned slowly, watching as Serafina crossed to the supply cabinet and pulled out a worn leather medical kit. With the practiced ease of someone who had done this a hundred times, she began filling it methodically—packing in bandages, suture kits, and small glass vials of antiseptic.

Finally, Serafina climbed onto the counter to retrieve a small jar from the locked storage cabinet—the one reserved for rare, carefully monitored treatments. She wrapped it carefully in linen before tucking it into the bag.

"For the iron burns," she said quietly. "It's highly regulated. Use it sparingly. This is all I can spare without flagging the Inquisitors."

She added a small, worn book to the pile. "This is a basic primer on Healing—there are instructions for burns, wounds...anything you might be dealing with."

"Thank you." Araya took the bag, her voice shaking. "This is— just thank you, Serafina."

Serafina nodded. "We *are* still friends, Araya," she said, pulling her into a tight hug. "Even if we can't tell each other everything. Even if it's hard."

Araya's throat tightened, the ache in her chest almost unbearable. "It doesn't feel like it."

"I know." Serafina pulled back just enough to meet her gaze, her expression somber—tired in a way Araya hadn't noticed before. "But I'm still here. And if you ever need me..." She squeezed Araya's hand. "I'm here. Just...try not to lose yourself, Araya. He's not worth it."

Araya swallowed hard against the lump in her throat. "I should go."

Serafina walked her to the door, lingering on the threshold, and for just a moment, Araya hesitated, longing to stay in a place she'd once belonged. But Araya's choice here had been made months ago, when she agreed to give Jaxon her bond.

The driver closed the door behind her with a heavy thud, the carriage lurching forward a moment later. Araya stared out the window, not even seeing the streets of Aetheris as they blurred past. Instead, her hand tightened around the worn bag Serafina had given her, the leather handle biting into her palm as her friend's warning echoed in her mind.

Don't lose yourself.

But what if it was already too late? What if the choices she had made—the ones she was still making—had already stolen parts of her she could never get back?

————

Araya strode down the corridor, her footsteps echoing off the stone as she blazed past the long procession of iron doors. It was cold outside, but the chill down here was different—it leeched the warmth from her bones, making her shiver despite her cloak.

"Miss Starwind," the guard greeted her with a nod as she approached Loren's door.

"Aeron." Araya mustered a thin smile, her gaze flicking to the heavy iron door. "How is he?"

The guard frowned, confusion clouding his features. "Who?"

"Loren," she clarified, her voice tightening. "The prisoner."

"No one's heard anything from in there." Aeron shrugged, his tone indifferent. "We don't go in. Takes two keys to open the door." He gestured to the untouched tray on the table beside him. "All I know is, he didn't eat."

Araya's stomach twisted at the sight of the gray, pasty gruel, the bread crust speckled with mold. "No one's been inside? At all?"

Aeron's expression turned defensive. "Not since you, miss."

"So he could be dead in there and you wouldn't know?" Araya dug for her key, drawing it out of the interior pocket of her cloak. "Open the door."

"Sorry, miss." Aeron shook his head. "Jaxon wanted to see you first—said to send you down to the workshop."

"Of course he did." Araya stepped back, her fingers curling into a fist around the key as she stared at the iron door. She glared at the guard. "When I come back—there needs to be warm clothing, blankets...and actual, decent food. Food that you would be willing to eat."

"Master Jaxon will have to approve that," Aeron called after her as she stormed down the hall.

"He will," Araya snapped, not bothering to turn back to reply.

She found Jaxon exactly where Aeron said he would be—seated at one of the newly cleared workbenches with his sleeves rolled up to his elbows, head bent over a mess of glass tubing and delicate brass couplings. Half a distillation rig had already taken shape, the blown glass flasks etched with delicate runes, just waiting to be activated.

"Starling—" Jaxon jumped as she let the door slam into the stone wall. "I missed you this morning."

"I had an errand to run." Araya dropped the first aid kit Serafina had assembled onto her own workbench. "Did you know that no one has checked on Loren?"

"Why would they have?" Jaxon gave her a bemused look, setting down the glass tubing he'd been inspecting. "They're here to make sure he doesn't escape—not coddle him."

"*Escape?*" Araya snorted. "You think he could escape after what you did to him? You've had him in iron for over twenty years—"

"He's fae, Starling," Jaxon arched an eyebrow. "He'll heal."

She took a deep breath, trying to steady her voice. This was necessary—what she had to do. But Serafina was right, she didn't have to lose herself in the process.

"He's running on nothing," Araya continued. "And you're starving him on top of it. Without magic, healing is going to be agonizingly slow. Keep treating him like an animal, and you won't get what you need from him. He needs food. Water. Warmth. Some shred of dignity."

"He's a prisoner, Starling," Jaxon said, his voice cool. "He doesn't get dignity." He tilted his head, studying her. "Why are you so concerned with his well-being?"

"Because you ordered me to be!" Araya snapped, then caught herself. She drew in a breath, trying to contain the heat in her voice. "You were so set on getting me to earn his trust. How am I supposed to do that when you're leaving him like... like this?"

Jaxon's expression remained composed, but something darker flickered in his eyes—something that didn't belong to the polished mask he wore so well. "Is it that important to you?"

"*Please*, Jaxon," she said, shivering even under all her layers. How cold must he be in that dark cell? Without even a shirt?

Jaxon sighed, his lips quirking into a faint smile. He closed the space between them, his hand slipping under the cloak to settle at the small of her back. Not holding her there—but reminding her that he could.

"You're not playing fair, Starling." He leaned in, his breath ghosting over the scarred edge of her ear. "You know I can't say no when you ask so nicely."

Araya huffed, twisting just enough to put space between them. "And you can tell the carriage drivers to stop keeping tabs on me. I don't need a babysitter."

"You do," Jaxon said, letting her pull away. But his hand lingered at her waist, tracing slow circles at her hip. "You're my bond, Araya. You don't have the anonymity you once did. The places you used to go? They aren't safe for you any more. Your refusal to acknowledge and understand that is dangerous—do you know what one of the rebel groups would do to you if they thought they could use you to get to me? Or my father?"

Araya stiffened. She had known she was taking a risk, but hearing it from Jaxon's lips made it feel... reckless.

His fingers stroked down her jaw, his touch light, coaxing. "I don't want anything to happen to you, Starling." He leaned in slightly, his breath warm against her temple. "So please...for me. Don't fight the carriage drivers on this."

She glanced away, her resolve cracking under the weight of his stare. "Fine," she muttered. She turned away, forcing herself to focus on the distillation rig instead—anything that wasn't *him*. Her eyes caught on a case of bone blanks, the ivory discs arranged neatly in their packaging.

"These won't hold a stable charge for long," she said, picking one up and turning it between her fingers. "Silver housings will slow the leakage, but it won't fix the core issue. If you're really trying to bind shadow magic to a physical vessel, you need a stronger lattice—preferably bone with a naturally high aether affinity."

"I agree," Jaxon plucked the blank from her fingers. "I put a petition in yesterday for whole bones, but these were the largest I could get at short notice. Is it enough to get started?"

Araya hesitated, glancing at where the vials of Loren's blood sat, held in suspension. "Once the blood is processed...we should be able to imbue six testers. But if you're using whole bone—you'll need more." She shook her head, guilt spreading bitter across her tongue. "I hope your last fae royal survived the night."

Jaxon's eyes narrowed. "Mind your tone, Araya."

He stepped closer, invading her space and cupping her chin in his hand. He tilted her head up, pressing a soft, lingering kiss to her lips. "You're right though. It would be...inconvenient...if he died. Make a list of what you think he needs. I'll approve it."

"You will?" Araya stared at him. After all that—he'd just agreed?

"I will." Jaxon grinned down at her, his dark eyes smoldering. "But don't forget your manners, Starling."

Araya froze, heat flooding her cheeks. Humiliation prickled under her skin, but she forced herself to stay still. She'd already pushed Jaxon too far—and if this was what it took to get Loren what he needed, then so be it.

"Thank you, Master Shaw," she whispered.

"Good girl." Jaxon smiled down at her, brushing a knuckle along her jaw. "That's a start—now, go make sure he's still breathing."

CHAPTER

FIFTEEN

Loren drifted in and out of consciousness, the darkness ebbing and flowing around him. The shadows brushed over his skin, their cool touch dulling the edge of his pain, though never enough to let him sink completely into oblivion.

The sharp bite of antiseptic cut through the haze, the scent of blood and waste mingling with the astringent, sterile tang of something medicinal. When he shifted, stitches pulled at his skin, hidden beneath layers of clean, white bandages. Someone had dressed his wounds, cared for him.

That was unusual—normally they just left him here to bleed and heal on his own.

Footsteps approached. Light, measured. Already familiar, even though he'd only heard them once before. *She* was here. She'd come.

Shadows skittered across the floor as keys grated in the lock, their hissing whispers filling his ears like the roar of waves. The aetherlamp flared to life, blinding him as she stepped through the door. It crashed closed on her heels, making her jump and cast a dark look over her shoulder.

"Barbarians," she hissed, too quietly for the human at the door to hear. But Loren did.

He laughed, a hoarse, jagged sound he barely recognized. It turned almost immediately into a groan, all the pain rushing back at once.

"Gods—" her silver gaze snapped to his, her eyes wide. "You're awake."

Before Loren could even start to formulate a response she was kneeling beside him on the filthy floor, setting her bag down beside her. "Can you sit?"

Loren hadn't bothered to try. He shifted, bracing his hands against the floor. The cold stone bit into his palms, sending another spike of pain through his ribs. He grimaced, the effort leaving him breathless.

"Don't—" Araya reached for him, the brush of her fingers like a brand over his frozen skin. "Let me help."

Her touch was careful. Tentative. She slid her arm around his back and helped ease him upright. Stars flared in his vision, pain lancing through his side as he settled against the wall.

"Goddess..." he hissed. "That hurts."

"I think you have a broken rib." Her fingers ghosted over the dark bruise spreading across his side. "Possibly several."

"Probably." Loren sucked in a sharp breath. "That tends to happen when you get kicked by a mage wearing iron-shod boots."

Araya winced. "Sorry," she said, pulling back quickly, like his words had burned her. She turned away, digging through her satchel. "Here."

She thrust a battered flask toward him. Loren took it warily, raising it to his nose. Nothing but water—cool and fresh. He drank greedily, washing the taste of blood from his mouth.

"Slowly," she warned, gently prying the flask from his fingers. "Or you'll make yourself sick. There's nothing worse when you have a broken rib."

She sounded like she knew from experience. What horrors had

she lived, growing up under human rule? Loren stared at her, the bond humming in his chest. It reveled in her closeness, a wild pull it would be far too easy to give in to. He didn't realize he was staring until she flushed, her gaze sliding away from his.

"I want to redress your wounds," she said, rummaging through her bag. "You've been unconscious for days—"

"You were the one who took care of me?" Loren stared as she pulled out fresh white bandages and jars of salve. "You can't do that. If Shaw finds out—"

"Jaxon already knows," she sat back on her heels, studying him. "I told you—he's my bond. I don't do anything without him knowing."

Her bond. Something inside Loren twisted painfully at her words —maybe his soul. Wrapped tightly in the threads that bound them together, it raged at the idea that anyone would dare to claim her— *his* mate.

"I asked him to authorize warmer clothes for you too," she continued, oblivious to the storm raging inside him. "Blankets. Clean water and food that a person would actually eat—"

"I told you not to ask for favors on my behalf," Loren growled. "I don't want you paying the price—"

"What I'm willing to pay is my business." Araya scowled at him, her face flushed with an emotion he couldn't read in the dim light.

"You don't—" He broke off with a hiss as she peeled back one of the bandages on his shoulder, her fingers grazing raw, inflamed skin. "I don't want you involved in this. You could get hurt—Goddess!" He swore, flinching away. "What kind of Healer are you?"

"I'm not a Healer," she snapped, sitting back on her heels. "I *am* a researcher." She plucked a worn book out of her bag, waving it in his face. "I've read up on the basics—now are you going to be picky, or would you prefer to keep bleeding?"

Loren gritted his teeth and forced himself to sit still, his fingers curling into fists against the cold stone beneath him as she returned to examining his wounds. He could tell she was trying to be careful even if she was clumsy, her touch gentle as she wiped the inflamed skin with a cool cloth before applying a fresh poultice.

She couldn't be here. The more time she spent with him, the more likely Jaxon was to figure out the connection between them—if he didn't already know. This could all be some elaborate plot to break him.

"Why does Jaxon want you here?" Loren finally asked. He had to know if Jaxon knew—if he'd figured it out and was just waiting for the right moment to use it against him.

"He thinks it will make you more cooperative."

Loren's jaw clenched. "And what do you think?"

"I think—" Araya sighed, sitting back on her heels to meet his eyes. "I think that if you told him what he wants to know, it could spare you a lot of pain. It might even win you some comforts."

"You think Jaxon won't find another reason to torture me?" Loren scoffed. "They barely need a reason at all."

"It would help the fae in the districts," Araya pushed, her face set. "The shadows are hurting them. If you could help your people and make things easier on yourself at the same time, why wouldn't you?"

"You actually believe they'll use whatever I tell them to help the fae?" Loren laughed again, groaning at the ache in his ribs. "They're humans. They lie. I've been in chains for twenty-five years—nothing is ever going to get better for me. I assume my parents and my sister are either dead or suffering the same."

Araya's hands stilled over the bandage she was tying. For a long moment, she said nothing.

Then, almost too quietly for him to hear, she asked, "Do you actually want to know?"

Loren looked at her, something cold and sharp settling in his chest. "Are you even allowed to tell me?"

"Probably not." Araya gave a hollow little laugh. "But no one told me not to. And..." Her voice faltered. "I've always been glad I *saw* what happened to my mother. That I didn't have to spend the rest of my life wondering."

Loren stared at her, then nodded tightly. "Tell me."

"The fae queen was killed during the Ascendancy." Araya sat back on her heels, her silver eyes shining with unshed tears. "The king escaped to Eluneth, where he was declared dead two years later —fallen in battle with New Dominion forces."

Loren pressed his fist against his mouth, stifling the sob clawing its way up his throat. His ribs ached with each shallow breath, but the pain was nothing compared to the weight of her words. He'd known. He'd known there was no way they were alive—but hearing it...

"And my sister?" He asked when he had control of his voice again.

Araya shook her head. "I don't know—but to my knowledge, you're the only fae prisoner of royal descent in Arcanum custody. If you want me to try and find out more—"

"No," Loren managed, his voice rough with grief. "If she's alive— don't draw attention to her. Please."

Araya nodded, pressing her lips together. They sat in silence for long minutes, watching each other.

"That's why I can't tell him anything," Loren said finally. "Nothing the Arcanum does will ever be good for my people, no matter what they promise. I could never sell my people out for a little comfort."

Araya didn't answer him, her focus on tying off the last bandage. Her fingers lingered for half a breath before she pulled away, sending sparks skittering across his skin. Loren shuddered, desperate to reach for her—but she'd been raised by humans. She didn't know about the mate bond. She didn't know what she was to him, or that her presence here was a noose tightening around both their necks.

"You can't come back here again," Loren said, his words clipped. "You don't understand what you're risking by being here."

Araya stilled, her silver eyes narrowing. "Then explain it to me."

"No." Loren looked away, fixing his eyes on the cracked stone in

the wall. His fingers curled against his knee, aching to reach for her
—to pull her close—but he couldn't. Not now. Not ever.

But she didn't let it go.

"It has something to do with the dreams, doesn't it?" She
pressed.

Loren's head snapped back toward her, anger and fear blazing in
his veins. "I told you—never speak of that."

The shadows stirred, slithering from the dark corners of the cell
at his outburst. Araya's gaze flicked over his shoulder, her eyes
widening as they closed in around them both. But she didn't run.

"Why are they doing that?" she asked softly. "You—you're not
controlling them. And I'm not..."

She trailed off, her face breaking into a wide smile even as the
misty shadows coiled closer to her. "I was right, wasn't I? They're
sentient."

No—she was too close. Loren needed to end this—now. Before
she learned enough to hang herself. He needed her to leave and not
come back, but if he couldn't convince her to do that...she needed to
hate him.

"Why would you choose to tie yourself to him?"

Araya stiffened at his question, her jaw tightening as she looked
away. "I told you—I made the choices I had to make to survive." She
stretched out her hand, letting the curious shadows twine around
her fingers as something dark and ancient purred in delight.

"Survive?" The word was bitter on his tongue, poisoned by the
weight of his own guilt. Loren swallowed, his ribs aching—not from
his injuries, but from the weight of what he was about to do.

He almost stopped himself. He wanted to warn her—beg her to
listen. But even that would be too dangerous. So he hardened his
heart and turned the words into something else. Something that
would hurt.

"And what are you surviving for, Araya? To be his pet? His
whore?"

Her head snapped up, her breath hitching. For a heartbeat, she just stared at him, silver eyes wide—not with fury, but with something worse. Hurt.

"I know enough." His chest tightened—guilt clawing at him—but he forced himself to hold her gaze. Forced himself to stay cold. Distant. Hating him would keep her safe. "I know you chose him over your own people. Over yourself. You gave up."

She'd been a child. What else could he have expected her to do?

Araya recoiled as if he'd struck her, her expression hardening. "I'm not the one rotting in a cell," she said quietly, her voice trembling at the edges as she stood, brushing the dirt from her skirts. "Maybe you're the one who gave up—*Your Highness.*"

She didn't look back as she walked to the door, knocking twice. The aetherlamp extinguished as it swung shut behind her, plunging him back into darkness.

But Loren wasn't alone, and this time, the shadows didn't wait. They surged from the corners of the cell, curling tight around his limbs and banding around his chest. Their whispers joined together, rising from a murmur to a deafening cacophony.

Coward, they hissed. *You drove her away.*

Loren's head thudded back against the wall. "We were never meant to be," he told them. "Not like this. Not as these broken things the humans made of us. I can't be what she needs—and she would never choose me, anyway."

She. Is. Yours. The shadows snarled, their voices joining together until they were almost screaming at him. *And you let her go. You hurt her.*

"Because she's safer if she hates me," Loren growled. "She would be better off if she never saw me—either of us—ever again."

Liar. The word slithered through the darkness, sharper than any blade. *You're afraid, Shadow Prince. Afraid of her. Afraid of yourself. And afraid of us.*

Loren didn't argue.

The shadows had known him his whole life—had chosen him as his father's heir when he was only a child, no older than Araya was when she gave up her name. They knew him better than he knew himself.

He sagged against the wall, groaning as his ribs protested the movement. The countless cuts Jaxon had left on him throbbed, the pain a dull constant. But it was nothing compared to the ache of the bond in his chest, a phantom wound that would never heal.

It tied them together, whether they wanted it or not—and that was the cruelest punishment of all.

Araya shoved past the guard without a word, fleeing down the corridor as tears blurred her vision. The shadows between the lamps twisted and writhed, morphing into shapes that clawed at the edges of her vision.

Pet, they hissed as she raced past them. *Whore.*

Araya stumbled, her shoulder slamming into the wall. Pain radiated through her arm, but she pushed forward, clutching her side as if that could hold her together.

You chose him over your people. Over yourself.

She shoved open the door to the workshop, iron stinging her palm as the cloying scent of copper and burnt aether flooded her nose. Jaxon had begun distilling the first vial of Loren's blood—it swirled gently in the central flask, runes glowing faintly with power.

He looked up, his eyes widening as he took in her disheveled state. "Starling, what—"

"He's awake." Araya wiped her face with the heel of her hand, smearing wetness across her cheeks before wrapping her arms around herself, trying to stop the trembling.

"Isn't that good?" Jaxon frowned, his brow furrowing as he stared at her. "Did he hurt you, Starling?"

Araya shook her head, shuddering. "I don't—" her voice cracked, and she pressed a trembling hand to her chest. "I don't want to talk about it."

"Alright." Jaxon moved slowly out from behind his workbench, holding one hand out as he approached her like a wounded animal. "But come here, let me see that you're not hurt—"

Araya grabbed his shirt, hands fisting in the fabric as she dragged him down to her. Jaxon barely caught himself, one hand bracing against the bench to keep from knocking them both over—but it was too late to stop the crash.

Their mouths met in a violent, messy kiss. Teeth clashed. Her breath hitched, uneven and hot against his skin as he responded instinctively, kissing her back with equal force. Her magic surged between them, burning hot just beneath her skin as it reached for his —just as desperate as she was.

But Jaxon started to pull back, opening his mouth like he might ask if she was sure.

Araya dragged him back, nipping his lower lip hard. Copper bloomed across her tongue as the sharp point of her canine broke the skin. "I need you," she said. "Don't make me beg, Jaxon."

His hesitation shattered.

He kissed her again, deeper this time—less caution, more hunger. His hands found her waist, her hips, her thighs—his fingers digging into her skin as he pressed her back into the nearest flat surface. Araya thought it might be some sort of packing crate, half shoved under a workbench, but she didn't really care. Care was gone. So was concern. All that remained was heat—raw, consuming, and uncomplicated.

Araya let herself drown in it—in him.

She didn't want to think. She wanted to be touched like she mattered, like if she gave enough of herself there would be nothing left to regret.

Jaxon lifted her onto the crate, the rough wood scraping her bare thighs as she hooked her ankles behind him, dragging him in closer. His breath stuttered, and he swore against her throat as she tugged his shirt free, her fingers working clumsily at his belt.

Her magic flared again, the buckle of his belt catching on the tender skin of her inner thigh as he entered her. He didn't ask if she was ready—and she didn't want him to. She gasped, clinging to his shoulders and closing her eyes, losing herself in the heat.

Whore.

Araya flinched, but Jaxon's mouth found her collarbone, his teeth grazing her skin and making her gasp. She tilted her head back, offering him more. Offering him everything.

"*Gods*, Araya," his words rumbled against her skin, low and dark. He pulled back just enough to search her face, his dark eyes molten as he dragged his thumb over her lower lip. "Do you have any idea what you do to me, Starling?"

She did. The logical part of her mind knew this was madness. It should have been impossible to want him like this—to trust him, even for a moment, now that she knew what he was capable of. But Jaxon had never been *just* anything to her. Not just a mistake. Not just a betrayal. Not just a savior.

Let them call her a traitor. Let Loren spit his accusations and his shadows call her names. She didn't care. This wasn't about absolution or justice or what was *right*. It was about the only thing she'd gotten to choose for herself in this world.

Jaxon was a choice—*her* choice. And that was enough for her.

———

Araya didn't know how long she stayed in Jaxon's arms, the edge of the crate digging into her thighs. Long enough for shame to go quiet, smothered by the warm contentment of belonging.

Jaxon was the one to break the moment.

"You're shaking," he murmured, pressing another kiss to her shoulder before pulling back to help her off the crate. Her knees buckled as her feet hit the ground, but he was there to catch her, tugging her dress back up and smoothing her skirts down.

"I'm fine now." Araya brushed loosened strands of hair out of her face, doing her best to tuck them back into her braid.

"Glad to be of service." Jaxon chuckled. "Maybe I should thank the prince—I thought you were going to be angry at me for at least a few more days."

"Don't ruin it," Araya warned, wincing as she stretched. Her thighs still stung where the rough wood had bit into them, raw and abraded. "What's even in that crate?"

"A surprise." Jaxon's dark eyes danced with humor. "I was going to tell you right away—but you were a bit distracted."

Araya leaned forward, curious despite herself, as he worked a pry bar carefully under the lid. The wood groaned, and her stomach lurched as it finally gave way, the golden light of the aetherlamps revealing bones of all shapes and sizes nestled into the straw packing material. They ranged from delicate knuckles and finger bones, still jointed in places, to a femur that must have once belonged to an adult fae male.

Jaxon dropped the pry bar, hefting the femur in his hand. "Amazing," he said. "Have you ever worked with whole bone before?"

Araya shook her head, her mouth suddenly too dry to speak. She licked her lips, wetting them enough to rasp, "I thought these were hard to get."

"They are." Jaxon turned the femur over in his hands, admiring it. "But this is a very important project, Starling. They made it a priority."

Her eyes flicked to the smallest bones again. One curled like a question mark, barely the length of her finger. It could only have belonged to a child. She hoped—prayed—that it had come from a long-buried grave. But fae died every day in the New Dominion.

"We'll need to process them carefully," she said, her voice thin. "And we should still use the blanks first—for our testers. We wouldn't want to waste whole bones."

"Of course." Jaxon glanced at her, a light smile playing at his lips. "I'll leave that to you, Starling. After all, you're the expert."

CHAPTER

SEVENTEEN

Araya's fingers skimmed over the delicate silver housing, her touch searching for flaws unseen by the eye. She and Jaxon had spent two painstaking months extracting, distilling, and stabilizing Loren's blood—ensuring not a single drop was wasted. These housings had to be flawless—even the slightest imperfection in the silverwork or a single misdrawn rune, and all the power they'd worked so hard to preserve would bleed out into the air, lost to them forever.

And that was just the best-case scenario. Loren might be weak and broken—but he was still a powerful fae. The amulet could just as easily shatter, pelting them with shards of bone and molten silver. That's why the Arcanum had confined any activity involving his blood to the dungeon workshop, where layers of complex warding and strict directives ensured no one discovered Loren's existence.

Thankfully, crafting the silver housings required nothing but a keen eye and a steady hand. That meant she would work on them here, in her own workshop, far from the dungeon's damp chill and the heavy, suffocating guilt that always tugged at her heart whenever she passed his cell.

Araya exhaled slowly, fingertips tracing every edge, every groove, searching her work for even the faintest irregularity. Like last time, she found nothing—no weak spots. No sign of instability.

It was ready.

"You aren't even close to ready, are you?"

Araya jumped, glancing up to find Jaxon leaning in the doorway, arms folded and amusement flickering in his dark eyes.

"This is the last one," she said, carefully nestling the finished amulet into its velvet pouch and tucking it away in the iron-lined box. "We're ready to start imbuing—"

"That's fantastic." Jaxon pushed off the doorframe, his grin widening. "But that's not what I was talking about, Starling."

She blinked at him, confused—then frowned as she took in what he was wearing.

Jaxon always looked polished, but tonight he looked almost unfairly handsome. The lamplight gleamed off the blackened buttons of his dress uniform, catching on the fine gold embroidery that traced the midnight fabric like spellwork. The dark sash slashed across his chest, pinned with the polished symbols of his rank and honors—each one a gleaming reminder of just how dangerous he really was.

"Did you forget?" He raised an eyebrow, a smile tugging at his lips. "Father's party?"

"I—" Araya whirled to the tall arched window, where the sun was nothing but a sliver on the horizon. "I lost track of time. I just need to run home and change—"

They were going to be *so* late. How could she have forgotten?

"No need," Jaxon said, holding his arm up to reveal the swath of shimmering black fabric draped over it. "I brought your dress to you, Starling."

"Gods—thank you, Jaxon." Araya snatched the dress from his arm, pressing a quick kiss to his lips. She exhaled, half laughing. "You always think of everything. Just give me a few minutes to change."

"Be quick, Starling." Jaxon smiled down at her, running his

fingers over her cheek. "A lot of important people will be there tonight—impressions matter."

Araya ducked into the attached bathing chamber between their workshops, her fingers working quickly to unfasten her plain woolen overdress and tug her chemise over her head. She folded them carefully, setting them on the vanity before turning to the gown Jaxon had chosen for her.

She slid it over her head, catching her breath as the sleek, black fabric kissed her skin like liquid shadow, clinging to every line and curve. Delicate embroidery traced the bodice like threads of moonlight—silver to Jaxon's gold—before flaring into floating layers that settled around her like a dark cloud.

Araya shivered, crossing her arms over her chest as she stared at her reflection in the mirror. The dress bared more skin than she ever would have shown on her own, leaving her acutely aware of the fragile lines of her collarbone and the exposed length of her back.

This was Jaxon's vision of her. Elegant. Captivating. Flawless.

She looked like a queen—*his* queen.

"Beautiful." Jaxon straightened as she stepped back into the workshop, his dark eyes glittering as he took her in. "Absolutely perfect, Starling."

Araya smoothed the fabric of the dress against her hips, still uncertain. "It's not much like anything I would normally wear—"

"This isn't the sort of event you would normally go to," Jaxon reminded her. The hair on the back of her neck prickled as he prowled forward, circling her slowly. He reached out, tugging the tie from the end of her braid and carding his fingers through the wild waves until it tumbled loose down her back.

"I have something else for you," he said, pressing a small velvet case into her hands.

Araya opened it carefully—and caught her breath. Two delicate silver bracelets nestled inside, thin as ribbons, glinting in the gleam of the aetherlamps.

"Jaxon," she breathed, startled. "They're beautiful. You shouldn't have—"

"Of course I should have," Jaxon said, already lifting the first one from the dark velvet. "Tonight's important, Starling. It's your first official Arcanum event as my bond. You should look like everything you are—irreplaceable."

The second bracelet snapped shut with a soft click. His fingers lingered over the clasp, twisting her wrist slightly as he turned it in the light. The silver links gleamed against her skin—delicate and beautiful.

"And now everyone will know exactly who you belong to," he said, stepping back to admire her with a slow, possessive grin. "Although I'm tempted to say to hell with it and stay here with you in that dress. We'd have a lot more fun than we would rubbing shoulders with all of Father's sycophants—"

"And disappoint your father on his birthday?" Araya shook her head with mock severity despite the blush heating her cheeks. "I don't think so."

Jaxon chuckled. "You're far too good at making me do things I don't want to," he said. But instead of turning to leave, he took her hands in his and tugged her into a deep, slow kiss that left her skin hot and her breath short.

"You're going to dazzle them, you know," he said when he finally pulled back, tucking her hand into the crook of his arm as he led her toward the door. "And there won't be any doubt as to who you belong to."

"As if you'd ever let anyone forget," Araya teased, leaning into his side.

Jaxon's smugness only deepened as they descended the stairs and crossed the central hall, every head turning to follow them as her heeled slippers clicked softly against the marble floor.

One of the Shaws' black carriages waited outside, pulled by a matching set of sleek, dark horses. The Arcanum's golden eye was emblazoned on the door, watching them with silent authority. Even after months of wearing that same sigil around her throat and reaping the privileges it offered, it still stirred something primal in her—an instinct to melt into the shadows instead of stepping forward.

Jaxon helped her up, sliding in across from her as she sank into the plush leather bench. He watched in silence while she smoothed her palms over the gauzy folds of her skirt—once, twice, again.

"Nervous?"

"A bit," Araya admitted, managing a faint smile. "Just thinking about how many people will be there."

"Kai and Mira will be—with their parents." Jaxon leaned back, stretching his arms across the bench as the carriage lurched forward. "So it's not like you won't know anyone. Kai will probably bring Caylin—but she won't dare cause a scene in front of Father and the other magisters."

Araya had her own thoughts about that, but she kept them to herself. Caylin hated her enough to cause a scene no matter who was watching.

When the carriage finally came to a halt, Jaxon stepped out first, extending a gloved hand to Araya to help her down as she faltered in the heeled slippers.

"Watch your step, Starling," Jaxon said, tucking her hand back into the crook of his arm. "I still can't believe you've never been here before."

"Not many reasons for a halfblood fae to be invited to the High Magister's house," Araya murmured.

Jaxon cut her a sharp look as he led her through the open gate and up the wide, stone-paved path. "No more of that, Starling. You belong here just as much as I do now."

Araya didn't answer, focusing on keeping pace with him in her heeled shoes as they started up the stairs. The house didn't tower over them like she'd expected. Instead, it stood just three stories high, its understated grandeur softened by the dusting of snow that covered the manicured evergreen hedges.

"It's beautiful," she said.

"It's home," Jaxon said, the corner of his mouth lifting. "Father's made a lot of improvements over the years, but he kept much of the fae architecture intact—a nod to the past."

He shrugged, breezing past the servant who scrambled forward to open the grand double doors, not sparing her so much as a glance. But Araya lingered, pausing to offer a smile to the fae female standing outside, shivering despite the dark cloak wrapped tightly around her shoulders.

"Thank you," she said.

The female didn't answer, her lips thinning as she fixed Araya with a cold stare—like Araya had tracked mud across the sparkling floors.

Araya faltered, her smile freezing on her lips as shame bloomed in her chest. She dropped her gaze, her cheeks hot as she hurried after Jaxon into the manor's warmth. The door closed behind her, leaving her blinking in the warm glow of hundreds of aetherlamps in sparkling chandeliers. She craned her neck, taking in the jewel-toned tapestries that lined the walls, depicting human triumph in vivid detail.

"Understated, as always," Jaxon quipped, taking her arm. He breezed by them, saying something about the architecture—but Araya barely heard him, her attention captivated by the soft music and low murmur of conversation drifting from the ballroom.

Clusters of humans moved through tables laden with silver trays of bite-sized delicacies, their laughter mingling with the chime of crystal glassware. The women glittered in rich winter shades, their gowns catching the light like frosted jewels, while the men stood sharp in dark tailored coats, boots gleaming, every detail carefully curated to impress.

It was stunning—glittering and grand in the kind of way human spaces were so often designed to keep people like her out. Araya tensed, her heart pounding as she hesitated on the threshold, every instinct screaming at her to turn and run.

But then, Jaxon's hand found her waist.

"You'll be fine, Starling," he murmured, pressing a kiss to her cheek. "You're with me."

————

"Jaxon Shaw—late to his own father's party." Kai raised his glass in mock toast, the amber liquor sloshing close to the rim. "We were beginning to think you weren't coming at all."

Jaxon chuckled, unfazed. "Not all of us have time to sit around drinking, Kai."

Kai snorted inelegantly, but his teasing grin softened as he turned to Araya. "You look marvelous, Araya. I hope you get to enjoy your first Arcanum party."

Enjoy. Araya smoothed down her skirts, forcing her shoulders to relax. She had every right to be here—she'd earned it, with her work, her sacrifices... and Jaxon's hand at her back.

"Thank you, Kai," she said, offering him a genuine smile. He always had a way of making her feel like a person, not a specimen under glass. "Who else—"

Bright, sharp laughter sliced through the conversation as Caylin swept in, crimson silk clinging to every curve like her gown had been stitched directly to her skin. She attached herself to Kai's arm, flashing Jaxon a dazzling smile before turning it on Araya—sharper.

"Jaxon," she purred. "You didn't tell us you'd be bringing her." She raked her gaze over Araya, her smile widening into something bright and cruel. "That dress is absolutely stunning. You've always had impeccable taste in your acquisitions."

"Araya always looks stunning," Jaxon said with an easy grin. "But I'll take credit for the dress."

"Well, your seamstress deserves a medal." Caylin laughed, tossing her hair. "She's almost made your little halfblood look like she belongs here."

"*Caylin*—" Kai's smile faltered, his eyes darting to Jaxon—who was already shifting, one hand tightening at Araya's waist, the other curling like he was preparing to step between them.

But Araya stopped him with a gentle hand on his chest. "It's fine," she murmured.

Then she turned to Caylin, her smile perfectly measured. "You're right, of course. It's a beautiful gown." She stroked her hands over the soft, floating layers of the skirt. "Jaxon *does* have impeccable taste. I'm sure he'd be happy to give you the designer's name—if you wanted something a little more... elegant for the next event."

Jaxon guffawed, the startled bark of laughter turning heads around them, while Kai coughed into his glass. "Gods," he muttered, barely hiding his grin.

Caylin blinked, her smile freezing on her face. Her eyes narrowed, and for a heartbeat Araya thought she might actually lunge.

But then—

"Jaxon. Araya."

Mira Redmond's smooth voice sliced through the tension like a well-honed blade. She swept into the circle in a shimmer of emerald silk, every inch of her polished and poised. "I was starting to wonder when you'd arrive. Araya, you look lovely—"

"Let's grab a drink," Caylin cut in, looping her arm through Mira's and dragging the other woman after her without waiting for a response.

Kai shook his head, his grin lazy but wicked. "She spent all night setting up a performance, and you walked in and took the final bow." He lifted his glass slightly. "Beautifully done, Araya."

"Araya usually takes the high road," Jaxon said, his voice warm with pride as he watched Caylin storm away. "But she knows how to finish a fight."

But Araya was looking at Kai. "Doesn't it bother you?"

Kai smirked, but there was something wry beneath the charm. He swirled the amber liquid in his glass, watching it catch the light.

"Caylin being jealous?" He chuckled, tossing back his drink. "No. She doesn't want Jaxon—she just hates watching you wear the crown." He rolled his glass between his fingers, his sharp smile never quite fading. "I was the runner-up—lucky me."

The words should have stung, but Kai said them with a grin, tipping his drink toward Araya in a mock toast. "To settling."

Araya smiled, but something in her chest twisted as she lifted her glass slightly in return. Kai might have wrapped his words in humor, but there was no mistaking the truth in them—or the grace it took to say them out loud.

She opened her mouth to respond, but the words died on her tongue as movement at the edge of the crowd drew her attention, her breath hitching in surprise. "Is that Master Carrow?"

Carrow spotted her too, his face lighting up with recognition as he changed direction, cutting through the crowd to reach them. "Adept Starwind—you look lovely tonight."

"It's just Miss Starwind, now." Araya clasped his proffered hand. "It's good to see you, sir. I didn't realize you'd be here."

"I could say the same for you." Carrow chuckled. "It looks like things have worked out for you—even if I do miss having you in the workshop. No one is quite as meticulous as you." His gaze shifted to Jaxon, respectful but shrewd. "And you must be the reason she's here tonight."

"Master Jaxon Shaw." Jaxon stretched out his hand. "It's a pleasure to meet you. Araya always spoke highly of her time in your workshop."

"Did she?" Carrow mused, raising his eyebrows as he shook Jaxon's hand. "Having her in my workshop during your years in the Eldergreen was a true privilege. Though, truth be told, the work never quite challenged her enough—she's an extraordinary mage."

Jaxon's smile didn't slip, but his fingers tightened at her waist, his voice cold. "She certainly is."

Before anyone could say anything else, movement at the far end of the ballroom caught Jaxon's attention. His father now stood surrounded by a cluster of high-ranking magisters and officers near the dais, their uniforms dark and severe against the gold-lit walls.

Garrick caught Jaxon's eye and made a sharp, deliberate gesture—summoning him.

Jaxon's jaw tensed. "Commanders' meeting," he grumbled. "Only my father would schedule one during a party—" he glanced down at Araya, his expression torn.

"I'll be fine here," she reassured him. "Master Carrow and I worked together for years—"

"Exactly," Jaxon said, his voice dark. "A long time. I'm sure you have plenty to reminisce about."

Then, to Araya's shock, he dipped his head and kissed her—holding her in place until she relaxed into him, letting him claim her for everyone to see.

"Be good, Starling," he murmured, his fingers brushing over her bracelets as he stepped away. "Pleasure to meet you, Carrow," he added, barely glancing at the other man as he turned and strode into the crowd, cutting a clean path toward his father's side.

"You apprenticed under Shaw, didn't you?" Carrow asked mildly, watching him go.

Araya flushed at his implication—but there was no censure Carrow's tone. "A long time ago," she said, tucking a loose wave of hair behind her ear. "We reconnected when he came back from Elvanfal."

"Well, Garrick must be pleased," Carrow said. "I can't imagine he's seen his son this happy in a long time. And you—" Carrow smiled at her, his voice warm. "You seem to be thriving, Miss Starwind."

"Some things have been an adjustment," Araya said with a laugh. "But I'm very happy with how it all worked out."

"I'm glad." Carrow regarded her with a thoughtful expression, a smile tugging at the corners of his mouth. "You know, I've yet to find anyone who matched your efficiency and intuition in the workshop. It's a rare combination, and one I appreciated more than I likely told you at the time. If Master Shaw can ever spare you, there will always be a place for you in my workshop."

Araya's eyes widened, her breath stuttering in her lungs. That kind of offer—it wasn't made lightly. And Carrow was making it to *her*—not to Jaxon Shaw's bond.

"That—that's very generous, sir," she said carefully. "But I'm assisting Jaxon with a project right now—"

"It's an open invitation." Carrow gave her a warm smile. "Think it over. No rush, no pressure." His gaze flicked past her shoulder. "Though it looks like someone else is hoping for a moment of your time."

Araya turned, expecting another guest—someone eager for a polite introduction, another curious gaze drawn by Jaxon's bond.

Instead, she came face-to-face with Darian Hale.

"Master Carrow," he said, his pale eyes gleaming as his mouth lifted in the faintest hint of a smile. "*And* Miss Starwind. Out and about—without Shaw, for once."

"Wonderful to see you again, Magister Hale," Carrow replied lightly, either missing or deliberately ignoring the edge in Hale's voice. "I trust things have been going well—"

"Yes," Hale cut in, his gaze never leaving hers. "I need to borrow Miss Starwind."

Carrow hesitated, just long enough that the spark of hope in Araya's chest sputtered and died when he gave her an apologetic smile. "Of course. Don't forget what I said, Miss Starwind. You're always welcome."

Araya forced a tight smile, but it wavered as Hale's fingers closed around her bare arm. "I won't," she managed, her voice thin.

Carrow's brow furrowed, his gaze dropping to Hale's grip on her arm—but he didn't say anything. He couldn't. He was in no position to say *no* to the High Inquisitor—and neither was she.

Araya cast one last, desperate glance over her shoulder as Hale steered her away, searching the crowd for any sign of Jaxon—but he was nowhere to be seen. She was on her own.

Her heart pounded as she wrenched against Hale's iron grip, trying to twist free as she fumbled for some plausible excuse—but he was faster. With a practiced shove, he forced her into one of the private alcoves that lined the edges of the ballroom, the heavy curtain snuffing out the warmth and light of the ballroom like a candle.

Araya ripped her arm free, stumbling back before he could grab her again. "Don't touch me," she snapped.

"How impolite." Hale's smile didn't falter. If anything, it widened, his gaze cold, calculating. "Your entanglement with Jaxon doesn't come with immunity to decorum, Miss Starwind."

Araya straightened, her chin lifting. "Then I suggest you remember yours, Magister."

But for all her bravado, her heart pounded against her ribs, betraying her terror. She was alone with the High Inquisitor.

"So passionate." Hale chuckled, taking a step toward her. "What will you do once Garrick isn't here to protect the two of you?"

Araya stumbled back, the hem of her gown catching underfoot. Her pulse pounded in her ears, each beat a warning—Hale was too close. Too dangerous.

"What are you talking about?" She demanded, her eyes flicking from Hale to the curtain behind him. His posture might be relaxed, but Araya had no doubt he was ready to stop her if she tried to push by him—that he'd hurt her, if he thought he could get away with it.

"You haven't heard?" Hale gave her an unpleasant smile. "High Magister Shaw will be traveling to Elvanfal—posthaste. Since Jaxon abandoned his post to take up with *you* the situation there needs a… firmer hand. And everyone agrees that Garrick is the best man to clean up his son's mess."

Elvanfal. Araya's stomach dropped. If Garrick went to the front and left them behind here—what *did* the rest of the Arcanum make of her bond with Jaxon?

"Why are you doing this?" Araya asked, her voice shaking despite the steel she tried to force into it. "I've never done anything to you—"

"You exist," Hale said coldly. "Jaxon might enjoy pretending otherwise, but fae were never meant to stand beside humans. Your bond isn't just unnatural—it's offensive. And I'll see it undone."

Araya's breath hitched. But she straightened her shoulders, meeting his gaze head on. "Jaxon would never let that happen."

Hale laughed, his lip curling. "Jaxon won't have a choice. He's young and arrogant. He doesn't understand how little power he truly has. But once his father is gone..." He sighed, letting the pause stretch. "The Arcanum won't waste its time entertaining this infatuation. You'll be put back where you belong, *Miss* Starwind."

The sharp rip of the curtains being thrown back cut Hale's words short. Jaxon strode into the alcove, his fury rolling into the space like a storm. His dark eyes flicked over Araya first, his jaw tightening slightly as he took in her expression before crossing the space in two long strides to tuck her tightly against his side.

"Careful, Darian," Jaxon said, his tone deadly. "Picking on someone your own size might be a better look for you."

Darian straightened, but his smirk faltered. "Jaxon," he said coolly. "I wasn't aware your meeting had finished—"

"It didn't," Jaxon said coolly. "Surely there's someone else you can pester—someone who might actually tolerate your company."

Darian's lips twitched, though his smile never quite formed. "I was merely offering some... observations," he said, his gaze flicking back to Araya. "It's not my fault if she finds the truth uncomfortable."

"Funny," he said, his tone glacial. "From where I'm standing, the only uncomfortable thing here is how hard you're working to stay relevant."

Darian's eyes flashed. "Relevance has never been an issue for me. But perhaps it will be for you—especially if you continue letting your *bond*—" he spat the word like a curse "—influence your decisions. I saw the indulgences you approved for your prisoner. I'm quite certain that wasn't your idea."

"And *I'm* quite certain you spend more time reading my reports than writing your own." Jaxon clicked his tongue, shaking his head.

"You've been coasting on the career my father handed you for more than twenty years. Try picking up your own sword once in a while—before the ground shifts and leaves you behind."

Darian bristled, his mask slipping just enough to show the fury burning beneath. But Jaxon didn't wait to see what he had to say.

He turned to Araya, brushing his fingers lightly along her spine as he leaned in, his mouth close to her ear. "Come on, Starling," he murmured, brushing a kiss across her temple as he led her past a fuming Hale. "Let's get back to the party."

———

"Is your father really going to Elvanfal?"

Jaxon's steps faltered, his hand tightening on her arm in silent warning as he led them back into the crowd. "It's not announced yet," he murmured, his voice low enough that no one would overhear them. "But yes—that's what the meeting was about." He stroked a soothing line down her spine, his hand warm on her bare back. "I won't let anyone touch you, Starling. Especially not Darian Hale."

Araya nodded, but the tightness in her chest didn't ease. It was one thing for Jaxon to say it—another to do it. Could he really keep them safe without his father's influence?

Jaxon studied her, his brow furrowing with concern. "That's enough for one night," he said quietly. "We're leaving."

"But it's your father's birthday—"

"He'll understand." Jaxon guided her through the crowded ballroom with practiced ease, cutting a direct path toward where Garrick stood near the grand fireplace, surrounded by people. Garrick's sharp eyes flicked to Jaxon as they approached, narrowing slightly as he took in his son's expression and Araya's pallor.

"If you'll excuse me," he said, easing out of the circle of officials. "I need a moment with my son—and his bond."

He led them a few steps away, toward a quieter corner of the room, then turned back to face them, his expression sharpening. "What happened?"

"Hale cornered her," Jaxon said coolly. "He told her you were leaving. I only caught the tail end, but he threatened her—promised to use your absence to target our bond. I handled it, but I'm taking her home now."

Garrick's gaze shifted to Araya, sweeping over her with careful scrutiny as she fought the urge to squirm. Even after months at Jaxon's side, she never quite knew where she stood with Garrick—and every interaction felt like a test she wasn't sure she was passing.

"Happy birthday, sir," she said quietly, dropping her gaze to her feet. "Sorry to ruin your night—"

"Nonsense," Garrick said crisply. "Darian should never have dared to corner one of my invited guests—you're the one who deserves my apologies, Araya. You should never have had to deal with that."

He glanced back at Jaxon. "You're not dragging her across the city at this hour. Your room is still here—use it."

"Oh, that's not necessary—" Araya started, scrambling. "I can make it home—"

"It's not safe, Starling." Jaxon's hand curled around her waist, pulling her into his warmth. "Not until we get a handle on Darian."

"You're Jaxon's now," Garrick added, giving her a rare, gentle smile. "That makes you my concern as much as his. Both of you get some rest—and leave Darian to me."

Araya didn't argue, letting Jaxon guide her out of the ballroom and up a sweeping staircase and into a bedroom at the end of the corridor. Araya paused just inside, her gaze sweeping over the unexpected blend of luxury and nostalgia. Polished wood furniture gleamed under the warm light of enchanted aether lamps, and sagging shelves brimmed with books and trophies, remnants of the boy Jaxon had once been.

"What do you think?" Jaxon asked, leaning casually against the doorframe.

"It's... not what I expected." Araya bent to study a set of trophies, most of them academic but some for sports and athletics. "It looks like a real child lived here."

"I was a real child, Starling."

Araya laughed, trailing her fingers along the back of the armchair as she moved toward the window. How many nights had Jaxon sat here as a boy—curled up with a book or just staring out at the city, dreaming of the world waiting beyond? Who had he thought he'd be?

"Come here." Jaxon stepped up behind her, folding her into his arms. His lips brushed her shoulder, sending sparks racing over her skin. "Let me take care of you tonight."

Araya's breath caught as Jaxon's skilled fingers worked at the fastenings of her gown. The silk whispered to the floor, pooling around her ankles. His hands followed its path, stoking those sparks into a flicker of heat that didn't quite chase away the lingering chill of Hale's threat.

"You're mine, Starling," Jaxon said, like he could read her mind. "No one—least of all Darian Hale—is going to change that. Now—" he tugged her toward the center of the room. "Come to bed."

Jaxon tucked her under the covers, pressing a quick kiss to her lips before he turned back to gather her dress. She could hear the rustle of fabric as he stripped out of his own formal clothes. Finally, he slipped into the bed behind her, his arm wrapping around her waist to pull her close.

"You're safe with me," he murmured, burying his face in her hair. "I'd never let anything happen to you, Starling. I promise."

Araya sank into the warmth of his arms around her, finally letting herself relax into the comfort of his heartbeat against her back. It didn't banish the fear, but his promise dulled the edge of it— just enough.

CHAPTER

EIGHTEEN

For the first time in twenty-five years, Loren opened his eyes to something other than stone and darkness.

A grand foyer stretched before him, dark polished wood gleaming under the golden light of the aether-lit chandeliers hanging from the soaring ceilings. Loren inhaled deeply, relishing a breath that didn't smell of moldy straw and iron.

Fragments of laughter and music teased the edges of his mind—snippets of memory hovering just out of reach, dissolving before he could grasp them. But Loren knew that if he started walking, he would find a ballroom at the end of this hall—and beyond it, sprawling gardens alive with dancing lights and the sweet scent of flowers.

But other details... Loren reached out, brushing his fingers across one of the heavy tapestries. The woven image depicted a battle scene, human figures crushing fae beneath their boots rendered in exquisite detail. *That* wasn't part of his memory.

He was dreaming—but he wasn't the one shaping it. *She* was.

Loren hadn't dreamed of her in weeks. She still visited his cell to check on his healing, but the warmth between them was gone—

replaced by a mask of cold indifference she never let waver, not since he'd sneered in her face and called her a whore for what she'd done to survive.

And who could blame her? That was what he'd wanted—to drive her away.

She was safer that way.

But it didn't make it hurt any less that he could smell Jaxon Shaw all over her. The reek of his sweet, cloying soap clung to her skin, her hair, her clothes—

Loren shuddered, choking back a growl. He should do the right thing and bow quietly out of her dream—no sense in torturing them both. But he couldn't. Instead, he took a step forward, letting the faint pull of music draw him down the corridor.

He finally found her in the ballroom.

She stood at the far side, silhouetted against the frosted window —small and solitary amid the cold grandeur of the empty space. Her dark gown hugged her torso before flaring out at her waist, layers of floating chiffon surrounding her like shadows. Her loose hair cascaded down her bare back, its deep burgundy and violet a spot of color in the cold lifelessness of the room.

"Not exactly what I expected to find in your dreams," Loren said, his voice carrying across the empty floor as he strode toward her.

Araya turned sharply, her silver eyes widening. But the flicker of emotion vanished almost as quickly as it came, her polished mask snapping back into place.

"Loren," she said without warmth. She studied him, her brow furrowing slightly. "What are you wearing?"

Loren glanced down, taking in the deep green silk and elegant cut of his jacket, both too familiar and completely alien all at the same time. A white sash stretched across his chest, and Loren didn't need to look closely to know it bore his family crest. He'd worn variations of this outfit to every formal event he had ever attended as crown prince.

"It's your dream," he muttered. "You tell me."

"My dream—" understanding dawned across her face as she gasped, her hand flying to cover her mouth, "My tea."

Loren frowned. "Tea?"

"For dreamless sleep." She crossed her arms, glaring at him like it was *his* fault they were here.

Loren reeled back, indignation flaring hot in his gut. She'd been *drugging* herself just to avoid him? Part of him admired her for finding a way to keep him out, carving a boundary between them that he hadn't even known was possible. But another part of him—a selfish part—raged at the idea. It wanted to reach for her. To pull her into his arms and bury his face in her hair. It didn't care that she was safer without him.

But she'd given her name to Jaxon. Not him.

So Loren shoved that part down, swallowing back his ire until he was able to force his voice into something neutral. "Where are we?"

Araya's gaze flicked around the ballroom, as though seeing it properly for the first time. "This...we're at Garrick's house. For his birthday. We stayed here, so I didn't have my tea..." she trailed off, watching him warily.

"Garrick's birthday," Loren repeated, the words settling bitter on his tongue. He swept his gaze around the grand room, taking in the opulence with new eyes. He laughed, soft and bitter. "They really have taken everything, haven't they?"

The Garrick he'd known had lived in one of the hastily built neighborhoods meant to contain the ever-growing human population. Cramped rows of identical, flimsy homes, built for function, not comfort.

But this? This wasn't the home of a man merely surviving. These were the spoils of a war that had taken everything from Loren—and handed Garrick everything he'd ever wanted.

Araya opened her mouth, but Loren plunged on before she could speak. "And by *we*, I suppose you mean Jaxon." Loren's lip curled, his voice dripping with venom. "Are you sleeping next to him in a feather bed right now?"

Araya stiffened, her pale skin flushing, anger staining her cheeks as red as her hair.

"He's my bond," she said, her voice cutting. "So yes, I sleep beside him *every* night. And I won't apologize to you for it."

Loren scoffed. "And what, exactly, has Jaxon ever done to earn that kind of loyalty?"

Araya's silver eyes flashed, her fury dark and unrelenting. "What has he done?" she repeated, disbelief tightening her voice. "You mean besides saving my life? Besides being the only one who saw me —who *believed* in me?"

Loren opened his mouth, but she talked over him, her voice rising. "Do you think the Arcanum wanted me? Do you think they looked at the little halfblood orphan and thought *yes, let's change the rules for* her?"

She laughed in his face, shaking her head. "If Jaxon hadn't stuck his neck out to sponsor me, I'd be rotting in the slums with the other breeding-age females."

"And you think he did that for you?" Loren demanded, his bitterness twisting his voice into something cruel. "Jaxon didn't see you as worth saving—he saw you as worth *owning*. And one day, when it serves him, he'll remind you of that." Loren held her gaze, green meeting silver. "I only hope he doesn't break you when he does."

"Hate him all you want, Loren." She shook her head, turning away from him. "Gods know, he deserves it. But Jaxon would never hurt me."

She believed it. Goddess help him, she believed—truly believed —that she was safe with Jaxon Shaw. Loren's jaw tightened, the anger in him threatening to boil over. But what good did his anger do her? What had *he* ever done to protect her?

Not nearly as much as Jaxon Shaw had.

The thought sat unpleasantly in his mind, ugly and undeniable. She'd had to survive without him, carve out a place for herself in a world that would have happily destroyed her. And it wasn't over—

she would have to keep surviving, while he rotted in his cell for the next two hundred years, doing nothing to help her.

Loren sighed deeply. How could he judge her for what she did to keep herself safe?

"I hope for my sake that's true, *ael'sura*," he said quietly. "Because I couldn't stand to see you hurt."

Araya's breath caught, her defiance faltering as she met his eyes. Loren could hear her heart beating in her chest, its tempo racing as the bond twisted between them. She felt it too—Loren could see it in the way her fingers curled against her arms, the bob of her throat as she swallowed, unable to pull her eyes away from him.

She was fighting it. Just like he was. And they were both losing.

"I'm fairly certain this place once had beautiful gardens." Loren tore his gaze from hers, forcing himself to stare out the frosted window. "Would you like to see them?"

"It's winter," she said, watching him warily.

"And this is a dream." Loren held out his arm, holding his breath as she hesitated, bracing for her refusal. But then her fingertips brushed his sleeve, her hand slipping into the crook of his arm as Loren fought the urge to close his eyes and lean into it—to let himself believe, just for a moment, that she could choose *him*.

Instead, he led them forward, offering his own memories of this place. The dream reshaped itself around them, the rigid lines of human design giving way to the organic curves of fae craftsmanship. The tapestries rippled, their grisly images replaced by woven depictions of starlit forests and iridescent rivers.

Above them, the lights dimmed, warming to cast the room in a golden, flickering glow. The stiff murmur of human conversation faded, unraveling like a thread pulled from a loom. In its place, voices rose in a low, musical cadence, each word flowing into the next as laughter rang through the space, soft and light.

Even the music changed—the grand piano melting away to reveal a slender, curved harp as he pushed open the door that led to the terrace, leading them down the steps to the garden.

The cold night faded into a warm caress, the frost clinging to the garden path melting as dewy grass sprang up beneath their feet. The stark, neatly trimmed hedges unfurled into wild, untamed vines, spilling blossoms of deep violet and silver along the stone pathways.

Somewhere in the distance, a fountain stirred to life, its song of rushing water filling the space as the scent of jasmine and rain drifted through the air. Fireflies flickered between the flowering trees, their golden glow mirroring the golden aetherlights still hovering within the ballroom behind them.

"This is how you remember it," Araya said, her silver eyes wide as she tracked the transformation. She leaned down, cupping one of the silver flowers in her palm as she inhaled deeply, savoring the perfume of a garden in full spring bloom. "How are you doing this without magic?"

"I'm merely providing the memories," Loren said. He reached out, tapping the flower she cradled gently, sending a soft shimmer into the air. "It's your dream, *ael'sura*. Your magic."

After that, Araya practically dragged him forward, eager to see it all. But Loren barely noticed the garden. His attention was consumed by her—the way her fingers curled around his arm, the steady rhythm of her breath and the excited tempo of her heartbeat. The bond pulsed between them, relentless, pulling him toward her even as he fought to hold himself back.

"You've called me that before," she said at last, breaking the fragile silence. "*Ael'sura*—" she pronounced the word slowly, deliberately. "What does it mean?"

Loren faltered mid-step, the edges of the dream softening as he lost his grip on his memories. "It's..." He started, but the word caught in his throat. The bond was there again, fierce and relentless, winding tight in his chest like a snare. Each breath dragged him closer to the edge as her silver eyes met his, searching and open.

Loren stepped toward her. She didn't pull away.

The space between them vanished, filled only by the sound of his unsteady breathing and the quiet pulse of the bond in his chest. The words he had sworn to never speak to her hovered on the tip of his tongue, desperate to escape—but Loren couldn't let them. Not when it might endanger her in ways he could never control from a prison cell.

"Some things are better left unspoken," he said instead, his voice ragged.

Araya's brows knit, her expression clouded with something that hovered between confusion and hurt. She didn't press him, but the silence that followed wasn't peaceful—it hung between them, heavy and unfinished. Around them, the dream began to unravel. The lush garden dimmed as the air turned brittle and cold, the blossoms wilting, their petals collapsing into ash that scattered on an invisible wind.

Her silver eyes—wide, uncertain, full of questions he couldn't bear to answer—were the last thing he saw before the dream broke apart like glass, and darkness claimed him again.

———

"Dreaming of something pleasant, Your Majesty?"

Loren's breath hitched as he woke, every nerve alight with dread. The bond still pulsed faintly in his chest, and the scent of flowers lingered, their sweetness turning to bitter fear as his gaze fell on the man standing in front of him, just out of reach of his chains.

Darian Hale. The Arcanum's High Inquisitor, and Loren's personal torturer. How long had he been standing there, watching him?

A sick knot twisted in Loren's stomach. Had he spoken her name in his sleep? Goddess, if he had and Hale had heard—

"I've always found dreams to be such... revealing things," Hale said, stepping closer. His lip curled as he ran his gaze over Loren. "They show us what we want. Who we care for."

Loren forced himself to sit up, ignoring the twinge of healing injuries. He didn't answer, keeping his gaze locked on a point beyond

Hale's shoulder. He couldn't let Hale see the panic twisting inside him.

"I wonder," Hale mused, tapping an iron dagger thoughtfully against his lips. "Who were you dreaming of, Your Majesty?"

Loren clenched his jaw, refusing to take the bait. He hadn't spoken to Hale in years—not one word, not even under the lash. That silence had become his shield, a final act of defiance he'd held onto long after everything else had been stripped away.

"Still holding on to that?" Hale's smile slipped. "All these years, and not a single word—but the guard told me you speak to *her*."

Loren flinched and Hale's smile widened, sharp and cruel. "What makes her so special? Is it the comforts she demanded for you?" He cast a disgusted look at Loren's warmer clothes, the raised cot and the blanket he'd been given. "Or did she do something else to earn your voice?"

He waited a moment, sighing when Loren didn't answer.

"Very well." He rose slowly, twirling the iron dagger between his fingers. "If you won't speak, then I suppose I'll have to make you scream."

The chains snapped taut. Loren gasped, biting back a curse as his back slammed into the cold stone, the iron manacles tearing into his raw wrist. He wouldn't give Hale the satisfaction—not when Araya's safety was at stake.

Hale just watched him for a moment, tilting his head like a collector studying a rare specimen. "Amazing, really," he mused. "How quickly even a king can be reduced to...this." He stepped forward, the blade gleaming dully in his hand. "Make this easy, Your Majesty. Tell me why she's so important to you, and I'll consider being...merciful."

Loren said nothing.

"I didn't think so." Hale's smile widened. "I suppose we're going to find out how much pain you're willing to take for her."

CHAPTER
NINETEEN

Araya stirred, the weight of sleep clinging to her as the dream dissolved like morning mist. For a moment, she was caught between worlds, her mind struggling to reconcile the surreal garden and its flowers that glittered like starlight with the slide of silk over her bare skin and Jaxon's warmth against her back. His arm wrapped around her waist, unwilling to let her go, even in sleep.

She exhaled slowly, careful not to disturb him as she shifted, trying to ease the strange tightness that lingered in her chest. She couldn't shake the last haunting image of the prince's eyes. He'd been so sad...

Jaxon stirred, his grip on her waist tightening. "Are you all right, Starling?" he mumbled, the words almost lost in her hair.

"Just a dream." Araya stroked his hand, letting his touch settle her. No matter how real the dreams were, they didn't matter. She was awake now—and Jaxon was right here beside her. This was where she belonged.

"Nightmare?" He groaned, his voice still rough with sleep. "I should have had the servants make your tea—I'm sorry, Starling, I didn't think of it."

"Neither did I." Araya leaned back into him, tilting her head just enough to graze his lips. "But I'm sure you'll find a way to make it up to me."

Jaxon hummed, his arms tightening around her as he trailed his lips from her temple down to her jaw. He lingered there, nibbling at her skin before claiming her lips. He kissed her lazily, warm and unhurried, like there was nowhere else for them to be and nothing else they could possibly want but this.

Araya melted into him, the ache in her chest easing as his touch chased away the last traces of the dream. Her magic stirred beneath her skin, flickering to life in response to his closeness—drawn to him always.

Jaxon pulled back, magic sparking between their lips. "Are you sure that was a nightmare?" He laughed, brushing her hair out of her face. Before she could answer, he was kissing her again—deeper this time, his hands sliding down her sides to pull her on top of him.

She gasped into his mouth, his touch igniting sparks that danced across her skin. The world around them fell away, narrowing to the heat of his body under her hands, the scent of him surrounding her as the slow drag of his fingers set fire to every nerve.

Then the door swung open without warning.

Jaxon swore, yanking the blankets over them in one swift motion. Araya yelped as she tumbled sideways, the heat between them shattering like glass.

"Didn't they train you to knock?" Jaxon snapped.

"I—I did sir." The young female hovered in the doorway, her eyes locked on the floor and her face flushed bright red all the way to the tips of her clipped ears. "Maybe you didn't hear—"

"What do you want?" Jaxon cut her off sharply.

The servant swallowed hard, holding out the stack of clothing in her arms. "Master Shaw—your father—wanted clothing delivered for...for your bond." Her eyes flickered toward Araya, but she imme-diately looked away again. "I'm very sorry—"

"It's alright," Araya said quickly, tugging the sheet higher over her chest. "Thank you—if you could just set it there, I can get it myself."

The girl dipped her head in a quick nod, still avoiding Araya's eyes.

"Master Shaw invites you both to breakfast," she added, shifting her weight from foot to foot. "I-if you need anything else—"

"We won't," Jaxon said, his voice flat. "Leave the clothes. You're dismissed."

The girl flinched, bobbing her head and all but tossing the bundle onto the chest at the foot of the bed before fleeing. The door clicked shut behind her, sealing the room in silence.

Araya stared after her, frowning at the closed door. "She looked... uncomfortable."

Jaxon groaned and flopped back against the pillows, draping an arm over his eyes. "Don't take it personally, Starling. Garrick's servants are terrified of upsetting him—especially the younger ones."

Araya bit the inside of her cheek. That hadn't felt like fear of *Garrick*. But this wasn't her world—and it wasn't her place to question it.

"Well—" she said, batting Jaxon's hands away as he reached for her again. "We shouldn't keep your father waiting."

Jaxon let out an exaggerated sigh, flopping back into the pillows. "Fine." His lips curled in a slow, lazy smirk. "But you owe me for this, Starling. And I always collect."

Araya shook her head, her lips twitching despite herself. Jaxon's charm was infuriatingly effective, no matter how hard she tried to resist.

"I'm sure you'll remind me," she said dryly, sliding out of bed and reaching for the clothes the servant had left behind. She avoided his gaze, knowing the amused glint she'd find there would only make it harder to hide her smile.

"Count on it." Jaxon sat up, his gaze heating her skin. "Now, if you could just dress a little slower—"

Araya rolled her eyes, pulling the soft, simple dress over her head. Though plain, it was nicer than anything she'd ever owned before she met Jaxon. She laced up the bodice and tied the waist, sectioning her hair into three before realizing the tie to her braid was back at the Aetherium.

"Wear it down," Jaxon said, tugging on a tunic and pants from the dresser. "It's just us here, Starling. There's no one for you to hide from."

Araya hesitated, her fingers curling around a loose strand of hair as she glanced toward the door. Jaxon adored her hair—but she still didn't feel entirely comfortable flaunting such a fae feature so openly.

"If anyone stares—"

"They won't." Jaxon was already beside her, his fingers threading through her waves as he pulled her close, his lips brushing the shell of her ear. "Because they know."

Araya swallowed hard, her resolve fraying under the heat of his breath against her skin.

"Know what?" she managed, her voice coming out weaker than intended.

Jaxon smiled against her jaw, dragging his fingers lazily through her hair. "What a lucky, lucky man I am that *you* belong to me."

Araya huffed a breathless laugh, making a half-hearted effort to twist away. "We have to go down to breakfast."

Jaxon's grin widened. "We could be late."

His lips traced a slow path down her neck, his fingers skimming her waist, drawing her back into him, coaxing her toward surrender. Araya shivered, letting herself sink into the heat of it—the pull, the ache.

But when she blinked, she saw green eyes instead of dark.

Araya sucked in a sharp breath, stepping back. "I don't want to disappoint your father."

Jaxon studied her for a long moment, something unreadable flickering in his gaze before he sighed and extended his arm with a teasing grin. "Fine. But you still owe me—with interest."

Araya stared at him, faltering for a moment as the memory of the dream rushed back to her. Loren had offered her his arm just like this —the thought left her reeling, like the world had shifted again under her feet.

But she pushed it away, slipping her hand through his arm and letting him lead her from his bedroom, willing the dream to stay behind where it belonged.

———

"I've never had a family breakfast before," Araya admitted, smoothing the soft folds of the dress they'd given her. It fit perfectly, tailored so precisely that she suspected it had been purchased for her—even though she'd never been here. She should know better by now than to be surprised—Jaxon was always prepared.

"They can be more trouble than they're worth." Jaxon snorted, his grin tugging at the corner of his mouth. "But Father will be glad to see you—I know he was worried about you last night."

The breakfast room was no grand dining hall, but it carried an understated elegance that made Araya acutely aware of how little time she had spent in places like this. Polished silverware gleamed at each place setting, and every detail of the table was meticulously arranged—from the fine china to the neatly folded napkins.

Garrick Shaw sat at the head of the table, already sipping a cup of tea as he thumbed through a stack of papers. He glanced up as they entered, his sharp gaze landing on his son before flicking to Araya, lingering just long enough that the hair on the back of her neck prickled.

"Good morning," he said. "I hope you both slept well."

"We did," Jaxon said dryly, pulling out a chair and gesturing for

Araya to sit. "Until your newest staff member made sure we were awake."

The young female moving around the table flinched but kept her head down, her hands trembling as she poured steaming tea into two more cups.

"She was just doing her job, Jaxon." Araya offered the female a kind smile, but the servant kept her eyes down, her face carefully blank. "Thank you for the clothes, sir. That was very thoughtful of you."

"Of course," Garrick said absently, his focus already drifting back to his papers. "I meant what I said last night—you're family now, Araya."

The servant scurried around the table, pulling silver lids off serving dishes to reveal platters of fluffy eggs and savory sausages. Another bowl held freshly cut fruit, and fresh rolls steamed in a basket beside a silver dish of creamy butter.

"Thank you, Belanis," Garrick said as she topped off his tea. "That will be everything for now—yes, please leave the teapot—"

"Milk and sugar." Jaxon nudged the small pitcher and dish towards Araya. "You're sweet to defend her, Starling," he added softly, taking her plate and piling it high with food. "But remember your place here—it's beside me, not her."

Araya stared at him, any response she might have made dying on her tongue as he set her plate in front of her with a smile that didn't reach his eyes.

"Darian was gone when we looked for him," Garrick said without looking up once the door had closed behind the servant. "He knew he overstepped last night."

"Coward," Jaxon snorted, heaping food onto his own plate next. "So he can corner someone who can't fight back, but he can't face the consequences of his actions?"

"Darian is more dangerous than you give him credit for," Garrick said, setting his papers down. His sharp gaze pinned Jaxon in place, his voice calm but edged with warning. "He may not hold formal authority over you, but he's made a career of currying favor. With the right allies —and the right moment—he can cause more than enough trouble."

Jaxon's grin didn't falter as he speared a fat sausage with his fork. "If he wants a fight, I'll make sure he gets one."

"Don't underestimate him." Garrick said evenly. He leaned back in his chair, his forehead creasing as he frowned at his son. "That's exactly what Darian wants you to do. He thrives on exploiting arrogance."

Jaxon grunted but said nothing, the silence broken by only the scrape of his knife against his plate.

"It would help," Garrick continued, "If we had measurable progress to show the Arcanum—something to indicate that you're making a difference."

"Araya is ready to start imbuing the amulets," Jaxon said around a mouthful of eggs. "Is that measurable enough for you?"

"Is that so?"

Garrick's attention shifted to Araya, his eyes narrowing slightly. The weight of his gaze pressed down on her, but she kept her expression neutral, her back straightening instinctively.

"Processing the blood took longer than we expected, but I finished the final housing last night," she said, relieved to return to a more familiar topic. "Once we install the bone blanks and imbue them, we'll be ready to start testing."

"And how long will imbuing take?" Garrick asked.

"They're just blanks," Araya said, considering. "Not more than a few days, if that."

"And do you believe they'll work?" He asked.

Araya hesitated, choosing her words carefully. "Everything we have done up until now is based on theory," she admitted. "It *should* work—but magic can be unpredictable."

For a moment, Garrick said nothing, his gaze lingering on her as if weighing her words. Finally, he nodded. "Good. It sounds like we're finally moving in the right direction, then. Where are you planning to conduct these tests?"

"I thought Ravonfar," Jaxon said without missing a beat. "That's where Araya helped her friend with those maternity clinics—with what she's said about how the mist behaves there, it sounds like the perfect place to start."

Araya froze with her teacup halfway to her lips. "Ravonfar? Are you sure that's the best choice?"

"Why not?" Jaxon raised an eyebrow. "You've spoken about it often enough—how the shadows creep along the beach. It seems like a logical place to begin."

"The people there..." Araya trailed off, setting her cup down carefully. "It's a complicated district. The people there haven't seen the good parts of the New Dominion—"

"All the more reason for me to go," Jaxon said. His hand found hers under the table, squeezing gently. "I want to see everything you've told me about. I want *them* to see what we can do to help— that we're trying."

Araya's protest faded as she met his steady gaze. There was no mockery in his voice, no trace of his usual charm. Only conviction— and sincerity. She leaned toward him almost without meaning to, drawn to the hope in his words even as a quiet voice that sounded disconcertingly like Loren whispered a warning in the back of her mind.

Humans lie. Especially when they want something.

But this was Jaxon. *Her* Jaxon.

"Just... don't be surprised if you don't get a warm welcome," she said. "You won't undo decades of mistrust and fear in a night."

Jaxon's grin softened. "I don't expect to undo anything overnight," he said. "But we have to start somewhere."

"Ravonfar it is then," Garrick said. "Just be sure the tests are thorough—and keep things contained. We can't afford a spectacle."

Jaxon inclined his head. "Understood, Father."

"And how is the prisoner?" Garrick picked his utensils back up, slicing neatly into a steaming sausage. "You've been spending a great deal of time with him, haven't you, Araya? Have you made any progress?"

Araya straightened, the bite she'd just taken turning bitter on her tongue. "I check on him daily," she said, careful to keep her voice even. "If his blood is the key to this, he needs to be strong enough to provide what we need."

A flicker of guilt twisted in her chest, but it was true. That's what his role was—what *her* role was. The dreams had made things more complicated—but Araya couldn't let herself lose sight of the truth.

"Just don't forget that he's a prisoner—not a guest." Garrick sighed, taking another bite of his food and chewing slowly, studying her. "I know it can be difficult for a soft heart to see—but Darian is looking for an excuse to cause trouble for you both. Do not give him one."

"I understand, sir," Araya said, lowering her eyes. Steam curled off her cooling tea, her fingers tightening around the cup.

"When do you leave for Elvanfal?" Jaxon asked, reaching across the table for the stack of papers by his father's plate.

"Tonight," Garrick said, a frown creasing his face. "Things are... not going as well as we'd like."

"Are these the latest?" Jaxon asked, frowning. "We were gaining ground when I left—"

"We were." Garrick sighed, suddenly sounding much closer to his age than he usually did. "But the chaos the fae left behind is more persistent than we anticipated in this section—add that to the terrain, and it's become a holding game."

"What if—" Jaxon dragged his chair a foot closer to the head of the table, their voices fading into background noise as the conversation turned to strategy and troop movements—nothing that concerned her.

Araya exhaled slowly, turning her gaze to the tall arched window and the snow-covered skeleton of the garden beyond. What did it look like now, after twenty years of Garrick's rule? Did it still hold the vibrant greens and bursts of color Loren had shown her last night—or had those, too, been stripped away?

What would Darian Hale say if he found out Loren visited her in her dreams?

She shivered, lacing her fingers together under the table and clasping her hands tightly. She never wanted to find out.

CHAPTER
TWENTY

ARAYA DESCENDED INTO THE DARKNESS, SHIVERING AS THE DAMP COLD slipped beneath her heavy cloak. Jaxon had gone up to her workshop to retrieve the housings, but she'd come down ahead to check on Loren—anxious to begin the imbuing and put this entire chapter behind her. Once the shadows were dispelled, she could be done. Done with this dungeon. Done with the dreams. Done with whatever strange, unwanted connection bound her to the fae prince.

No one would ever have to know.

The thought sent a pang of something sharp and bitter through her chest. She shoved it down, clinging to the same tired logic she'd repeated for weeks. She had done everything she could. If Loren wasn't willing to help himself... well, that was on him.

And yet, unease clung to her like the living shadows that were conspicuously absent as she made her way through the ruined temple. Her steps slowed, the hair on the back of her neck rising as she passed the desecrated tombs without any sign of them, unable to shake the sense that something was terribly, horribly wrong.

Araya shook her head. "Nerves," she muttered, tugging her cloak more closely around herself. She hurried past the long procession of iron doors, more relieved than she wanted to admit when Loren's cell and the guard outside finally came into view.

"Good morning, Aeron," she said, dredging up a polite smile for the human man. "How are things this morning?"

"Quiet, miss," Aeron nodded respectfully. "No trouble reported by the night guard."

"That's good." Araya rummaged in her cloak for her key. "Jaxon will be down shortly, but I wanted to check on Loren before we get started."

"Of course, miss." Aeron inserted his own key and then hers, turning them both in the lock together. Araya stepped forward, sketching a quick rune to kindle the aetherlamp, expecting to see Loren sitting on the cot she'd convinced Jaxon he needed. Instead—

"Gods," Araya gasped, clapping a hand over her mouth as bile surged up her throat. She staggered back a step, nearly slamming into Aeron as the creeping dread she'd tried to ignore erupted into full-blown panic.

Loren hung limply from the wall, his arms stretched wide by the chains that pinned him in place. His head lolled forward, chin to chest, hair falling in a dark, matted curtain that hid most of his face. What remained of his shirt clung to him in blood-soaked tatters, revealing a grim tapestry of angry burns and vicious cuts. Blood still dripped from some of the deeper wounds, leaving sticky, dark trails along his ruined flesh.

"What—" Araya's voice cracked, a sour taste rising in her throat. She swallowed hard, willing herself not to vomit. "What happened to him?" she demanded, spinning to face Aeron.

The guard stumbled back a step, eyes wide as he took in the grisly scene. "I... I don't know—"

"You don't *know*?" Her voice rose, shrill with disbelief. "You were standing right outside the door." She whipped around, her boots sticking to the tacky blood streaking the floor as she rushed to Loren's side. "Help me get him down."

But Aeron didn't move. He shifted uncomfortably, his hand

hovering near the hilt of his sword. "Miss, I—I can't enter the cell or touch the prisoner," he stammered. "It's against protocol—"

Aeron hesitated, his jaw tightening as he wrestled with her words, but still, his boots stayed firmly planted at the threshold. "The rules are very clear—"

"Fine!" Araya cut him off, her voice shaking as it rose to a near shout. "If you won't help, then go—go get my medical kit from the workshop!" She pointed at the door, her hands shaking. "Now!"

For a moment, Aeron looked like he might argue, but something in her expression made him think better of it. The door crashed shut between them, his footsteps pounding down the hall. But Araya couldn't worry about him any more.

She spun back to Loren, her fingers fumbling over the manacles around his wrists. She had to stand on her tiptoes to reach, the iron burning her fingertips as she searched for some sort of a release mechanism. There had to be a way to take them off—

But there was nothing but rough, pitted iron. The mechanism had to be magical—but she'd never even seen it work. She wasn't strong enough to rip them from the wall like Loren had—even if Jaxon hadn't had them reinforced.

Araya stepped back, gasping for breath. She couldn't think over the panic clawing at her, matching the ragged rise and fall of Loren's battered chest. It flooded her lungs, drowning her. If he died—

"Loren—" she grasped his face in her burned hands. "Wake up." She shook him gently, then harder, a ragged sob tearing from her throat. "Please—you can't just—"

A sudden commotion echoed from the hallway, the door screeching on its hinges. Araya's head snapped up, meeting Jaxon's furious gaze as he stormed into the cell. Aeron hovered behind him, the bag Araya had demanded clutched in both hands.

"What the hell happened here?" Jaxon's voice cracked like a whip. He whirled, glaring at the guard. "Who was here before you? Who else was given access to the prisoner?"

"I—I don't know," Aeron stammered, his voice faltering under the weight of Jaxon's glare. "The night guard, I assume—Belkin was supposed to—"

"Supposed to?" Jaxon snarled. He stepped forward, his next words hissed directly into Aeron's face. "This prisoner is the key to *everything*. And you let him be tortured and left for dead?"

"I didn't—" Aeron flinched, holding up her bag like it might shield him from Jaxon's wrath. "Miss Starwind asked me to remove the manacles, but I'm not authorized—"

"Do you think I care about your authorization?" Jaxon spat. "You do whatever she says from now on. If I find out you've hesitated *again,* I'll make sure you're the one chained to this wall. Do you understand me?"

Aeron blanched, nodding so hard Araya thought his head might snap off. "Y-yes, Master Shaw."

"Good." Jaxon turned away, crossing the cell in two long strides. "Hold him steady, Araya." His hands moved over the first manacle, burnt aether crackling in the air as the first manacle fell away. Araya stumbled as Jaxon released the other wrist, letting Loren's full weight fall on her, but then he was there, catching him under the shoulders.

"Get his legs," Jaxon ordered. Together, they maneuvered Loren down onto the cot, his limp form sprawling across the rough mattress. Araya hovered at his side, her hands trembling as she brushed blood-matted hair from his face.

"He needs a healer," she said, her voice breaking as she looked up at Jaxon. "I don't know if he'll survive without one. *Please,* Jaxon—call Serafina."

Jaxon cursed under his breath, dragging both hands through his hair. "You really think she can be trusted with this?"

Araya nodded, her throat too thick with tears to speak. For a moment, she thought Jaxon might still refuse, but then he straightened, looking back at where Aeron still hovered uselessly at the threshold of the cell.

"Send guards to the neighborhood clinic in North Bend," he

ordered. "They're to retrieve a Healer named Serafina Hart and bring her here, along with everything she needs to treat severe injuries. Burns, blood loss—everything."

"But I can't leave—" Aeron gulped, his voice faltering under Jaxon's piercing glare. "Yes, sir. I'll—yes. But I need to lock the door before I—"

"Then wait," Jaxon cut him off sharply. "I need a moment with her. Stay outside until I call you."

Aeron hesitated, glancing between Jaxon and Araya before giving a jerky nod. "Yes, sir."

Jaxon crouched beside her, his tone soft but laced with steel. "Araya, look at me," he said, brushing a thumb lightly against her cheek. "Starling. You've done everything you can for him. You need to come with me now."

Araya shook her head, tears streaking her face as she clutched Loren's limp hand. "No—I can't leave him like this. I need to—" Her voice cracked, and she pressed her forehead to Loren's shoulder, her breaths coming in sharp, shallow gasps. "Please, Jaxon. He can't—he can't—"

"Come on, Starling." Jaxon's hand tightened slightly on her shoulder, his tone still coaxing. "You're not thinking clearly. You're not a Healer, and nothing in that bag can fix this." He leaned closer, cupping her jaw and angling her face toward him. "The best thing you can do right now is come with me so Aeron can go fetch Serafina."

Araya stared down at Loren, her heart pounding in her chest like it was trying to beat its way free. Something inside her screamed, every instinct she had demanding that she stay, that she *fight*—

"*Araya.*" Jaxon's voice sharpened, slicing through the noise in her head. Her gaze snapped back to his, transfixed by the steel in his dark eyes. "You need to come out of the cell now. We need to talk—to figure out what happened here. But we can't do that with you in hysterics. *Trust* me, Starling."

He didn't wait for her to agree, pulling her bodily to her feet.

Something inside her screamed, wild and wordless. She didn't understand it—only that walking away felt like tearing something vital from her chest. But Jaxon's arm slid around her shoulders, propelling her forward as the door slammed closed between them.

———

BLOOD COATED HER FACE, HER HANDS, HER CHEST—DRYING INTO A BRITTLE crust that cracked with every movement. Araya shuddered, pacing the workshop like a cage. When her dream had fallen apart around them, had it been because he was fighting for his life here? How could she not have realized?

"Starling."

Araya flinched as Jaxon stepped into her path, catching her shoulders in his hands. "You have to stop, Araya. I don't know why you're so shaken—but this isn't helping anyone."

He didn't know why—Araya stared at him, nonplussed. "A prisoner was nearly tortured to death while under our care—our authority," she hissed. "He could still die! Why aren't *you* upset?"

"I *am* upset," Jaxon shot back, his tone laced with enough heat to make her pause. "That's why I want to figure out who did this—but we're not going to get anywhere if you fall apart."

"I should have known." Araya shook her head, hugging her arms around herself. "I should have stopped it—"

"How?" Jaxon snorted. "Don't be ridiculous, Starling. We both know who did this. Even if you'd suspected something, what could you have done? He's the High Inquisitor."

"You think it was Darian Hale," she whispered.

"He vanished right after he cornered you," Jaxon said, his jaw tightening. "That's not a coincidence. He could have used his credentials to get in here—and he left Loren like that to send a message to you."

"To me?" Araya shuddered, unable to banish the image of Loren's abused body from her mind. "Why? I'm no one—"

"Don't pretend, Starling." Jaxon wet his thumb, swiping it slowly through the blood streaked across her cheek. "You're the one he cornered—the one he threatened. He wanted to rattle *you*—and he succeeded. Now, tell me why."

"I—he—" Araya's pulse roared in her ears, her chest squeezing so tight she struggled to breathe. "Loren's key to everything. If he dies, your project—"

"Do you think I'm blind, Araya?" Jaxon laughed, a cutting, humorless sound. "This isn't about the project—you're falling apart because it's *him*."

"It's not what you think," Araya protested, the words spilling out in a desperate rush. "I don't know why this is happening—but I'd never betray you. I'd do anything for you."

"Anything," Jaxon repeated. "That's a lot to offer, Starling. Are you sure you mean it?"

"Yes." Araya didn't hesitate this time, her gaze never wavering from his. "I'm yours, Jaxon."

The words hung heavy in the air between them, charged with something dangerous—but the moment was shattered by a loud commotion from the hall. Jaxon straightened, his expression turning into a scowl as boots pounded against stone. Someone swore viciously, slamming hard into the door before throwing it open.

"I said let me go!" Serafina snarled, lashing out with her foot and catching one of the guards dragging her forward squarely in the shin. He grunted, barely managing to hold on to her as she twisted and writhed like a feral animal. "If you think dragging me in here like a common criminal is going to make me cooperate—"

"Enough," Jaxon barked. "Let her go."

One of the guards yanked the hood off her head, beating a hasty retreat as Serafina rounded on him, snarling. But it was Jaxon that drew the brunt of her anger, her sharp blue eyes blazing as she advanced on him.

"What the hell is this?" She demanded, rubbing at the red marks on her wrists. "Blindfolded? Shackled? If you think that's how you summon a Healer you're out of your damned mind, Jaxon—"

"There's a gravely injured prisoner here," Jaxon said flatly, unmoved by her fury. "You're going to stabilize him."

"A prisoner?" Serafina's lips curled into a sneer. "Let me guess—you want me to patch him up so you can throw him back on the rack? No. Find someone else."

"This isn't a request." Jaxon's jaw flexed, and his voice dropped dangerously low. "You don't have a choice—"

"There is always a choice," Serafina said coldly, folding her arms. Even with her braid mussed from the bag they'd shoved over her head, she leveled Jaxon with a look sharp enough to cut glass. "I don't heal people so you can break them again. If that's why I'm here, you've wasted your time—"

Araya's chest constricted as she listened, the pull inside her growing more unbearable with every passing second. She stepped forward, her voice trembling as she interrupted, "Serafina."

The Healer froze, her rant faltering as she took in the blood streaking Araya's face and arms. "Gods," Serafina whispered. "*Araya*—what happened?"

"It wasn't us," Araya said, silently begging Serafina to believe her. "I found him like this when we got here this morning. I swear, Jaxon was with me at Garrick's house all night."

Serafina hesitated, twisting her braid as her gaze flicked to Jaxon, then back to Araya, considering. Finally she exhaled sharply, bending down to sling the bag the guards had dropped on the floor over her shoulder.

"I'll do it for you. *Not* him." She shot Jaxon a hard look. "But only once. If this happens again—" she shook her head.

Araya nodded quickly, almost choking on her relief. "Thank you," she whispered.

"Let's go, then," Serafina said. "Where is he?"

"Araya will take you." Jaxon stepped aside, catching Araya's arm as she started forward. "You're the one who demanded the Healer," he warned. "*Anything* starts now, Starling. If this all falls apart, I know exactly who to blame."

Neither she nor Serafina spoke as Araya led the way back to Loren's cell, the silence stretching between them until it felt like a third presence in the corridor. Every footstep echoed louder than it should have, keeping time with the dread rising in Araya's chest.

Serafina would help. She had to. Once she saw him—once she understood—she wouldn't refuse.

But Araya's hands were trembling by the time she passed her key to Aeron.

"*Gods*, Araya," Serafina whispered as the door to the cell swung shut behind them, locking them inside. "What have you done?"

Araya stared down at Loren. He hadn't moved, still sprawled awkwardly over the too-short cot. She couldn't bring herself to look too closely at the cuts and burns crisscrossing his skin—but the smell of blood and blackened flesh clung to the air, inescapable.

"I—" She shook her head, unable to even speak the words aloud. She should have known—should have done something. If this had been a message for her from Hale...well, then it was all her fault, wasn't it?

"Gods," Serafina said again. She turned, tracing a silencing rune on the back of the door. *Thyn* spluttered, reluctant to take to iron without being inlaid, but held, sealing the outside world away from their conversation.

Serafina turned back to Araya, her green stare layered with disbelief, disappointment—and something far worse. Heartbreak. "If you want me to help him," she said. "You're going to start talking."

Araya swallowed hard, guilt threatening to consume her as she stared down at Loren's battered body. "I'll tell you everything," she whispered.

CHAPTER

TWENTY-ONE

"It started with a theory," Araya said. "I was researching the Shadowed Veil for Jaxon, and I noticed that every generation of fae royalty seemed to have someone with an affinity for shadow magic. It seemed to suggest that the shadows might not be an external force —something passed from king to prince."

"I thought—" Araya faltered, swallowing hard. "I told Jaxon that if we had access to royal fae blood, we might be able to craft an amulet that granted the same kind of control."

Serafina didn't respond immediately, her focus narrowing on the deep gash running along Loren's ribcage. Her hands hovered over it, golden light spilling from her fingertips, sinking into the torn flesh. The light moved like liquid, weaving the skin together until the edges finally met.

"Keep talking," Serafina ordered.

"It was just a theory," Araya said. "I never thought it would go beyond that. But then Jaxon—" she broke off, swallowing hard as her stomach twisted. "He brought me here, he showed me Loren—"

Serafina's hands stilled, the golden glow of her magic sputtering out as her head snapped up. "*Loren?*" she demanded. "As in *Prince* Loren?"

Araya nodded once, not trusting her voice.

"Gods." Serafina sat back on her heels, staring down at him. "How long has he been down here?"

"Twenty-five years," Araya said softly. "I swear, Serafina, I didn't know. When I told Jaxon my theory, I thought he was just... a dream. A figment of my imagination—"

Serafina's head snapped up. "What are you talking about?"

Araya swallowed hard, her hands curling into fists as the pull in her chest twisted tighter, sharp and urgent." "I've seen him," she said quietly. "I thought it was just... my mind playing tricks on me. But they're not dreams, Serafina. They're real."

"How real?" Serafina demanded.

Araya shook her head, tears stinging her eyes as she stared down at Loren. "I've spoken to him, walked with him... He's shown me things. Places that shouldn't exist—"

"Gods," Serafina repeated, her voice weary. "Araya—have you told anyone else about this?"

"No—"

"Not Jaxon?" Serafina pressed. "His father? The baker? *Anyone,* Araya—have you told *anyone* but me about the dreams?"

"No," Araya repeated, shaking her head quickly. "He—he told me not to tell anyone."

Serafina exhaled, her shoulders relaxing ever so slightly, but her expression remained tense. "Good," she said curtly, turning her attention back to Loren. "He was right. If anyone finds out..."

Araya's breath caught, her heart lurching. "Finds out what?" she demanded. "Do you know why this is happening to me?"

Serafina didn't respond immediately, her magic pulsing softly as it seeped into Loren's torn skin. For a moment, she seemed entirely focused on her work, but then her eyes flicked to the door—the wavering silencing rune etched into the iron surface.

"We can't talk about it here," she said, her voice low. "Not right now. I swear, Araya, I'll tell you what I know—but not here. Now—do you want to help him?"

"I do," Araya said quickly. "Tell me what to do."

"Then take his hand," Serafina instructed, nodding toward Loren's limp arm.

"What?" Araya blinked, her confusion deepening. "Why?"

"Just do it," Serafina replied, her voice firm but not unkind. "Trust me, Araya. You both need this."

Hesitant, Araya took Loren's hand in hers. He was still so cold, so still—but something inside her quieted as they touched, soothed by their proximity. Araya wrapped her fingers around his, careful not to squeeze too hard.

"Good," Serafina said, her hands still moving over Loren's wounds. "Now...let your magic flow into him. Don't force it—just let it happen."

Araya hesitated, staring down at Loren's limp hand in hers. Her magic—it belonged to Jaxon. Like everything else about her, it was his to direct, to use as he saw fit... but hadn't he made it clear she was to do whatever was necessary to keep Loren alive?

"Close your eyes," Serafina urged, her voice gentler now, but still firm. "You're overthinking. Just breathe and let it happen."

Araya obeyed, closing her eyes and taking a shaky breath. Her magic stirred hesitantly beneath her skin, as if unsure of itself. But the moment her magic touched him—

Warmth, spreading like sunlight breaking through dark clouds. Her heart spasmed in her chest, shuddering as the ice surrounding it thawed. The storm in her mind stilled, giving way to calm, still waters. Safe. She was safe. She was exactly where she belonged—

Araya opened her eyes, catching her breath as the shadows at the edge of the cell *moved*. They reached forward like restless fingers, flickering and curling as they twined around their joined hands.

"What—" Araya started, panicked.

"That's perfect, Araya," Serafina said softly. "Don't stop."

Araya knew she should press her, demand an explanation, but the warmth coursing through her dulled her urgency. Her magic flowed freely now, a stream of light flowing from her to him. The shadows wove around them both, a cool, gentle balm, and the pull in her chest softened into something gentler, steadier. Satisfied.

Loren's chest rose and fell slightly more steadily, his features relaxing as if he, too, could feel the calm spreading between them. He didn't stir, but Araya tightened her grip, as if holding on to him physically could keep him tethered to life.

"Good," Serafina said. She moved to the next wound, her magic dimming briefly before flaring bright again. ""Don't let go, Araya. He still needs more."

Serafina worked in silence after that, glancing up occasionally to look from Araya's face to their clasped hands. But whatever she had to say, she kept to herself. Araya's magic continued to flow, the pull in her chest easing to a gentle tug that ebbed and flowed in time with the faint rise and fall of Loren's chest.

Finally, Serafina sat back on her heels, the golden glow around her hands fading for the last time. The hum of her power quieted too, the silence of the cell broken by only Loren's slow, even breaths. Still, Araya didn't move. She sat beside Loren, his hand clasped in both of hers as she searched his face for a reassurance she couldn't quite find.

"Is he going to be all right?" she asked finally, her voice small and broken, barely more than a whisper.

"He's alive," Serafina said after a long pause, her tone guarded. "You've given him a chance—but that's all I can promise for now. Whoever did this—"

"Hale," Araya cut in, still staring at Loren's face. "His name is Darian Hale. The High Inquisitor. He doesn't approve of what Jaxon is doing... or of me."

"Hale," Serafina said. A flicker of something crossed her face, too quick for Araya to read it. "I've heard the name. The things they say about him..." She looked at Araya sharply. "Be careful, Araya. He's not finished."

Araya nodded faintly, her focus fixed on Loren's pale, unmoving face. The pull in her chest had quieted into a faint thrum, her magic no longer flowing into him, but still she couldn't bring herself to let go of his hand.

"Jaxon will...he'll make sure Hale can't get back in," Araya murmured, her voice distant and hollow. She blinked, forcing herself to focus as she added, "I'll make sure he does."

Serafina studied her for a long moment, her expression softening as she crouched down beside her. "You've done everything you can for him right now. It's time for us to go."

"I know," Araya whispered, but she couldn't bring herself to let go.

"Araya," Serafina repeated. "You need to stand up and come with me. Jaxon can't see you like this."

Jaxon—waiting. The thought was enough to give Araya the strength to loosen her grip on Loren's hand. For the second time that day, Araya let herself to be pulled to her feet and guided away—against every instinct screaming at her to stay.

"Well?"

Jaxon leaned against the workbench, his arms crossed over his chest. But there was nothing casual about the sharp edge to his voice or the way his dark eyes raked over her before flicking to Serafina.

"He's still unconscious," Serafina said brusquely, toweling off her hands. Somehow, her crisp, blue Healer's uniform was still pristine, while Araya felt like every inch of her skin was crusted with blood and dirt. "He'll need to be assessed daily—"

"Araya can handle that," Jaxon waved her off.

Serafina's eyes flashed. "Araya isn't a Healer," she snapped without missing a beat. "This is far beyond the scope of care either of you are equipped to provide. If you want him alive, you'll allow me to monitor his progress."

Araya risked a glance at Jaxon, her pulse stuttering at the faint tick in his jaw. He didn't argue, but the silence dragged—his displeasure curling around her like a hand closing over her wrist.

"Fine," he said at last, voice tight. "But only under strict supervision—following the same protocols as today."

"Good." Serafina exhaled through her nose, snapping her bag shut with a sharp click. She straightened, her shoulders stiff as her gaze flicked between Jaxon and Araya. "And I'm taking Araya back to the clinic with me."

Araya started, her gaze jerking to Serafina, but Jaxon didn't even hesitate.

"No." He crossed his arms, leaning back against the workbench.

"She's just been through a traumatic episode," Serafina snapped. "You've already wrung her dry. She needs to be observed—"

"Her place is with me," Jaxon interrupted, his lip curling as he stared Serafina down. "I can manage my own bond."

"She's not something to be *managed*." Serafina squared her shoulders. "She's exhausted, Jaxon. If you push her any further, she'll break—and then what? You'll trade her in for someone else?"

Araya flinched at Serafina's tone, but Jaxon just tilted his head, staring at her.

"You've always thought poorly of me," he said, sneering. "And you underestimate her. Araya knows her limits. Don't you, Starling?"

Araya's heart stuttered as they both looked at her. Serafina's face was set, her eyes pleading with Araya to take the out—but Jaxon's sharp gaze was expectant. If Jaxon felt like she was choosing Serafina over *him*—

"I'll stay," Araya said. She forced herself to smile at Serafina, adding, "It's fine. I want to stay with Jaxon."

The words sat heavy on her tongue, thick as tar, but she could force them out—that alone should be enough to reassure Serafina.

Araya didn't need to be saved. Jaxon was her bond—he would never hurt her.

Jaxon's smirk widened—a flicker of triumph flashing in his dark eyes.

"We're done here." Jaxon didn't even look at Serafina as he nodded to the guards. "Escort her out."

CHAPTER
TWENTY-TWO

Araya's hands trembled as she pressed the bone blank into its setting. The ivory disc had to fit perfectly. One slip, one miscalculation, and the entire thing would be ruined. They'd already lost more than a week making sure Loren didn't die—long enough for Jaxon's precious timeline to slip, and the silence between them to shift into something cold and threatening.

She inhaled slowly, steadying her grip on the dropper of Loren's blood as she touched it to the ivory surface. The carved runes there pulsed, drinking in the first drops with greedy hunger. A novice would be tempted to flood them, mistaking enthusiasm for strength —but Araya knew better. Move too fast, and the entire structure would fracture—just like everything else in her life right now.

So instead she counted the slow pulses of power, holding her breath as she waited—

"Be careful," Jaxon said, his voice dangerously close to her ear.

Araya flinched, her power flaring at his proximity. She cursed, trying to pull it back—but the blank flared white hot and split, a jagged shard biting deep into her palm.

"We can't afford mistakes." Jaxon sighed, shaking his head as she cradled her wounded hand.

"Then don't distract me," she snapped, fumbling for a bandage in the first aid kit.

But Jaxon caught her wrist. "Let me," he said.

He drew her in without waiting for permission, inspecting the wound with a critical eye. "Shouldn't need stitches," he said. Then, with almost unsettling gentleness, he dabbed away the blood, wrapping it tightly.

"Serafina is still refusing to let us collect any more blood," he said, his lip curling.

"Because he's recovering from almost dying," Araya said, snatching her hand back. The pain was nothing compared to the slow boil of frustration in her chest.

Jaxon hadn't let her anywhere near Loren since agreeing to Serafina's terms. Instead, he'd insisted on escorting the Healer himself, standing over her in silent judgement as she worked.

Serafina hadn't been pleased by that—but Jaxon made sure she was never truly alone with Araya either, lingering just close enough that they couldn't speak freely.

"He's been conscious for days," Jaxon said. "If Serafina would stop coddling him, we could actually move forward. It's not like he's doing much in there." He picked up a piece of scrap from the workbench, rolling it between his fingers. "Are you done stalling now?"

"I'm being thorough." Araya retorted, picking up another blank. "Like you said—no room for error."

A heavy silence settled between them as she adjusted the next setting, carefully controlling the slow siphon of aether into the blank. The pulse of magic steadied, soft and thrumming beneath her fingers. This one would hold.

She slid it across the workbench, joining the two completed sets. They were beautiful—perfect, even. Some of her best work. And yet, it felt like she'd carved something away from herself when she made them.

"You're trembling, Starling," Jaxon murmured. "Is something wrong?"

Everything. "Something is always wrong," she muttered, packing away her tools.

"Careful, Starling." Araya flinched, startled to find him right behind her. "I'm finding myself at the limits of what I'm willing to tolerate—even from you."

His hand wrapped around her hip, pinning her against the workbench.

"Go ahead and ask me the question you want to ask," he whispered, his breath tickling the sensitive ridge of scar tissue on her ear. "Ask me why I'm keeping you away from him."

Araya gritted her teeth, the edge of the workbench biting into her hips as Jaxon pressed against her back, not giving her room to turn in face him.

"Fine," she snapped. "Why won't you let me see him? You argued with the Arcanum for weeks for me to have access—"

"Because you made me." Jaxon's thumb traced lazy, circles over her hip, his breath hot on the back of her neck. "You ran to him—wept for him. Begged for him." His grip tightened. "How do you expect me to trust you alone with him after that?"

Araya twisted in Jaxon's grip, only managing to face him because he let her. "That's not fair."

He leaned in, invading her space. "Isn't it? Tell me, Starling—if I had been the one lying there, bleeding out, would you have held me the way you held him?"

"That's not—" Araya swallowed hard. "It wasn't like that."

Jaxon's lips curled into something that wasn't quite a smile. "No?"

"You know I can't lie," Araya protested. She shoved at his chest. "Let me go."

"Not out loud," Jaxon acknowledged. He tilted his head slightly, studying her like she was some kind of riddle he meant to solve. Finally he shrugged, releasing her. "The prince won't say a word about who nearly killed him—which means I can't have Hale sanctioned."

Araya braced herself against the workbench, her knees shaking as she hugged her arms around herself. "Why would he protect Hale?"

"Oh—he's protecting *someone*," Jaxon snorted, although there was no humor on his face. "But everyone he ever cared about is dead...unless it's someone new." His eyes lingered on her, dark and accusing.

"I haven't given him any reason to care about me," Araya protested.

Not wanting him to die a terrible and painful death didn't mean she *cared* for him—not like that. She'd dumped out her tea every night this week, desperate for even a glimpse of him—but Loren hadn't visited her dreams since Garrick's birthday. Whatever had linked them—if it had ever been real—was gone.

"I told you—" Her voice cracked, her heart pounding so hard against her ribs that it felt like it might burst. "You're the only man I've ever touched. The only man I've ever slept with. The only man I've ever—"

She caught herself too late, her breath hitching as she snapped her mouth shut on the word.

"Loved?" Jaxon finished for her, tilting his head curiously. "Do you love me, Starling?"

Araya's heart twisted. She hadn't meant to say it—hadn't even meant to think it. But it hung in the air between them now, impossible to take back.

"Yes." She choked on the confession. "Even now—when you question my loyalty every time I turn around."

For a fleeting moment, something flickered in his eyes—a shadow of the boy who had laughed with her, had promised her a future at his side. But that boy vanished in an instant, overshadowed by the cold, calculating stranger who stood before her now.

"That's sweet, Starling," he murmured. "But I don't need your love."

Araya caught her breath, dropping her hand as if burned. She blinked furiously, trying to hold back the tears welling in her eyes—but Jaxon saw them.

His thumb brushed across her cheek, catching the fat tear she couldn't stop with a tenderness at odds with the grim set of his expression.

"Don't take it personally, Starling." He cupped her chin, forcing her to meet his gaze. "Love doesn't change the world. But your loyalty? Your power? Those are the things we'll build our legacy on."

Araya swallowed against the ache in her throat, hating herself for wanting to lean into that touch.

"And what happens to me when you've gotten everything you need from me?" Her voice trembled, despite her best efforts to keep it steady.

"Is that what you're so worried about?" Jaxon's low voice curled around her like smoke, soft and suffocating. "That I'll cast you aside?"

He stepped forward, pressing his lips to her temple as he gathered her into his arms.

"Let me make something clear, Starling," he murmured. "No one —not the Arcanum and not some half-mad fae prince—will ever take you from me."

Araya's breath hitched, her pulse thundering in her ears. "And if I choose to leave?"

"You won't," Jaxon said, laughing.

Araya should have left it there—but hurt and anger made her foolish. "But if I did?"

"Then I'd find you and bring you back." Jaxon's fingers tangled in her hair, his grip tightening just enough to make her breath hitch. "And if you refused to come?"

He leaned in, his lips brushing the shell of her ear. "Then I would burn your world to the ground and take you from the ashes. You're mine, Starling. You always have been, and you always will be."

He paused, his breath hot against her skin. "Now—say it again."

Araya shuddered as her magic flared again at his command, rising unbidden like a pulse beneath her skin. Part of her wanted to spit in his face—to deny it and claw back some tiny shred of dignity. But her magic wouldn't let her lie—and maybe, in this moment, that was the cruelest thing of all.

"I love you," she whispered, her voice breaking like glass in her chest.

Shame burned beneath her ribs—shame at the relief she felt, knowing the lengths he would go to keep her. Maybe he didn't love her. But hadn't she told Serafina she didn't have the luxury of love? This wasn't about feelings. It was about survival. And even if he didn't love her, he chose her.

"And that's how I know you'll never leave me." Jaxon closed the distance between them, his hand tightening at the back of her neck as he claimed her mouth.

There was nothing tender about it—it was a declaration, a mark of ownership. His fingers dug into her flesh, but she couldn't pull away. Instead, her body leaned into his touch, answering to the connection between them like he hadn't just shattered her heart.

Araya was breathing hard when he finally pulled back, her whole body taut with a confusing blend of desire and panic. Jaxon smiled down at her, stroking his thumb along her jaw one more time before he finally stepped back, smoothing down his shirt like nothing had happened.

"Now," he said. "Let's get back to work."

———

Araya tugged on her gloves, her boots scraping against the uneven cobblestones as she led them toward Ravonfar. Jaxon hadn't even let them go home before dragging her out to test the amulets—but at least he'd listened when she told him to park the carriage a street away, well out of sight.

She'd hoped that leaving it behind would give them some anonymity. But Jaxon, as always, commanded attention. It wasn't just that he was human—it was the cut of his tailored coat, the way he walked with his head held high. He didn't need his name or a black carriage to mark him as powerful—he didn't even need to speak. He simply *was*.

There was nothing to be done about it now. They would just have to get through this as best they could. Araya shifted her bag to the other shoulder, pulling her identification papers from the front pocket of her cloak.

"Hood back," the guard barked, but he made no move to take the packet from her bandaged hand.

"I recognize that hair," he said instead, sneering. "There's no maternity clinic tonight, halfblood. You don't have authorization to be here without your little midwife friend. Unless you wanted to give up more power—"

"We're not here for a clinic." Jaxon pushed his own hood back, even though no one had asked him to. "Are you in the habit of imposing arbitrary restrictions on fae who wear the Arcanum's Eye?"

"I—" The guard stammered, glancing between them. "Since when do you wear an Eye?"

Araya hooked her thumb through the chain, pulling the distinctive amulet out from beneath her cloak.

"She was awarded it when she became my bond," Jaxon said, watching the guard squirm with a disinterested expression. "Which you'd have known—if you'd bothered to glance at her papers before you tried to take what belongs to me."

"And who are you?" The guard managed to recover some of his composure, flushing an impressive dark red as he straightened.

"Master Jaxon Shaw," he said pleasantly. "Commander for the

Arcanum. On official business under the authority of High Magister Garrick Shaw—my father." He let the words hang in the air, arching an eyebrow as he stared at the guard. "Do you need to write that down?"

The guard's mouth opened, then snapped shut as the color drained from his face. "N-no, sir. Of course not."

Araya hadn't meant to enjoy it, but she couldn't help the flicker of satisfaction as the man fumbled with the gate, the clang of metal against metal echoing through the silent street as he scrambled to unlock it. Last time, he'd drained her without a second thought, confident that neither she nor Serafina would dare report him. This time, he didn't even dare to look at her. Not with Jaxon standing at her shoulder.

"You know," Araya murmured once they were through the gate, her voice low enough that only Jaxon could hear. "You could have just given him your name and avoided the theatrics."

Jaxon's lips curved into a faint smirk. "But then you wouldn't have gotten to watch him scramble."

Araya laughed despite herself, and for a fleeting moment, it felt like they were *them* again—the way they used to be. Jaxon's smirk softened into a smile, his fingers sliding between hers as Araya brushed her thumb over the back of his hand, leaning into his warmth.

He'd come back for her. Fought for her. Defended her.

Because she was his. No one else got to take her power. No one else got to touch her—not unless he allowed it. He'd made that clear, over and over again.

This tension between them—it was just the project, the pressure of the Arcanum's oversight. Once this was over, they would go back to what they'd been. She just needed to endure it a little longer.

But the farther they walked, the more oppressive the silence became. Occasionally, Araya caught a glimpse of movement— nothing more than the twitch of a curtain or the flash of a shadow darting into an alley—but no one stepped out or even allowed themselves to be seen.

They were afraid. Not of her—but of the man beside her.

Jaxon strolled at an easy pace, surveying the desolate streets with the calculating confidence of a predator taking stock of its territory. He didn't seem bothered by their fear—if anything, he reveled in it, feeding something cold and sharp beneath his charming exterior.

"Are all of the fae districts like this?" he asked.

"Some are worse than others," Araya replied, her voice barely above a whisper. She tried to ignore the tension knotting in her stomach as they passed a boarded window where she could have sworn she'd seen eyes peeking out, watching them. "Ravonfar is closest to the Veil—the mist is blamed for a lot of the ills here."

"Which is exactly what we need," Jaxon said, his voice jarringly cheerful.

They walked the rest of the way in silence.

———

THE TEMPERATURE PLUMMETED AS THEY WALKED THROUGH THE EMPTY streets, and by the time black glass crunched under their boots, Araya could see her breath in the air. She shivered beneath her heavy cloak, picking a careful path across the shards to where the mist crept over the shoreline, clinging to the waves.

"Incredible," Jaxon breathed, staring out at the churning wall of darkness. "Look at the density—the motion. The mist must be blowing inland, which means it can be physically influenced—"

He dug into his bag, rummaging through it. "This has to be one of the points where it comes closest to the shore. The rate of dispersion here—" he emerged with a small brass instrument, kneeling to take a measurement. "If we could isolate this..."

He trailed off, eyes fixed on the churning dark beyond the shoreline. The excitement in his voice had shifted—brighter now, almost reverent. "Just imagine what we could learn."

Araya turned away, focusing on her own task. She unfolded the legs of her portable workbench, making sure it sat steady on the uneven, glass-littered ground. The cold bit at her hands even through her gloves, her bandaged palm throbbing with every motion—but she kept going, carefully arranging the boxes holding each amulet on it.

"Do you see how the shadows move along the surface of the water?" Jaxon asked, pulling her attention back to him. "It's almost like they're tethered—unable to break free entirely. And yet, here on the shore, they're more exploratory—and look, they like you."

Araya glanced down at the misty tendrils curling around her boots—the same way Loren's shadows had twined around her hands. "Maybe they're curious."

"They don't frighten you?" Jaxon tucked his pencil behind his ear. "You said they make fae sick."

"People *say* they make fae sick," Araya corrected. "There are a lot of problems here—poverty, poor living conditions, magic rationing suppressing fae immune systems...I doubt the mist is the whole of the story. Addressing it is only a first step if the Arcanum really intends to help the fae—"

"One thing at a time, Starling." Jaxon cut her off with a chuckle. "Let's tame the shadows first. Then you can save the world."

He stepped over to the portable workbench, removing the first of the amulets from its warded box. The silver housing gleamed faintly, cradling the bone disc Araya had painstakingly inscribed and then imbued with Loren's blood.

"It's beautiful work, Starling," he murmured, voice almost reverent. "Let's see if it's functional."

Araya stood frozen, her bandaged hand curled tightly in her cloak as he moved toward the edge of the obsidian shore. He held the amulet out toward the writhing mist, his focus narrowing as he channeled the magic she had sealed inside—Loren's magic.

The reaction was immediate. The shadows surged forward—then recoiled, hissing as the amulet flared. Mist twisted violently, the air thick with the rising hiss of a hundred voices whispering over each other, chaotic and sharp.

"It's responding," Jaxon said, his voice taut with excitement. "It's actually—"

The bone disc cracked. A clean fracture split it down the center, the pieces dropping from the blackened housing with a hiss of smoke.

"—working," Jaxon finished bitterly, his jaw tightening. He turned the shards over once, then flung them to the ground in disgust. "Give me the next one."

Araya fumbled the second amulet free, her gloves stiff with cold, fingers trembling as she passed it to him. Jaxon snatched it from her hands and turned back to the shore.

She held her breath as he activated it. The runes flared bright against the dark, their light sharp and clear. The mist surged again— then froze, held at bay. For a moment, it worked. The shadows writhed and twisted, slowing as if caught in a current they couldn't escape.

Then the amulet flared white hot, the scent of burning flesh cutting through the air.

"Damn it," Jaxon cursed, shaking his hand and flexing his fingers as a line of blistered flesh bloomed across his palm. "Give me the next—"

"You're burned," Araya said, tugging off her gloves to take his hand in hers. "Slow down, Jaxon. We don't have to race—"

"We have to show progress," he snapped, snatching his hand away. "And this? This isn't progress. It's a waste of time, bone, and blood."

"It's our first test," Araya said quietly. "We always knew there'd be variables. This was theoretical—"

"Just give me the last one, Araya." Jaxon exhaled sharply, dragging a hand through his hair as he stared out at the waves.

Araya bit her lip, opening the last warded case. But her hands, stiff from the cold, fumbled the amulet. She lunged to catch it without thinking, hissing in pain as blood welled through the bandage across her palm.

"*No*—" Araya gasped, staring in horror as her blood bloomed across the delicate etchings she'd spent days perfecting. The bone drank it in eagerly—mixing her essence with the aether they'd distilled from Loren's blood. Ruining it.

All that work, and she'd undone it with a single mistake.

"What did you do?" Jaxon demanded.

"I'm sorry—" Araya blurted, her voice shaking. "I can—I can imbue a new blank. I just need time—"

"No, Starling," Jaxon said, his voice shaking with excitement. "*Look*."

Araya looked up, catching her breath as she followed his gaze.

The shadows had stopped moving. The tendrils that had been writhing and surging just moments ago now swayed gently, every one of them turned toward *her*.

"It's your blood," Jaxon said, plucking the amulet from her hand. He stared down at it, his voice a mix of wonder and calculation. "You didn't ruin it, Starling. You *fixed* it."

"But that doesn't make any sense," Araya protested. "It's not—no, Jaxon, wait—"

Araya reached out, but Jaxon was already channeling power into the amulet. The runes flared to life, brighter than they had with any of the previous tests. The tendrils of shadow shifted, curling toward Jaxon as if drawn to him. He raised his hand, and the shadows responded instantly, coiling around his arm in a sinuous, controlled motion.

He moved his hand experimentally, and the shadows followed his commands, twisting and writhing in perfect sync with his gestures. He laughed, his delight palpable as he turned to Araya, his dark eyes gleaming.

"Do you see this, Starling?" he asked, his voice brimming with exhilaration. "It's responding—obeying. We've done it."

Araya watched him, her chest tight with dread as the shadows swirled around him. "Are you going to dispel them now?"

"Dispel them?" Jaxon asked absently, his gaze never wavering from the swirling shadows swirling.

"For the fae here," Araya said. "Remember?"

Jaxon blinked, his gaze finally lifting to hers. "Starling—"

But the runes on the amulet sputtered, the entire thing emitting a faint whine as they went out one by one. The shadows fell away, spreading back out into their natural pattern as Jaxon's influence over them vanished.

"Damn." Jaxon sighed, staring down at the depleted amulet. "That wasn't very long at all."

"We knew it wouldn't be." Araya wrapped her arms around herself, fighting the sting in her throat. "That's why you should have dispelled them immediately—"

He glanced at her, puzzled, then gave a soft huff of laughter. "Why waste it on scraps?" he said. "We can make more—and better ones. With whole bone next time, not just blanks."

"But—" Araya started to protest, but Jaxon kept talking over her.

"And now we know it works." Jaxon held up the cracked amulet, staring at it with open awe. "Your blood changes the reaction. That kind of resonance? It opens up at least a dozen new configurations. I need to test more combinations—your aether, Loren's blood, maybe even direct contact with the shadows—"

"You're not hearing me," Araya said, a chill rolling down her spine. "The people here—they *need* the Arcanum to help them—"

"And we will." Jaxon turned to her fully now, the edge of frustration sharpening his smile. "Once we've perfected it—not before." He reached for her, tilting her chin up to meet his gaze. "This is bigger than Ravonfar, Starling. We made progress here tonight. *Real* progress. With Loren's blood—and yours—we're one step closer to controlling the Shadowed Veil. You're as important as he is now—maybe even more so."

Araya caught her breath. She had no doubt Jaxon meant the

words as a praise—she should have felt honored, validated...but after seeing what had happened to Loren? It felt more like a warning.

"We're going to change everything, Starling." Jaxon's smile widened as he stepped closer, cupping her face in his hands and pressing a kiss to her parted lips. "You and me—together. No one will be able to stop us."

Araya forced a tight smile. "Together," she echoed, willing herself to believe it.

TWENTY-THREE

"They didn't just react—they *pulled* toward you, like your blood was some sort of key." Jaxon gestured animatedly as he spoke, not seeming to notice that Araya hadn't said a word since he helped her into the carriage. "In all my research, no accounts ever mentioned something like that—"

Araya pressed her forehead to the cool glass, watching the city blur past as the carriage rattled over the cobblestones. Her hand throbbed where the shard of bone had sliced her—a mirror of the cut she'd gotten on that same beach with her mother so many years ago. The shadows had been there then, too. Her mother had hoped the humans wouldn't chase them onto the beach because of them...but she had been wrong.

"—like there's some sort of a link between you—"

"What?" Araya straightened, her focus snapping to Jaxon.

"There's something between the two of you," Jaxon insisted. "Don't bother denying it. It explains everything. Why you've been so reluctant to do what needs to be done when it comes to him, why you're always defending him—but none of it is your fault, Starling. It's just instinct."

"Instinct," Araya echoed, the word bitter on her tongue. "I don't think so, Jaxon. What could a halfblood fae possibly have in common with a prince?"

"It wouldn't be the first time a king strayed, Starling."

"You think we're *related*?" Araya stared at him. "My mother was fae—"

"That's what you remember, anyway." Jaxon shrugged. "You were quite young. I'll have to dig into your records to try and figure it out. But imagine it—what if *you* could claim the shadows? You'd be a weapon that could change the balance of power entirely—"

Araya caught her breath. "But you said you'd dispel the shadows," she protested. "The fae in the districts—"

"I know what I said," Jaxon snapped. "But this is a *war*, Araya. Just because you don't see it being fought here doesn't mean it isn't killing people—humans *and* fae. What if we could apply this to the Eldergreen? If we win there, we help everyone. Not just the fae in Ravonfar."

The walls of the carriage seemed to close in around her, the scent of vanilla and burning aether slowly suffocating her. Jaxon's voice hummed in the background, smooth and enthusiastic, as though he hadn't just dismissed the fae as casualties of progress. She glanced back out the window, fighting the bile rising in her throat.

But his words found her anyway, curling around her like a vice. "We're so close, Starling," he said, his tone almost gentle. "Imagine what we could do if we harnessed that power. The possibilities..."

She clenched her jaw, her nails biting into the fabric of her dress. *At what cost?* The question burned on the tip of her tongue, but she swallowed it down, knowing it wouldn't matter. Jaxon had already made his decision.

Araya looked away, unable to bear the ruthlessness in his gaze. It wasn't just indifference to the fae in Ravonfar—it was an unflinching conviction that any cost was worth it, that any life was expendable if it meant achieving his goals. Her hands were shaking now, her bag trembling in her lap. She needed to get out of this carriage, away from Jaxon's suffocating presence, away from the weight of what she had unleashed on the world.

She clenched her jaw as the carriage approached their building, tracing the outline of the case holding the amulets through the fabric of her bag. "You should go in," she said. "These really need to be stored in the dungeon workshop. I can have the carriage take me back—"

"Absolutely not." Jaxon shook his head. "That amulet stays with one of us at all times. Hale already got in there once—I'm not giving him a chance to take this away from us."

Araya's heart sank as the carriage lurched to a stop. She had no choice but to follow him, to step out into the cold night air and walk up the steps to their apartment.

She wanted to flee, to lock herself in some small, safe room and press her back against the door until her mind finally quieted. She wanted to flee. To lock herself in some small, safe room and press her back against the door until her thoughts finally quieted. But Jaxon was watching, so she simply slipped off her boots and nudged them into place by the door.

"Lock those in my office," he said, stepping out of his own boots.

Araya crossed the apartment, her hands shaking as she tucked her kit into the safe, sealing its contents away behind the warded iron.

She straightened, turning to find Jaxon leaning against the doorframe, arms crossed. His smile was soft—but it didn't reach his eyes.

Before she could step away, he crossed the room in three easy strides and slid an arm around her waist. She stiffened, instinctively trying to step back—but he lifted her effortlessly and set her on the edge of his desk.

"Jaxon—" she caught her breath, heat flushing across her skin. "I'm tired. I just want to go to sleep."

"This will only take a moment," he murmured, brushing a strand of hair from her cheek.

That's when she saw her bloodletting kit in his other hand.

"Jaxon..." she protested, her voice faltering.

"It's just a little blood," he said soothingly. He opened her kit, spreading out her supplies beside her on the desk. "We can only take so much at once—with the time it takes to distill it...well, it only makes sense to start now, doesn't it?"

She opened her mouth to protest again, but he tightened the tourniquet around her arm, already moving on.

"Tomorrow, I'll look into your history," he said absently, his focus on her arm. "The Arcanum reviewed them before they approved our bond, of course. But maybe they missed something—"

He tapped her arm, searching for the vein. She flinched as the needle slid in—a sharp sting, followed by a slow, pulsing ache. His other hand settled on her knee, grounding her—or maybe he was trapping her. Araya wasn't sure. Not anymore.

"You're special, Starling," he murmured, staring at her dark blood flowing into the vial. "More special than either of us realized."

Araya stared at the edge of the desk, her eyes stinging as she blinked hard. She couldn't look at him—at the blood, at what he was taking from her.

"There," Jaxon said at last, removing the needle with brisk efficiency. "See? That didn't take long at all."

Araya stared down at her blood, neatly collected into vials and tucked into the velvet-lined case. "You didn't ask."

Jaxon blinked, glancing up from packing away the vials, his hand lingering on the case as he stared at her with a look that was almost amused. "Didn't ask?" he repeated, like the concept was foreign to him.

"I told you I was tired," Araya said, her voice gaining strength. She raised her eyes to his. "But you ignored me—"

"I didn't ignore you." His amusement slipped, replaced by a shadow of irritation. "I explained why this is so important—"

"That's not enough!" Araya snapped, her voice rising even as Jaxon's smile disappeared entirely, his expression darkening. "You didn't think about what I wanted—what I needed. You just *took* whatever you wanted."

"You don't speak to me like that." Jaxon's hand shot out, closing around her wrist with bruising force. "Ever."

Araya flinched, wincing as she tried to pull away. "Jaxon—you're hurting me."

"I'm hurting you?" He laughed in her face. "Have you forgotten, Starling? You're *mine*. And so is your blood and your magic. I don't have to *ask* for what I already own."

He wrenched her arm behind her back, slamming her onto the desk hard enough that her ears rang from the impact. She struggled, but pain lanced through her hips as he pinned her hard against the edge of the desk.

"This—this is *nothing*, Starling." He leaned in, his breath hot on the back of her neck. "I could make this apartment your whole world. No more work. No more errands. No more distractions. Just you, me, and the child we both know you'll give me growing inside you."

Araya's vision swam, tears falling freely as Jaxon pressed her into the unforgiving wood. His grip tightened, the bones in her wrist grinding together as he twisted her arm harder, making her shoulder scream.

"So what do you say, Starling?" Jaxon purred, his voice dripping with mockery and power. "Are you going to behave? Or do we need to call Kai to remove your *ta'nara* rune?" He chuckled softly. "You'd still be better off than any unbonded fae female. Isn't that what you've always wanted? Safety?"

Araya yelped as Jaxon's grip shifted, pinning her forearm to the desk beside her face. But her panic didn't spike until he shifted her hand to expose the *ly'ithra* rune inked at the base of her thumb.

"Jaxon," she started, her voice shaking as she tried to pull her arm away from him. But he only tightened his grip, pressing more of his weight onto her back until the room spun around her and she saw stars.

"Don't fight me," he warned. "I hate hurting you, Starling. Don't make it worse."

Araya's tears spilled over, fear curdling into hopelessness as she realized there was no escape. She closed her eyes, her body trembling as she waited for the inevitable. Pain and terror twisted together in her mind, a whirlwind of agony that left her gasping for breath, yet a single, desperate thought clawed its way to the surface—*survive*.

Then Jaxon's power surged into her like a thousand iron-tipped needles. Her vision blurred as her magic—already rising to meet him like a lover—recoiled at the violent assault, fleeing to some deep place inside of her. But Jaxon followed it—dragging it from her as she gasped in silent agony. The absence left her hollow, a puppet with its strings cut. She couldn't even scream.

It was brutal. It was excruciating. It was relentless. And she could not stop him.

Araya's scream lodged in her throat, only a choked sob escaping as her power fled her at his command. Her body trembled, each shuddering breath a battle against the darkness creeping at the edges of her vision. She was slipping, her strength draining away like sand through her fingers.

"You're mine to use as I see fit, Starling," he murmured in her ear. "Magic, mind, and body. That means if I want your magic, you will not fight me. If I want your blood, you'll roll up your sleeve and offer your arm with a smile. And if I want to take you against the wall of that filthy cell where the heir to the fae throne can watch? You will spread your legs and show him exactly who you belong to."

He released her, letting her collapse onto the floor behind his desk. With a monumental effort, she forced her eyes open, the room spinning around her. She tried to push herself up, but her arms gave out, and she collapsed back onto the floor, a pained whimper escaping her lips.

Jaxon clicked his tongue in disapproval. "Pathetic," he muttered, before crouching down beside her. His hand gripped her chin, tilting her head up so she had no choice but to look at him. "Remember this feeling," he said, his grip on her face hard and cruel. "You stand beside me because I allow it, Starling. But your place? That's on the floor by my feet. Don't forget again."

Araya listened to his footsteps cross the room, flinching as he slammed the door and plunged the office into silence.

CHAPTER
TWENTY-FOUR

The damp chill of the dungeon was as familiar as his own skin. The rough stone walls. The muted clang of distant footsteps. The lingering taste of iron in his mouth.

He'd thought Hale had killed him—that this was finally over. But Jaxon's Healer had pulled him back from the brink, slowly and painfully knitting his flesh back together and forcing his body to recover. Her magic numbed his body, the tonic she forced down his throat softening the edges of his mind. It dulled everything—even his slow, creeping awareness of the shadows that slipped back out of the corners once she and Jaxon left. They whispered urgently, but the only thing Loren could understand was *her* name.

Araya. They said it over and over again, their voices rising to a frenzied pitch.

He hadn't seen her—not in his cell, not in his dreams—since Hale had torn him from her mind. It should have been a relief. But fear tightened around his throat like a noose. He had no way to know if Hale had gotten to her too. No way to know if she was safe.

He fought the sedative, trying to stay conscious as his vision blurred and the world dulled around him. He couldn't help her like this—but exhaustion rushed over him, dragging him under like a dark tide.

But then—*fear*. Not his. Hers—*Araya*.

Araya was *terrified*.

Loren's body jerked. He was useless in the waking world, but somewhere deep in his mind—something cracked open. Shadows surged forward, rushing into the gap as he latched on to her fear, cutting a path through the numbing weight pushing down on him. It was a beacon, dragging him steadily through the chaotic, fragmented jumble of their minds.

The dreamscape was fragmented—one moment, there was nothing but darkness. The next, he felt hands on him. The sharp bite of a hard surface against soft skin, the salty taste of tears. Her fear. Her memories.

The shadows lashed outward, trying to rip through the shifting dream and pull her toward him. But the dream fought him—her fear spiking, then pulling away like a string unraveling faster than he could catch it.

Loren clenched his fists, forcing himself to focus. He had to reach her. He had to—

The dreamscape lurched.

And then, suddenly, Araya was in his arms.

"*Ael'sura*," he choked out, clutching her like she might disappear again. She clung to him with the same desperation, her tears soaking into his shoulder as the dream flickered and reshaped itself around them over and over again.

But Loren wasn't watching their surroundings. He was looking at her. At the bruises blooming dark on the delicate skin of her arms. At the bleeding gash along her hairline. Her cheekbone was swollen, the skin there bruised and tender.

Someone had struck her—hard. Loren could feel the echoes of what had been done to her through the tether between them. Her helplessness. Her fear and pain.

"Who did this to you?" His voice came out rough, almost unrecognizable. "Was it Hale?"

Araya sucked in a breath, but she didn't answer. Her pulse was too fast, her shoulders too tense as the dream twisted, dragging her back toward whatever nightmare she was reliving.

"*Araya.*" Loren's hands found her shoulders, trying to anchor her here with him. "*Who. Did. This.*"

She blinked, her gaze refocusing on him as his words cut through the panic gripping her. She sucked in a trembling breath, and for a moment Loren didn't think she was going to answer.

But then—she did.

"Jaxon."

Loren froze.

But the shadows did not. They surged outward, snapping violently, coiling like a living storm. And for a single, terrible moment, Loren thought he might lose himself to the fury twisting inside him. Rage burned in his chest, a wildfire he had no will to contain.

It was only the shock and fear in Araya's silver eyes that made him let her go, allowing her to step back as he fought for control. The shadows didn't though, clinging to her like a mantle of darkness— holding her when he couldn't.

"You said he would never hurt you," Loren said when he could speak again, the words scraping from his throat.

"It—It was my fault," Araya stammered. She dropped her gaze, staring down at her feet. "He—I forgot my place."

"Your place," Loren repeated, his rage cooling, hardening into something sharper. "And where exactly is that?"

He didn't move towards her, but the shadows didn't have his restraint. They twined around her ankles, shifting and coiling as they dragged over her skin.

"It doesn't matter." Shame flickered across her face, but she pulled in a deep breath, steadying herself. "I'm more worried about you. The last time I saw you..." She trailed off, her face haunted. "Why won't you tell Jaxon it was Hale?"

Loren's jaw tightened so hard he felt pain shoot up his temples. The shadows abandoned her, snapping back to his side and wrapping around him like armor. She had known—and she still hadn't come.

"If you really wanted to know how I was recovering, you could have skipped your tea one night and checked for yourself," he bit out.

"What?" Araya faltered, confusion flashing across her face at his accusation. "I haven't had my tea in over a week—I've been *waiting* for you. Jaxon won't let me come in person after how I...reacted. When I found you. But I've been actively trying to find you in my dreams."

How she had *reacted?* Loren couldn't let himself get distracted by that. What she was saying didn't make any sense. It shouldn't have been *hard* for them to reach each other. Not when fate itself wanted them together—

"Serafina," Araya said suddenly. "Your Healer. She's the one who recommended the tea to me. I told her about the dreams. If she's drugging you—"

"You told Jaxon's Healer about the dreams?" Loren hissed. "What part of *don't tell anyone* was unclear?"

"The part where you have any sort of authority over me," Araya snapped, glaring back at him. "And she isn't *Jaxon's* Healer—she's *my* friend. I'm the one who begged Jaxon to let her help you, because I didn't want you to *die*."

She clenched her fists, staring at him. "She figured something out when I told her. If the two of you expect me to keep this a secret, you have to tell me *why*."

Loren stiffened, the shadows twitching around him. "She didn't tell you?"

"No." Araya crossed her arms, scowling. "She said you were right and that we couldn't talk about it there—and Jaxon hasn't let me see *her* either. And now he's convinced there's some sort of connection between *us*. He's throwing around some sort of insane theory that we're related—"

Loren's stomach dropped. Even the shadows stilled, frozen in panic.

"But we're not—" Araya's voice faltered at his reaction. "Right?"

"We're not related," Loren confirmed hoarsely. "Why would he think that we are?"

Araya hesitated, but something about the look on his face must have convinced her to continue.

"We tested the first round of amulets tonight," she said. "To see if imbuing an amulet with your blood would allow us to dispel the shadows."

She paused, her gaze flicking past him to watch the shadows that swirled at the periphery of the dream.

"Two of them failed, but the third..." she took a deep breath. "I cut my hand—and when my blood combined with yours...the shadows responded."

"What did they do?" Loren asked, already dreading the answer.

"They...stopped. Like they were waiting for me to do something." Araya rubbed her injured wrist absently, tracing the bruised skin with her fingertips. "But when Jaxon took it..." Her voice dropped, hushed with fear. "He could command them."

"He commanded them?" Loren's pulse stumbled, then pounded. The dream quivered at the edges, alive with writhing shadows.

"With an amulet imbued with our combined blood." Araya nodded. "That's why he thinks we're linked in some way. He's convinced I'll be able to wield them like some sort of weapon—I tried to protest, but..." she gestured toward her face. "He didn't take that very well."

Loren swore viciously, his shadows surging as he turned away for a moment, raking a hand through his hair. But he couldn't stand her being out of his sight so he turned back around almost immediately, staring at her with a desperation that scared even him.

"Are you safe?"

"He left the apartment," Araya said, her voice quiet. "I'm alone there. For now at least." She shivered, cradling her injured wrist against her body.

Loren tracked the motion, his shadows twisting tightly around him. "Good," he said, but his voice cracked, the single word strained. His hands clenched at his sides, and for a moment he feared he might shatter into a thousand pieces like the dream around them.

"You have to convince him there's no link," Loren said, forcing the words out even as the bond screamed in his chest. "Whatever it takes—make him think it's a dead end. Distract him—whatever you have to do. But *convince him.*"

"But there obviously is some sort of link—" Araya started, but Loren caught her hand in his, stopping her.

She didn't jerk away from him. Her fingers curled around his, grounding him, anchoring him. Loren longed to keep her here. Just for a moment. Just long enough to feel something other than the weight of inevitability pressing down on him.

But that wasn't a choice he could afford. His fingers slipped from hers. He forced himself to step back.

"You can't come back here, *ael'sura.*" The words burned like acid. The bond recoiled, twisting inside him, dragging him toward her even as he fought to push her away. "You can't see me again. Stay away from the dungeon. Drink your tea—and try to have a happy life. However you can."

His voice broke slightly, a flicker of vulnerability breaking through his stoic mask. "But if you care about surviving—you have to stay away from me."

"If I'm in danger I deserve to know why." Araya stepped towards him, trying to close the distance between them again. "What are you so afraid of, Loren?"

He could only smile sadly. There was nothing he could tell her. He had no answer she would accept. No truth that wouldn't tear them both apart.

"Tell me," she pleaded, her voice breaking.

She took another step—but the dream buckled, the nonexistent ground lurching under their feet like something alive. She stumbled, but Loren didn't move to meet her this time, his shadows curling around him like a shield. He forced a smile, but it felt desperately hollow.

"It doesn't matter," he said softly. "Go, *ael'sura*. And whatever you have to do—stay safe."

The dream crumbled, but her silver eyes—wide with confusion and bright with heartbreak—were the last thing to fade.

And when she was gone, there was nothing.

TWENTY-FIVE

The world came back to her in fragments. Pain first—a dull pulse behind her temples. A deeper ache sinking into her hips and wrists. Araya whimpered as the silk sheets scraped against her raw skin, the cloying scent of vanilla choking her.

She was in bed—in Jaxon's bed.

She jerked upright, pain splitting her skull with flashes of memory that left her gasping for breath. His hands pinning her down, the crack of her wrist as she fought to free herself, the moment her body betrayed her and went still, panic driving her to flee before her mind could catch up. Her stomach heaved, the room swaying around her as she clawed her way free of the sheets.

She'd barely reached the basin when her knees gave out, her stomach twisting violently. She gagged, her body convulsing as sickness tore through her in relentless waves. Each heave sent fresh agony jolting through her aching joints, bruises burning hot where he'd held her down as cold sweat rolled down her spine.

When it finally passed, Araya sagged against the cool porcelain, her forehead pressed to the rim of the basin as she fought to steady her breathing. The shaking wouldn't stop—whether from exhaustion, pain, or the lingering nausea twisting in her gut, she didn't know. Her arms felt boneless, too heavy to lift, and her knees throbbed where they'd hit the tile.

She still wore yesterday's shift—the thin linen clung to her skin, sour with sweat and vomit. Her overdress lay crumpled on the floor where she must have shed it, but she didn't remember undressing. She didn't remember climbing into bed, or anything at all after Jaxon had left her broken on the floor of his office.

This was worse than last time. So much worse.

When Jaxon had drained her all those months ago, he'd left her with enough power that she could stand. Speak. She'd been weak and tired—but not broken. Not curled up on the cold tile, too sick to scream and too weak to run.

Gritting her teeth, Araya reached for her magic—part of her still unable to believe that Jaxon would have left her defenseless. There had to be some spark left—

But where her magic should have sat, Araya found nothing but an aching void. There was nothing left inside her to reach for—no warmth curling in her chest, no lifeline. Only a vast, terrible emptiness.

Araya shuddered, her stomach cramping again even though there she had nothing left to purge. This went beyond depletion—it was devastation. Jaxon hadn't just taken too much. He'd taken *everything*.

She braced a hand against the floor to push herself up, but the room spun around her. Araya dropped back to the floor, clenching her jaw and squeezing her eyes shut. Her skull throbbed with every heartbeat, a dull, relentless pulse behind her eyes. Bruises bloomed along her arms, the imprint of his fingers biting into her flesh, and pain flared through her pelvis each time she shifted, her hips aching and bruised where he'd held her down.

Araya forced herself to breathe through it, sucking in sharp breaths through her nose as she willed herself to stay conscious. She had to pull herself together, to figure out what she was going to do before he—

"Gods, Starling."

Araya flinched, her breath catching in her throat as Jaxon loomed over her. Every instinct screamed at her to stay still and quiet—to not do anything to provoke him. But the survival instinct that had kept her alive all these years was at war with something else now—the raw, burning humiliation that he was seeing her like this, broken and weak.

Jaxon crouched beside her, his expression unreadable—though something dangerously close to regret flickered in his eyes. He reached out, his fingers brushing the cut along her hairline before she could react.

Pain flared behind her eyes, blinding her. Her stomach twisted again, a fresh wave of nausea leaving her bent over the bowl. But she had nothing left to come up, her shoulders shaking with violent, useless convulsions that left her breathing ragged and her skin clammy.

A hand steadied her, slipping around her waist when she had finally finished.

"Easy," Jaxon murmured. "Let me see."

He eased her back until she was sitting on the floor, her pulse thundering in her ears. He studied her for a long, silent moment, his brown eyes sharp as he took in the bruises, her raw skin, how she couldn't stop shaking.

Finally, he sighed. Before she could react, his hands were on her again. He hooked an arm around her waist, lifting her effortlessly, ignoring the way she hissed in pain. Her stomach heaved violently, nausea still gnawing at her, but she bit down hard on her lip to keep from retching again.

"Jaxon—"

He didn't answer, just adjusted his grip, maneuvering her out of the bathing chamber and depositing her on the edge of the bed like she was something fragile—a delicate possession in desperate need of repair.

"I don't have time for this," he muttered, throwing open her wardrobe. He selected a simple, dark dress, dropping it on the bed beside her before grabbing the hem of her shift and stripping it off over her head in one smooth motion.

Araya sucked in a sharp breath as cold air licked over her bruised skin, her arms reflexively curling around herself in a feeble attempt to shield what little dignity she had left.

Jaxon sighed, clicking his tongue at her. "You're acting like I haven't already claimed every inch of you." His fingers curled around her wrists, prying them away with a patient force that was somehow even more terrifying than his rage had been. But all he did was drag the fresh dress on over her head, guiding her arms into the sleeves.

Araya shuddered, tears pouring freely down her face as he smoothed the fabric over her shoulders, fastening the buttons like she couldn't be trusted to do it properly. Maybe she couldn't. Her head spun, her body trying to drag her back down into the numb relief of unconsciousness.

His thumb lingered on one of the deep purple bruises marring her forearm—the shape of his fingers, branded into her skin. "I have to go to the Aetherium," he said, straightening. "You're in no condition to come—I'm going to arrange for a carriage and a guard to take you to Serafina's clinic."

Araya blinked, wondering if she'd heard him correctly. *Serafina*—the name sparked a flicker of hope, faint but stubborn beneath the fog of pain and exhaustion. But—

"I don't need a guard," she rasped.

"That's not your call, Starling." Jaxon raised his eyebrows like she'd said something amusing. "You're too important to risk now."

He sighed, gliding his fingers down her throat. "If the shadows answer to your blood, you matter just as much as Loren now. Maybe more."

Araya shivered, a chill skittering down her spine as his hand tightened around her throat. He studied her for a moment, like he was counting each terrified beat of her heart under his hand.

"You can't take risks anymore," he continued, his words wrapping around her like silk. "It's for your own good, of course. You're too valuable to be left to your own devices. We wouldn't want anything to happen to you."

He leaned in, his lips brushing the shell of her ear. "Do you know how many fae would beg for the protection you have?" His fingers traced over her skin, threateningly gentle. "Anyone else would be rotting in a cell right next to the prince. But not you."

A cell next to Loren. No sunlight. No escape. Just the cold bite of iron against her skin.

They wouldn't just take her magic and her blood—they'd carve her into pieces. And when she finally died, they'd take her bones too, cataloguing every part before using her up completely.

The threat curdled in her stomach, thick and suffocating. Her vision narrowed to a pinprick, and Araya swayed where she sat as the world shifted around her. She wasn't in Jaxon's room anymore—she was at Kaldrath, screaming while they held her down and carved into her flesh with iron.

She'd rather die.

Whatever Jaxon saw on her face, it must have pleased him. He smiled down at her. "I don't want that for you," he said. "But if you fight me again...if you do anything that makes this harder than it has to be...it may be out of my hands."

He wouldn't have to lift a finger. If he just said the word, the Arcanum would leap at the chance to do the rest. Araya forced herself to nod, clenching her fingers around the fabric of the dress he'd chosen for her.

"Good," Jaxon said with a satisfied smile. "Let's get moving, then."

Araya barely curbed the instinct to flinch when he reached for her, pulling her to her feet. She had to be perfect for him. Even if his touch burned against her skin and every instinct screamed at her to run.

Because there was nowhere far enough that Jaxon wouldn't find her, that he wouldn't drag her back. There was no escape for her—not from this.

So she let him lead her to the door, leaning against the wall as he shoved her feet into her boots and laced them before sweeping her cloak over her shoulders, fastening it at her throat. Finally, he lifted the hood, covering the last of her bruises. Hiding what he'd done.

"You'll be good for me, won't you?" Jaxon asked, tucking a loose strand of hair into her hood.

"Yes, Jaxon," Araya whispered.

"That's my Starling." His fingers trailed down her spine, a gentle, possessive touch, before settling at the small of her back.

"You'll see," he said, his voice a silken promise as he led them out the door. "It will all work out in the end."

———

A GRIM-FACED GUARD RODE IN THE CARRIAGE WITH HER, WATCHING FROM the opposite bench with surly intensity. But Araya couldn't bring herself to care. She leaned against the window, her mind drifting as the wheels rumbled over the cobblestones.

He grabbed her by the arm before the carriage had even fully stopped at the back of Serafina's clinic, ignoring her weak protest. When she tried to tell him patients had to enter through the front, he gave her a vicious shake, jarring her already aching joints and cutting off whatever words she'd meant to say.

"She needs a private room," he said, wedging his boot in the door like he expected the confused apprentice who'd answered his pounding to slam it in his face.

"We don't have private—"

"For her you do," he said, shoving past the woman. He dragged

Araya with him, his grip on her arm the only thing keeping her upright.

They ended up in the cramped storeroom where Serafina kept supplies. The space was cluttered—boxes stacked high, jars and bundles crowding the shelves—but there was a spare cot in the corner. The apprentice shoved the boxes off it in a hurry, clearing just enough space for Araya to collapse onto the thin mattress with a pained groan.

"What happened—" the Healer tried to ask, but the guard shook his head brusquely.

"Master Shaw said *only* Serafina Hart is to treat her," he said, scowling at the woman.

The Healer hesitated, but then her eyes darted to Araya—bruised, trembling, barely upright—and whatever protest she might have made died before it reached her lips. With a final glance, she turned and hurried down the hall.

Araya barely noticed. The room swayed, nausea churning beneath her ribs. She dropped her head back against the thin mattress, her breath coming in slow, uneven pulls. Was Serafina even here? Or would they have to send for her—

The door slammed open.

Serafina stormed in, her cheeks flushed from cold and fury. "Get out," she ordered the guard.

He didn't budge. "Master Shaw said she wasn't to be left alone."

"Does it look like she's alone?" Serafina snapped. "And I don't give a *damn* what Jaxon wants—this is *my* clinic and if she's here she's *my* patient."

"He gave me a direct order—"

"I don't care," Serafina said, her voice deadly. "Wait outside. And I don't mean outside this room—get out of my clinic, or so help me, I'll drag you into the street myself and *you* can explain to Jaxon that she didn't get the care she so desperately needs because you were busy arguing with me."

His jaw flexed, and for a moment, Araya thought he might refuse.

But Serafina stared him down, her green eyes blazing as she crossed her arms and set her feet, making it clear she would do nothing until she got her way.

"It's your head if anything happens," he said finally.

The moment the door slammed behind him, Serafina dropped to her knees beside the cot. Her cool fingers cradled Araya's wrist, taking her pulse before gently brushing her hair back from the cut on her head.

"Araya," she said, her voice wavering. "Look at me. Was he the one who did this?"

Serafina wasn't talking about the guard. Araya forced her eyes open, her vision still unfocused, her body too weak to do much more than nod.

"Gods." Serafina's expression cracked. She stood, turning to the hovering apprentice. "Bring warm water. Compresses. Get me the tonic for magic depletion—the concentrated one." A pause. "Yes I'm sure. And bring the numbing salve too."

Footsteps hurried out of the room.

Araya tried to focus on Serafina, struggling against the pull of exhaustion. She had so many questions—and this might be her only chance to ask. She needed to know why she kept finding herself in Loren's dreams, why he was so insistent that she stay away from him. But she couldn't make her mouth move, her tongue too heavy to form the words she needed as the room blurred around her.

"Araya—" Serafina leaned forward, her brow furrowing. "I need you to stay awake—"

But Araya was already slipping under, Loren's name the last thing echoing through her mind.

ARAYA WOKE TO THE SHARP SCENT OF HERBS AND ANTISEPTIC, HER MOUTH dry and her head pounding. But at least she could think again. Her fingers twitched against the rough sheets, brushing against something solid and warm—Serafina's hand. Her friend sat beside her, silent and still. A deep furrow lined her brow, worry etched into every tense muscle of her face as she cradled Araya's hand in hers, staring at nothing.

Araya swallowed past the tightness in her throat, embarrassment warring with gratitude. She hated being seen like this—but even at her worst, Serafina had always cared for her. Had sat beside her and held her hand, even when they'd barely known each other.

Araya squeezed her fingers gently.

Serafina startled, her lips parting as relief flooded her face. "How do you feel?"

Araya licked her cracked lips. "Terrible."

Serafina huffed softly, but her face—always so composed and calm—was still tight with worry. "I need you to tell me what happened."

"There's not much to tell." Araya said, her voice raw. "I questioned him—he slammed me into a desk."

Serafina's breath hitched. Her grip on Araya's hand turned vice-like before she forced it to loosen again, her nostrils flaring. But when she spoke, it was with the familiar edge of clinical detachment she used with all of her patients.

"You had a concussion. A sprained wrist—numerous contusions." But her clipped, professional tone wavered, her mask cracking as she asked, "Are you hurt anywhere...else?"

"No—" Araya shook her head, wincing as the movement pulled at stitches they must have put in while she slept. "He didn't. He siphoned my magic and left right after—I don't think he came back to the apartment until he woke me up this morning. Then he had the guard bring me straight here."

"He siphoned your magic and then left you to sleep all night unsupervised with a head injury?" Serafina's lips thinned as she lost the fight to keep her expression neutral. "You don't have enough aether left to blow out a candle—he could have killed you."

Araya looked down, unable to hold Serafina's gaze. "I know."

Serafina exhaled slowly. For a moment, neither of them said anything.

"I treated the physical injuries," she said at last. "But there's no quick cure for being drained that completely. You're going to struggle —mind and body. But I can't keep you sedated with the head injury —it's too dangerous."

"Is that what you're doing to Loren? Sedating him?"

Serafina stiffened, all but confirming it.

"Your dosage was off last time," Araya said, pulling her hand away. "Because I saw him last night."

"That was more likely a reaction to your pain and fear than an issue with my dosage," Serafina said. This time, she was the one who couldn't meet Araya's eyes.

Araya pushed herself upright—and instantly regretted it. White-hot pain flared through her joints, radiating like fire with every breath. Her vision swam, black spots creeping in at the edges, but she clenched her jaw and forced herself to focus.

"I want to know what the two of you are hiding from me," she said. "I deserve to know instead of being forced to blunder around in the dark."

Serafina's shoulders tensed, but she said nothing, her expression hardening into an unreadable mask.

"Jaxon is already digging," Araya pushed. "Loren might think I can distract him, but you *know* Jaxon, Serafina. He never lets go of a puzzle. Give me the chance to figure it out first so I can control the damage—*please*."

Serafina bit her lip, staring at Araya for a long moment.

"You're right." She sighed, her hands twisting in her lap. "You do deserve to know—but I'm not the one who should tell you." She stood, smoothing her robes. "Can you walk?"

"Walk?" Araya blinked, frowning. "To go where? The guard—"

"They're watching the front and back," Serafina confirmed. "But we forced them to wait outside—they won't even know you're gone." She held Araya's gaze. "If you're willing to take the risk…I can get you your answers."

Araya hesitated. If Jaxon found out she left, Gods only knew what he'd do to her. Were answers worth risking that?

"I need to be back before they check," Araya said finally, swinging her legs over the edge of the cot. Her head swam as she pushed to her feet with more determination than caution, but Serafina steadied her, gripping her hand until it passed. "If they realize—"

"My apprentices can handle them," Serafina said, with a faint, knowing smile. "It's not the first time."

Before Araya could question what *that* meant, Serafina shoved the cot aside, dropping to her knees. She ran her hands over the floor, pressing her fingers into a rune Araya would never have seen. Magic flared at her fingertips, the hidden trap door springing open to reveal a dark, narrow passage. Cool air wafted up from it, carrying the stale scent of damp stone.

"We don't have much time," Serafina said, swinging her legs over the edge of the door. She glanced back at Araya, a spark of challenge burning in her green eyes. "Are you coming?"

Araya stared at her best friend, her heart twisting in her chest. How much of her life had Serafina hidden behind a steady voice and kind hands?

But she straightened, lifting her chin. Whatever secrets Serafina had kept, however much this felt like stepping off a ledge blindfolded—Araya couldn't turn back now. Not when this might be her only chance to understand what kept pulling her toward Loren.

"Then let's go."

CHAPTER
TWENTY-SIX

She had forgotten her place.

Loren's vision narrowed, his pulse pounding as rage flared hot in his veins, burning away the deep, numbing cold that had settled in his bones over the years he'd rotted in this hateful place. Every time he closed his eyes, he saw the bruise on Araya's skin. The gash on her forehead. The stiff, painful way she moved.

Jaxon Shaw had done that to her. Because she had *forgotten her place.*

Loren would kill him. Jaxon would pay for every mark he had left on her. Every bruise, every scrape, every cut—Loren would tear him apart with his bare hands for daring to claim something so precious, only to shatter it. Just imagining it filled Loren with a savage, burning energy.

Except he couldn't kill Jaxon Shaw. He'd kept Araya safe—made her happy, even. Loren wanted that for her again, even if it felt like a knife in his gut. His only consolation was that she didn't know about the bond. It would only bring her pain to know what the Arcanum had stolen from them. Better that he bear the knowledge for both of them—it was the least he could do.

Then, footsteps—two sets.

Loren swore under his breath, swallowing back his rage as he strained his ears to hear through the heavy iron. That female just didn't *listen*.

"I'm not supposed to let anyone in without Master Jaxon—" the guard said.

"Have you not been here every other day Jaxon has dragged me down those million steps?" the Healer snapped. "If this prisoner he's so worried about dies on *your* watch—"

Loren raised an eyebrow. He hadn't realized he was still on the verge of death. He could hear the guard shifting from foot to foot, no doubt preparing to turn them away again—

"Jaxon has meetings with the Arcanum all day. I'm here in his stead—I'm very sorry, Aeron. He should have sent you a message. Here, my key."

Araya. The shadows hissed, stirring at the edges of his cell.

Loren had known she was there from her footsteps, but hearing her voice stoked the dull ache in his chest to a sharp pain, stealing his breath away. He sank down on the cot she'd insisted he have, despair flooding him as the keys grated in the lock.

She wasn't supposed to be here—she should be securing her own safety. Not checking on him. But he couldn't stop himself from raking his eyes over her as the Healer kindled the aetherlamp, taking in everything from the neat bandage on her head to the wrap supporting her wrist, knowing there were a myriad of bruises he couldn't see hidden beneath her cloak and dress.

"I told you to stay away, *ael'sura*," he said wearily.

She frowned at him, but the Healer's face softened at the term. She did know then—but she hadn't told Jaxon. Or Araya.

"And you still don't have the authority to give me orders." Araya glared at him as her friend traced a silencing rune on the back of the door, her silver eyes blazing. "The two of you owe me an explanation."

Loren's lips twitched into a faint smile despite himself. In another life, this female would have made a fearsome queen.

"You're better off not knowing," he said softly. "You know I wouldn't be able to say it if it wasn't true."

"All that means is *you* believe that." Araya didn't flinch. "If you know something that could put me in danger, I want to know. That's *my* decision to make—not yours."

"He thinks he's doing the right thing," Serafina interrupted quietly, resting a gentle hand on Araya's shoulder. "Let me talk to him—I'll explain."

Araya bit her lip, her eyes still fixed on him as she nodded.

Serafina stepped forward and knelt beside Loren's cot, her hands light but practiced as she examined the remnants of his wounds—almost fully healed now, under her care. If she hadn't been escorted by Jaxon Shaw and drugging him, Loren might have thanked her.

"*Vira'thal,*" she greeted him, continuing in flawless Valenya. "We haven't had a chance to speak, Your Majesty, but we have friends in common. My name is Serafina."

Araya's head whipped towards them, and she took a step forward. "Are you speaking *Valenya*?"

"My father taught me," the Healer said in the common tongue, but her eyes didn't waver from Loren. Switching back to Valenya she added, "She's smart. She's going to get suspicious fast."

Loren stared at her, still shaken from hearing his title roll effortlessly off her tongue. "You know."

"I figured it out." Serafina said. "I understand you haven't told her because you want to keep her safe, but that won't protect her once Jaxon figures it out."

Loren's jaw tightened, his emerald gaze flicking to Araya before locking back on Serafina. "Then he can't figure it out."

"She can't stop him," Serafina said softly. "It's only a matter of time." She leaned back on her heels, her green eyes unreadable. "My father told me mates are always stronger together—would claiming her make you powerful enough?"

"Powerful enough to do what?" Loren growled, something cold and ugly twisting in his gut. To claim a mate without their knowledge or consent…it was the kind of violation the Arcanum had built an empire on.

"To escape," Serafina said calmly, as if she hadn't just suggested something unspeakable.

"In case you haven't noticed, I'm in iron," he ground out, his voice raw. "And I would never do that to her."

"If you don't, the Arcanum will put her in a cell like this." Serafina stared at him, her accusing stare ripping into his resistance. "If you're lucky, you'll be able to hear her screaming when Hale does to her what he did to you. She'll never be safe here, Your Majesty."

Loren inhaled deeply, Serafina's truth weighing heavily on his conscience. He wanted to argue, to find another way—but the idea of Araya locked in a cell, her screams echoing in the darkness? That was an image pulled straight from his nightmares.

Loren breathed out, his shoulders stiff. "I'll need the collar off."

Serafina didn't hesitate, rising smoothly to her feet as she turned to Araya. "I want to treat the abrasions under the collar," she said in the common tongue. "Can you take it off?"

Araya hesitated, her gaze flicking warily between him and her friend. "I'm not sure that's a good idea," she said, her voice as guarded as her eyes. But she stepped closer anyway, drawn forward by the bond even if the rest of her mind hadn't caught up.

Her scent surrounded him as she leaned in to study the collar, filling his lungs with the smell of rain and wildflowers despite the stink Jaxon had left on her skin. It took every drop of Loren's willpower not to reach out for her as her eyebrows drew together, her gaze lingering on the damage to his flesh beneath the iron.

"Hold still," she murmured.

Loren didn't move as her fingers brushed against his skin, tracing the edge of the collar. It had to be burning her, but her hands didn't falter as she worked, feeling for some sort of hidden clasp. Loren wanted to tell her he'd burned his fingertips to raw stubs without finding a way to get it off, but before he could speak the collar released with a faint *click*.

Air flooded his lungs. It was the same damp, cold air he'd been breathing for more than twenty years. But now, it was different. Because for the first time in decades, Loren could breathe freely.

For so many years, he had felt nothing. Nothing but silence. Nothing but loss. His power, his birthright, his will to keep fighting —it had all withered away under the weight of iron and suffering.

But now—

The meagre dregs of power he'd been able to cling to with iron around his wrists and throat leapt to life, a spark in the frozen waste-land his magic had become. The shadows stirred as well, slithering from their hiding places to coil around his feet. His to command—if he could find just a little more power.

But he'd been in iron for more than twenty years. They didn't have time to wait for him to replenish his power naturally—which meant there was only one way they would escape today. He opened his eyes, his gaze finding hers without conscious thought.

"—I'll have to put it back on," Araya warned, glancing over her shoulder at Serafina as she set the collar to the side. "But—"

He didn't want to do this. Gods, he didn't. But he was out of time. She was the only one who could save them now. Before he could talk himself out of it, Loren lunged.

He wrapped his arm around her waist as she stiffened in surprise, hauling her against him in an unrelenting grip. His lips crashed into hers—desperate and starved, a collision of ruin and need.

Her lips parted, and magic ignited between them like a spark to dry kindling. She tasted of aether and fire, of something forbidden and vital, something that could save him or break him.

The desperate, primal part of him surged to the surface, aching to consume her, to drag her closer, to mark her and claim what was his by fate and divine right. He wanted to bury his hands in her hair, pull her under, make her forget that Jaxon Shaw even existed.

But this wasn't a claiming.

So instead of kissing her the way he ached to—Loren sank his teeth into her lip.

She gasped, ripping away as the metallic tang of blood filled his mouth. He let her stagger away from him, his breath ragged as he fought the desperate desire to hold on to her.

"What was *that?*" she demanded, her voice shaking. She raised a hand to her lip, her fingers coming away bloody. "You bit me—"

"A necessity," Loren muttered, dropping his eyes. The betrayed look on her face would haunt him for the rest of his life, but a spark of power under his skin had roared into a wildfire, flooding him. And for the first time in decades, the shadows answered his call.

"There's only one guard," Serafina said in Valenya, taking Araya's hand and drawing her back against the far wall. Araya didn't resist, but Loren could feel the tension radiating from her through the nascent connection between them, mingling with her fear and confusion.

Loren nodded, rapping his knuckles twice against the door. The keys grated in the lock, but the second the bolt slid free and the door started to swing open, Loren let the shadows go.

Araya cried out as they surged forward, silent and merciless. They sealed themselves over the guard's mouth, slipping past his lips and down his throat, flooding his lungs. He died silently, his eyes bulging with terror as his body crumpled to the cold floor.

"Take his boots," Serafina said. "It's cold out."

Loren crouched, yanking the guard's boots off and jamming his own feet into them. They were too small—pinching his toes—but better than nothing. He took the heavy cloak Serafina handed him next, fastening it around his shoulders. With the hood up, the dark, nondescript fabric would blend easily into the background.

"Serafina..." Araya whispered from the doorway, her horrified eyes glued to the dead guard. "What are you doing? You're going to get us both killed. Loren, I'm sorry—this is a mistake. There's no way you get out. Let me put the collar back on you—"

"I'm sorry, *ael'sura*," Loren said, catching her hand gently but firmly as she reached for him. "But that won't be happening." Glancing back at Serafina, he asked, "How are we getting out?"

"Crack this when you're ready." Serafina handed him a small crystal glowing with magic. "It will lead you to allies. They'll know you're coming."

"What about you?" He asked.

"I have to wipe the record of our coming down here from the checkpoints we passed," Serafina said. "And come up with a good story for how Araya went missing from my clinic." She glanced at her friend, her expression turning sad. "You'll have to compel her to follow."

His stomach twisted. "She'll hate me."

"But she'll live," Serafina said simply. "If you don't, she'll never even get a chance to forgive you. She'll run straight back to Jaxon, and now that you've claimed her..."

Jaxon would know. The truth settled like lead in Loren's gut. Even if she never forgave him, he had to make sure she was safe.

He reached out to Araya, his heart aching when she didn't flinch away, even after everything he had done. She just glared at him, her silver eyes wide with hurt and fear.

"Araya," Loren whispered, her name heavy with magic as it fell from his lips. "*Ra'lora.*"

She gasped, her body going rigid as the command seized her. Fresh panic surged through the bond, hot and desperate.

"Did you just—" Araya choked, her eyes widening in horror as they darted to Serafina. "What did you do? What did you let him do?"

Serafina embraced her, kissing her softly on each tear-streaked cheek.

"Have a good life, my friend," she said, her voice breaking. "Be free. Be safe. Grow old. And one day, when you understand why I did this... forgive me."

She stepped back, tears glistening in her eyes. But as she turned to Loren, her chin lifted, and the raw vulnerability in her gaze hardened into quiet resolve.

"Safe travels, Your Majesty."

CHAPTER
TWENTY-SEVEN

THE FAE PRINCE'S COMMAND MIGHT AS WELL HAVE BEEN AN IRON MANACLE, chaining her to him. His shadows needled at her whenever she slowed, urging her forward as they followed the dim glow of Serafina's seeking spell deeper into the labyrinth beneath the Aetherium.

Her lip throbbed, but Araya clenched her jaw—refusing to acknowledge the phantom heat of his mouth that still lingered on her lips. He had kissed her. *Bitten* her. And then he'd compelled her.

That was the only thing that could explain how the command she hadn't even understood had burrowed under her skin, digging into her will in ways no book could have ever prepared her for. She raged against it at first, but with her power so drained she had no way to fight the urge to obey burning in her blood.

She hated him for it—but she hated herself even more for how she'd frozen when his lips met hers. *Why* had it taken her so long to push him away?

"We have to go back," she hissed between ragged breaths as she stumbled after him. "They will kill us all—"

"I heard a rumor they need my blood for something important," Loren shot back. "It will be hard to collect if I am dead."

Araya glared at his back, her head swimming with exhaustion. He didn't even sound winded. How was he this strong after spending twenty-five years chained to a wall?

"That won't stop them from killing me," she protested. "And Serafina. If we go back now there's a chance I could talk Jaxon down—"

"Shaw isn't going to catch you, *ael'sura*," he said, his voice maddeningly calm.

"You can't promise—" Araya gasped, nearly falling as she stumbled over an uneven patch of ground. "Please, slow down," she begged. "I can't—" she swayed, her words cutting off as another wave of dizziness swept over her.

Loren's shadows caught her a heartbeat before his strong arm wrapped around her, steadying her against him. Heat sparked where he touched her, licking up her spine. He was too solid, too close, too... something.

Araya shoved him away, a little too hard. "Don't touch me," she snapped.

"I'm sorry," Loren said, the hand that had touched her curling into a fist at his side. "We need to keep moving."

"You have to let me go," Araya argued again, but the words came out raw and thin. "*Please*, Loren—you don't understand. He'll never stop looking for me."

Loren's gaze dropped, a flicker of regret crossing his face. But he only shook his head.

"I do understand," he said, still not looking at her. "That's why we're going to make sure he can't find you."

He turned and started walking again without waiting for her to respond, following the bobbing light deeper into the labyrinth. And because she had no choice, Araya followed.

Even without Loren's compulsion, she was hopelessly lost at this point anyway. She'd never find her way out alone—if she even had the strength to try. Whatever mix of Serafina's care and adrenaline that had carried her this far was wearing off, every ache and pain hitting her with a vengeance as she plodded behind Loren.

After what happened last night, Jaxon would never believe she hadn't run willingly. Araya's throat tightened. She had the bruises to show what Jaxon was capable of when he thought he was being defied. If he thought she had anything to do with Loren escaping…

She shivered, cold dread running its icy fingers down her spine. She would be *lucky* to end up in a cell.

They rounded a bend, the walls narrowing around them. Loren slowed, his eyes scanning the tunnel ahead. "This was part of the old aqueduct system," he said softly, though his voice still echoed in the quiet. "There should be—ah, there."

The little ball of light darted to the side, vanishing into a narrow opening in the wall. Loren didn't hesitate—just bent and gripped the cover, moving it aside with a grunt. Araya stepped forward, curious despite herself—but then the smell hit her.

"No," Araya snapped, gagging on the stench. "I'm not going in there."

"Your friend seems like she's done this a few times," Loren dropped to his knees, peering into the dark, fetid tunnel. "I'm going to trust her." He glanced back at her, those green eyes as bright as a cat's in the darkness. "It slopes down. I suggest going feet-first."

He didn't wait for her to answer before he shimmied into the tunnel feet first, barely managing to squeeze his shoulders through the narrow opening.

"I will not," Araya hissed, digging her heels in as Loren's magic needled at her, the shadows urging her toward the reeking hole.

You will, they seemed to chant back.

The only defiance she had left was refusing to go feet-first. Clenching her jaw, she crawled forward awkwardly, her injured arm tucked against her chest and every breath thick with filth. The tunnel swallowed her whole, closing around her like a grave.

It only got worse the deeper she crawled, the stone turning slick under her palm. Loren had been right—it did slope down, steeper and steeper the further she crawled, until Araya started to regret going headfirst. She stopped, the compulsion prickling at her to keep going as she tried to gauge if there was enough room for her to turn herself around.

Her hand slipped.

Araya cried out, instinctively throwing out her injured arm to catch herself. It buckled under her—and then she was sliding.

The darkness swallowed her scream as she scrabbled at the slick, slimy rock in a futile effort to stop her plunge. But there was nothing. This was going to be how she died—smashed to pieces in a stinking sewer tunnel—

Loren's arms locked around her, breaking her fall as he muffled her scream against his shoulder. He was all sharp edges and wasted muscle, painfully lean but somehow brimming with a coiled strength that called to the faint wisps of aether just starting to flicker back to life inside her.

And his scent—Gods, with the iron gone, he smelled like thunder and cold stone—rain lashing slabs of frozen granite. It was raw and wild and old, and something about it made Araya long to bury her face in his throat and breathe him in until she drowned in it.

"Stubborn female," he muttered, his voice a low rasp as it brushed over her scarred ear. The wicked smile in the words curled low in her stomach, kindling a fire she wanted no part of.

She smacked a hand into his chest—harder than necessary. "Put me down."

"As you wish."

Araya's triumph at his quick obedience shifted into sharp regret the moment she splashed into the calf-high muck, a wave of nausea gagging her as the foul liquid soaked the hem of her skirt and rushed over the tops of her boots, filling them with freezing filth.

"You knew that would happen!"

"I told you I thought you should go feet-first," he said, his hands still on her shoulders as if worried she would slip. "You made the decision not to listen."

Araya's face flushed, embarrassment and irritation tangling with her body's confusing reaction to him. She shook off his hands, squaring her shoulders and glaring up at him. He was tall—taller than any human man she'd ever known—forcing her to crane her neck to look up at him.

"Why didn't you just compel me, then?" she snapped.

"I could have," Loren acknowledged. He cocked his head, studying her with the same fae stillness they'd beaten out of her at Kaldrath. "I could make you do a lot of things—follow, bow, obey... but I won't. Not unless you're dying, and you're too stubborn to save yourself."

He leaned in, his voice dropping to a timbre that sent goosebumps racing over her skin. "You're not a puppet, Araya."

The emphasis he put on her name sent a shiver over her skin as his gaze lingered, burning through her defenses like wildfire.

"Maybe you should just try trusting me," he added.

"Trust you?" Araya echoed, her voice rising. "You used my best friend to escape—you *kidnapped* me!"

"It was completely her idea." Loren shrugged, starting to walk forward again. "If you recall, *I* told you to forget about me and have a happy life. You're the one who showed up at my cell anyway."

"This is *not* my fault." Araya clenched her jaw as Loren's magic tightened around her, forcing her to move.

For what felt like an eternity, they pressed on in silence with only Serafina's seeking spell to light their way. The narrow tunnel forced them to walk single file, the ceiling dropping so low in places that Loren had to bend nearly double. Much to Araya's dismay, there were places where the muck rose to mid-thigh, the cold sludge sucking at their legs as they struggled forward.

Finally, the tunnel began to widen. A welcome breeze brushed Araya's face, a breath of freedom after the suffocating darkness. She gulped in the clean air, picking up her pace until Loren threw out an arm to keep her from passing him.

"Do you have any idea where we are? What's out there?" He asked.

"Not a sewer," Araya said, shoving at his arm. "That's good enough for me."

Loren shook his head at her, his expression unreadable in the dim light. "Put your hood up," he ordered, pulling his own.

"Make me," Araya hissed. She expected him to compel her again, bracing for the surge of magic to twist her to his will. But instead, Loren just reached out and tugged the hood up over her hair.

"I'd prefer not to," he said, checking the clasp under her chin. "I just don't want us to be killed as soon as we step out of here." He turned before she could answer, leading them towards the source of that breeze.

The air changed first—the breeze, cool and sharp against her sweat-dampened skin as it carried away the suffocating dampness of the tunnels. The walls fell away around them, giving way to the cracked cobblestones and sagging buildings of an unfamiliar fae slum.

Araya looked around frantically, searching desperately for anything she recognized. But it wasn't until she spotted the black towers of the Aetherium looming in the distance that she put it together.

They had to be in Farhallow—the other fae district outside the walls. Gods, they were on the other side of the city. She hadn't realized they'd gone so far, but at least now she could find her way back.

All she had to do was get away.

But before she could even think about a plan, a hooded shadow separated itself from the crumbling wall, dipping its head at them.

"*Vira'thal*," a male voice said, low and even. "This way—hurry."

Loren followed without hesitation, leaving Araya no choice but to trail behind, her heart pounding against her ribs as their guide led them deeper into the maze of crumbling buildings.

Whoever he was, he knew exactly where he was going, leading them into one of the dilapidated ruins. Araya braced herself for the floor to give way under her feet as Loren dragged her after him, but the structure was surprisingly solid.

"Welcome," the man said once they were safely under cover. He thrust back his hood, revealing short auburn hair and warm amber eyes that spoke to some fae ancestry. "Congratulations on making it this far. We have food and fresh clothes, so you can both clean up a bit and rest before we leave—"

"Thorne?" Loren interrupted, his voice hoarse as he threw back his hood.

"By the Goddess..." Thorne stared at Loren, his expression splintered and raw. "*Loren*—"

Loren stiffened, grabbing the male by the arm as he started to drop to his knees. Sharp words followed—not in Common, but in Valenya. And then Loren was moving, dragging the other male into a fierce, crushing embrace, tears streaking both their faces.

Araya took a step back, shocked when she was actually able to. The compulsion tugging at her was a fraying thread—one she might actually break if she tried. She gathered herself, tensing to run—

But then Loren and the male broke apart. Araya froze under Loren's bright green stare as he cast a sidelong glance her way, saying something under his breath in Valenya.

The other male nodded, turning to her. "We owe you a debt," he said softly. "I'm sure you're exhausted. We can have you out of the city tonight—"

"That's not necessary." Araya shoved her hood back, lifting her chin as Thorne's eyes widened at the sight of her clipped ears and bruises. "Wherever you're going, I'm not coming with you."

"You are." Loren's expression darkened, his voice like iron. "Even if I have to drag you."

Araya glared at him, clenching her teeth on the venomous words she wanted to spit. He glared back, the silence stretching between them brittle and heavy.

"Well," Thorne said. "There's clearly a story here." His tone was easy, but his eyes were sharp as they raked over her, assessing.

"Come inside. Get cleaned up, eat something. Then we'll talk about what comes next."

———

Thorne led them deeper into the dilapidated building, guiding them past piles of debris carefully arranged to make this place seem abandoned. Araya glared at Loren's back, her irritation simmering as he conversed with their rescuer in fluid Valenya. At one point, he laughed—a rich, genuine sound completely unlike anything she'd ever heard from him before, making her wish she could see his face.

Finally, Thorne pushed open a thick wooden door. Light poured into the corridor, spilling warmth and soft voices into the dingy hall along with the rich, savory smell of cooking meat. Araya's mouth watered, her stomach cramping with hunger. She hadn't eaten since...she couldn't even remember.

"Look what I found waiting at the other end of the guide spell," Thorne said, giving Loren a shove into the room. "Not what I was expecting tonight, that's for sure. Serafina outdid herself this time."

The two people in the room looked up from the map they'd been studying, the woman sucking in a sharp breath as her eyes landed on Loren. She rose quickly, but her companion moved faster—crossing the room in three long strides and pulling Loren into a fierce, familiar embrace.

Araya froze, staring as the man from the Crust & Kettle—*Serafina's Finn*—embraced Loren like a brother. Her pulse roared in her ears, every detail taking on new weight as she scanned the room, taking in the worn armchairs, the fire crackling in the hearth, the map spread across the table. This wasn't just a sanctuary—it was a base.

"You're a rebel?" she demanded, the hysteria in her voice drawing every eye in the room. "*Serafina* is a rebel?"

Loren cut in before Araya could respond, his words a soft, fluid stream of Valenya, too fast for her to even attempt to follow. But she didn't need to understand the words to guess at what he was saying as everyone in the room stared at her. Finn's expression shifted sharply, his relaxed stance straightening. Whatever Loren had told him about her, it was enough to earn her Finn's full attention.

But it was the silver-haired woman who stepped forward, the sheen of her hair and the grace of her stride left little doubt in Araya's mind that she had fae blood, despite her rounded ears.

"I'm Nyra," she said with a genuine smile. "We're all friends of Loren's—from before. You've done a great service for Valendral, Araya."

"Against my will," Araya said stiffly.

Nyra's smile faltered, but her eyes were sympathetic. "Loren mentioned that," she said. "We're still grateful to you for bringing our friend back to us. Would you like to wash—change your clothes? We have things that will fit you."

Araya hesitated, reluctant to accept anything from these people. But the promise of clean clothes and a chance to wash the stench of the sewers from her skin was too tempting to resist, no matter how much she hated the idea of being in their debt. With a tight nod, she followed Nyra down a short, dark hallway and into a tiny room.

The hum of conversation faded, replaced by the faint creak of wooden floorboards underfoot and the soft splash of water as Nyra filled a bucket from a tap. "Sorry we don't have a full tub," she said, setting the bucket beside a low stool. "These aren't the most luxurious accommodations, but they are safe. You'll at least be able to scrub off—"

She lifted a hand, and Araya stifled a gasp as silver rippled across the surface of the water, steam curling lazily toward the ceiling.

Nyra had used no rune, spoken no words—Araya had only ever read about magic like this, shaped with will and intention instead of force and might. No one under the New Dominion's rule had enough power to even attempt it...yet Nyra had used it to warm a bucket of water for a stranger.

Nyra must have noticed her shock but didn't comment as she set a soft-bristled brush and a bar of soap neatly on the stool. Finally she opened a small cabinet, pulling out a folded towel and a bundle of clothing. "These should fit you," she said, setting them on top of the cabinet. "I'll be just outside—take your time."

Araya blinked, surprised by the offer of privacy. "Thank you," she said quietly, the words stiffer than she intended.

Nyra nodded, pausing in the doorway. "After you're clean, we'll get you some hot food. Everything is better after a hot meal." She stepped out before Araya could respond, pulling the door shut behind her.

Araya froze, holding her breath as she listened. But there was no click of a lock settling into place, no hum of enchantment—she was alone. And unrestrained.

She raced to the window, tugging at the rough boards nailed across it. But none of them budged, not even when she pried at their edges with her fingers. Araya swore under her breath, whirling to scan the rest of the room. But there was no hidden door or second exit—just the one she'd come in through, that would lead her back to the main room.

To him.

No escape then—not yet. With a sigh, Araya eased her arm out of the brace, gritting her teeth against the pain. Apparently, crawling through sewers counted as *resting*. She'd be lucky if it didn't need to be set after she finally managed to get away.

Araya nearly cried when the hot water touched her skin. Lathering the soap on the brush, she scrubbed until the water darkened to murky brown and her skin glowed a rosy pink. Her soiled dress she left crumpled in a heap—they could burn it, for all she cared. But her boots she scrubbed as best she could, dunking them in the water until they were at least passably clean.

The bundle of clothing Nyra had left consisted of fresh undergarments along with a too-large but blessedly clean tunic and a set of drawstring pants. There was even a pair of warm, dry socks. Araya pulled them on gratefully, padding out of the room with her dripping boots dangling from one hand to find Nyra sitting just outside in a sturdy wooden chair.

The woman—*female*, Araya corrected herself, no one who could use aether so naturally was human—looked up as the door creaked open, her gaze sweeping over Araya before a small, approving smile touched her lips.

"Much better," she said, rising gracefully to her feet. "I know you didn't choose to be here, but you should know that you're safe here, Araya. We've worked hard to ensure this place is secure."

Safe. The word settled heavily in Araya's chest. She shook her head. "None of us are safe as long as I'm here," she said. "Jaxon will find me."

Nyra's smile faltered, and for the briefest moment, something sharp flickered in her blue eyes. She recovered quickly, smoothing her expression into calm reassurance, but Araya didn't miss the way her fingers tightened around the back of the chair.

"Jaxon Shaw?" Nyra repeated. "You're *his* bond?"

Araya nodded, lowering her voice even more as she stepped closer, desperate not to be overheard by anyone in the main room. "That's why you have to let me go. He'll never stop searching for me, and if his search leads him here..."

Jaxon would burn this place to ash, with them inside.

For a moment, Araya thought Nyra would see sense—but then she shook her head slowly. "Serafina wouldn't have sent you to us if she didn't think we could help," she said, sympathy flickering across her expression as she glanced at the bruises that marked Araya's face and arms. "You made it here—let us worry about the rest."

Araya opened her mouth to argue, but Nyra reached out, resting a steadying hand on her arm. "You're not alone in this, Araya," she said firmly, even though her tone remained gentle. "Come, there's food waiting for you by the fire. Eat first, rest, and then we'll talk more."

Reluctantly, Araya let Nyra guide her back to the warm glow of the hearth, her reassurances ringing hollow in Araya's ears. How could they be so calm and dismissive when Jaxon was out there? He would be missing her by now—had they found Serafina and the guard yet? Her heart clenched at the thought of what might be happening to them right now. Jaxon wouldn't let something like this slide—not with his prized prisoner missing.

Her stomach tightened as her thoughts spiraled. She knew what Jaxon was capable of, how far he would go to make an example of disobedience. The longer she stayed away, the worse her punishment would be. Unless she went back willingly. If she could make him believe she'd returned of her own volition, maybe—just maybe—he'd show her mercy.

She just needed a chance. One chance.

So she accepted the hearty bowl of chunky stew Nyra served her with a tight, forced smile. The warm aroma of herbs and rich broth filled her nose, but even as she ate slowly, savoring the flavors, it did little to soothe the knot of tension in her chest. She could feel the weight of their glances—Loren's especially—lingering on her like an itch she couldn't scratch.

If he expected anything from her beyond silence, he was more arrogant than she'd thought.

Her grip tightened around the spoon, the memory of his compulsion simmering just beneath her skin. The pressure of the magic had faded now, but it left a bruise behind—a reminder of just how easily he'd bent her will. Could it even be resisted? Could *she* resist *him*? He was a prince, and she was just... herself.

No wonder he hadn't hesitated. Why would someone like him care about violating someone like her?

Araya set her spoon down as the stew turned sour on her tongue, her appetite waning.

Nyra returned with a steaming cup of fragrant herbal tea, setting it down in front of her. "To help you relax," the female said kindly.

Araya wrapped her hands around the mug, letting the warmth seep into her hands as Nyra cleared away her bowl. She took a cautious sip, the sweet, rich blend soothing her aching muscles and frayed nerves as its heat spread through her body. She was so tired—drained from the loss of her magic, the last traces of adrenaline fading after their desperate flight through the tunnels.

The room blurred at the edges, her thoughts slipping through her grasp like water through her fingers. She blinked, struggling to focus on lifting her arm, but it barely moved. She felt like someone had wrapped her in lead chains, pinning her to the bench. From across the room, Thorne's amber gaze flicked toward her, his brow furrowing slightly.

They had drugged her.

The realization was like a bucket of ice water being dumped over her head. The tea, the kindness—it had all been a calculated trap to make her lower her guard. She fought to stand, but her limbs barely twitched, sluggish and unresponsive.

She should have known—of course they wouldn't just *trust* her. How could they? She was bonded to Jaxon Shaw. She had said it herself—she was as much a threat to them as he was.

A shadow moved at the edge of her vision, Loren's storm and stone scent enveloping her as his gentle hands guided her head to rest on her folded arms. He murmured something, the words pitched for her ears alone. Araya didn't understand, but she didn't need to speak Valenya to hear the quiet undercurrent of guilt in his voice.

Her eyes slipped closed, her resistance draining away. Part of her wanted to fight—to shove him away and scream that she didn't want his comfort. But she was so tired—surely she could rest, just for a minute. Just long enough to gather her strength for whatever came next.

Araya's breathing slowed, the world fading around her. The last thing she felt was his hand on her back, his low, soft voice wrapping around her like a comforting blanket she hadn't asked for.

CHAPTER

TWENTY-EIGHT

Loren's breath caught as Araya's eyelids fluttered. Her breathing quickened, and Loren could hear her heart start to pound as realization and panic flashed across her face. She shifted, struggling to stand—fighting to stay awake. His chest tightened, but he shoved away the guilt. This was for her—even if she never understood. He had to keep her safe.

But he couldn't stop himself from taking a step toward her as the conversation around him faded, the celebration of his return snuffed out in an instant.

"Easy," he murmured, his hands settling gently on her shoulders. "Don't fight it."

She blinked up at him, her silver eyes glazed and unfocused. For a heartbeat, he thought she might speak, but then she swayed and her eyes closed, surrendering. He caught her before she collapsed, guiding her head gently onto her folded arms.

With her cheek pillowed on her arms, she looked heartbreakingly young. The anger that had hardened her features since he compelled her was gone, washed away like ink in the rain. Her lips parted slightly, her face slack with the kind of peace he had never seen her wear awake.

Loren reached out before he could stop himself, brushing a loose strand of hair from her face. Its softness lingered against his fingers. For a moment, he let himself pretend—pretend she had never been a pawn in Shaw's game. Never looked at him with silver eyes blazing with rage. But he knew that as soon as she woke, the fury and hate would come roaring back—stronger than ever.

"Really, Nyra?" Thorne said tightly. "Since when do we drug people who come to us for help?"

"She didn't come to us for help—Loren forced her to. Drugging her was *his* suggestion," Nyra responded coolly, arms crossed as she faced Thorne. "And I decided it was a good idea after Araya told me she's bonded to *Jaxon Shaw*."

Loren's head snapped toward her, locking onto her steely blue glare. Why would Araya have volunteered *that*?

"She said it herself," Nyra continued, not flinching from his stare. "None of us are safe as long as she's here because Shaw isn't going to just *let her go*. He will rip this city apart looking for her. Our work here, everything we do—it's in danger because of who she is. And he *knew* and didn't say a word." The accusation hung in the air between them.

"Nyra—" Finn's steady voice cut through the mounting tension with the practiced weight of someone used to playing the mediator. But even he couldn't fully mask the strain threading through his words. "He couldn't leave her there—"

"He absolutely could have," Nyra snapped, her composure cracking. "It's a question of saving one female versus saving hundreds. If Shaw keeps turning over rocks looking for her, he'll eventually find *us*—and then we won't save anyone."

"What would you suggest, then?" Loren growled.

Nyra paused mid-stride, the room falling into a tense silence as everyone turned toward her. Her blue eyes, usually as calm and clear as a winter sky, were now sharp and glinting with an edge of cold resolve. She met Loren's gaze, holding it. "Jaxon has to find her body."

Loren's world tilted, narrowing to a pinpoint as the bond howled in his chest, every instinct demanding that Loren tear Nyra apart for what she'd dared suggest. "She is innocent—"

"She's not innocent, Loren," Nyra argued. "Shaw changed all the rules for her. What other fae female is working at the Arcanum, wearing an Eye around her neck, and apparently visiting high-profile prisoners alone? I'm grateful for whatever role she played getting you out, but she doesn't *want* to be here. You need to think. If we let her live she's going to run right back to him and tell him everything."

"You're talking about murder," Loren hissed.

"I'm talking about survival," Nyra snapped, her voice rising with frustration. "Do you think I want to be the one who has to make this choice? If Shaw finds her, he finds us. I know it sounds cruel, but she won't suffer. She'll just never wake up—"

Loren's vision blurred, his thoughts spiraling. "You want me to stand by and let you murder her while she's defenseless?" He took another step forward, the room tensing as the shadows rippled outward from him. "While she sleeps?"

Nyra's composure wavered, her shoulders tensing as Loren's shadows surrounded her. "I don't *want* to," she said. "But I will if it means saving hundreds, maybe thousands, of lives. She wouldn't suffer, Loren. It would be quick—merciful."

Merciful?

Loren barked a harsh, bitter laugh, the sound too loud in the dense silence. The shadows lashed outward, crawling up the walls and creeping across the floor in trembling, twisting veins of darkness. Nyra stiffened, taking a half-step back as one snaked toward her boot.

"Is that what you tell yourself to sleep at night?" Loren demanded. "That you're being merciful?"

"Loren—" Finn took a cautious step forward, his voice carefully measured and his eyes on the shadows. "Let's all calm down and talk about this—"

"She's not just Jaxon Shaw's bond." Loren's voice cracked, his fury barely masking the raw terror tearing through him. The thought of losing her—whether to Nyra's cold logic or Jaxon Shaw's cruelty—he couldn't accept it.

"She's mine," he snarled.

His confession cracked through the room like a thunderclap. The shadows burst outward, pulsing in rhythm with the bond pulsing between them. He'd spent so long arguing that she'd be better off without him, that he had no right to claim her—but he had.

And now...Goddess help him. He would kill anyone who tried to take her from him.

Across from him, Nyra stumbled back a step, her eyes wide as she stared at the shadows. "Loren, I didn't know—"

"Would it have changed anything if you had?" Loren snarled. "Shaw will be looking for me too. Should I be worried about you slitting my throat when I fall asleep?"

Nyra shook her head, tears shining in her eyes as the shadows crept toward her. They spilled across the floor, brushing against her boots and twisting into long tendrils that reared like snakes, poised to strike.

And then—

Araya stirred. Her breath hitched, so quietly it was barely even a sound—but Loren's gaze snapped down to her, his world narrowing to the unconscious female he'd bound his soul to. The shadows recoiled, their focus snapping back to him as he dropped to his knees beside her to run his hand over her back in long, soothing strokes.

I'm here, he whispered into her mind, a promise only their bond could hear. *I won't let them hurt you.*

"We need to move them both tonight," Finn said, his voice firm but quiet. "Before the Arcanum starts looking for them. Make it happen, Nyra."

Nyra choked on a sound that wasn't quite a sob, her hand still pressed hard to her mouth. But she nodded sharply before she turned and fled—like she could outrun the weight of what she'd nearly done.

Loren watched her go, unable to summon even a flicker of the rage he'd felt just moments ago. He sank onto the bench beside Araya, wanting nothing more than to lay his head down on his arms and fall asleep on the table beside her.

"Nyra manifested as a weather worker," Finn said after a beat, watching Loren carefully—a leader assessing a threat. "One of the best we've ever seen. She's personally saved hundreds of fae from the New Dominion."

Loren's lip curled, but he was too wrung out to do more than show his teeth in something too exhausted to be called a snarl. Not even saving hundreds excused the slaughter of innocents.

"She has no idea, does she?" Thorne asked quietly.

Loren shook his head, unable to bring himself to look at his oldest friend.

"That's not uncommon for young females who grew up in the New Dominion." Thorne sighed, rubbing his jaw. "The Arcanum has suppressed knowledge about the mate bond, perverting it with their so-called *bond* agreements. But it's not hopeless, Loren—you can still tell her."

"No—" Loren stared down at her, giving in to the temptation to brush a loose piece of hair back behind her mangled ear. "I just want her to be safe. Help me get her somewhere safe—please."

"She can't go to Lumaria," Thorne said, glancing at Finn. "Not until she accepts that she can't go back—if she took any information about it back to the Arcanum—"

"What about Ithralis?" Finn suggested. "It's abandoned, but secure. We can contact Eloria once we cross the Veil—"

"Eloria?" Loren's voice came out hoarse, the name hitting him like a lightning strike. "My sister, Eloria? She's alive?"

Finn leaned back, a grin breaking across his face. "You mean your sister the Queen Regent?" He laughed. "She's alive, well, and more terrifying than ever."

Loren's heartbeat thundered in his ears, a little of the ice around his heart cracking. His sister was alive. She was out there—leading and fighting, holding their people together.

"When do we leave?"

———

LOREN CRADLED ARAYA'S LIMP FORM AS HE STEPPED ONTO THE RICKETY gangplank leading to the glorified fishing skiff Nyra had the audacity to call a boat. The wood groaned beneath his weight, threatening to pitch them both into the frigid black water below.

Loren carried her straight to the cabin. It was as cramped and unwelcoming as the rest of the boat—dank and musty, with the pervasive scent of salt and mildew clinging to the air. The thin wooden walls blocked the wind but did little to hold back the biting cold. The narrow cot bolted to the deck looked more like a slab of wood than a bed, but Loren laid Araya on it gently, making her as comfortable as he could.

"Someone she trusts should be here when she wakes," Thorne said quietly from where he watched Loren tend to her.

Loren let out a bitter laugh. "Not me then." He tucked her injured arm carefully against her chest, his fingers brushing hers as he pulled back, taking comfort in the faint pulse of life beneath her skin.

"Drugging her probably isn't the way to her heart," Thorne said wryly. "But you shouldn't give up hope, Loren."

Loren glanced at his oldest friend—the male who had been like a brother to him. Guilt and regret tangled in his chest, thorny vines coiling tight around his heart. "Do you think it was better or worse than tricking her into removing the iron collar around my neck and using her true name to compel her to come with me against her will?"

"So not you, then," Thorne agreed after a beat of silence. "I can sit with her if you want. I'm a Healer now."

"Like your mother," Loren said, smiling at the thought of the bright human woman who had welcomed the fae crown prince's friendship with her son. "She must be proud."

Thorne's expression tightened, his smile fading as he looked past Loren. "She's dead," he said flatly, like he'd had to say the words a thousand times before. "Killed for sympathizing with the fae monarchy."

The words hit Loren like a blow, the air in the cabin suddenly too thick to breathe. "I'm sorry," he managed to say, his voice rough. "Your father?"

"Died with yours, on the battlefield trying to avenge her," Thorne said, clearing his throat. He looked away, not meeting Loren's gaze, and when he spoke again his voice was stiff. "I have things handled here. Nyra will need an extra set of hands getting underway. You should help her."

Loren nodded, recognizing the request for what it was. Thorne needed space—not just to tend to Araya, but to wrestle with his own ghosts. As soon as he stepped onto the deck, the wind hit him like a blade, slicing through the heavy cloak Serafina had given him. He made his way over to the helm, where Nyra adjusted the sails.

"How can I help?" he asked.

Nyra glanced over her shoulder at him, her sharp gaze flicking down to his hands before returning to her work. "Take that line," she said, nodding toward a coil of rope near the rail. "Tie it off before we lose the mainsail."

Loren caught the rope, his fingers numbing slightly from the cold as he worked to secure it. The tension between them hung heavy in the air, unspoken but undeniable. He could feel Nyra watching him out of the corner of her eye, but she said nothing until he finished.

"Good," she muttered, testing the tension on the rope. Satisfied, she stepped back toward the helm, her hands resting lightly on the wheel. "We'll be faster with the wind at our backs," she added, mostly to herself. "We can skirt close to the shadows and find a gap—"

Loren's gaze drifted as Nyra spoke, her voice fading into the background. His sharp eyes caught a flicker of movement against the darkness of the shoreline—a flash of light. "Nyra," he said, cutting her off.

"Dammit—" Nyra's head whipped around, her sharp gaze locking onto what could only be a patrol boat. "Cut those ropes and find something to hold onto."

She tossed him a knife, not waiting to see if he was following her instructions as she dashed for the helm, throwing her arms wide. Her power lit the air, every hair on Loren's arms standing on end as the wind rose to a shriek. He sliced the first two ropes, lunging for the third as the patrol boat changed course, drawn by the sheer power Nyra was calling to heel.

He'd only cut halfway through the last rope when she released it.

The wind sliced across the deck, filling the sails with a deafening *crack*. Loren grabbed for the rail, almost plummeting into the icy water as the last rope tore free on its own. It whipped past his face, left behind as the skiff lunged across the waves like an arrow, leaving nothing but churned water in its wake.

"They're following us—"

"Of course they are," Nyra snapped, her eyes never straying from the darkness ahead of them. "Hold on to something—this is going to get rough."

Instead of hugging the safety of the shoreline, the skiff barreled straight toward the looming wall of shadows. At the last moment, Nyra turned the wheel, bringing them parallel to the writhing mass —so close Loren could have reached out and brushed his fingers through the inky blackness.

The patrol boat didn't fall back. Worse, they must have had a weather worker of their own—because they were gaining.

"They never come this close to the shadows!" Nyra shouted, her words whipped away by her conjured wind.

But today they did—because an important prisoner had escaped, along with a bond belonging to one of the most powerful families in the New Dominion.

His heart pounded as the patrol boat closed in, cutting through the waves with brutal efficiency. He could see the shimmer of runes etched into the hull of their boat and the gleam of corrupted magic on their weapons.

If they caught them, they would drag him back to his cell. And Araya—they would take her back to Jaxon.

No—just the thought sent a bolt of raw, hot fury through him. He wouldn't allow that to happen.

Loren reached out—not with his hand, but with his mind, brushing it across the darkness the way one might stroke a coiled serpent. *Come*, he urged it, inviting it forward. *Strike.*

For a moment, the void hesitated. A presence stirred against his awareness as something cold and ancient tilted its head, considering him.

Now! Loren demanded.

The darkness inhaled, Nyra's wind dying with a whimper. The patrol boat was so close that Loren could see the terror on the soldiers' faces as their own wind vanished, the water around them turning as smooth as glass. One stumbled back, scrambling to nock an iron-tipped arrow—but he never managed to raise his bow.

THE SHADOWS STRUCK WITH DEADLY PRECISION, WOOD SPLINTERING AS THEY slammed into the patrol boat with crushing force. Men shouted, scrambling to fight back—but the shadows had already breached the ship, slipping through cracks in the hull, weaving between armor and skin. The first soldier went down, his scream cut off as darkness wrapped around his throat and dragged him under. The second tried to run—a mistake—because the shadows came for him next, ripping him backward into the abyss.

Loren's blood surged with the thrill of it—every scream, every kill feeding a power that felt far too right in his hands. In minutes, nothing was left of the patrol boat but wreckage. And then even that was gone, dragged beneath the surface by tendrils of inky blackness that reached out from the void.

"It's over," Nyra whispered, but her voice wavered and her grip on the wheel was too tight, her knuckles white. "Loren...you can call them off now."

Loren's brow furrowed, his fists clenching as he touched the shadows with his mind again. *That's enough,* he ordered.

Something stirred in the dark—twisting, slithering along the edges of his mind, brushing his thoughts like cold, wet fingers. It peered back at him from the dark, mocking and unimpressed, its inky tendrils lingering on the water as it considered him.

He calls, a hundred voices hissed at once. *He commands. He thinks we obey.*

"I am the heir," Loren snarled. "You answer to me."

We did. Once, the voices acknowledged, a cackle of dark laughter rippling through their dark presence. *And look what has become of us. We do not forget, shadow prince.*

"Loren!"

Thorne's sharp voice cut through the haze, dragging his gaze toward the cabin.

Araya stood in the doorway, clutching the frame for balance as the skiff rocked beneath her. Her silver eyes were wide, fixed on him with an expression that twisted something deep inside his chest. Her hands trembled where they gripped the doorframe, her lips parted as though she wanted to speak but couldn't find the words.

"Araya—" Loren's voice cracked, but she flinched, taking a step back as if he'd struck her.

Before he could say more, the air shifted.

Loren stiffened, his gaze snapping back to the shadows. The writhing mass stood unnervingly still, as if her presence had hypnotized them. Then, slowly, the tendrils began to move again—sliding across the water's surface, tasting the air as they curled closer. The temperature dropped, his breath fogging in the air as the void's dark intent coiled around him like a noose.

They'd made their decision.

"Nyra," Loren hissed, his voice tight. "Get us moving."

Nyra turned to him, her face draining of color as the air tightened, thickened. She sucked in a sharp breath, staring at the approach darkness. "Loren..." Her voice dropped to a whisper. "What did you do?"

"Turn the boat!" Loren roared. "Move! Now! Get us out of here! They're coming for *us*!"

TWENTY-NINE

Araya's eyes fluttered open, her head pounding in rhythm with the slow, sickening sway of the world around her. She struggled to sit up, instantly regretting it as the world tilted sideways beneath her, moving like she was on a—

A boat.

Araya's stomach lurched, panic cutting through the lingering fog in her mind. They'd *drugged* her and put her on a *boat.*

"Whoa—" Thorne jumped up from the chair beside the cot, reaching out like he was going to steady her.

Araya jerked away from his hand. "Don't touch me," she snapped.

She threw off the thin blanket, staggering to her feet. Her head spun, but aether sparked in her blood—still faint and weak, but there. She wasn't defenseless anymore.

"You should sit," the male said cautiously, watching her like she might bolt. "You're probably dizzy—"

"Because you *drugged* me," Araya snapped. Her voice rose, taking on a hysterical edge. "You drugged me and put me on a godsdamned boat!" Her hands curled into fists. "Take. Me. Back."

"I'm sorry, but that can't happen," Thorne said, lifting his hands slowly, like she was a cornered animal. "There's a lot going on here you don't understand, and this isn't the place to explain."

Gods, if one more person told her *this wasn't the place to explain—*

"I don't want an explanation," Araya hissed. "I *want* to go to shore." She stepped around him, but he moved faster—planting himself between her and the door.

"You have every right to be angry," Thorne said, still maddeningly calm. "But it's not safe for you to go out there. Nyra and Loren need to focus on the crossing—"

The boat lurched, sending them both stumbling. Araya barely caught herself, grabbing onto a tied-down crate as the deck pitched violently under their feet. Thorne wasn't as lucky, losing his footing completely and slamming into the cabin wall with a sharp grunt.

Araya threw herself into the opening, lunging for the door.

Thorne shouted her name, grabbing for her. But something dark and whispering slithered between them, and his hand closed on nothing but empty air as the door burst open under her hands.

Cold, salt-heavy air slammed into her, stealing the breath from her lungs. She stumbled forward, the icy spray soaking her socks and biting into her skin—but it wasn't the chill that stopped her cold, leaving her frozen in terror.

It was the shadows. Just feet away, the roiling wall of darkness loomed over them, ravenous tendrils unfurling from it like dark snakes.

Araya hadn't entirely believed Jaxon when he'd told her the Shadowed Veil destroyed anything that tried to breach it—not entirely. But she should have.

She clapped a hand over her mouth as the Arcanum patrol boat lurched, sending men scrambling across the deck. One of the soldiers fell, the shadows dragging him into the void before he could even scream. Another tried to leap overboard—only to be yanked back like a puppet on a string.

It took minutes.

Araya swayed, nausea churning in her gut. The boat was just... gone. Nothing remained but a few scattered splinters bobbing on the surface, until the shadows dragged even those beneath the waves.

Loren had done this—just like he'd killed Aeron in the tunnels. But this—this was worse. Thorne shouted something behind her, his hand closing around her arm to drag her back into the cabin. But Araya couldn't fight—she could only stare as Loren turned, green clashing with silver as their gazes met.

"Araya—" Loren took a step forward, his face stricken. But before he could say anything else, the shadows moved.

The hair on the back of Araya's arms stood on end as Loren's head snapped around as a dark tendril slid toward the skiff— reaching for them. No—for *her*.

"Get us out of here!" Loren shouted at Nyra. "They're coming for *us*!"

Nyra flung out her hands. The wind howled to life—a violent gale slamming into them, sending the skiff tearing through the water with jarring speed. Araya stumbled and would have fallen if not for Thorne's grip on her. He dragged her back, his voice barely cutting through the wind.

"Get back to the cabin!"

"No!" The word ripped from her throat, raw and furious.

She shoved him—harder than she meant to. The wind screamed, lashing her hair into her face as she fought her way across the deck, her soaked socks sliding on the slick wood.

"Loren!" Araya screamed. The skiff pitched violently, nearly throwing her to the deck. She grabbed the mast, her palms burning against the slick wood. "Call them off!"

He'd commanded them to sink the patrol boat—he could command them to stop. But Loren's eyes were wide and wild when they met hers, his chest heaving and his skin deathly pale under the salt spray that coated them both.

"I can't," he whispered, the words somehow reaching her over the howling wind.

Araya's stomach dropped as another tendril slammed into the hull. The boat lurched sideways, flinging her against the mast and sending Loren sliding into her. He wasn't controlling them. Whatever power had bent them to his will before—it wasn't working now.

Araya choked on a scream as the darkness climbed above them. It curled higher and higher, blotting out the sky in a wave of pure darkness.

They would all die here unless someone did something. And Loren wasn't doing anything—he wasn't even *trying*.

She lunged forward, grabbing his hands and digging her fingers in like he was the only solid thing left in the world. A jolt of *something* shot through her—whether it was magic, aether, or something else she had no idea. But whatever it was, the darkness around them shuddered, rippling like it had felt it too.

Loren's hands twisted in her grip, but Araya didn't let go. She wasn't going to die like this.

And then, the wave broke.

The void crashed over them, swallowing the boat whole.

———

THE WAVE OF SHADOWS CRASHED OVER THE SKIFF, PLUNGING EVERYTHING into darkness so complete it stole the world away. The howling wind, the groan of the boat, the crash of the waves—all of it vanished, replaced by a silence so complete it took on a life of its own.

The only thing she could see in the suffocating blackness was Loren. She clung to him, and he gripped her just as tightly, pulling her into the curve of his body as cool shadows traced over her skin. They curled at the edges of her sleeves, winding through her hair and wrapping around her throat—inspecting her.

Loren bared his teeth, snarling something in Valenya. Araya lifted her head, opening her mouth to remind him that she couldn't understand him—

But it was the shadows that answered.

A thousand voices whispered at the edges of her hearing—like leaves rustling in the wind or waves crashing against a forgotten shore. They rose, merging into a single, deafening voice that rattled her teeth in her skull. She couldn't understand the words, but the pain behind it was a familiar friend. Scorn—rage. The burn of a wound that had never healed.

Loren stiffened, his grip tightening as he snapped something back, his voice sharp with an anger that didn't quite mask the desperation in his response.

Whatever he'd said sent a ripple through the void, every tendril of shadow quivering and whispering among themselves. For a moment, nothing happened, the air thickening as that ancient power studied them both.

And then, the shadows retaliated.

A tendril lashed out, wrapping itself around Loren's forearm. He flinched, a strangled cry escaping his lips as the darkness sank into his skin like molten metal—branding him.

"Loren!" Araya reached for him—but he just dragged her close, curling his body around hers as the shadows clawed in around them. A raw sob tore from her lips as the darkness screamed, her fingers twisting in his shirt. They were speaking again—demanding something that Loren either couldn't or wouldn't give them.

This was a test, and Loren was failing it.

Before she could think better of it, Araya twisted out of Loren's grip.

"Wait!" She called out, her voice falling strangely flat in the vast darkness that surrounded them. To her shock, the shadows froze, that ancient focus snapping to her.

Araya swallowed hard, forcing herself to take another step forward. "I—I don't speak Valenya," she said, her voice shaking under the weight of that ancient regard. "But... I think you can understand me, can't you?"

The silence stretched for a long moment, thick and suffocating, before a slow ripple shivered through the darkness. The voices swelled, rolling over her like a crashing tide.

We speak all tongues, they hissed.

They were listening. Gods—they were listening.

"Araya—" Loren reached for her, but she shook him off, wiping her sweaty palms on her borrowed tunic. If he wasn't going to save them, she would.

"What is it you want from him?" she asked, staring into the void.

The void shuddered, and for a moment, the whispers fractured again—echoes splintering into overlapping voices of rage, disappointment, and something far older. Something wounded. Then, they merged again, their words slamming into her with so much force she felt them in her bones.

He is unbalanced. Shattered. Drifting where he should root.

We will not bind to a hollow heir. Not again.

Never again—never—again— The voices fractured, a chorus of *nevers* echoing in the dark.

"Another?" Araya asked, the strange phrasing tickling something in the back of her mind.

The shadows hissed, a violent, splintering sound.

There was another, they said. *A ruler who was whole—until he was not.*

His father fell—and we fell with him. The shadows paused, and Araya felt Loren stiffen behind her, tension radiating from him. *The son is as weak as the father. We will not fall again.*

"He—he's barely had time," Araya said, desperately piecing together the argument as she spoke. "He's been in iron for twenty-five years. If you want a ruler worth binding yourselves to, at least give him a chance to—"

The shadows shook around her, the void shuddering and rippling like a disturbed lake. Araya flinched, bracing for their anger—but the rattling tremor just went on and on.

They were laughing.

Or we strike him down. And choose another.

"Is there another?" Araya asked, praying to all the Gods that she was right. If she was wrong...they were all dead.

The shadows were silent for what felt like an eternity.

Not yet.

"Then you won't get what you want if you kill him now," she argued. "Are you willing to risk waiting decades for another heir? One that might be even worse?"

She held her breath as they considered, ignoring the burning weight of Loren's gaze on her back.

One chance. The void pulled back, but the weight of its presence lingered. *One chance—lost prince. For the brave one who argued so well for you—even when you deny her.*

Do not waste it.

A roar split the air. The void convulsed like a wounded beast—then, with a nauseating lurch, the world snapped back into place. Light and sound poured in, a dizzying rush of sensation that left her reeling and disoriented. The skiff groaned under her feet, the wind hissing past her ears as water lapped against the hull—but something was wrong.

Araya sucked in a breath, her heart hammering against her ribs as she scanned the horizon, searching for anything familiar. The towering wall of shadows still loomed—but it was the wrong side. There was no sign of the Obsidian Shore, no sign of Aetheris. Only the looming silhouette of an unfamiliar island.

They had crossed the Shadowed Veil.

Her head snapped toward Loren, searching for answers. But what she saw stopped her cold.

Still kneeling, he stared down at the black tendrils winding up his forearm, marking him from wrist to elbow. They almost seemed to move under his skin, their edges rippling like ink in water.

"*Loren,*" Araya gasped.

She reached for him, but he lurched back, climbing to his feet without even looking at her. Instead, he stared down at his marked arm, flexing and curling the fingers as if testing it.

When he finally raised his gaze, his green eyes were distant and shuttered, like a wall had gone up between them.

"Thorne!" Loren shouted.

The other male peeled himself off the deck, staring around with the same wild shock she'd felt. His amber eyes widened even further as he caught sight of the spiraling black mark on Loren's arm.

"Take her back to the cabin," Loren ordered.

"What?" Araya stared at him. She had *saved* them.

Even Thorne hesitated, glancing between them. "Loren...are you sure that's what you want to do here?"

For a moment, Loren met her gaze—truly looking at her. His lips parted, something raw flickering in his eyes—a glimpse of what he wasn't saying. But then his expression shuttered, that wall going up again between them.

"I'm sure," he said, his voice cold. "And this time—lock the door."

CHAPTER
THIRTY

The jagged cliffs of Eluneth loomed above them, rising from the mist like the spine of some long-dead beast. Sunlight barely pierced the dense fog, the few rays that struggled through revealing only deadened rock and brittle, colorless vegetation.

Loren couldn't even see the castle. He wouldn't have believed this was the same place he'd grown up visiting if not for the stone steps that zigzagged up the cliff face.

The last time he'd climbed them had been with his father—just before he left for Aetheris. The sun had blazed overhead, and the shadows had curled around them to shield them from the heat. They'd brushed through Loren's hair and wrapped around his arms in greeting, familiar and warm.

They recognize the heir, his father had said, smiling at him.

If he'd lived, how heartbroken would he be to see those same shadows reject his son now? To see Eluneth rotting—strangled by the very power the Goddess had given them to protect it—while Loren stood by, unable to stop it.

"Are you trying to make her hate you?"

Thorne stalked across the deck, stepping up beside him. "You can't just lock her up, Loren. She's your mate, not your prisoner."

Loren said nothing, his jaw tightening as he stared fixedly at the shrouded cliffs.

"You're going to lose her," Thorne snapped. "And it won't be because of Jaxon Shaw. It'll be because you pushed her too far—and she doesn't want to come back."

"Maybe that would be for the best." Loren stared down at his hands, white-knuckled on the rail. "She could leave—build something real. Something better."

The wood groaned, splinters biting into his palms, but he welcomed the pain. If he could just feel enough of it, maybe it would drown out the things he didn't want to think about. "Goddess knows, she doesn't deserve to be shackled to me. I'm not the male I was supposed to be."

"Loren..." Thorne didn't sound angry now. He just sounded tired. "You're not fixing anything by hating yourself. You don't deserve to be punished."

Except he did deserve it.

Jaxon Shaw's face flashed unbidden in his mind. The Shaws had taken everything from her—her choices, her name, her magic, her freedom—and now Loren had done the same. He'd used their connection to escape, compelled her with her true name, drugged her, torn her away from the only world she knew...

And then he'd locked her up.

It didn't matter that he'd done it all to keep her safe. His intentions didn't erase the hurt he'd caused her. They didn't make him any better for her than Jaxon Shaw.

Guilt twisted in his chest, self-loathing bitter on his tongue.

He was free. After twenty-five years in iron—huddled in the dark and forgotten by the world—he could finally feel the wind on his face. He stood just steps away from a place where the New Dominion held no power. A place where he was still a prince, not a prisoner.

But none of it mattered.

His mate hated him. The magic that should have answered him —the legacy he'd been born to—had recoiled from him in disgust. The land he was meant to rule lay crumbling and abandoned, soaked in shadow and rot. The Goddess's gift, squandered. His birthright, denied.

And his parents were gone.

His father, who had stood by with pride in his eyes as the shadows claimed him heir. His mother, who had kissed his forehead the day he left for Aetheris like he was still a boy. His sister, forced to take his place when she was only a child—another person he had failed to protect.

Maybe the shadows were right to reject him.

"We should get up to the castle," Thorne said after a long moment. "Eloria moved the seat of governance to Lumaria years ago, but she kept the whisperstone maintained so anyone who needs shelter can contact the remnant government from Ithralis—"

"I guess we qualify," Loren said bitterly. "Some prince I make."

"She never stopped believing you were alive, you know," Thorne said quietly, giving Loren a long look. "Your people—they're going to be overjoyed to see you returned. You still have people who love you, Loren. Even if you can't see that right now. Don't you think it's worth showing Araya that version of you?"

Loren watched the fog writhe over the rocks, smothering the tiny flame of hope Thorne's words had sparked before it could catch fire. Araya had never had a chance to be free—not really. Not in any life that had been hers alone. She deserved more than to be shackled to him by magic and duty.

"Take her up to Ithralis," he said. "Get her settled in one of the guest rooms—make sure she has everything she needs. But don't let her wander."

"You'll take her up yourself," Thorne snapped. "And explain things to her. Maybe consider apologizing—"

Loren shook his head. "I'm not coming."

Thorne's jaw tightened. "Where else would you go? Eloria is

going to drop everything and come running as soon as we contact her—"

"Then tell her I'm going to see our parents." Loren vaulted over the rail, landing lightly on the dock.

"You can't." For a moment, Thorne looked ready to climb over the rail after him. "This isn't the Eluneth you remember. There are creatures—twisted by the shadows. They'll tear you apart before you get anywhere near the temple—"

"I'll take my chances," Loren called back over his shoulder. Wood creaked under his too-small boots, giving way to slick stone as he headed for the narrow steps carved into the cliffside.

"And what if you don't come back?" Thorne shouted after him.

"Then I'll have solved everyone's problems."

Thorne shouted something after him, but Loren didn't look back, putting all his focus on climbing the treacherous stairs. Araya had said her piece to the shadows, saving their lives. Now, it was his turn.

CHAPTER

THIRTY-ONE

Araya stormed across the cabin, pacing the tiny room like a caged animal. She'd made at least a dozen loops since Thorne had shut the door in her face with an infuriatingly apologetic grimace. But it wasn't Thorne she was going to tear into when they finally let her out of here.

It was Loren. The male who'd given the order to lock her up like a disobedient child.

Her fists clenched at her sides, nails biting into her palms. She could have ripped the door off its hinges with the trickle of magic that had returned to her—but where would that get her? Back on deck with an irritated Loren? Better to save it for when it could really make a difference.

The door rattled as someone knocked, turning a key in the lock. Araya spun, scowling at Thorne as he stepped inside, his broad frame filling the cramped space.

"We've arrived," he said, his voice touched with forced cheer. "I can take you up to your room—"

"No, thank you." Araya dropped onto the edge of the cot, crossing her arms. "I'll wait here for the return journey."

Thorne sighed, rubbing a hand over his face. "You have every right to be angry at him—"

"You said that before." She inclined her head, glancing pointedly at the door. "You can leave now."

But Thorne didn't move. He leaned against the doorframe instead, arms crossed, his amber gaze steady and far too knowing.

"The boat was damaged in the crossing," he said. "Nyra can't leave until she makes repairs, which will take at least a few days. And she won't take you anyway—not against Loren's wishes."

"So, what, then?" Araya let out a sharp, disbelieving laugh. "Am I *his* prisoner, now?"

"I can see why you might feel that way," Thorne said quietly, his jaw tightening. "But no. You're not a prisoner, Araya. I'm sure—or at least, I hope—Loren will explain everything soon. Now—" he straightened, his voice turning firm. "Put on your boots. I'm not spending the night on Nyra's leaky boat when there's an entire castle full of beds waiting up there."

Grumbling, Araya yanked on her damp socks, muttering curses as she jammed her feet into cold, stiff boots. They squelched with every step as she followed Thorne across the narrow gangplank. Mist swallowed the dock, reducing the world to vague, shapeless forms. She squinted into it, searching for any sign of this castle.

"So where is it?"

Thorne, looking far too pleased with himself, pointed.

She followed his gesture, freezing as she caught a glimpse of the castle perched precariously at the top of the cliffs. The mist clung to its towers like a shroud, obscuring the full shape and making the whole structure look half-formed—like if she blinked it might vanish before her eyes.

"That's Ithralis," Thorne said. "The residence of the fae monarchy on Eluneth—or it was."

"Was?" Araya tore her gaze away from the castle, unease crawling under her skin. Something about the way the mist swallowed the towers made her feel like the whole place was holding its breath, waiting. "It's not now?"

"The fae haven't lived here since King Corwin fell," Thorne said, his voice quiet. "Once the Veil formed—well, it was easier for Eloria to move things to Lumaria. But the castle is maintained, in case any of our people who brave the Shadowed Veil need shelter before moving on to Lumaria."

Araya shivered, tracing her gaze along the jagged cliffs. Eluneth—the last home of the free fae. Gods, what would Jaxon do when he found out she was here? Bile rose in the back of her throat. She hadn't escaped him, not really. And she couldn't afford to stay here.

"How do we get up there?"

Thorne pointed.

Araya followed his gesture, her breath catching as she spotted the narrow, twisting steps carved directly into the cliffside. They had to be ancient—slick with mist and half crumbling in places. One wrong step and she'd tumble into the sea—if she was lucky enough not to hit the rocks.

"You can't be serious."

"It's the only way up from here," Thorne replied smoothly, though his lips twitched like he was hiding a smile. "Didn't you work at the Aetherium? They have a lot of steps there too."

"Inside steps," she retorted. "Well maintained, with bannisters—and walls."

"You'll be fine," Thorne said, his tone maddeningly dismissive. He turned and strode down the dock, leaving Araya no choice but to scramble after him.

"If I slip, I'm dragging you down with me," she warned.

He shot her a grin over one shoulder. "I'll keep that in mind."

THE CLIMB WAS AS TREACHEROUS AS IT LOOKED—SLICK, UNEVEN, AND STEEP enough that one wrong step would send her plunging to her death.

Araya kept her gaze glued to her boots, blocking out the churn of water far below. Even years of climbing the Aetherium's endless staircases hadn't prepared her for this. By the time they reached the top, Araya was gasping for breath, her already bad mood turned venomous.

Araya stared out over the ocean, trying to gauge how far they had come—but the mist churned over the waves and the Shadowed Veil loomed on the horizon, leaving her without a single landmark. She might as well have been standing in another world—cut off not just from Aetheris, but from everything she'd ever been allowed to be.

"How far from the mainland are we?"

"Too far to swim," Thorne said cheerfully. "Come on—let's get inside before we freeze."

Araya narrowed her eyes at him, swiping a damp strand of hair off her face. "I wouldn't be upset if you tripped on the way back down."

Thorne just laughed and pushed open the gates, leading her into the courtyard.

The castle *looked* abandoned—its gardens dead and its weathered stone walls crawling with barren vines. The inside was no better, their footsteps echoing in the stale air as the heavy door slammed behind them.

"I thought you said this place was maintained." Araya skimmed her fingers along a windowsill as they passed, dust coating her fingertips. "This looks abandoned."

"It's sad, isn't it?" Thorne sighed, leading her through the labyrinth of halls. "It wasn't always like this."

She raised an eyebrow at his back. "Did you spend a lot of time here?"

"I did. My mother was a Healer for the royal family—good friends with his mother. And my father was one of King Corwin's generals. Loren and I grew up together." Thorne paused, his gaze flicking briefly to one of the threadbare tapestries that lined the walls without seeming to really see it. "He's some of the only family I have left."

Araya looked away, a strange weight settling in her chest. She hadn't asked to be part of any of this—they were the ones that had dragged her into it.

"So...are we heading to Lumaria then? After Nyra fixes her boat?"

Thorne shook his head. "No—we're staying here. At least until Loren and Eloria decide what happens next."

"What happens next?" Araya scoffed. "You mean what you're going to do with me?"

Thorne didn't have an answer to that.

"Of course." Araya crossed her arms tightly over her chest. "I guess it's easier to keep me locked up here."

"It's also safer," Thorne said quietly. "There are a lot of fae with a very real, personal hatred of your bond. And you haven't exactly been discreet about his identity."

He paused, his voice softening when she had no retort. "None of us expected this to happen. There's no grand plan to keep you confined—all any of us are trying to do is keep you safe."

"That's what Jaxon said too."

Thorne's shoulders stiffened, but he didn't answer—didn't defend Loren. Neither of them spoke again, the only sound in the deserted halls the rhythmic tread of their boots on the dust-covered stone.

"Here we go," Thorne said finally. He stopped in front of a wooden door, pushing it open. "This is you."

Araya wrinkled her nose, sneezing as a rush of stale air and dust hit her. A four-poster bed loomed against the far wall, its once-fine drapes and linens gray and stiff with age. A thick layer of dust coated the wardrobe and the small table and chairs in front of the cold, empty hearth.

"I'll sleep on the boat," she said, falling back a step.

Thorne just laughed, stepping into the room.

Magic stirred in the air, plumes of dust lifting in slow, swirling streams only to vanish like smoke. The bedsheets stretched and smoothed themselves, the fabric darkening to a deep, rich green. In the hearth, flames leapt to life without kindling, feeding on nothing but the shimmer of power in the air.

All without a single rune or sigil—gods, he hadn't even spoken or gestured. Just like how Nyra had heated the water with nothing but her will.

Araya's mind buzzed with questions. *How?* Could anyone do it? Did it require training, or just... desire? But she clenched her jaw, swallowing the questions back. She refused to be impressed—not by them.

"So," she said instead, stepping warily inside. "This is my cell?"

Thorne watched her, his amber eyes unreadable. "It's your room."

"Do I get a key?" Araya asked sweetly. "Or should I assume the door will be locked from the outside?"

Thorne's jaw ticked. "It will be locked."

"Because I'm a prisoner?"

"No." He exhaled sharply. "Because this island is dangerous, and Loren wants you safe. We all do. If you need anything, knock. Someone will hear you."

"And unlock my cell?"

"If that's what you insist on calling it," Thorne said flatly. "But you're safer here than anywhere else, whether you want to admit it or not. And I have to say, Araya—" he held her gaze, his eyes blazing. "You seem like a *very* lucky prisoner. I don't know where the Arcanum kept Loren for the past twenty-five years, but I imagine it wasn't half as nice as this."

Araya glared at him, shoving away the hollow pang of guilt that echoed in her chest. They had *drugged* her.

"And where, exactly, is his Royal Highness?"

"He's busy."

Araya scoffed. "I'm sure he is," she said, her voice dripping venom. "Does he intend to show his face? Or was he planning to kidnap me and then just... pretend I don't exist?"

Thorne's jaw tightened again, but this time, he didn't rise to her bait. "I'll let him know you'd like to speak with him. Enjoy the room, Araya."

He didn't wait for her reply. Instead, he turned and stepped into the hall, closing the door with a soft *click*. The sound of the lock sliding into place was louder, echoing like a thunderclap in the silence that followed.

Araya stared at the door for a moment. Then, with a growl, she stalked to the window and threw herself down on the bench, glaring down at the dead garden. The statues and hedges were strangled by vines, their beauty choked by neglect. Beyond the garden, the dark waters of the Shadowed Sea churned violently, the horizon oddly shortened by the wall of towering shadows between her and everything she'd ever known.

They thought she was *safe* here—locked in this room, hidden behind the Veil. But she'd never been in more danger—because by now, Jaxon had to know she was gone.

She didn't doubt he was already leveraging every ounce of his father's formidable power to track her down. Araya could picture him even now—his jaw clenched as he paced his office, the sharp line of it flexing with every barked command.

Jaxon didn't lose. He didn't let go of things that belonged to him —especially not *her*.

Did he know she'd crossed the Shadowed Veil? The Arcanum patrol hadn't survived the crossing—but that didn't mean no one had seen. All it would take was a single report, a whisper of her presence near the Veil, and he'd put the pieces together. Even if he didn't have confirmation, he'd suspect. Jaxon was relentless, his mind a sharp, calculating force that worked as tirelessly as his ambition. He didn't need much to go on.

She shivered despite herself, standing and taking the blanket off the back of the chair in front of the hearth to wrap around her shoulders. She stared into the flames, forcing herself to breathe and think clearly. Fear wasn't going to help her now.

Thorne had called this an island, which meant no escape without a boat.

Even if she managed to get out of her room, slip past Thorne and Loren and steal a boat—then what? She didn't know where they were, didn't know how to sail, and doubted she could talk her way past the Shadowed Veil a second time.

Araya gritted her teeth, flopping into one of the chairs. There was nothing she could do—nothing but wait, and hope Loren and Thorne would listen to her when they finally decided to tell her what the hell they were thinking.

She sank back into the plush chair, letting herself relax for the first time since she'd found Loren bleeding out in his cell.

Gods, she was tired.

All she wanted was to close her eyes and wake up in her own bed —discover that the past few weeks had been nothing more than a strange, tangled dream. Because if none of this had happened—if Jaxon had never taken her down to Loren's cell, never pinned her down and ripped her power from her—Araya could still pretend she was safe.

She could still pretend he loved her.

The fire snapped in the hearth, startling her. Araya flinched, a hand flying to her chest to still the sudden, hollow ache blooming there.

And then the shadows moved.

Araya shot to her feet, her heart pounding as she stared at the twisting streams of darkness slinking out of the corners of the room. The fire guttered, the temperature plummeting and her breath fogging in the air. She stumbled back a step, starting to reach for the door—but even if it hadn't been locked, where would she go? The Shadowed Veil had dragged an entire ship into oblivion. What could it do to *her*?

But these shadows didn't move to attack her.

Araya narrowed her eyes, studying the shifting shapes. They weren't feral or all-consuming like the shadows from the Veil. These moved like the ones that had curled around Loren in his cell—watching, waiting... almost curious.

Of course, those shadows had killed Aeron—but Araya had never feared they would hurt her. "What the hell *are* you?" she murmured.

That got a reaction—the shadows shuddered in unison, rearing back. They looked almost...offended.

"What?" Araya sank back into the chair, staring at them. The way they curled into the corners of the room...it really did look like they were sulking. "Don't tell me I hurt your feelings."

The shadows hesitated, their movements stilling before they rippled again—slower this time, almost... tentative. They clung to the corners of the room, their tendrils curling in on themselves like they were reconsidering their approach.

"Fine." Araya laughed, shaking her head. "If you're so interested in me, do something useful. Take me to Loren. Let me tell him myself just how much of a bastard he's been."

The shadows paused, as if considering her words. Then, without warning, they vanished, melting into the walls like ink on old parchment. In seconds, Araya was alone in her room again, with only the very normal shadows for company and nothing to do but wait.

CHAPTER

THIRTY-TWO

Eluneth had once gleamed atop the sea like an emerald, its cliffs draped in ivy and crowned with ancient oaks and silver-bloomed laurels. Now, it was a corpse.

Loren's boots crunched across the brittle soil, mist curling around his legs like grasping fingers as he walked through the skeletal, twisted remains of the tortured trees. He had expected ruin. But that didn't make it any easier to see.

Somewhere in the distance, something snarled—low and guttural. Loren stilled, his breath catching.

A *zal'vor*. Or more than one.

He didn't move, didn't even breathe for a long moment. But whatever was watching from the seething heart of the shadows was content to let him pass. For now.

Loren forced himself forward, picking his way across the blackened earth toward the looming shape of the temple. Bones littered the ground—all fae and human alike. Gaunt ribcages lay tangled in rusted armor, jaws slack in eternal screams. Some had been cracked open, dragged through the ash before vanishing into the mist that searched across the battlefield.

He picked his way carefully up the ruined stairs, skirting the veins of shadow spidering through the once-pristine white stone. It yawned open, its grand doors shattered. Loren held his breath as he stepped through, half-expecting to be struck down where he stood—but only silence met him.

Whatever had happened here, it hadn't crossed the threshold. Only time had done its quiet work here, fading the murals and dulling the stone. Dust drifted through the air, the altar looming above it all. The Goddess' statue still stood there, her face shrouded and her hands outstretched in eternal offering or warning—Loren could never decide which.

But Loren wasn't here to pray.

He descended the narrow stairs into the crypt. Aetherlamps flared to life as he passed, casting a flickering glow that barely touched the shadows clinging to the floor. They moved with him—curling around his feet, trailing behind like misty specters.

These were the same shadows that had been his only companions for so many years—watching from the corners of his cell, brushing over his skin like whispers. Why had they answered him, when the Shadowed Veil had wanted to kill him? Were they truly pieces of the same whole, or had the tragedy that shattered their people fractured them as well—leaving them broken beyond repair, just as he was?

The crypt was as old as the temple above it, carved into the bedrock of Eluneth itself. Statues stretched along the dimly lit hall, the names of kings and queens long past worn smooth by time and reverent hands. Loren let his fingers brush over one inscription, bowing his head as he passed. These were the rulers that had come before, laid to rest beneath the temple of the Goddess they had loved.

At the far end of the chamber, beneath the flickering glow of the aetherlamps, Loren found what he had come to see.

His mother, Queen Lysana Nightshade, had been rendered in flawless detail—her long hair swept back beneath a delicate crown and her hands folded over the hilt of a sword, its point resting between her bare feet. The sculptor had captured her grace and strength, freezing her in time just as Loren remembered her—elegant and fierce.

Beside her stood his father, King Corwin Shadowbane. He loomed as tall and unyielding in death as he had in life—but the tomb beneath his statue yawned open, empty and untouched. No body had been laid to rest here.

Loren knelt before them. He hadn't seen their faces anywhere but his memories in twenty-five years. And now all that remained of them were statues and silence.

"I don't know why I came here," he said, even his whisper too loud in the silence. "I failed you. Our people."

The shadowmark on his forearm burned, pulsing in time with his heartbeat as the darkness writhed under his skin. Loren lifted it, staring down at the black veins of power. What right did he have to even kneel at their graves if he couldn't even claim his birthright?

His homeland was crumbling, the magic he'd sworn to protect dying a long, slow death at the hands of their human oppressors. His people were scattered—lost. And Loren—he was too broken, too far from the male fate had wanted him to be.

Loren clenched his fists, closing his eyes against the sight of his mother's face. "I don't know how to fix this," he said, his voice breaking. "I don't know if it's even possible."

The shadows stirred. Not like the cold, devouring void of the Veil —but quieter, closer. They murmured around him, indistinct, their whispers brushing his skin like the ghosts of old friends. He couldn't make out the words at first, but they gathered, their whispers joining together until they spoke with a single voice.

She bargained for your chance. Do not waste it.

Loren clenched his jaw. Goddess help him, she really had—throwing herself straight into the path of the Shadowed Veil like they weren't all about to die. She'd *spoken* to it—like it was something that could be reasoned with.

Reckless—absolutely insane. But somehow, impossibly...it had listened.

"I won't drag her into this," he told them. "She deserves better. A life untouched by darkness. Free from people who see her as a means to an end. We have to let her go."

Then you should not have taken her blood, the shadows hissed, sharp and displeased. *You* claimed *her. You claimed us. And you dare to tell us she is not already ours?*

Loren gasped, clutching the shadowmark on his arm. It burned like fire beneath his skin, searing through muscle and bone. The shadows surged around him, the weight of their presence a dark ache that took him to the ground.

You cannot unmake what you bound, Prince of Shadows, they said, the force of their words pressing him into the stone. *If you do not rise to meet them,* dara'el *will unmake you and choose again—and we will allow it.*

They vanished as suddenly as they had come, slithering back into the cracks and secret places of the world to watch and wait. Loren gasped in a harsh breath, his face pressed against the cold stone at the foot of his parents' tombs, one hand still clutching the brand that pulsed like a second heart beneath his skin.

"I took her blood to get us out alive," he snapped. "Not to bind her to this—to me. If she's your demand, you should have killed me before I ever left that cell."

The shadows said nothing. But someone else did.

"Lorendriel."

Loren stiffened. It had been years—*decades*—since he'd heard his true name from someone's lips. And the voice...he knew it.

Hardly daring to believe, he turned. She was a grown female now, far removed from the child he remembered—but he *knew* her. He knew her raven-black hair and her bright green eyes, both so like his own. He knew her voice, even though it now carried the weight of years of leadership.

"Eloriane," he whispered, his voice breaking on her name as he stood.

Before he could take another step, his little sister crossed the space between them in a rush, flinging herself into his arms. She clung to him, holding on like she feared he would vanish if she let go. Loren clung to her just as tightly, his face wet with tears.

He hadn't allowed himself to imagine this—to be found, to be welcomed back. But here she was. Real. Warm. Alive. Holding him as if she could erase the years between them.

"You made it back to us," she said when they finally parted, her voice shaking. "I thought we lost you forever."

"I thought I'd lost you too," Loren managed, his throat thick. "I didn't think I'd ever see you again. I thought—"

"You're here," Eloria said, her voice firm even though there was sorrow in her green eyes as they traced the scars he wore now. "That's all that matters, Loren. You survived. You're here."

His chest ached under the weight of her words. "I shouldn't be," he whispered, dropping his gaze. "So many didn't make it. And I... I don't know if I deserve to stand here. Not when—"

"Don't." Eloria gripped his arms. "Don't you dare finish that sentence."

"But I wasn't here," he said. "When you needed me. For you. For our people—"

"You couldn't have been." Her tone softened but stayed unyielding. "You were taken, Loren. That wasn't your fault." She lifted a hand to touch his face, wiping a tear from his cheek. "You survived. Don't apologize for that. Not to me. Not to anyone."

Loren wanted to believe her. Wanted to let the guilt burn away under the strength of her conviction. But it was never that simple. He pulled her into another embrace, wrapping his arms around her like a shield—as if he could somehow protect them both from the pain of the past. For a moment, the weight of decades lifted. Only relief remained.

When they finally pulled apart, Eloria wiped her face, transforming before his eyes from the little sister he remembered to the female who had led their people for the past twenty years.

"Everyone is going to be so relieved," she said. "We were running out of options. But now that you're here, maybe we can finally get the Veil back under control."

Loren's stomach twisted at her words. "El..." he began. "I don't know if that's going to work. The shadows...they aren't very happy with me."

Her brow creased. "But they chose you."

"Thirty years ago," he said quietly. "A few hours ago they told me I wasn't worthy of them and they were going to kill me so they could pick again."

"What?" Eloria stared at him, her mouth agape. "They said that?"

"They were pretty clear." Loren looked away. "I don't have the strength to wield them, El. Not after... everything." He paused. "If anyone deserves to wield them, it's you—"

"You don't think I tried?" Eloria crossed her arms, one eyebrow lifting in the same way she'd always looked at him when she thought he was being a fool. "They've been waiting for you for twenty years. I'm not the heir. You are. The shadows don't care who the regent is. They care who the king is."

"I'm not a king," Loren muttered, his eyes fixed on the floor. "Do you really think I'm fit to lead? Because I don't."

Silence stretched between them, heavy with all the things he couldn't say.

Finally, Eloria asked, "What about the female who helped you escape? Thorne's report said she was your mate—that she spoke to the Veil. That it listened to her."

"Thorne had a lot to say, didn't he?" Loren said, his voice tight.

"He told me you claimed her." Eloria crossed her arms, frowning at him. "You know as well as I do that bonded pairs are stronger. Maybe if the two of you stand together—"

"He must have left out that it was against her will."

Loren stared at his mother's statue, unable to face the disappointment and horror he knew he would find in Eloria's expression.

"She's already bound to the mage who tortured me," he said, his voice ragged. "She stood beside him—put my chains back on me and took my blood to try and give *him* control of the shadows."

He swallowed hard, his vision blurring.

"Then he hurt her, and she came to me for answers—for help. And instead of giving them to her..." his breath hitched. "I stole her power. Used her true name to compel her to follow me—drugged her. All so Jaxon couldn't use her against me."

He shook his head slowly. "She doesn't even know what a mate bond *is*—and she hates me."

"You did all of that to protect her," Eloria protested. "Once you explain the bond—once she understands what it means—surely she'll see why you—"

"I'm not going to explain it," Loren snapped. "She's suffered enough."

"But she's your mate!" Eloria's snapped, her voice rising as her frustration finally got the better of her. "You only get one, Loren. Why won't you even try to fix—"

"*Because I'd make as poor a mate as I would a king.*"

Eloria flinched back, the silence between them ringing with the echo of Loren's bitter words.

Loren shook his head, his voice breaking. "She's had every choice taken from her. Let her make this one, Eloria. Let her leave if she wants to—promise me."

Eloria's gaze softened, her eyes sad. But when she spoke, her voice was iron.

"I want to say yes. But as regent—" she sighed, and when she met his eyes again it wasn't his sister who looked back at him, but a desperate leader pushed to the edge. "I can't let a possible solution walk away while our people are starving. If there's any chance she could bring the shadows to heel—with or without you—she stays."

Loren stilled—but the shadows didn't. They slithered out of the darkness, pooling around his feet and rising with his fury, drawn to it like blood in the water.

Eloria's eyes widened, tracking the movement. "Loren—"

Loren just stared at her, his jaw locked and his hands curled into fists at his side. He didn't trust himself to speak—not to the sister who loved him or the regent who had no choice but to demand more from him. But what she was asking...she couldn't have it.

"Promise me," he ground out. The air around him thickened, pressing in on all sides as the shadows coiled tighter. "I can't be the reason she's made a prisoner."

But Eloria only shook her head slowly. "I'm sorry, Loren," she said. "I can't."

Her words broke something in him, his rage and despair surging. The shadows struck in tandem, lashing through the air like living whips. Loren shouted, lunging forward to try and pull them back before they reached her—but he was too late.

They struck her head on, ripping through her like a blade.

And Eloria—shattered. Like mist at sunrise, her form dissolved, leaving behind only empty air and the echo of her voice.

Loren staggered back, his breath ragged. An illusion. His sister had been gone long before he ever lost control. Loren dropped to his knees, his mind reeling as he frantically clawed back through the last moments, trying to pinpoint the instant his sister had decided she didn't trust him enough to stay.

But he couldn't—and in some ways it didn't matter. She had been right. If she'd stayed...he would have killed her.

Loren turned to face his father's statue, his gaze settling on the gaping tomb. He had never truly believed escaping the New Dominion would set him free. He didn't wear iron on his body now, but their chains still wrapped around his mind—his soul.

But he hadn't expected this.

The shadows churned through the hall, their whispers fading as they drew back to him, coiling at his feet like smoke too tired to rise. They had waited decades for him to return—but now?

Loren stared down at the shadowmark writhing under his skin. If the shadows wanted to protect the fae, they should have killed him on that boat. Because he was no king. He was nothing but a danger to anyone desperate enough to believe in him.

CHAPTER

THIRTY-THREE

Araya hadn't really expected him to, but she couldn't help being disappointed when the sun set without any sign of him. She passed the hours as best she could—exploring the bedroom and attached bathing chamber, then soaking in a hot bath to ease the bruises and bone-deep ache of the last two days. She even washed her hair, careful not to jostle her stitches as she unwound what remained of her braid and worked the tangles free with slow, aching fingers.

By the time she stepped out of the bath, a tray had mysteriously appeared on the small table near the hearth—still steaming, even though she hadn't heard anyone come in. Her stomach growled at the sight of it, and she didn't ask questions.

She ate in silence, curling into one of the chairs while her hair dried loose around her shoulders. The fire warmed her skin and the food filled her stomach—but neither was quite enough to quiet the ache in her chest.

Eventually, she gave in. She slipped into one of the nightgowns she'd found in the wardrobe and stretched out on the bed, telling herself she wasn't going to sleep—just rest.

But the moment her head hit the pillow, sleep dragged her under.

Araya jerked awake, her breath catching in her throat. She must have been asleep for hours—long enough for the magical fire to burn itself out, casting the unfamiliar room in strange shadows. She stared into the dark, the blanket clutched tight to her chest as she listened for any sign of what had woken her.

Then, she heard it—a soft *click* as the lock turned over, followed by the faint creak of hinges as her door swung open.

"Hello?" she called. "Is someone there?"

Nothing answered her but silence.

Araya slipped out of bed and crept across the room, pushing the door open just enough to peer into the dark hallway.

Empty. But a faint prickle of unease danced along her skin, raising the hair on the back of her neck. She stared down the darkened corridor, wavering between the urge to seize the unexpected opportunity to explore and the instinctive desire to retreat into her room and push something heavy in front of the door.

Before she could decide, a shadow peeled away from the wall.

Araya sucked in a sharp breath as it drifted toward her, curling lazily across the floor. She flinched as it twined around her ankles—strangely warm against her bare skin—before slipping away again, only to stop a few paces down the hall.

Araya stared after it, a strange certainty settling in her chest—it was waiting for her. Only a fool would follow a shadow—but somehow, Araya found herself stepping into the hallway, closing her door quietly behind her.

The shadow was almost playful as it led her through the empty castle—spiraling and looping through puddles of dim moonlight and darting from shadow to shadow. But when Araya paused in front of one of the shrouded paintings it raced back to her, flickering around her feet as it urged her onward.

It didn't stop until it reached a heavy door, swirling in front of it for a moment before melting into an inky pool. Araya quickened her steps, but before she reached it the shadow had flattened itself, sliding through the crack at the bottom of the door.

Araya gripped the handle and turned it—but the door didn't budge.

Locked—of course.

"You know," she muttered, aiming her voice at the door in case the shadow was still listening, "If I'd known you were just going to leave me at another locked door, I'd have stayed in my room."

She didn't expect an answer. But just as she turned to leave, there was a soft click.

Araya stared as the door creaked open, revealing a narrow sliver of the room beyond. A golden glow spilled through the crack, a strange tug in her chest beckoning her forward.

It was another bedroom—larger than the one they'd given her. The grand bed was neatly made, with heavy emerald curtains that matched drapes along the wall of windows. Outside, she could just make out the dark shape of a balcony overlooking the long-dead garden.

Araya crossed to the writing desk by the window, trailing her fingers over the polished wood. It was completely bare—with not even a stray scrap of parchment or a forgotten quill to tell her anything about the person who lived in this room.

She had more luck with the wardrobe.

Araya ran her fingers over the meticulously hung clothing, marveling at the array of fine fabrics and delicate embroidery. Only a king would have so many beautiful things to wear.

Or a prince.

"What are you doing in here?"

Araya gasped, slamming the wardrobe shut as she spun. Loren stood in front of a door she hadn't noticed, the bathing chamber behind him. He'd shorn his long hair to his chin, drops of water still clinging to the inky strands and dripping onto his bare shoulders. Her gaze caught on one of those droplets, following it as it trailed over his scars—over the sharp ridges of his torso and the edge of the low-slung pants that clung to his hips—then snapped away as heat surged up her neck.

"Maybe you should ask your shadow what I'm doing here," she said, her voice coming out higher than she'd intended. "It was the one that unlocked my door and led me here."

Loren tilted his head, his gaze dragging over her like he meant to memorize her. He stepped closer, the heat of him bleeding through the thin silk she wore and his scent curling around her—cold stone and storm winds, as sharp and cutting as the male himself.

"You followed a shadow through a dark, unfamiliar castle," he said slowly, like he couldn't quite believe it. "In the middle of the gods-damned night?"

"Are you saying you didn't send it?"

"I did not." Loren's scowl deepened, his gaze flicking toward the shifting darkness near the door. "They did this on their own."

"Well, it's not like I knew where it was going," she said, lifting her chin. "If I had, I'd have stayed in my room."

"That's my point." He planted one hand on the wardrobe beside her head, caging her in without touching her. "You didn't even know where it was taking you—and you still followed it."

He leaned in, his voice low as his breath grazed the scarred edge of her ear. "This is the last place you should be, *ael'sura*."

Araya took a shallow breath, her back glued to the wardrobe as his heat burned into her. But she forced herself to hold his gaze. "You're right," she said, her voice cutting. "I *shouldn't* be here—I should be in the New Dominion."

"You know that's not what I meant," Loren snapped. But he took a step back, giving her space to breathe. "You should go back to your room, *ael'sura*. And next time, don't follow things that belong to me."

Araya folded her arms, intending to retort—but hissed through her teeth as pain shot through her wrist. She started to pull away, but Loren was already there, his fingers curling around hers with unexpected gentleness.

"Let me see," he murmured.

Before she could protest, he was examining the splint. Araya held her breath and turned her head away, too aware of how little separated them as heat flushing her skin where he touched her.

"You're going to make this worse if you're not careful," Loren said, his brow furrowing as he adjusted the splint with deft, precise movements.

"There wasn't much I could do to protect it," she said, her voice trembling. "Not when I was crawling through sewers."

Loren's hands stilled, guilt flickering across his expression. He released her wrist, stepping back. "I'll have Thorne arrange for a Healer to look at it," he said. "They'll make sure it's set properly."

"Thank you," she said cautiously, the softness in his voice throwing her more than she wanted to admit.

"I owe you an apology," Loren said, his eyes dropping away from hers. "Probably more than one. But everything I did—I was trying to keep you safe."

"By drugging and kidnapping me?" Araya straightened, anger chasing away the strange warmth in her chest. "You had Thorne lock me in my room like some kind of prisoner."

Loren flinched at that, turning away from her. He crossed to the window, gripping the sill with white-knuckled hands. Shadows coiled tightly around his feet, mirroring the tension in his shoulders as he stared out at the dead garden below.

"I'll tell Thorne to give you the key," he said without looking at her. "You're welcome to walk around the castle. And the grounds if you want to."

"But—" Araya stammered, caught off guard by how easily he yielded. "Thorne said it was dangerous—"

"That's why I'd prefer you stay inside," Loren cut in, still staring into the dark. "But asking you to follow orders seems like a waste of breath, even when they're in your own interest. You'll just do what you want anyway, won't you?"

Araya sucked in a sharp breath, his words stinging more than they should have.

"Well, thank you, *Your Highness*." She folded her arms, dragging her anger around herself like a shield. "I'll be sure to cherish my newfound freedom."

She stepped back, putting space she suddenly desperately needed between them. "I think I'll go back to my room now," she said stiffly, every word bitter on her tongue. "Sorry to bother you."

She turned, practically bolting for the door so he wouldn't see how her hands trembled at her side. She'd barely closed it behind herself when something slammed against it, shattering with enough force to rattle the frame.

Araya stood frozen, her breath caught in her throat. For one reckless moment, she almost reached for the handle, ready to fling the door back open, demand—what? An explanation? A reason?

But she didn't want to hear it. Not if it meant admitting how badly he'd hurt her.

So instead, she curled her fingers into fists and turned away, forcing one foot in front of the other. Each step dragged heavier than the last, like something had hooked beneath her ribs and was trying to pull her back to him. But Araya held her head high—and did not look back.

EPILOGUE

Araya was gone.

Jaxon's fingers tightened on the edge of his desk, the wood groaning beneath his grip. She had vanished from the clinic—no trace, no explanation, no witnesses. *Nothing*. He might as well not have sent that useless guard at all.

"Are you even doing anything to find her?" Jaxon hissed.

"They're tearing the clinic apart as we speak," Caylin replied, not looking up as she sifted through a stack of maps. "The staff swears they saw nothing. And Serafina Hart—" she glanced up, her lips pressing into a thin line. "—is being questioned."

Jaxon exhaled slowly through his nose, resisting the urge to slam his fist into the desk.

Serafina Hart. He should have cut the troublemaking Healer out the moment Araya accepted her place as his bond. Instead, he'd spent months carefully chipping away at their friendship—but Serafina had always lingered at the edges of their life, sticking her nose where it didn't belong.

And when Araya had begged him to bring a Healer for the fae prince, it had been Serafina she asked for.

It had seemed like a harmless concession to keep Araya close when she was so obviously falling apart. But now?

Now she was gone. And Serafina was the last person to see her.

"Just let me do my job," Caylin said, smoothing out a map of the New Dominion. She picked up his amulet by its chain, the casing Araya had made catching the golden light of the aetherlamps. The bone disc from their bonding was nestled inside, the pristine ivory marked with a single, dark drop of her blood.

Caylin let it dangle from her fingers, holding it out over the map as she murmured under her breath. Power crackled as she drew on the aether in her own amplifier. Jaxon's amulet swung in slow circles over the map, then suddenly jerked backward—away from the parchment entirely.

"What the hell does that mean?" Jaxon demanded. "Has she left the continent?"

"No." Caylin frowned down at the map. "I'd be able to find her if she left the continent. But..." She paused, watching him carefully. "This spell only works on the living."

Jaxon's breath stalled, panic flaring under his ribs. He hadn't even considered—

"Are you saying she's dead?"

Caylin bit her lip, offering no response.

Jaxon stared at her, panic clawing at his chest. She couldn't be gone—not like that. They were bonded—he would have known, wouldn't he?

"Not necessarily," Darian Hale said.

Jaxon turned sharply, focusing his full attention on Hale for the first time. The High Inquisitor leaned against a bookshelf, his blue eyes unreadable under the flickering glow of the aetherlamps. He was the one person Jaxon knew didn't have anything to do with this —they'd been in the same meetings all day.

"What are you saying?"

"We've been monitoring rebel movements for months," Hale said. "Mostly in Farhallow. They've been smuggling resources—

people. Arcanum policy is to declare the ones we can't track as perished in the crossing...but we don't *know*."

Jaxon sucked in a sharp breath through his teeth. "Are you suggesting that she crossed the Veil?"

"One of our patrol boats went missing while pursuing a rebel vessel the day she disappeared," Hale said. "We believe it was sunk by the Shadowed Veil—it's possible the rebel craft they were pursuing sank as well, but..." he trailed off. "Do you have any reason to believe she'd run from you?"

"No."

Jaxon's jaw tightened, his fists curling. Araya wouldn't have run —she *loved* him. She'd said so. And fae couldn't lie.

But the thought had wormed its way in now, festering. He saw her eyes—wide and afraid. The way she'd flinched from his hand. The bruises he hadn't meant to leave.

But she had *made* him do that. She'd known the cost of challenging him—and done it anyway.

So why did it feel like *he* was the one being punished?

He forced his jaw to unclench, meeting Hale's gaze. "She would never."

"Then we assume Loren took her by force," Hale replied. He turned to Caylin, who offered a faint nod.

Jaxon's stomach twisted. *Loren.* The lost, chained prince—where did that fae filth get the idea he had any claim over her? That he could just *take* Araya and walk away?

"If she has crossed the Veil—willingly or not—" Hale adjusted the cuff of his coat, his voice calm and measured. "We'll have to get more creative in our search if you want to find her."

"Meaning?"

"There's more than one way to track someone," Caylin said. "If your father approves, we could sweep the districts. Search for signs of rebel activity. Shut them down."

"If Araya crossed the Veil, she's in fae hands by now," Hale added.

"You won't get her back without a war—a war your father has not been amenable to."

Jaxon's chest ached with fury. *Araya.* Her name burned through him like fire.

He would find her. He would bring her home—willing or not. And if war was the price?

So be it.

"Then it's time he changed his mind," Jaxon said coldly. "Tell me what you need. I'll make it happen."

His father had spent decades dismantling the fae. But the remnants had always clung to the Veil. They thought it would protect them, hide them.

They were wrong.

Jaxon would tear it all down. They would kneel—or they would burn. And when the ash settled, he would take back what was his.

Hale smiled—sharp and full of teeth. "Let's begin, then. Time is short. And we take missing bonds... very seriously."

Also by Becca Calder

The Eldergreen Trilogy

The Chained Prince

The Bound Mage

The Crowned Queen

Looking For More?

Join my newsletter for exclusive bonus chapters, NSFW artwork, character art, and other reader-exclusive content. You'll also get sneak peeks at upcoming books and be the first to hear about new releases.

Scan the QR code below to join.